GHOSTANIAZ

SON OF DRAGONS

TESSA DAWN

Published by Ghost Pines Publishing, LLC
Volume III in the Pantheon of Dragons Series by Tessa Dawn
First Edition Trade Paperback Published November 15, 2022
10 9 8 7 6 5 4 3 2
First Edition eBook Published November 15, 2022

Ghost Pines Publishing, LLC

CREDITS AND ACKNOWLEDGMENTS

Ghost Pines Publishing, LLC., *Publishing*
Damonza, *Cover Art*
Reba Hilbert, *Editing*

Passing Mentions

The enemy of my enemy is my friend is an ancient proverb which *appears* to have originated with the Indian philosopher Chanakya (also referenced, Kautilya) Arthashastra around the fourth century BCE. It was also spoken by Winston Churchill during WWII.

"[*It's all*] *sound and fury, signifying nothing.*" ∼ William Shakespeare, *The Tragedie of Macbeth*, first published in the *Folio* of 1623, first performed circa 1606.

The Wonderful Wizard of Oz, written by L. Frank Baum in 1900.

"*Time flies over us but leaves its shadow behind.*" ∼ Nathaniel Hawthorne, born in the early 1800s in Salem, Massachusetts.

The Planet of the Apes, a novel written by Pierre Boulle in 1963 and adapted to film in 1968.

"Fortune favors the brave." ~ Publius Terentius Afer, a Roman playwright known as Terence (c. 190–159 BC). First use in the play *Phormio* (161 BC).

The Twilight Zone ~ original television series, 1959, created by Rod Serling.

"The lady doth protest too much, methinks." ~ William Shakespeare, *Hamlet.*

"Fear is the main cause of suffering." ~ Buddha.

PANTHEON OF DRAGONS

Before time was a recognized paradigm, seven dragon lords created a parallel primordial world for their glory...and their future offspring. They harnessed seven preternatural powers from seven sacred stones and erected the *Temple of Seven* beyond the hidden passage of a mystical portal that would lead back and forth between Earth and the Dragons Domain. And finally, they set about creating a race of beings—the Dragyr—that would exist on blood and fire, and they gifted their progeny with unimaginable powers, unearthly beauty, and immortal life.

For all of this, the dragon lords required only one thing: *absolute and unwavering obedience* to the *Four Principal Laws*...

1. Thou shalt pledge thy eternal fealty to the sacred Dragons Pantheon.
2. Thou shalt serve as a mercenary for the house of thy birth by seeking out and destroying all *pagan* enemies: whether demons, shadows, or humans.

3. Thou shalt *feed* on the blood and heat of human prey in order to reanimate your fire.

4. Thou shalt propagate the species by siring *dragyri* sons and providing the Pantheon with future warriors. In so doing, thou shalt capture, claim, and render unto thy lords whatsoever human female the gods have selected to become *dragyra*. And she shall be taken to the sacred *Temple of Seven*—on the tenth day, following discovery—to die as a mortal being, to be reborn as a dragon's consort, and to forever serve the sacred pantheon.

And so it came to pass that seven sacred lairs were erected in the archaic domain of the dragons in order to house the powerful race begotten of the ancient gods, each lair in honor of its ruling dragon lord:

Lord Dragos, Keeper of the Diamond
Lord Ethyron, Keeper of the Emerald
Lord Saphyrius, Keeper of the Sapphire
Lord Amarkyus, Keeper of the Amethyst
Lord Onyhanzian, Keeper of the Onyx
Lord Cytarius, Keeper of the Citrine
& Lord Topenzi, Keeper of the Topaz

While a *dragyri* may appear to be human, *he is not.*

While a *dragyra* may appear to belong to her mate, *she does not.*

While the Dragyr may be fierce, invincible, and strong, they are *never* truly free...

PROLOGUE

Octo ber 31st...

Halloween...

It had always been one of Bethany Reid's favorite holidays.

Even at the age of twenty-nine, she kept with the yearly tradition of meeting up with a handful of her best girlfriends from both high school and college—*their friendships had lasted that long!*—dressing up in elaborate costumes as they tried to outdo each other, and frequenting the scariest haunted house they could find. Afterward, they would go out for drinks, tell scary stories, and end up at one or another's living room, watching classic horror flicks until they crashed on the couch or the floor.

At this point in her life, and even though she was now a well-paid, successful administrative assistant to a smart, if not demanding, finance company CEO, she just couldn't let go of the custom...or the nostalgia. It wasn't so much about the costumes or the holiday—she had pretty much grown out of her love for being scared witless and having to sleep with the lights on for a week—but the easy, unrestrained comradery and banter, the chance to

1

reconnect with lifelong friends and solidify those bonds. As the only child of a gorgeous African American mother and an upwardly mobile German-and-English father, Bethany's girl-friends were her family, the sisters she'd never had.

But tonight had been different...

Heaven help her, had it been different.

This Halloween had been a true, waking nightmare, and Bethany was still too terrified, confused, and disoriented to wake up.

She didn't want to wake up, lest she find that the skeletal man with the long, wispy white hair was real: the dark, malevolent presence at the Arapahoe County fairgrounds, the one who had emerged from the fog in the haunted house, wrapped its long, spindly arms around Bethany, and dragged her into the shadows, separating her from her friends. The man who had stabbed her in the arm with a syringe before she even knew what was happening, injecting her swiftly with some sort of tranquilizer.

At first, she had thought it was part of the act, someone from the crew who ran the haunted house; and since she and her friends prided themselves on not screaming, never showing fear, she had giggled nervously and glanced around in the darkness, waiting to see what would happen next.

The syringe had answered that question.

Next was going to be too late.

Next, she had felt like she was falling...spinning...traveling at some ungodly speed through time and space.

Next, she was being carried into some garish fortress, like a gothic castle from a vampire novel, and dragged to the base of a nightmarish, red velvet throne.

Next, she was staring into a pair of impossible glassy eyes—diamond irises framing phantom-blue pupils—and the powerful, muscle-bound creature who owned them was glaring back at Bethany like she had stolen his firstborn son.

* * *

Ghostaniaz Dragos watched as Wraith Sylvester, one of Lord Drakkar's loyal shadow-walkers, a soul eater, dragged a stunning human woman with thick, wavy, dark brown hair and terrified yet exotic dark brown eyes, the pupils rimmed in gold, to the base of the pagan king's throne and presented her to the ruler of the underworld.

Lord Drakkar appraised the woman from head to toe and then gently inclined his head in a nod, which meant the female was acceptable—he would receive her as a replacement for the beautiful human slave Ghost had drained to the point of exsanguination...expiration...*death*—just four weeks earlier.

It hadn't been Ghost's choice, or his fault, feeding on the human slave like that—

Trader Vice had left Ghost no choice.

Ghost, too, had been captured...taken...exploited by the Pagan Horde, ensnared in an earthside trap, a creek bed filled with hexed, paralyzing quicksand, and snatched away to the underworld, one month prior. And Trader had used that abominable hand, the one that was missing a palm, a thumb, and all four fingers, the one that had been replaced with the head of a turquoise-and-black tiger snake, instead, to force Ghost to feed, to evoke his dragyri instincts.

What was done was done.

Ghost didn't have the time or the pleasure to entertain regrets.

His every breath was now about survival: finding a way to withstand and eventually escape this gods-forsaken realm.

True: The night he had been captured, he had been feeling reckless, suicidal—he had left the Pantheon and traveled through the portal, alone and by his own accord, amped up and looking for trouble. But he had gotten a helluva lot more than he had

3

bargained for. He had never intended to end up as Lord Drakkar Hades' favorite pet, a tool to be used and tortured for the dark lord's amusement, a way for the pagan king to strike back at the Seven, his ancient co-creators who had chosen another life.

Ghost's top lip twitched, and he restrained a feral snarl.

Since he had arrived in the underworld, he'd had every bone in his powerful body broken. He'd had several organs ripped from his torso, only to be returned, restored, and regenerated. And the demons had likely split his skull open a half-dozen times—Ghost had quit counting.

What he had learned with a quickness was that eternity was going to be a very long time if he didn't get his shit together, formulate a plan, and do something—anything—to stop the incessant torment.

Ghost was a *hard-ass* by nature—tainted, broken, way beyond cynical—and there wasn't much he couldn't endure.

But this shit?

Nah, this was way beyond the pale.

And the way Ghost figured it, he had to have something of value, something he could barter, something he could offer Lord Drakkar in exchange for a *cease-fire* on all the beatings. The bludgeonings. Ghostaniaz Dragos was a Dragyr male, an embryonic hatchling from the first of the dragon lords, the Genesis Son of the diamond dragon, Lord Dragos, first of the sacred Dragons' Pantheon—in a sense, he was Lord Drakkar's nephew, just a thousand years removed.

But whatever.

Point was: The Pagan Horde was powerful—both demons and shades had wicked supernatural powers—but a dragyri was stronger...faster...superior. And that gave Ghost an advantage. It made him both a scourge and a celebrity in the underworld. Furthermore, he had a sacred amulet hanging around his thick, corded neck, and at least when earthside, he could use that

4

amulet to open a portal, gain access to the Pantheon, a place Drakkar and his minions couldn't travel. Ghost had knowledge about the Dragons' Pantheon, the lairs, and the Temple of Seven, and if he could sell the fact that he hated his lineage—that he despised his dragon daddy, which wasn't that large of a stretch— he might be able to win Lord Drakkar's favor.

The enemy of my enemy is my friend...

Maybe Ghost could convince his uncle Drak that they weren't entirely on opposite sides of the cosmic spectrum, that Ghost might have more value as a spy or an informant than a punching bag or a flesh-and-blood play toy.

Slowly, but surely, the plan was working, although Ghost had almost lost track of all his lies. In truth, he might be coerced to screw with Lord Dragos, but he would never betray his Diamond Lair brothers; nor would he expose the Pantheon to a full-on demon attack—so basically, he was walking an extremely dangerous line: giving the pagans just enough information to be credible, but never enough to be lethal.

And now—this night—Lord Drakkar had summoned Ghost to the throne room to ask him something about the various regions in the Pantheon: the grasslands or rolling hills; the mountain regions and the Garden of Grace; the white, sandy beaches with their ocean of fire; the dry desert in the east; and the tropical flatlands, also known as the plains. He had wanted to know the precise positions of all seven lairs so Killian Kross, his chief counselor, could add them to the topographical map the shadowwalker was creating.

And that's when Ghost had seen the girl.

The beautiful human woman, first carried into the dark throne room, then set on her feet and dragged before Lord Drakkar.

That's when Ghost had rolled his shoulders, popped his neck, and waited for the stupid, inane scene to unfold with cold indifference—Drak's human slaves, his personal or abhorrent proclivities, were none of Ghost's concern, and he was never going to get out of that damnable place if he let minor underworld politics distract him.

But that was also when Ghost had seen the quick *flash*...

Less than a second, really, maybe a heartbeat or two at the most.

That was when the stunning, half-drugged woman's dark brown eyes had flashed as diamonds, their color shifting from umber to crystal and phantom blue. And that's when Ghost's diamond amulet had heated to a searing spark and burned an indentation in his chest.

He had quickly covered the gemstone with his hand, appraising Lord Drakkar and his nearby minions to see if anyone else had noticed—it didn't look like they had—and then he had stared the woman down like he had been alone on a deserted island for a century, and this was his first astounding contact with other sentient life.

Hell's fire and brimstone...

Literally.

The shit had just hit the fan!

Ghostaniaz Dragos was standing in the Pagan Underworld, of all places, the prisoner of an ancient, savage, demonic king, and he was staring at his *fated*...his dragyra...and the woman was Lord Drakkar's newest slave. As if that wasn't horrific and unthinkable enough, Ghost only had ten days to somehow get this lady out of the underworld and into the Temple of Seven.

CHAPTER ONE

THE PANTHEON

Perched on a white, sandy beach inside a private cove, just north of the Diamond Lair, Lord Dragos, Keeper of the Diamond and ruler of the same, threw back his massive, bestial head and snorted before sniffing the clean sea air. He had been flying, circling, soaring, and diving since seven o'clock that All Hallows' Eve—the earthly Halloween—when the sun set in the Pantheon, and the dragon moon rose...

Since the waves became as flames, undulating in the sea...

Roiling in dazzling cascades of diamond, emerald, and sapphire; of Amethyst, Onyx, Citrine, and Topaz; mystical fire, embedded in crests, rising and blazing as liquified gemstones.

He had been anxiously pacing the beach whenever his wings grew fatigued.

And always...*always*...he had been thinking of his dark, insolent, insubordinate son, Ghostaniaz Dragos, and the horrific fate that had beset the dragyri one month past: Ghost had traveled through the portal alone—and against the Seven's orders—in a reckless, if not suicidal, frame of mind. He had gone to check up on Axeviathon Saphyrius, a fellow Dragyr from the Sapphire

Lair, after dipping subtly into the mercenary's mind and finding Axe and his mate to be in distress: Like the wild, recalcitrant loner he was, Ghost had flown to the rescue, descended into a trap, and he had ultimately been captured by Lord Drakkar's Pagan Horde.

Ensnared in a pit of malicious, demonic quicksand.

Paralyzed and rendered as helpless as a dove.

Bested and taken to the underworld by the Pantheon's most formidable foes.

Lord Dragos whipped his massive head from side to side as if trying to dislodge the painful memories. The time for mourning had come and gone—the time for filling the Pantheon's skies with rage-filled flames and grief-stricken cries had long since grown redundant...and futile. No, Lord Dragos could not...would not... lament any longer. The time had come for decisive action.

Only, there was little the powerful dragon lord could do, for he held no sway in the underworld, and his powers were no greater, nor lesser, than Lord Drakkar Hades'.

He stomped a clawed foot into the sand, kicking up a virulent storm of dust, and sniffed the air once more, trying to retrieve— and recall—her scent.

The human woman's...

Bethany Reid's.

Ghostaniaz's *fated*—his dragyra.

Lord Drakkar had done all that he could...

Along with the remaining six dragon lords, he had initiated the unthinkable, what had yet to be done since time immemorial. The Seven had accelerated a dragyri's claiming, located his pre-chosen mate, and set the ten-day clock into motion prematurely, a decade before Ghost's mating was due.

It was of no matter.

What was done was done.

Nearly two weeks earlier, during a fitful dream, Lord Dragos had felt his youngling's essence—he had awakened with a start, simply knowing...*sensing*...detecting Ghost's amulet, so far away. The original hatchling was still alive! Wounded, perhaps. Distressed, even broken. But by all that was wicked, or holy, or divine, Ghostaniaz still lived. And that's when Lord Dragos had entreated the Seven to take matters into their own immortal hands: That's when the Seven had consulted the Oracle Pool and scoured the earth for Ghost's promised human female.

And now, more recently, for the past seven days, each of the dragon lords had visited Bethany Reid in a dreamscape, though she had no memory of the same. They had drenched her aura in power and magnetic force; they had coated her essence with gravitational attraction, camouflaging her very being in all seven sins. For all intents and purposes, they had covered Bethany's pure, innocent spirit like a caramel apple, encasing her core in an overpowering lure, a delectable shell formed of lust, gluttony, greed, and sloth...wrath, envy, and pride.

No, Bethany would not become tainted by the same—sin and disharmony was *always* a choice—but her very scent, her pheromones, her vibrational allure would transmit like a satellite to every sin eater and soul eater for a million miles. Yea, if a demon or a shade passed Bethany by, the draw to the female would be irresistible. And Lord Dragos could only hope they would not strike her down, that the desire to have her, the temptation to keep her, would be powerful enough to induce them to take her all the way back to the underworld.

In truth, Lord Dragos would have done anything—risked anything—to reach his ill-fated son: After all, what in hellfire did he have to lose!

Staring out at the ocean, beyond the cove, which was now eerily calm—several hours had passed since moonrise—Lord Dragos let his weary diamond-eyes drift shut and curled back his snout in a snarl. As his tongue snaked forward, and his lips recoiled, he whispered a solicitation, a prayer, a *command* to his long-lost son trapped in the Pagan Realm: "Find the girl, Ghostaniaz! Remember what and who you are. Fight like the devil, you son of a bitch, and claw your way back home. If love and lust do not appeal, then do it out of arrogance—do it out of honor—do it to flaunt your superior bloodline. And if you're forced to walk through the flames of hell, for the sake of your lineage, command your destiny as if you rule the fucking place!"

As Lord Dragos reopened his eyes, a blood-red wave crashed against the shore, an anomaly to be sure. If the ether could hear the dragon lord's prayer and respond with a crimson tide, then perhaps his son could hear it as well and respond with blood, rebellion, and fire.

CHAPTER TWO

B ethany fell to her knees on the cold stone floor of a dark, medieval bedchamber and froze like a rabbit, too traumatized to move, as if trying to blend in with the limestone.

What the hell had just happened!

That white-haired, skeletal creature had attacked her in the haunted house, injected her arm with some sort of tranquilizer—falling, spinning, *traveling?*—before he had dragged her into a creepy gothic castle and tossed her on the ground, forcing her to kneel before a garish red throne. "My liege," he had nearly purred in a sin-laced tone, "I present to you this flawless human female as a replacement for the servant you lost four weeks past. If it pleases you, my lord, we will train her to serve you."

And then...

And then...

Oh, sweet mother of mercy, and then some deranged, demented—hell, the guy had to be demonic—cryptic being, with deep-set eyes reflecting every color imaginable like a revolving kaleidoscope of gemstones, had glared at Bethany with undiluted hatred and contempt in his aberrant gaze: The monster...the *liege*...the king had shifted lazily on his throne before appraising Bethany from head to toe and nodding in arrogant assent.

Bethany had almost passed out.

But something far more terrifying had robbed her of that mercy, commanded her attention, and kept her fully awake: eyes made of glass—or supernatural moonstones—diamond irises framing phantom-blue pupils, the most stunning, resplendent, yet terrifying creature Bethany had ever seen. A powerful titan of a warrior, standing just to the left of the throne, had stared daggers straight through Bethany's soul, devouring her body, her features, and her eyes with an all-encompassing knowing, a far too penetrating scrutiny that had caused her to shiver from her head to her toes. And then, like a lunar eclipse, the sun slipping seamlessly behind a phantom moon, the titan's expression had waxed blank and inscrutable, and that's when a new, unfamiliar guard, a monstrosity with tree trunks for hamstrings and a thick iron piercing that resembled a rusty nail in his nose, had snatched Bethany by the arm, yanked her from the floor, and dragged her out of the throne room. She had kicked and flailed and screamed, all to no avail, while the brutal sentry had proceeded to haul her down a long, winding row of dark, craggy halls, until at last he had tossed her into an ominous, foreboding bedchamber and locked the door behind her.

Holy hell...

Her fear had become a living, breathing entity, and being locked away like a helpless lamb awaiting some horrific, unknown slaughter had not been the thing that terrified her most: That phantom-eyed titan, the one who had stared straight through her, had slipped out of the Great Hall to follow from a distance. Bethany had *felt* his presence as surely as one could sense a stranger entering a room or steam rising from a boiling kettle.

And now, as she knelt on the cold stone floor, still trying to grasp the horror, reorient to *Place* and *Time*, and process a new reality beyond her worst imagining, an odd, disconnected haze enveloped her mind, her senses heightened, and for reasons unknown, her eyes latched onto her splayed, trembling hands...

The texture of her skin.

The way her veins spread out in branches, toward—or away—from her knuckles.

The clear polish on her fingernails and the antique opal ring on her fourth, left finger, the one her beloved grandma Betsy had given her on her eighteenth birthday. The stone was visibly trembling, and Bethany's skin was visibly pale. She tried to slow her breathing—her breaths were far too shallow and much too quick—even as she struggled to gather her senses, free her brain from the fog, think clearly...*rationally*...and use her damn wits. She could not afford to retreat inside like a turtle stuck in its shell. She needed to back away from such an open, exposed foyer, put some distance between her body and the chamber's creepy, arched stone entrance, and find a place to hide!

Only, she didn't have a chance.

A sound!

Her ears perked up, and she drew to attention.

A moan—no, a scrape.

She angled her head to the side and listened.

The heavy, archaic handle on the enormous twelve-panel door creaked as it rotated slowly...clockwise.

Someone was turning the knob!

Without thought or preamble, Bethany scampered across the grotto, shot beneath a high, moss-and-granite archway recessed within its own private cove, and ducked behind the fall of an ancient silver-blue, velvet bedspread, on the other side of a large four-poster bed. She sniffed to fight back tears, even as her nostrils filled with a rising, pungent scent. Sulfur. Slowly entering the cavern, streaming beneath the chamber door, and permeating the dank, musty air.

In the space of a fleeting, thunderous heartbeat, her eyes shot left then right—up then down—as she absorbed every dark, terrifying detail of what felt like gallows closing in all around her: the great, circular iron chandelier above her, replete with at least a half-dozen raven-black tapers; the way the flickering flames merged with a macabre assortment of smaller, garish lanterns strewn about the room, each one affixed to a separate stony crevice, each crevice casting ghoulish shadows like haunted nooks and crannies; and the oppressive weight of the high, domed ceiling, the thick, looming, crisscrossed beams...the way the beams cast a menacing illusion, like hungry wooden vultures just waiting to swoop down.

Bethany couldn't breathe for all the heavy, sinister energy.

She held her breath instead.

Silent, perched behind the bed, and so alert she could've heard a pin drop—or more appropriately, a sharpened, rusty nail —Bethany waited.

And waited...

Until at last, a pair of heavy footfalls crossed the stony threshold, entered the bedchamber, and traversed the floor. She peeked above the mattress—she couldn't help herself; *not knowing* was its own form of torture—gasped, and ducked back down.

Oh shit, oh shit, oh shit!

She knew this familiar monster...

The skeletal being with long, wispy white hair and spindly arms, the one who had abducted her from the haunted house at the Arapahoe County fairgrounds. He cleared his throat and spoke out loud, his voice a harsh, bitter harbinger of dark things to come. "Allow me to introduce myself more formally. I am a shadow-walker, the soul eater known as Wraith Sylvester, and it is my duty to make you presentable and acceptable for Lord

Drakkar, to ensure your service to the king of the underworld is satisfactory in every manner imaginable."

Those last three words curdled in Bethany's gut like a container of milk left out in the sun, sending a fresh new wave of shivers down her spine. She gagged and held back the bile.

"Come out from behind the bed."

Bethany strained to listen, but she didn't move a muscle. If her heart beat any faster—or harder—it would explode in her quivering chest.

The soul eater cackled, and it was a hair-raising sound. "Girl, you do not seem to understand your plight. You are a new human servant in the world of the Pagan Horde, and from this moment forward, your very existence depends upon how well you serve... and please...Lord Drakkar Hades, creator and supreme ruler of the same. In less than ten minutes, he will enter this chamber to dine upon...to ravish and savage...his newest slave. And if you are not prepared, if you make even the slightest mistake, he will dine upon your entrails instead. He will ravish, savage, and feast upon your dying soul and hang your carcass from the parapets like rotting meat, as an example to his other human minions. Now then, I entreat you once again: *Come out from behind the bed.*"

Bethany's brain nearly rattled in her head.

Her ears were burning, her palms were sweating, and her heart was beating a dark, desperate symphony in her chest.

She parted her lips and gasped for air...

Come out?

Come out!

She couldn't come out.

Yet, if she hesitated much longer, she had zero doubts the monster would kill her right then and there.

Her head felt woozy, and her knees knocked together as she forced herself, against all better judgment, to crawl from behind the antique coverlet, clamber to the foot of the bed, and slowly push up to her feet. Only...she couldn't do it. Her legs were like two thin, rubbery strings of spaghetti, and she sank back to the floor.

"There she is," Wraith Sylvester drawled, drawing out the "S" with a hiss. "As beautiful as ever."

He raised his right hand, inadvertently placing it beneath the ambient light of a nearby candelabra, and following the light, Bethany's eyes latched on to several hanging garments, implements...monstrosities...each horrific article dangling from his forearm, finger, or fist.

She gasped in horror.

She audibly whimpered.

Then she studied the vile assortment, one by one...

The first article was obvious: a black and red, silk and lace, see-through negligee; only, *negligee* was too tasteful a word. A hooker wouldn't be caught dead in that garment. But it was the second object that caused Bethany's stomach to lurch and throat to retch—Wraith had some sort of grotesque gadget, like a gag with a spiked rubber ball in the center, draped over his right index finger, and as his hand rocked rhythmically back and forth, the ball swayed in the air like the hanging chime on a grandfather clock. He had a leather blindfold dangling from his pinky and a pair of rawhide straps twisted around his wrists. The blindfold had razor blades inserted into two eye-level pockets, and the straps had nails...blades...and rusty hooks sewn into the center of the rawhide.

"Remove all your clothing." He spoke like he may as well have been discussing the weather. "Put the garment and the blindfold on, then fasten the gag around your neck, securely. Lord Drakkar will insert the spikes in your mouth."

Bethany clawed the floor like a trapped wild animal, her fingernails scraping against large, uneven stones, even as she fought to swallow fresh bile. She blinked several times—Wraith was still talking, but she could no longer make sense of his words: something about sitting quietly on the edge of the bed, head bowed in reverence, hands folded in her lap. Something about never, ever saying "*No*," crying out, or resisting. Something about being so obedient—so compliant—that Lord Drakkar would want to keep her and, thus, heal any wounds he inflicted.

The words were like cotton stuffed in Bethany's ears...

Fuzzy, muddled, and distant.

And it really didn't matter—Wraith's instructions, that is—because she had already come to the most terrifying and tormented conclusion of her short twenty-nine years of life. The nails, the blades, the spikes...the razors imbedded in the blindfold, and that torturous, grotesque ball...all of them, some of them, at least one of them had to be sharp enough to sever an artery, and against her every instinct to survive, she shifted her focus inward, tuned Wraith out, and latched on, like a spider grasping for its web, to the only questions—and answers—that mattered.

The femoral?

The carotid?

Or the radial artery?

Which was she brave enough and strong enough to slice?

And how long would it take to bleed out?

Could Bethany disassociate from her body—and the pain—long enough to escape this living hell? And, heaven forbid, could Lord Drakkar somehow intervene? If he found her too soon, could he still save her life? Was he powerful enough to bring her back from the dead, and was he evil enough to try?

She glanced around the dark, ominous chamber, studying it strategically for the very first time: The domed ceiling was much too high, and the layers of mortar between the stones were too thin. She could never climb up, let alone reach the apex, in time to jump to her death. There was a narrow tin tub inside a private raised alcove, curtained and certainly deep enough to drown in;

but it was dry as a bone, and she saw no obvious plumbing or means to draw water. There was, however, an old, arched stained glass window, wooden and crisscrossed with black iron bars, on the other side of the chamber. It likely looked out upon the castle's exterior, and it was wide enough to slip through, if she could only turn the rusty crank and push it open.

Yes.

Yes…

Jumping from the window would be far, far easier.

A whole lot quicker and a lot less painful—besides, it would be a hell of a lot harder for Lord Drakkar to put the shattered pieces back together.

"Are you listening, girl!" the shadow-walker thundered, and Bethany's attention snapped back to the present, back to the unconscionable thing standing in front of her, and back to the implements he was now flinging across the bed.

She forced her head to nod. "Yes," she muttered. "I heard you, and I promise, as soon as you leave, I will do everything you asked, exactly as instructed." She didn't know where the words or the courage came from, but she was playing it by ear, just long enough to get to that window.

At this, Wraith brushed a long, flimsy lock of his parched white tresses behind his shoulder and curled his thin, reedy lips back into a scowl. "Do you really think I would leave this duty to my lord, unattended, unsupervised? Do you really think I don't intend to stay and watch? Hell, if it weren't for our king's insistence that he be the first to sample…to soil…the slaves, I would've already shoved those spikes in your mouth and bent you over that bed." He flicked his wrist in an over-the-top, condescending gesture, dismissing Bethany's humanity in a single flick of the hand, and as his long, black fingernails swept through the air, Bethany regurgitated in her mouth and spit the bile on the floor.

She wasn't getting out of this…

Wraith eyed the spittle with disdain before turning his attention back to her terror-filled eyes. "Humans are so incredibly... inferior," he snorted. "Listen, girl, and listen well. Welcome to hell, for this is your new home. Soon, you will come to seek and revere my counsel, for learning my lessons will lessen your pain. You will serve Lord Drakkar, you will serve him well, and you will do so until the end of your days." He paused for the space of a half-dozen demonic heartbeats, then continued in a discordant purr. "Tomorrow, I will begin to explain your duties in the throne room, in the kitchens, in the laundry...in the sacred Great Hall. You will be given several fresh garments to wear, and you will be taught how to properly bathe, how to festoon your hair, and how to walk, kneel, and bow before your new lord and master. But for tonight, you have no other duty than to offer your body as a sacrifice of pleasure to the king's every whim. Now then, do not make me repeat myself thrice: *Remove your clothing, and put that shit on!*"

CHAPTER THREE

Having slipped from the throne room to follow the human woman—his *fated*—Ghostaniaz Dragos stood outside the ancient bedchamber with his ear pressed against the giant door. In truth, he didn't really need the proximity or the extra effort to overhear the conversation, but he wasn't about to leave anything to chance. As it stood, all six of his senses were on high alert, and his mind was racing like the wind.

The fear emanating from his female on the other side of that door was palpable—he could feel that shit on his skin—and her tainted scent was undeniable; it was as if she had been drenched in *sin*, her very pores emitting the stain of lust, gluttony, greed, and sloth...wrath, envy, and hubris. Her capture by the Pagan Horde had not been an accident, but he'd turn that shit over later, figure out what it meant. Right now, what troubled him most was everything he had just seen and heard: Wraith entering the bedchamber with a foul-as-hell collection of barbaric sex toys, vulgar implements of torture dangling from his fingers and swinging from his wrist, the bastard telling Ghost's dragyra to get undressed for Lord Drakkar so the king could "dine upon, ravish, and savage his newest slave."

And all that perverse, demented savagery was headed the female's way in less than ten minutes.

Less than ten minutes...

Nah.

Hell fucking no.

Ghost may have been powerless in the underworld. He may have been a slave or a prisoner—an outsider, himself—but the thought of that nasty, loathsome demon king brutalizing Ghost's mate, torturing, maiming, and defiling her fragile human body, just to get his malevolent rocks off? Wasn't gonna happen. Not on Ghost's watch. Not even if he had to put both the girl and himself in an early, self-inflicted grave to prevent it.

His top lip twitched.

What the devil was happening?

Why in the name of the Seven had Ghost been given a mate anyway?

Even under normal circumstances—and these were anything but that—the dragyri wasn't capable, let alone ready, to take on that kind of a head trip. Ghost didn't possess compassion. He didn't do tenderness. And he didn't know love. He got his pleasure wherever he could take it, scratching an occasional itch with craven, broken women in back-alley nightclubs, and even then, he only sought release on rare, desperate occasions.

He never, *ever* got involved.

He never hit the same...source...twice.

And in a thousand years, he had never nuzzled, cuddled, or caressed anyone. Hell, he had never even looked a female in the eyes while he was thrusting inside her body. Sex, for Ghost, was like eating or breathing, just a basic primal need, and that was only one of the many reasons he knew he couldn't handle a mate. Bare-bones truth: He was about as capable of caring for a human female as he was unseating King Drakkar from the pagan throne and taking the monarch's place.

Nope.

Claiming a dragyra—under any circumstances—was just not in Ghostaniaz Dragos' repertoire.

Still...

Shit.

What was about to happen to that girl was foul.

Not on Ghost's watch—couldn't let it go down.

He had to think fast and act quick. Proceed like the mercenary he was, while shoving all the extraneous bullshit aside, burying that touchy-feely crap six feet deep. Steeling his resolve, he backed away from the oppressive wooden door, closed his eyes, and took a long, deep breath in an effort to draw power from so many centuries of living...

Learning...

Surviving as a Genesis Son.

Lord Dragos was Ghost's sire, and deviant or not, the dragon lord had taught Ghost well. At only five years old, Ghost had already learned to speak three languages, fluently, and without the aid of divination, cognition, or mental telepathy. Ghost had already gained powers his dragon father knew nothing about. Magical. Mystical. Alchemic shit. Some sort of instinctive voodoo that he had somehow managed to conceal from his sire. How much more did he possess now, just over 995 years later?

Done with the self-reflection and contemplating, he rendered his body invisible, even as he recognized it would only be a temporary fix; the vibrations permeating the underworld were so thick and dense, no one from a higher realm could hold an altered state for long. On top of that, he had learned a thing or two—or twenty—during his short, hazardous stay in purgatory as Lord Drakkar's unwilling guest: He had figured out that the pagans could smell him—they were like fucking black-hearted hound dogs—and if they didn't hear him, see him, or sniff him, then they could *feel* him at some point. In other words, as long as Ghost was anywhere within the Pagan Horde's vicinity, they could detect him, and Lord Drakkar was the powerful fountain from which all that shit sprang into being. So yeah, whatever reckless route he chose was more likely than not to fail, but what the hell did Ghost have to lose anyway?

He had never been that afraid of death.

Grasping on to an ad hoc, split-second plan, he shot down the long, winding stone hall like a rocket, wrenched open a heavy iron door at the end of the corridor, and bounded up the ensuing staircase, taking two or three granite stairs at a time. He emerged like a geyser, exploding atop the castle battlement, and bolted along a thick row of parapets, until he swiftly arrived on the side of the fortress, just above his dragyra's bedchamber. And then he extended his leathery wings and descended the castle wall, creeping steadily downward until he reached the ledge outside his *fated's* window, the translucent nature of his powerful form already fading fast.

Fuck.

He had been right about the invisibility thing, the fact that he would not be able to maintain it, and there, by extension, went the element of surprise.

So how the hell was he gonna pull this off?

As quickly as the question arose, the obvious and only answer followed, but it didn't sit well with his soul: Ghost would rather rot in the abyss than try to reach out to his loathsome father, so many spans removed. He would rather slide down a blade made of pantheon steel and land in a cauldron of alcohol than use his ancient mystic powers to try to draw on his connection to the first dragon lord, but what other choice did he have?

He spit out a string of curses, bit down on his lower lip, and clutched his sacred amulet, concentrating hard: Lord Dragos was epochs away. He and Ghost were universes apart. Nonetheless, energy was energy—timeless ether and boundless space—so the most powerful force in existence might just still apply...thought.

Thought.

The most basic building blocks of all galaxies...

All reality.

Beyond the elements, beyond quantum energy, above all that was known, contemplated, or built, *thought* was the true, most universal living substance. *Yes,* Ghost reassured himself, *pure, undiluted thought. The human female's eyes changed in the throne room. They flashed from dark brown to the color of diamonds, if only for a heartbeat, and that means the Seven's omniscient power, the timeless directive they brought forth at creation—brought forth through thought—is still material in this sphere of existence.*

So, think, Ghost, think...

Focus!

The Diamond Lair, the Temple of Seven, Lord Dragos perched on his opulent throne.

Reach, Ghost, reach...

Harder!

A sudden shiver ran up Ghost's spine, his temperature took a nosedive, and frost began to collect on his fingertips.

Yep, Lord Dragos can feel me.

The diamond deity was expunging Ghost's heat, if only just a scintilla, in order to insert a piece of his being inside his wayward son's soul, and the more he inserted, the more Ghost, the male dragyri, faded back into invisibility, the more Ghost, the son who hated his sire, wanted to pull back and recoil.

He ignored the self-destructive urge and clenched his amulet even tighter, breathing slowly, steadily, in deep, rhythmic ebbs and flows. "Third eye," he whispered. "Silver cord. Allow my soul to travel inside that bedchamber unnoticed." With that, he let go of all lingering resistance and conjured the full measure of his power. Then he streamed his essence into a silver funnel, careful not to break the life-giving thread, and passed his spirit right through his dragyra's stained glass window, emerging as a true ghost in her quarters, while leaving his body behind to hover...and wait...on the other side of the glass.

Wraith Sylvester spun around, immediately sensing a powerful, foreign energy. Yet he could not see Ghost's spirit, and the dragyri's body wasn't there.

Ghost knew he could not kill the soul eater without ultimately committing suicide himself and leaving his *fated* to twist in the wind—the pagans would retaliate with a vengeance—and he sure as hell couldn't take on Lord Drakkar, mano a mano, dragyri spirit to dragon lord. Ghost had not forgotten what it felt like to have his spinal column expunged from his body, just for kicks and to make a point: "*Leave your spine at the door when you enter my throne room...*"

Hell no...

Ghost wasn't going there again.

But perhaps, just maybe he could incite Lord Drakkar to extinguish Wraith himself.

If Wraith directly disobeyed an order, if Wraith touched the female first—what was it the vile soul eater had muttered? "*If it weren't for our king's insistence that he be the first to sample...to soil...the slaves, I would've already shoved those spikes in your mouth and bent you over that bed.*" Surely, a king, *a deity*, who ruled manifest over the seven sins would possess a truly enormous ego, an endless vat of pride, so Ghost just needed to stir the pot.

Without pausing to second-guess his latest ad lib—he didn't have time to waste—Ghost slammed into Wraith's chest like a battering ram, funneled his essence into the shadow-walker's mouth, and tunneled down his throat.

The soul eater gasped.

Breath is life, and life is breath, Ghost chanted in his mind, straining his consciousness, even as he sought to possess the soul eater's form and take hold of his entire loathsome body. *More power, Lord Dragos!* Ghost prayed in earnest. *Father, please...*

It was not enough, not nearly enough.

The soul eater was like a wild alley cat, trying to kick Ghost out—he certainly had never contemplated someone else eating his soul as it were.

A surge of pure anima exploded in Ghost's ethereal body, only it immediately propelled him backward, not forward, and he shot out of Wraith's resistant carcass like a cannonball that had just misfired.

What the hell?

Hovering above the stunned, angry soul eater as a scattered cluster of particles, then coalescing in the room, Ghost's spirit, still attached to his body by a faint silver cord, slowly floated up toward the ceiling, and he grappled to regain his bearings: Inanimate waves of light and vibration—topaz, citrine, and amethyst cells—were now swirling all around him, and then the light-infused cells swiftly tunneled downward, mutated into the shape of a dozen dark, spindly tics, and burrowed their tiny, seeking black heads into the flesh of the soul eater's body.

Wraith's flesh...

Somehow...

Someway...

Lord Dragos had linked his powerful essence with that of Lord Topenzi, Lord Cytarius, and Lord Amarkyus, and the dragon gods were uniting as one, usurping Ghost's perilous task. The gods were possessing Wraith's body themselves.

Holy shit.

They had the soul eater now and not a moment too soon.

Ghost could hear bold, heavy footfalls approaching the

chamber door. He could feel Lord Drakkar's dark, inky energy sucking out and replacing the very air in the corridor as the deity traversed the winding stone hall. The pagan king would enter the chamber any moment, and all Ghost could do was hover...and watch.

CHAPTER FOUR

"Do you really think I would leave this duty to my lord unattended...unsupervised? Do you really think I don't intend to stay and watch? Do not make me repeat myself again: *Remove your clothing and put that shit on.*"

Bethany's blood chilled, and her stomach sank like a heavy stone falling to the bottom of a filthy pond. Her mind swirled in desperation as she frantically searched for a way out.

The window!

She could never get there in time—the soul eater would catch her first.

The implements?

She couldn't slice an artery before Wraith Sylvester could stop her.

The door to the chamber, the hall, hiding somewhere in the Pagan Palace—no way could she escape! As for somehow appealing to the demon king, creator, and supreme ruler of the Pagan Horde?

Yeah, right—never gonna happen.

She couldn't cry, plead, beg, or reason with sheer, unadulterated evil.

All she could do was survive it...whatever was coming next.

But how?

So swept away in desperation and panic, Bethany hardly noticed the shadow-walker's sudden, drastic...dance, at least, not at first: the way he whipped his head to the side in the direction of the stained glass window; the way he gawked at the painted glass, eyes bulging in their sockets, madness glowing in his pupils; the fact that he took a violent, spasmodic stutter step backward and threw up his hands in a defensive posture—the sudden gasping, gagging, coughing, and spitting—and then the way he clawed at his skin as if it were suddenly on fire.

For all intents and purposes, the soul eater was flailing in place!

Twisting.

Shuddering.

Struggling...

Bethany finally found her footing. She stood and took several cautious steps back. As if being a soul-eating monster was not enough, Wraith Sylvester looked like he had just been possessed by an ancient maniacal spirit, and then, without warning or provocation, he grew eerily still, turned his head to the side in a robotic swivel, and fixed his gaze on Bethany. Only, his once coal-black stare was now glowing like a pebble beneath the shallow surface of a rushing river—topaz, citrine, amethyst, and bright, dazzling diamond—powerful, iridescent rays reflecting off the water's edge, swirling about the dark, tormented, stony pupils.

Bethany gasped, and Wraith's eyes changed back again.

Black.

Blank.

And inscrutable.

Yet this time, there was something else in their depths, stark desperation and unfettered...*rage*.

Whatever had possessed Wraith Sylvester had awakened his most base, animal instincts and removed all censure, reason, and self-control: The soul eater no longer cared about his place in the palace, and he didn't give a sinner's damn about Lord Drakkar's rules. He was going to have his savage way with Bethany before the king ever entered the room, and there was nothing she could do to stop it.

Absolutely...

Nothing.

An unbridled scream of horror assailed Bethany's windpipe, her hand flew up to her throat, and then the world went topsy-turvy.

A tug!

A rapid jerk.

The sensation of falling...*backward*...rising, lifting, shooting up into the air—it was as if she had abruptly left her body, and as she flailed, trying to catch her spirit's bearings, a pair of vaporous arms and a duo of equally ghostly hands seemed to encircle her waist, large, strong, unyielding fingers affixing to her rib cage.

Bethany hovered in the air, suspended beneath the thick, crisscrossed beams of the bedchamber ceiling, all the while locked in the grip of a ghostly...*sensation?*...yet staring down at her body below.

Far beneath her, as if in a slow-moving picture, the soul eater lunged, grasped Bethany's corporeal frame, and flung her onto the four-poster bed. He groaned, snarled, and clutched at Bethany's waist...her hips...her buttocks...her breasts. He tugged her beneath him and tore her shirt, shredding the thin, soft cotton like paper. Then he twisted, ripped, and sliced her jeans, tossing the ensuing ribbons across the chamber.

Her undergarments followed next.

He swiftly disrobed and covered her body.

It was all happening so fast—too fast—yet it seemed so far away.

Bethany's eyes grew wide—*her spiritual eyes*—as she watched the soul eater score her corporeal back with a pair of gnarled claws and swirl the tips of his fingers, the sensitive pads, in her fresh, crimson blood.

Bethany's blood!

She tried to close those same psychic peepers when he wrenched her hips forward, scored the curves of her waist down to her buttocks, and lifted her pelvis to meet his own seeking groin—but she couldn't look away. She was utterly transfixed. Paralyzed with panic. Rooted to the scene by morbid curiosity and an equal measure of horrified disbelief.

"Scream like this is really happening." A harsh, gravelly voice against her ethereal ear.

She startled, jolted, and began to fall from the ceiling, but the ghostly hands that had just been around her spirit's midriff tugged her back in place and tightened their grip. And then, as if on cue, the sentient body beneath her began to scream, loud, lingering, ear-piercing wails, trying to escape its assailant.

Wraith wrapped his blood-tinged digits around Bethany's throat, squeezed like he was juicing a lemon, and pressed down against her trachea to halt her incessant wailing.

Scream like this is really happening? Bethany thought. *It is really happening*—it was really happening—even if Bethany couldn't feel it! And if the body on the bed continued to scream, if Bethany continued to wail, the soul eater was going to kill her. He was going to strangle her to death.

Bethany's body tugged against Wraith's murderous grasp and began to pant instead.

"Now fight!" The same harsh, gravelly voice in her ear.

Bethany stared downward, numbly, trying to comprehend.

What the hell was happening?

And who...or what...was speaking in her ear?

"You're not strong enough to remove his hands from your throat, but you can easily break his little fingers if you isolate them first, then snap them with your fists."

Her spirit gasped as her body complied, as the woman on the bed ceased her struggles against the implacable chokehold, held her strangled breath, and began to feel in earnest for the soul eater's little fingers. She ran two trembling, seeking, pincer grasps along the length of all ten of the soul eater's clawed, spindly digits —thumbs, indexes, middle fingers, then ring fingers—until at last, she found both pinkies. Then she wrapped both fists around the small, bony, isolated digits, squeezed with all her might, rotated her wrists, and bent them backward. Just like the voice had instructed, the pinkies snapped like twigs, and the soul eater's murderous hands fell away from her body's throat.

A rage-filled roar of pain and fury filled the conical chamber, and just like that, the soul eater reared back, wrenched Bethany's knees apart, and exposed her thighs, her groin, and her most intimate, corporeal nature to the dank bedchamber air.

"Fight!" the disembodied voice thundered, his growl a harsh command.

Bethany's spirit cocked her head to the side, or maybe it just felt like she did—the entire scene was so befuddling, disorienting —and then she watched in both terror and wonder as the woman on the bed began to buck and twist.

To kick and resist.

To jackknife and bend—side to side, up and down—in frenzied, desperate, rebellious motions. And then the world, both above and below, went topsy-turvy again: The door to the bedchamber flew open, and the pagan king of the underworld stormed in, his deep-set eyes ablaze with madness. He flew like a gust of preternatural wind across the length of the chamber, dug all five fully extended talons into the soul eater's shoulders, and flung Wraith off Bethany's body onto the hard, craggy floor.

The king's nostrils flared.

His thin, reedy lips drew back in a crazed, sinister scowl.

And his distinct kaleidoscope eyes burned with ever-rising ferocity.

He glared beneath Bethany's open legs, gawked at the blood drawn from Wraith's fingers, now staining the coverlet and both of her thighs, and instantly drew the most obvious conclusion. "You dare to defile what was mine to take!" His terrible voice shook the stony rafters as he spun around to glower at Wraith.

The soul eater scampered to his knees, braced his rib cage in pain, and lowered his forehead to the cold medieval floor. "My liege—"

"*My liege?*" Lord Drakkar Hades thundered, mockingly.

"My venerable king," Wraith whimpered.

"Your venerable...*king?*"

"*Please.*"

"*Please?* Please what!"

"I-I-I wasn't in control—"

Lord Drakkar struck the cowering soul eater so swiftly, so violently, the walls in the chamber rattled, even as he spat the most vile, ancient curses in some guttural, bestial foreign language, then repeated them in English. The king fisted Wraith's parched hair in a dominant hand and wrenched him off the floor, tearing a large, uneven patch of bloody scalp from his skeletal head in the process. Then he flung the vile soul eater up into the air, like a cat toying with a helpless mouse, and held both hands upward, as if praying, while waiting for the vermin to come back down.

Before Wraith's body could hit the ground, the king struck with final fury. He removed the soul eater's entrails, sliced his jugular, and shredded his torso to ribbons—limbs, bones, and putrid organs—strewing each morbid heap about the chamber.

And just like that, Wraith Sylvester was dead.

Killed by his beloved lord and master.

And Bethany's spirit was back in her body.

Stunned, terrified, and dizzy with vertigo, Bethany instinctively clamped her thighs together, scurried backward on the four-poster bed, and raised both arms to shield her head in a cowering, defensive posture.

An eerie silence fell over the room, the calm before the storm, as Lord Drakkar Hades spun around on his heels, his powerful body still covered in gore, and fixed his hate-filled glare on the helpless, recoiling female.

"No...*no*...please no," Bethany muttered beneath panting breaths, even as she knew the effort was useless.

The pagan king inched closer.

Oh, God, make this quick—she said a silent prayer, then buried her head in her arms and waited.

Lord Drakkar leaned over her quivering form and bent to command her gaze. "Look at me, bitch."

Though every instinct in her body protested, Bethany slowly lowered her arms.

The king drew back his taut, narrow lips, exposing a lethal set of fangs, and then he stuck out his tongue, like a scenting snake, curled it inward, and slowly slid it over his lower lip. He flicked it in the air several times, like a tiny toy whip, flashed a grotesque, contorted grin, and hissed. And then the appendage—his tongue —snaked out even further, parted into eight even sections, and grew an equal number of spindly legs.

Legs!

His tongue grew freakin' legs...

Bethany's eyes bulged in their sockets, she gasped, and her stomach turned over in seasick waves as the most forward pair of spindly legs transformed into two grasping pedipalps, followed by a narrow, posterior, segmented tail. The end curled upward, stood erect, then bent back, and just like that, the entire tongue became a scorpion. Dark arachnid eyes looked out of the venomous invertebrate, reflecting a soulless tapestry, and Bethany's teeth began to chatter even as her eyes rolled back in her head.

Lord Drakkar drew closer and groaned.

He lowered the scorpion and allowed it to linger above her breasts, her stomach, down toward her thighs.

So, this was it.

Bethany froze, grit her teeth, and tried not to whimper.

She held her breath and closed her eyes.

Before this night was over, she would be somewhere else.

Unconscious?

Insane?

No longer alive...

Even if death had to take her, the nightmare would end.

It had to.

All nightmares did.

Determined to control her own passing, Bethany braced herself for the harsh transition as well as the inevitable, horrendous pain. She swallowed her cries, choked down her fear, and placed her full attention on her lungs and her breathing. She would regulate her respirations and count down the seconds—or the minutes—until final repose could take her. And if there was any mercy left in the universe, the ordeal would not take hours.

Her end would at least be quick.

CHAPTER FIVE

There were shitstorms.

And then there were...*shitstorms*.

And then there were the last five minutes in Ghost's *fated's* bedchamber, which was in a category all by itself: his female's spirit hovering beneath the beamed medieval ceiling, unknowingly grasped in Ghost's strong but ethereal hands; Wraith Sylvester, possessed by at least four of the seven dragon lords, losing his ever-lovin' mind, disrobing, and trying to help himself to the female's...inner sanctum, something he had no right to partake of; and now, Lord Drakkar, with a scorpion for a tongue, hovering over the terrified woman, lingering like a sadist in order to draw the shit out, and about to do gods-knew-what.

Shit!

Ghost couldn't track this hellish hurricane as fast as it changed directions.

And hovering above the worst of its fury like a useless, impotent rain cloud—safely ensconced in the eye of the storm, his spirit no longer in his body—had not been Ghost's intention

36

when he had scrambled to the end of the hall, scaled the castle wall, and climbed onto the ledge outside his *fated's* window.

Ghost had fully intended to mix it up...

Come hell or high water, no pun intended.

But that was then, and this was now.

The Seven had stepped in, the shitstorm had exploded, and Ghost needed to regain his bearings and do something *fast* before none of it mattered.

Father, give me back my body!

He streamed his essence toward the cavern's foyer, just so he would be facing inward with nothing at his back, the four-poster bed front and center—and then he waited.

C'mon, Lord Cytarius, Lord Topenzi, Lord Amarkyus! Lord Dragos—sire—*make this shit happen!*

A tug on the silver cord.

A whoosh of sound like an oncoming freight train.

Then a strange, tingling, whirring sensation, and Ghost was back in his body: corporeal, yet still invisible, and standing in the doorway of his *fated's* bedchamber. He glanced up at the ceiling, eyed the black iron bars on the arched stained glass window, then glanced down, once more, to inspect his heavy torso. Yep, all six-feet-five of him seemed to be there: thick, corded neck; dense, heavy muscle; and a spirit—or soul—packed betwixt all of it.

Inside it?

Within it?

Whatever!

The gods had deposited Ghost back in his body, his molecules were no longer scattered about the ceiling, and the silver cord was gone. More important than all that crazy, inexplicable, mind-numbing shit was the fact that the woman—*his woman*—was no longer bisected either. The human female had been back in her corporeal body since the moment Wraith Sylvester had been slaughtered, and unlike Ghost, his *fated* possessed a frail, helpless, human carcass, one that was about to be decimated by the supreme deity of the underworld. But enough of that sad, sappy reverie—it was time to focus—no feelings, no compassion, no emotion.

Ghost could not afford the weakness of passion, nor could he afford a single stray thought—not here, not now—not when he was about to announce his presence to the supreme ruler of the underworld. He relaxed his shoulders and slowed his heartbeat. He summoned the mercenary and the Genesis Son, the hatchling born of the Seven, the child, now a man, reared in blood and fire, and he focused his full, undivided attention on the depraved pagan king leaning over the bed, and the helpless female who was quivering like a leaf beneath him.

His mind clamped down like a vault—nothing in, nothing out—as Ghost reached behind his back, grasped the heavy, ornate handle on the bedchamber door, opened it quietly, then closed it briskly. He braced himself like a granite statue, willed his persona back into view, and cleared his throat to draw the king's attention as his flesh once again became visible. His *fated* could see him now, and so could Lord Drakkar. "You seen Killian or Wraith?" Ghost barked in the dark lord's direction, hoping the sudden, audacious, *clueless* enquiry would snap the king's mammalian brain stem out of its murderous frenzy and disrupt his primal, bestial drive to devour the prey before him.

As expected, the king spun around like a viper.

As hoped, Lord Drakkar Hades appeared too stunned by Ghost's presence, impudence, and stupid question to act or reply on impulse.

Good.

Ghost donned an even dumber expression. "Wraith?" he repeated, trying desperately to sell the ignorance. "Killian? Couldn't find them in the Great Hall's anteroom." In for a penny, in for a pound—he was prepared to give the desperate, reckless act his best Academy Award performance.

The king's ancient brow knitted into a gobsmacked frown, and he glared at Ghost like he had never seen a more foreign species. "What the fuck!?" the king finally bellowed, the scorpion darting in and out of his mouth.

Ghost held his blank expression, pretending not to notice. "Wraith," he repeated. "Killian Kross?"

"What...*how*...when the hell did you...boy, are you suicidal or just fucking daft!?"

Well, that about summed it up. "There's something I forgot to add to the map," Ghost said, barreling forward in the same careless direction, "and Wraith had a couple unanswered questions—thought I saw him head this direction."

The king practically snorted with incredulity. "Do you not see this woman!" Spittle flew from his contorted lips. "Do you not see this vulgar, bloody bedchamber?" He choked on the arachnid filling his gullet, until he was finally forced to swallow it whole. "Do you not comprehend both where you are and to whom you are speaking?" His eyes bulged in their black-hearted sockets, and his pupils flashed with delirium. "How dare you—"

"My bad," Ghost interrupted, all the while bracing inwardly to be slaughtered. "The castle. I still get turned around." He spared a glance toward the bed, toward his *fated*, and raised one shoulder in an indifferent, cocky shrug before holding both palms up and outward in a gesture of contrition. "Didn't mean to barge in or interrupt. No disrespect. Of course I know who you are...*my liege.*"

King Drakkar Hades blinked three times, words and reason eluding him.

Ghost's erratic behavior and asinine comments had elicited the intended effect: The demon king was caught off guard, he was momentarily befuddled, and the absolute mental incongruity of the moment had distracted him from his deadly purpose, defiling and destroying the female on the bed. Ghost flashed a devil-may-care smile. "Wraith?" he reiterated.

The king threw two angry hands in the air and gestured wildly. "I have no fucking idea where Killian went, nor why you are so intent on provoking my wrath; but *Wraith*, in case you haven't noticed, is all over the fucking floor!" He gestured at the blood, guts, and strewn intestines littering the stone and mortar.

"Damn." Ghost licked his thick bottom lip. "*Shit*...my bad. What the hell did he do?"

Swirling smoke and dancing flames eddied around the king's dark, gangly fingers, and literal steam wafted from his ears. He took a menacing step toward Ghost, and that's when the female on the bed began to scramble backward...sideways...eyeing the barred window and the chamber floor. She was obviously thinking of making a run for it.

Don't move! Ghost sent the telepathic command into his *fated's* head with all the gentleness of a battering ram, glowering into her eyes and stealing her full name from her hippocampus.

Beth.

So, his *dragyra's* name was Beth...

Bethany Kayla Reid.

Not one fucking muscle, Beth! he added to the telepathic order.

King Drakkar Hades raised one hand slowly, too slowly, and rotated the tips of his fingers toward Ghost.

Oh, shit...

He was about to smite the dragyri dead, right where Ghosta-niaz stood, and that's when Ghost changed tack. "Let me guess," he snarled, signaling toward the floor and away from his *fated*, "Wraith came into this chamber at your direction to prepare your newest slave for her duty, to get her ready for your...exploration, but then he had a change of heart." He cocked both brows in a sardonic gesture, hoping to prick the king's pride. "Decided to circumvent the whole make-her-ready-for-the-king bullshit and enjoy her for himself. You caught him. You killed him. And that's when I walked in." The king snorted, and a thin plume of fire escaped his nostrils, revealing his original, prehistoric genus; but Ghost didn't give him time to conjure fire, nor to think of his next reply. "But, my liege, that's only half the story. Truth is: The bastard had it in for you all along." He dangled the bait and waited. The king would either kill him right then and there, or Ghost would be given another few seconds to expound on his audacious accusation.

"*The bastard?*" King Drakkar chided. "You mean *Wraith?* One of my oldest and most loyal subjects, a soul eater who has stood at the right hand of my throne for the last ten centuries?"

Ghost shrugged his shoulders again, this time in a blatant, dismissive manner. "So loyal he was about to defile your newest slave. So loyal he didn't feel the need to follow your orders or even to watch the clock as he defied them. So loyal he was asking me questions about the Seven—but not where they resided in the Pantheon and not just for Killian's map—rather, he wanted to know which of the dragon lords might have more power than you, which ones might be open to persuasion...temptation...whether any of them had any mortal weaknesses. In other words, is there any way a dragon lord can be killed, and if you, as their brother, the eighth to the seven, shared the same vulnerability."

King Drakkar cackled, his loathing rising. "You're lying." The words were barely audible.

Ghost stared pointedly at the woman still cowering on the bed, and then glanced at the blood-strewn floor. "Am I?"

The king narrowed his hate-filled gaze. "*If* Wraith asked you such questions, then rest assured, it was to increase the Pagan Horde's base of knowledge. *If* he asked about...mortal weaknesses, it was to always and ultimately protect his lord."

"Maybe," Ghost muttered. "Maybe not. All I know is that Wraith wanted to know if an immortal Dragon Lord could be killed. He wanted to know if *you* could be killed. Perhaps just to further his body of knowledge...perhaps not. What I can attest to is that the whole damn time he was asking all those...shady questions...he just stared at that red velvet throne like a dog salivating over a bone. Kinda like a male consumed with lust and envy. Kinda the same way he stared at that woman when that dude with the rusty nail through his nose dragged her down the hall toward this chamber." This time, he pointed directly at Beth. "So yeah, maybe he didn't really want your throne, and maybe he didn't really want that female. Only"—he kicked a pile of bloody gore with the toe of his boot and grimaced—"looks like the part about the female is a bit hard to refute."

The king smirked, then laughed again, only this time his snicker was far more sinister. "And you, Ghostaniaz Dragos; you are sharing all this for what altruistic purpose? Out of the goodness of your heart? Out of your own undying loyalty?"

Ghost grinned from ear to ear. "Nah. *Neither.*" He growled like the dragon offspring he was. "Out of self-preservation, my liege. I followed Wraith to this room because I knew exactly what the son of a bitch was up to, and I thought if I could catch him in the act, myself, I might just get the pleasure of killing one of my captors, consequence free, as well as a chance to elevate my position. I have no friends here—you are all my enemies. But at least I'm smarter than Wraith, and I know who to align my fortune with...who to challenge...and who to suck up to. Who I can't defy or betray and still live to tell about it."

King Drakkar licked his bottom lip in a purely serpentine movement. "And who to lie to. Don't forget that neglected detail —did you not begin this conversation by asking if I had seen Killian or *Wraith?* Did you not just make up some pitiful falsehood about forgetting to add something to the map?"

"Touché," Ghost shot back. "Figured it'd be best to ease into the real subject. Couldn't exactly lead with '*Your right-hand man is a traitor.*'"

"I see. And now you figure...what? That I will dismiss your lying tongue and spare your hypocritical life because you shared some worthless morsel, according to the way you, a captive slave and enemy, see it?"

"Nah." Ghost shook his head. "I figure that at the end of the day, friends, allies, or enemies, blood is always thicker than water."

At this, King Drakkar drew back. He measured Ghost from head to toe then cocked his head to the side in equal measures of disdain and curiosity. "Blood?" he queried, his voice thick with suspicion.

Ghost nodded crisply. "Yeah, blood." He let the word linger for the space of several heartbeats. "Are you and my biological father not brothers? At least cut from the same cloth or split from the same primordial atom?" When King Drakkar didn't speak, Ghost pressed on: "Lord Dragos' blood is your blood. Lord Dragos' blood is my blood. Do you and I not share the same familial bloodline? And is that ancestry, that DNA, that ancient genetic lineage, not a closer pedigree—a stronger tie—than any you might share with every one of the demons or the shades you created over time immemorial?" He held up one hand. "Don't get me wrong, creation is a powerful thing, and indeed you have crafted a formidable army—but I'm talking about family... race...*pedigree*. One's people. Flesh of my flesh, bone of my bone, and yes, blood of my blood."

The corner of King Drakkar's mouth turned up in the semblance of a ghoulish smile. "Are you looking for a new daddy, Ghost?"

The words sent chills up the dragyri's spine—Lord Drakkar was not a monster to toy with—but Ghost was already in too deep. He shrugged a muscular shoulder and went in for the metaphorical kill, nothing to lose but his life at this juncture. "I despise Lord Dragos, and that is the truth. Make of it what you will. And I have zero shits to give whether I live in the Pantheon or this soul-forsaken cauldron of an underworld, as long as I'm reasonably comfortable. But what I am after is clemency, wherever I reside, a life free of endless torture and bullshit. As a cellular offspring of an original creator, I'm superior to a fabricated minion, however divinely manufactured, and you know it. What I want is a position of power and prestige, something worthy of my blood and my lineage. What I'm bargaining for, right here and now, is the girl—the one on the bed. A little pleasure, some regular carnal distraction, would go a long way toward endearing me to my pagan uncle and presenting the underworld in a whole new light. Why the fuck not? What have I got to lose? What do you have to lose? I'm no threat to you or your kingdom, but, my liege, Lord Drakkar, make no mistake: I *am* your flesh and blood. Your *only* flesh and blood in this entire Pagan Palace."

Silence consumed the medieval bedchamber, and Ghost struggled not to shift where he stood—to make a little more room in his denim for his gonads—because what he was doing was ballsy as hell. Even for a devil-may-care, reckless, suicidal mercenary, it was an audacious stretch, and he was shocked he hadn't just split the seams of his pants.

One could've heard a pin drop a parallel dimension away.

And then Lord Drakkar began to slink, more than walk, slowly, in Ghost's direction. He circled the Dragyr three separate times, and each time around, he tightened the circle. Ghost shuffled and followed suit, like they were dancing the paso doble, too terrified to speak, yet too wise to turn his back on the ancient pagan monarch.

At last, Lord Drakkar pressed a black, spindly finger against his own taut lips and let out a thin fissure of fetid breath. "I don't know whether to snatch the amulet from your arrogant neck and return your soul to the cosmos; to torture you, bit by infinitesimal bit, until epochs of time have recycled, and I have finally had my fill; or to meet your audacity, your unmitigated gall and disrespect, with a reward worthy of its boldness. I do know, however, that there has to be at least a semblance of truth in your self-aggrandizing, foolhardy words, because no one besides an original offspring could possibly have such enormous balls."

Well, shit...

The king had caught it too.

Lord Drakkar laughed out loud, a harsh, discordant sound. "And all of this for a place in my horde and a pretty piece of ass?" He spared a glance at the woman on the bed. "Flesh of my flesh and blood of my blood." And then he pressed his nose to Ghost's. "Clean up this chamber. Make it your own. And yes, you may defile and keep the human woman. Screw her into oblivion if you like—kill her if you wish. Just see to it that as long as she is breathing, she joins the other slaves in service to the castle and unerring obedience to my whims. You may continue to work with Killian on the map, but there will be no position of power and prestige, not at this early, unproven juncture. I will be watching...observing...measuring your every word, deed, and intention, discerning your fealty at every turn. Perhaps affection will grow in time. Perhaps it will not. But either way, know this, Ghostaniaz Dragos, blood of my blood and flesh of my flesh: If you deceive me, betray me, even glance at me sideways in a way that I do not approve of, you will rue the day you bartered with the all-powerful ruler of the underworld. You will eat every arrogant, narcissistic word, and you will pray for death—you will plead for the same—but death will not be forthcoming. Forever is a long time to suffer, so choose wisely, once and for all: death, right here and now at my hand, or the girl and life, forever in my service. And just to be clear about what the latter looks like, from this day forward, you will not just serve me—you will live for me, and *you will worship me* like your own flesh and blood."

Ghost gulped on his resolve even as he swallowed and tried to digest the king's words.

Fuuuck.

Talk about making a bargain with the devil.

His eyes swept the length of the bedchamber and then rested on his *fated*, his dragyra...

On Beth.

Her beautiful, dark brown eyes were wide as saucers, filled with equal parts dread, confusion, and revulsion, and as much as he wanted to save her, as much as something deep and elemental —something buried in his core—compelled him to do no other, Ghostaniaz Dragos also had zero shits to give about another living, sentient being.

No woman was worth selling one's soul.

No breath of life was worth this bargain.

Ghost retracted his neck, drew back his chin until his nose was no longer touching King Drakkar Hades', and then he squared his shoulders to the Father of the Pagan Realm, took a deep breath, and made the call. "I will not betray you," he grunted. "And I will keep our blood lineage at the forefront of all my decisions. But *live* for you, worship you like some lovesick, sycophantic bitch? Nah, don't have that shit in me."

Lord Drakkar recoiled, snarled, and then he moved so quickly, Ghost never saw the long, pointed nails on the gnarled, blackened hands moving toward him. The king snatched the cord on Ghost's amulet, tightened his fist around it, and yanked back so hard, smoke wafted from the amulet.

Only, nothing happened.

Interesting...

So, Lord Drakkar did not know everything there was to know about the Dragyr, the Pantheon of Dragons, or the inner workings of the Seven's creation. The sacred gemstone that infused Ghost with life, the permanent talisman he received at his formal induction into his adulthood lair, was, for all intents and purposes, indestructible. The only one who could remove it was Ghost's sire. And the only way for Lord Drakkar Hades to get it off Ghost's neck was to first remove Ghost's head. If Lord Drakkar wanted the life-giving umbilical cord, he would have to decapitate, incinerate, or dismember the dragyri first.

And therein lay the rub...

Ghost steadied his breathing and waited.

The shit could go either way.

Surprised, disappointed—*then curiously amused?*—Lord Drakkar released the cord and smiled the most wicked, duplicitous grin Ghost had ever witnessed. "Ah, I see. It would appear your beloved dragon papa decided to make his firstborn hatchling practically imperishable. *Practically*, not actually." He tilted his ear toward his shoulder. "Alas, I could remove your head, but then I think this demonstrates my previous point most brilliantly: Death will not be an easy out for you, *nephew*." He took a measured step back and regarded the Dragyr surreptitiously. "For now, you do not have to wholly worship me, but don't ever disrespect me again. If I tell you to grovel, you grovel." He extended his fingers toward the floor, and a glob of filthy, bloody sinew and innards floated into his palm. He twirled it in and out of his fingers, until the residue dangled from his flesh like sloppy, garish webbing.

In a swift, brutal sleight of hand, once again too rapid for Ghost's eyes to register, the king of the underworld pried Ghost's mouth open, stuffed the grisly entrails around his tongue and his teeth, then held the dragyri's lips shut until he instinctively swallowed in order to breathe. "Just a taste of your future, a reminder of Wraith...the equivalent of washing a recalcitrant child's mouth out with soap. You may be superior to a manufactured minion, though not by much, *not by much at all*, but your greatest powers are a stain on the chamber pot I shit in every morning, when compared to the least of my own." He glided toward the door and held up a forefinger. "Not another word, Ghostaniaz. Not. One. Single. Word."

Ghost bit his bottom lip.

"Kneel."

Ghost reluctantly dropped to his knees.

"Now kiss the filthy ground I just walked on."

Lips twitching, muscles straining, every cell in his body itching to protest, Ghost lowered his head to the chamber floor and touched the granite with his lips. Despite what his sire—and now Lord Drakkar—might think of him, Ghost might be brazen, hopelessly reckless, and even a shameless risk taker, but he wasn't irredeemably stupid. And gruesome midnight snack notwithstanding, filthy ground aside, he had more or less won this first round and pushed Lord Drakkar as far as he was going to get away with.

"Lick it."

Ghost's shoulders tensed, he pursed his lips, and his temples began to radiate with feral anger.

"I said, *lick it*."

Ghost drew in a harsh breath...

Wraith was dead. Beth was still living. And Ghost had managed to secure possession of his ill-fated dragyra, however temporarily, all while keeping his head on his shoulders.

The shit could've gone a whole lot worse.

He bent once more, extended his tongue, and touched the very tip of the same to the cold stone floor, barely making contact—he also had his limits.

"Good boy," Lord Drakkar spat caustically; then he exhaled a plume of red-hot vapor, turned on his heel, and vanished.

CHAPTER SIX

EARTHSIDE

K ari Baker, Joy Green, Nicole Perez, and Anne Liu hunkered down in a loose semicircle, sprawled like a tight-knit family at an outdoor picnic, all squeezed upon a modest blanket, only they were atop the soft, carpeted floor in the living room of Nicole's small, third-floor apartment. It was 12:45 A.M. All Hallows' Eve had officially ended forty-five minutes ago, and by Nicole's count, it was exactly two hours, forty-nine minutes, and a handful of seconds since Beth had disappeared from that horrifying haunted attraction.

Tragedy did not even begin to explain it.

Why had they gone anyway?

If they could only take that back...stay at home instead.

In the absence of obvious signs of foul play, an officer at the local precinct had informed Beth's *besties* that it was far too early to consider her missing, that they needed to contact everyone Beth knew—especially any male companions she could have taken off with—to first make sure there wasn't a simple explanation for her abrupt and puzzling vanishing act. Still, the law did not necessarily require twenty-four to seventy-two hours before an official report could be filed, and Nicole Perez, one of Beth's oldest and dearest friends, had been insistent, pressing the officer to take down Beth's information, even as Kari, Joy, and Anne got busy making phone calls, sending texts, and placing forlorn, desperate posts on social media.

Now, as the four women gathered in Nicole's quaint, tidy, one-bedroom bungalow, the Halloween movie marathon no longer on the itinerary, they tried to wrap their heads around what in the world could have happened. They tried to keep their fear in check.

"She wouldn't just walk away without a word," Kari insisted, pinching the bridge of her nose between her high-arched brows.

Nicole sniffed. She glanced out a pair of whimsical, sheer white curtains billowing beneath a half-open window, and stared at the haunting moonlight above. The dim white light shone through the tiny window, casting silver and gray shadows along the length of her indigo blue chaise and the soft white blanket strewn over the sectional's arm, the blanket Beth always snuggled beneath while the five of them devoured popcorn and huddled together. "She was in the wagon, maybe four carts behind me. We saw her go into the ride."

"But she didn't come out," Anne Liu responded, swiping a lock of thick, straight black hair away from her stunning eyes.

"We checked!" Joy insisted, twisting a finger through her naturally curly locks. "Over and over! We walked the full length of the tracks. We had the manager shut down the ride and flood the exhibit with LED lights. The guy even questioned every one of his employees, the actors in the haunted house, the ticket takers, hell, even the girl at the snack stand. No one saw Beth—how is that possible?"

"It's not," Nicole insisted. "It just...isn't."

"So then who took her?" Anne's voice began to shake.

"Took her or...or hurt her," Kari whispered.

Nicole tightened her hands into fists and crossed her arms over her stomach, leaning back against a large, overstuffed floor pillow before relaxing her fingers once more, only to nervously pick at the tufts in the stiff gray carpet. "There would have been blood," she offered matter-of-factly, flicking a tassel of nylon in the air and modulating her tone.

"She would've screamed," Anne said.

Joy nodded emphatically as if to convince herself. "There would definitely have been some sign of a struggle."

Kari's soft hazel eyes dimmed from worry, the color now matching the faint golden-red of her Irish lashes. She licked her bottom lip and shivered. "Unless she couldn't. Unless it all happened too fast."

"Who would hurt Beth?" Anne rushed the words as if she had to get them out before she lost her courage.

"No one, at least no one who knew her," Kari said.

"A stranger." Joy narrowed her eyes with a shudder.

"No." Nicole had heard enough, had enough. "None of this makes sense. Human beings don't just vanish into thin air." All three of her guests nodded. "Fuck!" She wrung her hands together, then tightened two fists. "Just...*fuck*." She pursed her soft, heart-shaped lips into a taut, angry frown, absently grasped at the silver cross she always wore around her neck, and whispered a faint prayer beneath her breath to Saint Christopher for protection. "We need to light some candles."

At this, Joy snorted. "Our lifelong friend, my sister of the heart, went into a freakin' haunted house and never came out—she just vanished into thin air on Halloween night, and that's what we're gonna do? Sit on the floor of this living room, discuss it like a casual therapy session, and light some fucking candles?"

"Joy," Kari admonished, "Nicole's just trying to be—"

"No, that's okay," Nicole cut in. "I get it. We're all frustrated. We're all scared. *We're all pissed*. And we all feel helpless. But we can't go back to the police station before morning, and I have to tell you guys—I dunno, but I can't shake it—to hell with therapy; there's just this...vibe. I don't even know how to explain it. I just have this really creepy feeling, and it's beyond the obvious reasons."

Anne sat up straight. Ever the peacemaker and one to avoid both conflict and too much conjecture, she tried to change the subject: "We should check the online post again. Maybe someone heard something, knows something. Maybe someone—"

"Wait," Kari interjected. "What Nicole just said." She paused for the space of several heartbeats. "Earlier tonight, when we first met up, you guys didn't feel it? I mean...nobody else felt it?"

"Felt what?" Anne asked, her skin a sudden pasty pallor.

"Sin," Nicole blurted, feeling instantly guilty for saying it aloud.

"Sin?" Anne echoed, her usually elegant features contorting.

Nicole shrugged apologetically, and that's when Joy leaned forward, rested one elbow on the coffee table, and placed the tip of a stunning manicured nail against her brightly painted bottom lip. "Oh, snap!" she said, as if suddenly receiving some deep revelation. "Nicole is right. *Sin.*"

Anne shook her head in confusion.

"What do you mean, exactly, Nicole?" Kari asked. "Sin's a pretty harsh term."

Nicole paused to weigh her words carefully—should she just blurt it out, or would it be better to hold her tongue? After all, Bethany Reid was the strongest...kindest...most compassionate person any of them likely knew. She wasn't soft or weak by any means, but she did have a heart of gold. Pure. Solid. Gold. Still... yeah...they needed to get this out in the open, and Nicole was the only one brazen enough to just spill the tea. "The seven deadly sins: lust, gluttony, greed, and sloth. Wrath, envy, and pride." There. She'd said it.

At this, Anne threw her dainty hands in the air. "What the hell are you saying, Nicky?"

Yikes; she'd used Nicole's nickname.

"Guuurl..." Joy nodded emphatically.

"I don't know how to explain it," Nicole said, "but it's like I almost heard those very words. Every time I glanced at Beth— every time I looked at Beth—there was just this sense...this impression...this almost audible narration, like a cartoon cloud hovering in the air, right above her head, and it was broadcasting the same three words: *the seven sins*."

"No way!" Anne stood up and glared at Nicole, Anne's petite, five-feet-four-inch frame visibly shaking. "So now Beth is some kind of evil or sinful person, and whatever happened to her in the haunted house is what? The wrath of some vengeful god? Karma gone awry? Enough with all the religious nonsense. I'm sorry, Nicole, but we're not all Catholic." She raised her voice, which was an extreme rarity for the kind, soft-hearted woman.

"Okay, you did *not* have to go there, little Miss Anne," Joy chided, flicking the same manicured hand in Anne's direction. "There's no need to get nasty."

Anne sighed. "I didn't mean...*nonsense*...just that maybe..." Her voice trailed off. "Nicole, we're just not all superstitious."

"Whoa!" Joy interjected, this time holding her palm in a clear, unambiguous signal: *Stop*. She took a deep breath, lowered her lids, and spoke in a thick, golden-toned voice, the soft yet authoritative power permeating the living room. "We all need to take a breath. Just chill. Think before we speak. Whatever is going on with Beth, we are *not* going to turn on each other. Understood?"

"It's the lust, the envy, and the wrath," Kari whispered. "It's still hovering." All three women turned to gawk at the reddish-haired beauty, and Kari slowly nodded her head. "Anne, I felt it too...heard it too...I dunno, maybe sensed it too, and I'm not religious." She swallowed a lump in her throat and held steady eye contact with Anne, her eyes revealing her apology. "It was like...it was almost impossible not to sense *something*, not like Beth was bad or evil, or even sinful—never, not Beth!—but like someone had poured that shit all over her."

"Like a virus," Joy added.

"Something attacking her," Nicole chimed in.

Anne sat back down, gathered her knees to her chest, and wrapped her arms around her shins for comfort. Shrugging slightly, she offered, "Well, I'm Buddhist, not Catholic, so I don't really have a concept of *sin*, per se—but it's funny, now that you describe it that way, because earlier, when we were on our way to the haunted house, the concept of the hindrances...the Kleshas... did cross my mind. Like more than once. I figured it was just a Halloween jitters thing. You know, the way we get ourselves all freaked out every year by the atmosphere, the way we celebrate... the way it plays tricks on our minds."

"Excuse me," Joy said, her dark eyes narrowing in both concern and concentration, "but what are the...*Kleshas*?"

Anne nodded circumspectly. "Sort of like a state of being... like mental states of mind that can afflict someone...make life or the spiritual practice more difficult."

"You mean like a bad mood or a nasty disposition?" Joy asked.

"Well, sort of," Anne said, "although that would be more like the result of—"

"And?" Nicole interrupted. "How does that relate to the seven sins?"

"The Kleshas are sensual desire, anger, and ill-will, sloth or torpor, restlessness or worry, and doubt."

"What's torpor?" Joy asked, cocking one brow.

"It's like apathy," Kari answered for Anne.

"Huh," Joy said.

"Not all that different," Nicole observed, shaking her head as if to dislodge some cobwebs. "I think the real point Anne is trying to make is that she felt something too." She glanced around the living room, eyed each woman in turn, and shuddered. "We all felt something really weird. Really...off."

"Unnatural," Kari said.

"And whatever it was—whatever we're calling it—it was following Beth?" Anne asked.

"It was *all over* Beth," Joy clarified, in her typical, no-nonsense manner.

"For the lack of a better word, it was haunting Beth," Nicole said.

Anne shrugged her slight shoulders. "So, what then? We light candles? Try to find a priest? I don't understand how this works or what this means."

"Oh shit!" Kari suddenly exclaimed, holding up her brightly lit cell phone, fingers clasped in a death grip around the soft, mint-green butterfly case. "There's a super creepy comment on our Community Social Circle post. Some guy named Bryce M. No picture, just an avatar, but check out what he wrote!" She held her phone up and outward to share the glowing screen; then she rotated it in a slow semicircle before turning it back around and bringing it up to her eyes. "I have no idea what happened to your friend, never met her, but I think I know where you need to look. Have you ever heard of the seven sins or the Cult of Hades? I have reason to believe your friend Beth might have gotten caught in that web..."

Silence hovered in the living room like a living entity. As everyone's mouths hung open, it circled and spread out like rings from a heavy stone plopped into a murky pond, until the absence of sound became positively deafening.

Finally, Joy broke the spell: "She *might have gotten caught in that web?* What the fuck!? This guy had something to do with it!"

"What does that even mean?" Kari said. "Beth would *never* join a cult."

"We gotta go back to the police station," Joy insisted.

"Wait a minute." Nicole spoke with caution, even as the hairs stood up on her arms. "I agree; this guy is sketchy as hell. Why would a total stranger, someone outside our network of friends and family, even read the post on our page, let alone share his two cents on the subject. But did you hear what he actually said?"

"Yeah," Joy replied. "He basically said Beth, a girl he's never met, was caught in a web. *Caught.* As in snagged, surprised... captured! *By him.*"

"Click on his profile!" Anne rocked forward onto her knees and straightened her back, pointing at the cell phone.

Kari tapped the screen several times, then scrolled from right to left. "There's nothing on it. No picture. No background info. No posts. Like he just opened an account five minutes ago."

"This is crazy," Anne said.

"He just asked us if we'd ever heard of the seven sins!" Nicole burst out, practically shouting. "You guys don't think that's weird?" She jumped up, made a beeline to the kitchen, where she kept a box of candles, and yanked hastily at a narrow drawer beside the oven. "I don't care if you're Christian, Catholic, atheist, or Buddhist—or if you just crawled out of the Dark Ages and still believe the earth is flat—but this shit just got next-level real. Yes, we need to go back to the police station and show them the post—to hell with waiting until morning! But first, we need to burn some candles and say a prayer for Beth!" She snatched a set of three candles, a small box of matches, and circled her wrist in the general direction of Kari and her now ominous smartphone. "And I also think we should write this Bryce M guy back, see if we can't get some more information out of him while he's talking."

"Like, who the hell are you?" Kari said.

"And what the fuck is the Cult of Hades," Joy added.

"Yeah," Nicole said. "All of that. This whole thing is just way too creepy."

"Oh my gosh," Anne mumbled beneath her breath. "Poor Beth..."

"What *exactly* should I ask him?" Kari said, placing her cell phone on the coffee table and moving some art and design magazines out of the way to make room for the candles.

"Ask him how he came across the post," Nicole offered.

"Should I try to get his full name?" Kari asked.

"*Yes*," Joy insisted. "Phone number...address...hell, social security number."

"Ask him if he would be willing to meet us at the police station," Anne suggested.

"No!" all three other women exclaimed in unison.

"You don't want to scare him away," Joy clarified.

Anne nodded, even as she clutched a pillow and scooted closer to the coffee table. "Nicole," she said sheepishly, watching her intently as if to read Nicole's feelings by each subtle expression. "I'm sorry for what I said earlier...about Catholicism...superstition. I was just worried. Upset. Completely freaked out."

"Don't worry about it," Nicole said softly. "I totally understand."

Kari closed her eyes and visibly shivered. "I don't think this is as simple as some weirdo abducting Beth, and I don't think it's about religion or any of us being superstitious. I think...I think... heaven help her, but I think something really, *really* awful happened to Beth tonight. Something totally...unnatural...and way beyond the scope of the police. And I can't even believe I just said that out loud."

Just then, an icy breeze swept through a crack in the half-open window, swirled around the living room, and left several brittle eddies of crystallized ice on the chaise, coffee table, and light gray carpet. Though the night was chilly, and it was supposed to snow later, what stood out to Nicole was far more frightening, eerie, and telling than the sudden, freakish breeze: It had not yet started raining or snowing.

CHAPTER SEVEN

THE PANTHEON

A girl—

No, a fated dragyra.

A boy named Bryce M—nay, a Dragyr male from the Diamond Lair.

Four human females, desperate to find their best friend.

Or...

A set of easily honed, soon to be finely tuned lures to hopefully hook a sycophantic member of Lord Drakkar's Pagan Horde.

So, the trap was almost set.

Lord Dragos paced like a wild thing, back and forth atop the magnificent glass floors in the enormous Temple of Seven, pausing only briefly to take in his own refracted, jeweled reflection before glancing at his dragon-lord brethren, each fearsome deity in turn. "He's alive!" Lord Dragos bellowed, snarling to emphasize the words.

Lord Amarkyus reclined against his brilliant amethyst throne and nodded his head ever so slightly, but he didn't say a word.

"Strong," Lord Topenzi offered.

"Indeed." Lord Cytarius narrowed his citrine eyes in certain agreement. "Ghostaniaz was going to try to possess the soul eater himself, before we intercepted his effort and took over Wraith's body."

"He's fighting!" Lord Dragos drew back his top lip in a sullen scowl, his tone as surly as his restless pacing.

Lord Topenzi clasped his hands in his lap and smiled, seemingly undaunted by Lord Dragos' demeanor, ever the most ascendant of the fold. "As is she, the human female, the *fated* we chose to activate early."

At this, Lord Dragos flicked his wrist in the air and snorted. "Well, thank the Oracle Pool and my own omniscient wisdom for convincing the rest of you to help me find the girl, prematurely, to visit her in her dreams, and to coat her essence in the seven deadly sins. And thank every bastard in the blasted underworld that the pagans took the bait!"

"Agreed," Lord Saphyrius said, likely in the interest of getting along, as well as brevity. "Yet, I would like it on the oral record that I still have reservations about sending such a pure, innocent soul into such an unholy place—such a tainted and dangerous realm—but alas, what is done is done."

He'd like it on the oral record! Lord Dragos rolled his large diamond eyes. What the fuck was an *oral* record, anyway, in a private, unrestrained conversation amongst dragon gods? So much for getting along...or brevity. Lord Dragos spun around on his ethereal tail, the majority of his persona being projected in human form, and a plume of smoke escaped his flaring nostrils. "The girl is insignificant," he barked. "What matters most is all we have achieved thus far." He ambled aimlessly toward the Oracle Pool, as if mere proximity with the pearlescent waters might enhance his patience and stabilize his mood. "We managed to get Bethany into the Pagan Palace, we were able to make fleeting contact with Ghost's soul before the connection was broken, and we were industrious enough to provoke Wraith's arrogance—the genuflecting minion's pure stupidity—until our wayward sibling killed the blasted idiot, himself." He smiled then, replaying the fateful moment in his head. "Yea, Lord Drakkar extinguished his own right-hand man. And Ghost! What can be said about my genesis offspring? He is clever, is he not? He will do what he has to do and say what he has to say. If there is a way...*any way*...to manipulate Lord Drakkar, Ghostaniaz will find it. He will exploit the king and find his way home. He will. *He must.* It is simply...imperative!" His words were met with a lethal silence, more expansive than the looming cathedral ceiling above, but Lord Dragos paid it no mind—he knew his Genesis Son. Ghost was a first-class heathen, to be sure, a hardass rebel with zero shits to give about anyone's rules, conventions, or even his own well-being, but that was precisely what made the dragyri exquisitely suited for the challenge that lay ahead of him. Perhaps Lord Drakkar had finally met his match.

The pregnant moment lingered until, at last, Lord Topenzi cleared his throat. "Might I remind you, my esteemed brother, Lord Dragos, first of the Seven, and father to a captured son—just as a matter of course, mind you—that what happens to the human girl is quite significant, indeed. Do not forget that Ghost has only eight more days to bring her to this very temple, that we must convert her by fire, or his life will be forfeit, and you will ultimately lose him just the same." He waved his hand in a gentle but dismissive arc before Lord Dragos could eat him for lunch. "That said...*that said*...your observations are correct: We were fortunate that Ghost reached out from the netherworld, that his soul cried out for help. It allowed us to enter the pagan realm, if only for a fleeting moment, to do what needed to be done, and through Ghost's eyes—through Wraith's eyes, at least for the duration of the soul eater's possession, at least until we set Ghost back in his body and stood him, whole, before the chamber door—we were able to see quite a bit. Only now, we are blind once again. Only now, we are here once again. Separate. Alone. Sequestered in this temple. Apart from Ghost and whatever is going on in the underworld." He rushed his next words before Lord Dragos could cut him off. "Yea, once again, we find ourselves tinkering with fate and infinite power to expose even more innocent souls to an incarnate evil. I agree with Lord Saphyrius."

Shiiit.

Lord Topenzi made Lord Dragos' head spin.

He could hardly follow all that eloquent yada-yada.

Speak fuckin' English—or even Dragonese—brother!

Still, if one could sift through all the fluff and nonsense, Lord Topenzi's words were usually packed with wisdom. Not to mention, the matter was far too serious, too critical, to become sidetracked with constant petty squabbles. Despite his usual inflammable temper, Lord Dragos considered all of Lord Topenzi's words carefully, and the more he considered, the more he pondered...the more he latched on to one particular sentence within the long, rambling diatribe: *We were fortunate that Ghost reached out from the netherworld, that his soul cried out for help.*

Ghost *had* reached out from the netherworld, but he had not reached out to the Seven!

Nay, he had reached out to Lord Dragos, specifically, to his sire, and he had actually said, *Father, please...*

Despite himself, Lord Dragos couldn't help but replay that singular memory, again and again, in his mind—whether out of morbid curiosity, prurient fascination, or timeless wonder, he couldn't say. Just the same, the moment was stamped into his serpentine hippocampus for all time, and the truth of it had shaken the ancient dragon to his core: Ghostaniaz had rendered himself invisible before leaving his body. He had made a choice to try to possess Wraith Sylvester himself, and in that stunning moment, that shocking, incomprehensible gap, Ghost had gathered the full power of his focused thought and reached out—nay, sought in earnest—the assistance of his cold, calloused creator. With the full measure and intent of his being, Ghostaniaz had, more or less, *prayed* to Lord Dragos—he had asked his *father* for help.

More power, Lord Dragos!

Those were Ghostaniaz's words.

Father, please...

Yes, Ghost had said *Father*; hell, Ghost had said *Please*.

Or at least he had thought it.

And because of Ghost's power, Ghost's intention, *Ghost's* unfathomable and transcendent connection to his sire, Lord Dragos had been able to cross a multitude of dimensions and step into another time and place. Lord Dragos had even been able to bring Lord Amarkyus, Lord Topenzi, and Lord Cytarius with him, at least when it had mattered most.

Such a feat was unheard of, unthinkable.

Such a connection—*between Ghost and Lord Dragos?*—was perplexing at best.

And yet, it had happened. Perhaps it could happen again. Or perhaps, with the aid of the four human women, such a second miracle would not be needed.

"Yes," Lord Dragos finally said aloud, disguising his internal consternation from his brethren, "I concede that the fated dragyra does have a purpose, a vital role to play going forward. I only meant that my son is obviously and substantially para-mount." He quickly shifted tack. "But let it be known for the *oral record*"—he snickered internally as he mocked the concept—"that I will not lose one ounce of sleep, nor will I pull any punches, in the interest of protecting four measly human females, their fate, their well-being, or whatever befalls them going forward." He lowered his head in a sarcastic bow, showing clear and sardonic deference to Lord Topenzi's annoyingly enlightened soul. *Sorry.*

I wasn't born that way, he thought, but he didn't say it aloud—his contempt spoke for itself. "As Lord Saphyrius so aptly put it, what is done is done. We have already involved the women. We practically stamped the words *Seven Sins* on each of their frontal lobes and painted the walls of that miniscule apartment with neon signs flashing *Lust, Gluttony, Greed,* and *Sloth. Wrath, Envy,* and *Pride.* For hell's sake, we had a Hindu woman reaching for the sins in her own religion."

"Miss Liu is Buddhist," Lord Onyhanzian pointed out, his dark onyx eyes flashing with annoyance.

Huh, Lord Dragos thought. *Since when did Lord Onyhanzian give a shit about humans and their myriad, divisive demarcations?* "So, the silent decides to speak?" He instantly searched out a pair of dark green eyes and flashed a wicked smile at Lord Ethyron, a soul whose...potential for iniquity...was closer to his own. "Brother, do you have anything to add from your emerald throne?"

Lord Ethyron smirked. "Hindu, Buddhist, Pentecostal—who gives a crap! They're human and yes, expendable. The true question is, can Jax do with them what we did with Bethany?"

Ah, yes, Jax...

Jaxtapherion Dragos, son of the Diamond Lair.

The mercenary dragyri who was calling himself Bryce —*Bryce M,* to be exact—at the behest of his lord and master. The member of the Diamond Lair who would hopefully meet with the girls, influence the girls, and stir up a dust storm worthy of Earth's infamous Black Sunday, thick with the seven sins...seven sins...seven sins!

The more the girls asked around, the more they bothered the human police, the more they searched and prayed and lit idiotic candles, unwittingly evoking unseen, spiritual elements, the more likely they were to catch the attention of the Pagan Horde.

To swiftly attract a wayward demon or a curious shade.

The more likely they were to land on Lord Drakkar's indirect radar, by way of his many Earth-traveling fiends.

And while the Seven could no longer see inside the Pagan Underworld, while they were neither directly connected to Bethany, nor Ghost, they had begun taking steps to address that shortcoming by planting clear and definitive supernatural seeds inside each of the human girls' minds—yes, the seven dragon lords could absolutely see through the eyes of Bethany's four mortal best friends. They could see through their eyes, hear through their ears, and smell through their nostrils if needed.

Indeed, the Seven had jurisdiction in many parallel dimensions: They could rule supreme in both the Pantheon of Dragons and anywhere on Earth. They could read minds, control energies, create miracles, or wreak havoc as they chose. And now—or at least, hopefully, soon—they would have four unknowing spies to manipulate and follow. Fixated upon the seven deadly sins and following Jax's instructions—going wherever Jax bid them and doing whatever Jax told them—the females would provide a much-needed psychic bridge between the Pantheon and the Pagan Underworld. And if the plan worked—*when the plan worked*—once the girls came in contact with various evil miscreants from Lord Drakkar's forsaken dimension, the Seven could leapfrog seamlessly from one species to another: from the girls' eyes to the pagans' eyes, from the girls' ears to the demons' and soul eaters' ears, from the females' minds to the pagans' minds. Yea, the Seven could learn more of Ghost's and Bethany's fate through any and all interactions between the four unsuspecting females and the lured demons and shades.

Can Jax do with them what we did with Bethany?

What?

Drench them in the seven sins?

It wasn't needed—they were already homed in like hounds on a scent.

Make the human women do his bidding?

Puh-lease...

Lord Dragos ceased pacing, leaned against a thick, jeweled pillar in the middle of the temple, and scoffed. The question was almost too stupid to answer, yet again, petty squabbles, brevity, and such...

He rubbed the flesh of his chin and lingered before answering.

A girl—

No, a fated dragyra.

A boy named Bryce M—*nay, a Dragyr male from the Diamond Lair.*

Four human females, desperate to find their best friend: Kari Baker, an Irish hottie with gorgeous, *come-fuck-me* hazel eyes; Joy Green, an African American bombshell with a killer set of tits; Nicole Perez, a fiery, devoted Catholic who had gobbled up the seven sins like she was guzzling the head of Jax's...whatever; and Anne Liu, an arousing, tiny, yet smart-as-a-whip Hindu—*correction, Buddhist!*—whose eyes saw more than most, whose eyes would make the most exquisite windows from which the gods could see much. She would ultimately skip mindlessly down whatever trail Jax and the Seven sent her along, much like Dorothy and her brainless scarecrow.

Yes...

A set of easily honed, soon to be finely tuned lures to hopefully hook a sycophantic member of Lord Drakkar's Pagan Horde.

The trap was almost set.

"Don't worry about Jax," Lord Dragos snorted, finally answering Lord Ethyron's question. "He is obedient, single-minded, and laser focused. He will do all his lords require of him. Besides, he has already set a meeting with the human women and will cross through the portal at sunrise."

CHAPTER EIGHT

THE PAGAN UNDERWORLD

I *nsanity.*
That's what they called it.
PTSD.

Having a nervous breakdown.

Going batshit crazy in the blink of an eye.

The haunted house, then the castle, being dragged before that red velvet throne...Wraith Sylvester trying to rape her...Lord Drakkar barging in...that arachnid, scorpion tongue—

Oh, wait, yeah...

There was also the ceiling.

Hovering beneath the ceiling, staring down at her body, and watching her...*Self*...writhe on the bed as two ghostly hands wrapped around her invisible waist and barked out terrifying orders.

But was it her waist?

Or her spirit's waist?

Or was it her actual—*her actual, what?*—as in what the actual fuck!

Didn't matter.

She was all one person now.

Bethany was all...one...human person, just trapped in a dark castle bedchamber in an alternate dimension, some shady, demonic underworld with a black-haired, muscle-bound titan, the guy from the throne room with the phantom-blue pupils and diamond-tinted eyes, the guy who was so obviously and hopelessly suicidal, he had just talked shit to a demon king—so much shit, in fact, the king had made him eat a handful of blood, guts, and innards, kneel before him, and kiss-lick the floor—the guy who had just made a deal with the devil in order to take possession of Bethany's all-one-human person.

Fuck!

She had well and truly lost her mind.

She gaped at the muscle-bound titan...

The guy...

The man...

They called him Ghost, but no, not a ghost—he was the son of a *dragon*.

Had she heard that correctly?

"It would appear your beloved dragon papa decided to make his firstborn hatchling practically imperishable"—that's what Lord Drakkar Hades had said, so yeah, a dragon...

A firstborn hatchling.

Sure!

Why the hell not?

Bethany was perched on a medieval four-poster bed, her breasts hanging out a ripped cotton shirt, her jeans and her panties somewhere on the floor, shredded to ribbons and presumably scattered amongst a dead pagan's flesh, guts, and organs, a soul eater who had called himself Wraith Sylvester—so why not add a dragon to the mix?

Her back and her thighs were bleeding.

Her cold, round ass cheeks bared to the wind.

And the one called Ghost was just standing there, about five feet away, staring her down like he was about to dissect her internal organs one molecular compound at a time, all six-feet-five of his massive, brazen, devil-may-care torso having just provoked and defied the ruler of hell.

Laughter.

Uproarious, unhinged, maniacal laughter.

Sounded like her own.

Bethany slid her fingers into her thick, wavy hair, scratched her scalp like she was mining for dandruff, then fell onto her side, pressed her knees to her chest, and laughed like a wild hyena.

Oh gods, oh gods, oh gods—

She couldn't stop laughing!

Her sides began to hurt, so she clutched them.

"Fuuuk!" she cried out as another wave of hilarity took her, and then she swiped her eyes as fresh, copious tears of mirth flowed freely.

Laughter.

Insanity.

Sweet, blessed release.

CHAPTER NINE

G host stared numbly at the hysterical human female still perched half naked on the bed, trying to make sense of what was happening inside his *fated's* addled mind: Not long after Lord Drakkar had left the bedchamber, Beth had turned her vivid, dark brown eyes on Ghost, only her pupils were enlarged, her irises were glazed over, and she had more or less gaped at him like he was a creature from outer space, an alien about to dissect—then eat—her human brain.

Her lips had moved rapidly, noiselessly, like she was murmuring to herself, and then she had scratched her scalp like a wild monkey, broken into delirious laughter, fallen to her side, and clutched her knees to her chest. She had screamed, "*Fuuuk*," loud enough to shake the rafters, all the while still cackling like a hyena, and that was to say nothing of the steady stream of tears now flowing down her mocha-colored cheeks.

What the actual hell?

"Beth." Ghost barked the shortened version of her name in a harsh, guttural tone, hoping to snap her out of her delirium.

Her glazed eyes grew twice as wide.

"*Beth.*" He tried a softer approach.

She froze for a second, her mouth dropped open, and then she started to laugh, even louder, even harder.

Ghost furrowed his brow and massaged the stress lines at his temples with his first two fingers. Round and round. *Just breathe, dragyri.* "C'mon, girl," he tried again. "We don't have time for this bullshit."

Her eyebrows shot up, her mouth formed a wide letter "O," and she gasped like a child reacting to the sound of a naughty word.

Damn.

Just...damn.

Ghost cleared his throat. "Bethany. Kayla. Reid."

She sat up abruptly, blinked several times, then snorted with a fresh burst of laughter. "Hello...*dragon.*" She waved her little pinky at him, then covered her mouth with the palm of her hand and continued to giggle, hiding behind it like a mischievous, two-year-old child.

"Fuck," Ghost spat.

"Fuuuk!" Beth echoed.

"*Stop.*"

"You stop." She laughed again.

"Beth!"

"Bethhhhh," she mocked, drawing out the T and the H.

With three long, purposeful strides, Ghost closed the distance between them, pressed one solid knee into the over-stuffed mattress, leaned in, and slapped her soundly across the side of one cheek, the harsh, open palm echoing throughout the stony chamber as a crisp retort. "Snap out of it, girl."

As if he had just stung her with a cattle prod, rather than a hand, she drew back abruptly, ran her fingers over her smarting cheek, and glared at him with murderous intensity.

"Beth?"

In the span of one or two seconds, maybe less, she rose to her bare, bloodstained knees, balled her hand into a fist, and landed one of the fastest right crosses Ghost had ever seen, at least for a human female: The flat of her knuckles connected squarely against the side of his jaw, the tip of her forefinger clipped the edge of his mouth, and she even managed to turn her wrist, smashing the flesh of his upper lip into his teeth. She leaned in and growled like some sort of angry, wounded animal. Then held his gaze in stark rebuke.

And then she caught him off guard a second time.

Following the right cross with a swift left uppercut, she slammed the same damn fist into the curve of his throat, twisted her wrist 180 degrees to force her knuckles deep into his gullet, and snarled, "Fuck you!"

Ghost jerked, recoiled, and threw up a hand to block her.

There wouldn't be a third assault.

Hell, he'd never had a mother, but if he had, he was certain she wouldn't have raised a fool—he took an obvious, generous, and cautious step back, placing a healthy arm's length between them, and then he measured her warily from a much safer distance: Her dark brown eyes were still flashing with fury. Her flawless, baby-fine skin was mottled along her left cheek, where he had regrettably slapped her, and based upon the stern, rigid set of her jaw—to say nothing of the fact that she was no longer laughing—Ghost hoped she had at least come back to her senses. He let out a long, deep breath and cocked his eyebrows. "Does that mean you're good?"

"Does that mean I'm *good*!?" If looks could kill, he would have been six feet under.

So much for coming back to her senses.

She sprang to her feet like some kind of ancient imperial ninja, jumped off the bed, rushed forward, and, for all intents and purposes, unleashed Armageddon.

Holy mother of—

She landed two swift kicks to the groin.

Whew! She *just* missed the family jewels.

At least ten sustained seconds of relentless fist pounding—wild, King-Kong-worthy thumping, swinging, and pummeling—trying to make mincemeat of Ghost's sternum and pecs.

So much for heading off a third, fourth—and fifth?—assault.

Yep...

Three more harsh, crisp slaps to the same cheek she had just struck moments earlier. "Fuck you! Fuck you! *Fuck you!*" Her chest was heaving. Her hands, which were still balled into fists, were trembling. And a deep, guttural sound, like a string of frantic, feral vowels, lingered in the back of her throat, raw, abused, and vibrating.

And that's when Ghost got it...

He relaxed his shoulders and stood in silence.

This woman had been kidnapped, dragged, terrorized, and defiled until nothing but primal fear and pent-up rage remained, until her most basic survival instincts had taken over, and nothing but *escape* or *attack* could register. Still, the shit had to stop before her mind was wasted.

Ghost moved so quickly, she never saw him coming.

He clasped both of her wrists in a single hand, wrenched them behind her back, and held them in place with superior, demonstrative power, while wrapping his free arm around her waist. He rocked her forward, locked her slender frame against his massive torso, then bent to her dainty, perfectly proportioned right ear and allowed her to distinguish, if only for a moment, what a true, bestial snarl sounded like.

"Look, girl..." His voice remained a guttural rasp. "I get it. I understand. You're pissed. You're rattled. And you're teetering on the edge of reckless and unhinged. In fact, from my vantage point, right about now, I'd say you're so damn desperate, your fight, flight, or freeze wires aren't just crossed—they're tangled into a gnarly mass of freak-the-fuck-out. *Got it.* But you need to find a way to chill. Take a deep breath. Visualize a beach or some shit. Just calm the hell down, shut the fuck up, and do *not* hit me again." He released her waist, let go of her wrists, and spun her around to face him. Then he took a healthy step back and waited.

Beth drew in a harsh, ragged breath.

And then another...

A third.

She licked her full bottom lip, rubbed her hands together, then measured Ghost from the top of his head to the tips of his toes, before staring fixedly into his phantom-blue peepers. Her own golden-rimmed orbs moved side to side, up and down, narrowing, then growing ever wider as she carefully scrutinized his odd diamond irises and pulsing, witchy pupils, haunted shadows flickering in soft, eerie lantern light, more likely than not glowing as pale blue coals inside the dim, ancient bedchamber.

Ghost steeled his resolve.

There was little he could do about his witchy appearance or the freaky-as-hell ambiance.

Besides, as long as she was looking, studying...taking it all in... she wasn't kicking, punching, or coming unhinged. "Just listen for a minute," he said in an even, measured tone, hoping to come across much less severe.

She didn't answer, but she did take a fourth drawn-out breath —in through her nose and out through her mouth—releasing the exhale gradually.

Good.

This was good.

Her heartbeat slowed down, and her full, pouty lips slowly parted. "Don't you ever slap me again," she said sternly, her voice as steady as a prehistoric rock, her tone as cold as a mountain stream in the dead of winter.

Ghost declined his head in a faint, almost imperceptible nod.

"Do you hear me?" she repeated.

He stretched his neck from side to side, popped a vertebra back into alignment, and grunted an affirmative reply.

"I'll take that as a yes," she said coolly.

He waited, still watching, while sands of time they didn't have time to waste flowed through an invisible hourglass. Finally, he cleared his throat. "You ready to listen now?"

She sniffed, ostensibly dispelling her rage while also displaying defiance. "Yeah, I can listen."

Her voice...

When she wasn't panicking...

There was just something in it. Something about it. Power. Inner fire?

When this woman wasn't freaking out, she was no-holds-barred...no-nonsense. "But first, tell me this," she continued. "Who the hell are you, *what* the hell are you, and what is this place? Why am I here? You told that evil, demonic king you wanted 'the girl on the bed...a little pleasure...and some regular carnal distraction.' What the hell did that mean?"

"*Shiiit.*" Ghost breathed the word beneath his breath. He counted backward from three to one, paused to organize his thoughts, then decided to hit the main themes first—besides, he didn't owe Bethany Reid any deep, moral explanations.

He had done what he had to do.

He had said what he had to say.

And, at least for the moment, he was still alive, as was his dragyra. Not to mention, the female was unmolested. Well, at least for the moment...

He crossed his arms over his stomach. "First things first: Who the hell am I? Well, I'll tell you who I'm not—I'm not Lord Drakkar Hades, king of the fucking underworld, and yeah, that's exactly where you are. You're in the bowels of hell, little lady, a lower, parallel dimension created by an ancient dragon lord for his illustrious Pagan Horde, and you're here at his behest. A replacement. A mortal servant. He keeps seven personal human slaves at all times, and he just...lost one...the other day, so he sent his minions earthside to replace her. As for *what* the hell I am? I'm the gnarly bastard who just flipped that script, the one who bargained with the devil to make you mine, instead of his. And that means I'm the only thing standing between you and a really, *really* nasty existence as an object of sex and torture for that same demonic king. No, Beth, I have no intentions of using you for a little carnal distraction. I said what I needed to say to stop what was about to happen."

"How did you know...how *do you* know my name?" she muttered absently, taking a generous step back, and then she shook her head as if she didn't care or no longer wanted an answer. She licked her lips in a nervous gesture, opened her mouth to say something else, then closed it, her dark brown eyes searching Ghost's earnestly, as if to discern the truth...or the falsity...of his words.

He cocked his head to the side and casually shrugged one shoulder. *I took the info from your mind* was teetering on the edge of too much self-disclosure, and if she didn't care to pursue it—well, sometimes silence was golden.

"If you did that," she croaked, "said what you had to say to spare me from a...nasty existence...then thank you."

He nodded, surprised, and then for the first time, he appraised her in turn, taking in the full remnants of her encounter with Lord Drakkar and the recently deceased soul eater. "You're bleeding," he said frankly. "And I can see your tits and your ass."

She blanched. "Oh my God, *are you serious?*" She cupped both hands over her breasts and pressed her knees together. "You asshole." She glanced at her torn cotton T-shirt, the stripes of blood still coating her thighs and her knees, then visibly cringed as her eyes swept lower—over her ankles, her bare feet, and her toes—before fixing abruptly on the forgotten, vulgar heap of monstrosities strewn about the floor all around her: a gut-spattered, black-and-red negligee piled atop a spiked rubber ball gag; a vile leather strap festooned with nails, blades, and rusty hooks lying amongst a garish heap of innards; and the horrific blindfold, fashioned with razors sewn into each eye patch, soaked and covered in a shallow pool of blood. Her stomach convulsed, she began to shake, and the corners of her eyes filled up with teardrops, only these weren't tears of crazed, unhinged laughter; they were tears of utter disgust and stark defeat.

She slowly inched backward, tiptoeing away from the grotesque sexual objects until the backs of her knees hit the edge of the bed, and gravity did the rest—she sat down silently and stared at her bloodstained hands.

"Ah, hell," Ghost grumbled.

She squeezed the frayed, torn edges of the battered T-shirt, held it together with her fists, then looked up at Ghost beneath desolate, lowered lashes; her expression, one part helpless, another part lost.

He reached for the hem of his own black, classic crew neck, tugged it over his head, and tossed it into her bruised, naked lap. "Put that on."

She reached for the shirt, eyed him warily, and waited.

He cocked his brows and raised an open palm.

"Well?" she said.

"Well, what?"

"Turn around."

"Seriously?"

"Look away."

"Little late for that, don't you think?" he groused.

She gestured with her chin toward a scant, loose-hanging

string of cotton fabric crisscrossing her chest like a meager shoe-string where she should have been wearing a bra, and sighed. "I still have to take what's left of this off. Turn around...please."

He didn't turn around.

But he did angle his shoulders and turn his head to the side. The fact that all dragyri males possessed enhanced peripheral vision was a morsel of truth he chose to keep to himself—his *fated* may as well have still been front and center, but if any of her injuries were worse than they looked, he needed to assess that with his own two eyes.

Beth tugged Ghost's shirt over her head...over the scraps of the shoestring T-shirt...and then she used the crew neck as a cover, like a tent, to shield her body as she shimmied out of the few, threadbare remnants and tossed the worthless scraps on the floor, beside the bed. And then she absently licked the pads of two fingers and tried to scrub the blood from her thighs, wincing each time the abrasive digits glided over an especially deep gash.

"Motherfucker," Ghost grumbled beneath his breath as he approached the female pragmatically. "Move your hands."

She jerked back.

"Just hold them up in the air."

She gulped, stared at him wide-eyed, and then slowly complied.

Without explanation or preamble, Ghost dropped into a squat, placed one large hand on each bare knee, and spread her trembling thighs.

"Don't!" she gasped.

"*Trust,*" he countered.

She eyed him with caution, but she didn't try to stop him.

He closed his eyes, focused on his inner dragon's fire, and began to bathe her legs in mystical blue flames. She blanched, squirmed, and shoved at his chest, but her efforts didn't budge him an inch. "Shh," he urged around the swirling blaze, "this is going to heal you, not harm you."

The dragyri male was like a mountain, anchored in place over epochs of time, as he placed his full focus and supernatural concentration on each of Beth's wounds, one at a time: the scratches, the gashes, the various punctures and bruises, all caused by Wraith Sylvester's calloused groping, until each slash had closed, each wound had healed, and every gnarly bruise had been erased.

He turned her on her side, held her hips against the bed, and repeated the entire process, ignoring the reactive gasps, plaintive whimpers, and stark, embarrassed groans she let out as he held her steady with the palm of his hand and tried not to stare at her ass. And then he turned her one last time, set her forward on the edge of the bed, and kneeled, yet again, between her legs. "Done."

She stared dazedly at her perfectly restored, unmarred flesh, running the pads of her fingers over scarless skin that had just been injured moments earlier. "Who are you?" she whispered breathlessly. "*What are you...really?*"

Ghost met her gaze and lowered his voice. "I'm Ghostaniaz Dragos, firstborn hatchling to Lord Dragos, first of the seven dragon gods. I am Dragyr...a dragyri male... The closest your kind can come to grasping the concept is perhaps part human, part vampire, part...dragon...all savage male, and in my case, broken to the core. Like you, I am here against my will. We have never met, Bethany Reid, but believe me, we are connected. You are what my kind calls a dragyra, a human female fated to be the consort or mate of one of my kind. Lord Drakkar doesn't know that—that's not why he took you—but it is the reason I saved you. The *only* reason I saved you. It is the reason I claimed you as my own. If I die, you will die. And if you die, I will die. The only chance either one of us has is to make it out of this underworld together, and to get to the Temple of Seven before the next eight days pass."

She nearly choked on her own shallow breaths, but to her credit, she restrained her emotion and focused on what mattered most: the dire situation before her and the details of Ghost's revelation. "Temple of Seven?" she asked, apprehensively. It was as good a place to start as any.

"It's in the Dragon's Domain, a world beyond a portal, a world not of Earth."

"Ghostaniaz...Dragos." She tried his name on her tongue.

"Ghost," he corrected.

She nodded. "Ghost." A hint of barely concealed fear shined in her eyes, her complexion grew pale and ashen, yet once again, she harnessed her dread and held her composure like a champion. If Bethany Kayla Reid had been certifiably insane just minutes before, she was perfectly lucid now, and her strength of mind was only surpassed by her defiant will and indomitable spirit. She leaned forward, braced her hands on Ghost's shoulders, and held his gaze in a penetrating stare. "Explain it, Ghost. All of it. *Specifics*. And don't leave a single detail out."

CHAPTER TEN

F ive minutes...

Maybe ten.

Or hell, it could've been hours, the time that had passed while Ghost had spun his terrifying tale: stories about dragon lords, a hidden pantheon beyond a portal, and mercenary sons required to hunt pagan enemies, *feed* on the blood and heat of human prey, and propagate their terrifying species by mating human women—those they called *dragyra*—thus siring *dragyri* offspring.

And then he had proven the truth of it, or at least made a pretty strong case for the entire narrative not being supernatural fiction: In order to get Bethany's attention, to save time, or to demonstrate why he believed Bethany was Ghost's dragyra, Ghost had pricked her forefinger, squeezed both sides to extract a droplet of blood, then spoken a haunting phrase in a low, cryptic tone: "Child of fire; daughter of flames. More than a woman; more than a name. Born from the soul of the Pantheon." The dark red droplet on Bethany's finger had begun to glow like a crimson light, and then the light had turned from phantom blue

TESSA DAWN

to pale silver to a brilliant diamond cast sparkling in the lantern light. With a sudden sizzle, it had erupted into a single white flame and continued to burn at the tip of her finger until Ghost had extinguished it with a swipe of his tongue.

Startling...

Petrifying...

Unnerving.

Yet all Bethany could think about was...*time*.

Time waits for no one.

Life can change in the blink of an eye.

"Time flies over us but leaves its shadow behind," a chilling phrase written by an arcane storyteller, Nathaniel Hawthorne, born in the early 1800s in Salem, Massachusetts. As odd as it was to be fixated on something so esoteric, in a moment, so surreal, Bethany could not get over all that had happened—all that had changed, indelibly—in such a short span of time.

Five minutes...

Maybe ten.

Or hell, it could've been a half an hour, the time it had taken Wraith Sylvester to abduct Bethany from the haunted house and alter her life forever.

Thirty minutes...

Maybe an hour.

The time it had taken a brutal sentry, with a thick iron piercing in his nose, to lock her in a castle bedchamber, for both Wraith, a shadow-walker, and Ghost, a dragyri, to follow down a dark, winding hall, and for Ghost to descend the castle wall and enter the chamber as an invisible, disembodied spirit through the barred, stained glass window. The time it had taken four of the Seven to possess the shadow-walker's form, provoke Lord Drakkar to kill his own minion, and for Ghost to hatch an implausible, farfetched plan.

Every neuron in Bethany's human brain was screaming: *You*

can still turn back the hands of time! This is only a dream, a God-forsaken nightmare. You are going to wake up! But every sense in her alert human body—whether taste, touch, smell, or feel—told her otherwise.

This was as real as real could get.

And any way Bethany turned it, she knew a cruel twist of fortune, an intractable moment in time, had already sealed her fate: She would never make it out of this house of horrors alive, not if she somehow managed to escape the castle and flee into the endless, demonic night, not if Ghost managed to get her out of the...Pagan Underworld...only to present her as a sacrificial lamb to the true dragon lords he was bound to obey—to be remade, reanimated, and transformed through *fire!*—and not if Bethany possessed the powers of Superman, Wonder Woman, and Spider-Man combined. There were too many battles to fight, too many worlds to navigate, too many horrific and terrifying land mines to steer clear of. And there was no one familiar, those she already knew and trusted, to help her: not her lifelong besties, not her parents, not even her boss. There was no human government—some well-armed cavalry—that could traverse space and time, enter a realm it was completely unaware of, and fight a colony of demons to bring Bethany home. And even if there were, the life of one twenty-nine-year-old, half German English, half African American girl from the suburbs of eastern Colorado would hardly warrant an interstellar fight.

No, Bethany was summarily screwed.

Her fate was sealed.

Her besties were likely going insane, and her parents had to be sick with worry.

Still...

Ghost had insisted that Bethany had a choice: If they managed to survive the underworld, as well as a mysterious journey through a duo of strange, unknown portals—from the abyss, back to Earth; from the earth to the Pantheon—then Bethany would have the right to say *Yes* or *No*. Yes, I will enter a terrifying temple and kneel before seven domineering dragon lords, or no, I will not. I would rather face some vague set of consequences—Ghost had not been clear at all as to what, exactly, those penalties looked like.

Still, the point remained: Bethany had free will.

And while death might be inevitable, at least in this singular moment in time, life was still an option. Only, she had to depend on Ghost: *Stay away from Lord Drakkar,* he had warned her. *Try to avoid the demons and the shadow-walkers whenever you can; obey any and all commands, and most of all, do whatever I tell you, exactly as I tell you...and pray to whatever God you believe in.*

Those were the broken dragyri's words.

And yeah, the male was broken from the depths of his pale blue, witchy eyes to his shattered-glass, hard-as-nails soul—hell, in one breath, he had saved her from a really, *really* ugly existence as the sex object of King Drakkar, yet in the next, he had casually pointed out her bare tits and ass. He had slapped her to shock her out of her PTSD, explained that he understood her terror, then told her to shut the fuck up. And then he had given her his crew neck and systematically healed her wounds. So yeah, all kinds of harsh, rude, disrespectful, and...broken...yet also curiously compassionate.

Bethany struggled to make sense of all the strange contradictions.

It was almost too much to process.

Still, if she was going to rely on him, she had to get a bead on him, at least a general sense of his person. *His person*—maybe that was the problem.

Ghostaniaz Dragos was not a person.

He was a different species: superior, yet uncivilized, enhanced, yet raw and uncouth. Most of all, he was transactional.

Reckless. Pragmatic. Somewhat protective, maybe even capable of being just south of kind and a tad east of gentle, then blunt, exacting, and equal parts brutal.

Broken to his core, exactly as he'd said.

Yet he was Bethany's only hope, this son of a dragon.

She shielded her eyes and stared at the floor, backing a bit further into the corner of the bedchamber, while Ghost continued to perform his...*dragon-ly*...work.

Fire.

This time, iridescent silver streaming in glistening waves from his thick, parted lips, as he bathed the floors, the walls, and the four-poster bed with stream after stream of the luminous flames: disintegrating bile, guts, and intestines; eradicating blood, gore, and entrails; cleansing, purifying, and sterilizing the whole of the bloody bedchamber with a mere mystical exhale of breath, while Bethany stood and waited in the corner, trying to figure him out.

Two minutes...

Maybe three.

But no more than five, and the heavily muscled, dark-haired son of the Diamond Lair spun around on his dexterous heel and pointed at the now empty yet still intact mattress atop the bed. "It's late," he barked. "You're exhausted. You need to try n' get some sleep. I'm gonna venture out, try to find some new bedding, some food, some water—you need to keep up your strength. But no matter how long I'm gone, try to stay in this chamber. Wait for my return. Lord Drakkar was crystal clear when he said, 'Just see to it that as long as she is breathing, she joins the other slaves in service to the castle.' I don't think he'll fuck with you anymore this night, or have one of his servants send for you this soon. Still, if you can help it, don't open the door. Not for anyone, Beth. Let me deal with the fallout from any disobedience. In the short term, I will work on getting you some fresh clothes and food, and in the long term—however I can, and whenever it comes up—I will work on establishing your position as mine in this castle: my slave, my female, my inviolable property, as in *hands off the fucking human merchandise*. But I can't promise that I can keep you away from the horde forever, from the other human slaves, or the underworld's various bestial inhabitants. Just the same, quiet as a mouse. Wait for me, Beth—do not venture out."

Bethany gulped.

Ghost had left out the second half of Lord Drakkar's wicked statement: Yes, he'd said she would have to join the other slaves in service to the castle, but he'd also said she would have to show unerring obedience to the king's every whim.

She shivered.

Couldn't think about that now...

Ghostaniaz Dragos and his foreboding orders were more than enough to handle.

She shrugged her slender shoulders in a gesture somewhere between *of course* and *no duh*. Where the hell could she possibly go anyway? And in that instant, the most curious thing happened: Ghost's phantom-blue pupils locked with Bethany's dark, seeking eyes, and a spark of intensity, like an unbroken wave of quantum energy, tangibly pulsed between them. Like a heavy curtain suddenly drawn back, it opened a window of pristine, see-through glass, magnifying each of their souls. And for Bethany, it was like gazing beyond the event horizon of a previously shrouded black hole.

Yes, Bethany was certain Ghost could see the full extent of her own terror, despair, and duplicity. He surely perceived all her mental calculations, including the part she wouldn't dare say out loud: Not only was death more than likely inevitable; if truth be told, it was probably preferable. And if they ever got out of the underworld, she would still try to escape her fate.

Somehow.

Someway.

She would go along to get along for now...

She would forge an unlikely alliance with Ghost, but if the opportunity ever presented itself, she would run—she would never enter that Temple of Seven.

Yet and still, the glass shined two ways, and Bethany could also see fragments...hidden, obscure, mysterious revelations... lurking in the shadows of Ghost's innermost darkness: something raw, something buried, something wholly devastated and ruined. Bethany had vaguely glimpsed the outline of a...*secret*. A truth so dark, so sinister, so painful, it dared not rear its ugly head, yet it held Ghostaniaz Dragos like an iron fist in its agonizing, murky grasp. It had absolute power over the son of a dragon, like a master ventriloquist over the doll on its knee, and not even Ghost was aware of its presence.

He was blind to its true identity.

Interesting...

Bethany strained to see the skeleton more clearly, but she could not bring it into focus.

Nonetheless, she could still recognize pain beyond measure, betrayal beyond conscience, and loss beyond reckoning when she saw it.

Bethany could see Ghost.

The dragyri male.

And she had seen more than enough to draw a harrowing conclusion: This supernatural being with all his unimaginable powers, this hardened mercenary with all his strategies and knowledge, this unequaled prisoner also trapped in the under-world, facing overwhelming odds, superior numbers, and impending peril with such bravery and defiance, was the only one of the two of them truly in shackles.

Wicked chains.

Heavy manacles.

Ancient, unyielding bindings.

To be sure, both Bethany and Ghost were summarily screwed —neither had a snowball's chance in hell of truly making it out of this alive—and torture, suffering, a slow, painful death were far more likely than a swift, humane end.

But...

Once it was over, however hellish and traumatic, Bethany's soul would at least be free.

Pray to whatever God you believe in—Ghost's cryptic words.

Indeed, Bethany didn't just believe, she *knew*.

She knew her creator, she knew her spirituality, and she knew no amount of unconscionable darkness could ever erase the ultimate well-being of her soul. But Ghost was another matter entirely.

His hell was within, not without.

And there was nowhere he could go—not in life, not in death, and not in the hereafter—to escape that endless black hole.

Five centuries...

Ten millennia.

Hell, eternity could repeat on an endless loop, and Ghostaniaz Dragos would still be a prisoner to the bitter, barren underworld he had harbored, masked, and buried inside.

"I'll wait for you," she said softly. What else could she do?

CHAPTER ELEVEN

EARTHSIDE ~ 10:00 A.M.

Jax Dragos planted the heel of one boot in a fresh, slushy puddle of snowmelt and ice as he took the curb with the other foot, strode confidently to the coffee-shop door, and wrenched the heavy glass panel open. A stiff gust of wind, carrying a circular eddy of fresh, falling snow, followed him into the establishment, and he shook out his tricolored hair—flaxen, espresso, and deep gold locks that fell to his shoulders in crisscrossing waves—to dislodge the frigid, frozen flakes.

No need for a hat.

In fact, if he hadn't been heading out to meet four human women, he wouldn't have bothered with a coat.

One step inside the bright, tiled entry, one glance toward the circular booth at the back of the quaint establishment, and his light green pupils, keen with diamond-colored irises, told him everything he needed to know: four mortal women, all wearing thick, heavy coats, huddled together with revealing, sad eyes. They appeared dazed and weary, their foreheads were creased with worry, and their shoulders were hunched in defeat. Hell, they could have collectively powered the overhead lights with all that anxiety and charged, nervous energy.

No matter...

It was time to do what the dragyri had come for: plant seeds, make suggestions, and prime the girls to start attracting pagans for the Seven.

Jax strode confidently to the apex of the hardwood table, stopped just short of brushing up against the smooth, beveled wood, and flashed his best cordial grin. "Hey, I'm Bryce M."

A sharp inhale.

An actual warble.

A double take—*a triple take*—and two nervous sweeps of hair behind cold, eager ears. *Yeah, human women, meet dragyri male.* Some shit was just as primal and instinctive as eating and breathing, and Jax had to give the women a moment to adjust to his rare and singular presence, his unusual, almost bestial energy, and the gift—or curse—the seven dragon lords had bestowed on all their powerful progeny: unearthly beauty that made it difficult at best to fit in with humans and nearly impossible to slip seamlessly into earthly shadows. The Dragyr stood out like bright, blazing comets streaming across a midnight sky.

He counted silently from ten to one, then, "Do you mind if I sit down?"

The gorgeous African American spoke first. "Not at all; have a seat." She absently flicked a thick cluster of lush, perfectly coiled blonde-and-black locks behind her shoulder, and the silky, full tresses bounced as they brushed the curve of her neck. "I'm Joy, by the way, and if you don't mind my asking: What does the 'M' stand for, Bryce?"

Ah, so Joy Green was confident, direct, and inclined to take the lead...

Good to know.

Jax took a seat next to Joy and smiled again, only this time he flashed a perfect set of brilliant white teeth—*yes*, he was deliberately accentuating every hard, masculine angle in his rugged jaw and chiseled cheeks, in an effort to evoke attraction, garner influence, and hasten yet unearned trust. "Nice to meet you, Joy." He extended his hand, and the moment she took it, he transferred a lightly banked heat through his touch. Nothing too coy or obvious. Nothing meant to overwhelm or compel. Just a slight, gentle nudge, a comforting warmth, to further manage the narrative: *All is well, you can trust me, please be at ease.*

Joy audibly gasped, drew back her hand, and scooted a few inches away from Jax.

So much for managing the narrative.

"The M?" she repeated, rattled but not dissuaded.

Jax chuckled beneath his breath. "My business," he said coltishly, "the M stands for *That's my business only.*"

Joy cocked her brows. "Oh, I see."

Damn, Jax thought, *she is clearly unimpressed.*

Fortunately, Nicole Perez leaned forward: "That's fine. Whatever. We're just glad that you came." She twirled a lock of dark, layered hair, flashed a welcoming smile of her own, and extended a graceful hand, presenting five long, elegant fingers. "I'm Nicole, but my last serious boyfriend called me Nicky." Her face flushed red, and she cringed in embarrassment, even as Joy visibly blanched, tucked in her chin, and turned up her lip in astonishment.

"Nicky." Jax took the blushing woman's hand, sent a soft, soothing energy into her fingertips, then held it a second longer than was proper. "Nice to meet you as well."

Nicky nodded. Then she gestured toward the redhead with soft hazel eyes. "This is Kari." She paused, then pointed at the petite Asian beauty with thick, straight hair nearly down to her waist, and eyes far too keen for her limited years. "And this is Anne."

Jax nodded at each female in turn. "Nice to meet you, Kari. Same to you, Anne." He made a point of holding eye contact with Kari, even as he refused to hold Anne's gaze a second longer than necessary—this one saw too much. It was as obvious as it was subtle and instinctive.

Both women smiled amiably and murmured their hellos.

"So," Joy cut in, "now that we have introductions out of the way, I hope you don't mind if we get right to the point: We would really love it if you could explain your Social Circle post in more detail"—she paused—"that's if you don't mind, Bryce My Business Only."

Jax exhaled slowly.

Yeah...

Perhaps a bit of mind control was needed with this one too, nothing too intrusive, just a light but persuasive compulsion—

"Sorry to interrupt." A waitress in a light blue dress, balancing a tray of sweet, gooey pastries in her outstretched left hand, sauntered up to the table, lowered the tray, and flashed her sweetest, please-buy-something smile. "Would anyone care for some dessert to go with your coffee?" She turned her attention to Jax. "Would you like something to drink, sir?"

Jax shook his head and waited while the females studied the tray; then he turned his attention back to the compulsion and silently tiptoed inside Joy's prefrontal cortex: *Joy Lynn.* He spoke her name tenderly, telepathically, even as he drew her in with unbroken eye contact. *You don't care about my last name, sweetheart. You will not ask me again. But you are very eager to get to know me, you trust me implicitly, and you will encourage your girlfriends to trust me as well.*

He pulled back softly, and she blinked three times.

Good.

It was done, and the compulsion was secure.

"Are you sure I can't tempt you? Any of you?" the waitress persisted, gesturing one more time at the items on the tray.

Kari and Nicky shook their heads, Anne made some excuse about a gluten-free diet, and Joy just turned up her nose.

The waitress smiled and sauntered away.

"So where were we?" Jax said. "My comment on Social Circle?"

"Um, yeah," Joy stuttered, appearing a bit befuddled, "if you don't mind sharing more detail. It's completely up to you."

"*Yes*," Anne persisted, studying Joy's features in earnest before turning an almost harsh, scrutinizing gaze on Jax. The perceptive female had noticed...*something*...but her logical mind could not define or make sense of it. To her credit, she had filed her suspicions away, for now, while insisting Jax remain on topic. "Your comment beneath Kari's post," she continued. "Let's just say it was a little unsettling. I believe you said something along the lines of you have no idea what happened to our friend, you've never met Beth, yet you think we should look into the Cult of Hades. Something about the seven sins. The fact that Beth may have gotten '*caught*' in some web."

Whew! Jax thought. *Talk about putting one's cards on the table.* Maybe he had tagged the wrong female as leader.

"Yeah," Kari said, raising her high, arched brows even higher. "You have to know that was really creepy, Bryce. I mean, like, if you did know Beth, you would also know she's the last person alive who would ever get caught up in a cult...any kind of cult."

"Agreed," Nicky said.

Bryce leaned back in the booth to slow the ladies' roll and recapture control of the conversation. After a few pregnant moments had passed, he slowly nodded his head. "Gotcha," he said congenially. "So, I freaked you all out?" He smiled. "I apologize. Sincerely. It's just..." He cracked his knuckles and decided to dive in—he would have to be far more direct with this audience. "Look, what are the police telling you? Was there any sign of a struggle? Have you heard even a peep from anyone who might have seen something, anyone who knows something? And as long as we're being both blunt and candid, tell me the truth—the seven sins—did that resonate at all with any of you? Or did it *only* seem creepy and off base?"

Nicky visibly shivered and absently clutched at a silver cross hanging from a thin, tasteful chain beneath her collarbone. "The police aren't telling us shit," she said brusquely. "We stopped by the precinct before we came here, and while I think they finally believe Beth is missing, they're handling the whole thing like a bunch of disinterested Keystone cops—I don't get it."

"Yeah," Kari agreed, "just a whole lot of backwards-ass fuckery."

Jax chuckled at the colorful description.

Anne crossed her arms in front of her stomach and appeared to be measuring her words more carefully. "The seven sins...the Kleshas...yes, we all felt it. That's one of the reasons we reached out to you, but it doesn't change what Kari said: Beth would never be attracted to some deviant sect. And if she'd had contact with anyone new, anyone that odd, we would've known about it."

Very well, Jax thought.

So, this was his entry.

Time to put Lord Dragos' cards on the table...

He leaned forward, braced his forearms on the wood, and held Anne Liu's intense eye contact without blinking or wavering. "The Cult of Hades isn't just one small group here in Colorado. It's a national, loosely knit organization, more like a religion: men and women who worship something they call the Pagan Horde, a deity they call Lord Drakkar Hades. You can always tell the diehard members because they have a hidden tattoo on the napes of their necks, usually just above the hairline."

"Yeah, I'm pretty sure Beth would've mentioned something like that," Anne said sarcastically.

"What kind of tattoo?" Kari asked, her hazel eyes deepening with concern.

Jax frowned. "A witch's pentacle on the pommel of a sword, a reversed numerical seven, just below the cross guard, the stem of the seven stretching down the length of the blade."

"Oh, hell no!" Joy exclaimed.

"Seven?" Anne asked, swiftly putting the pieces of the puzzle together. "As in the seven sins..."

"Is it some sort of witchcraft or...voodoo?" Nicky asked.

"Something like that," Jax said. "Thing is: Your friend's disappearance on Halloween was not...is not...all that uncommon. Different sects of the group are unusually active on All Hallows' Eve, and they have been known to case parties, haunted houses... informal gatherings...looking for people who seem innocent or pure—"

"What for?" Anne interrupted.

"To...involve them...in their ceremonies. Maybe rituals."

"And how the hell do you know this?" Joy asked.

"What kind of rituals!" Kari demanded, her eyes flashing wide with horror.

Jax lowered his voice and coated his light green pupils with moisture for effect—well, maybe not moisture, not actual tears, but close enough. "Religious observances, gatherings of veneration, prayers, petitions to their deity."

"Sacrifices?" Anne asked, her thin dark brows creased with shock and worry.

"No, nothing that brutal, at least not that I'm aware of. And I know this"—he leveled his gaze on Joy—"because my little brother, Jonas, disappeared on Halloween five years ago, when he was only seventeen years old. He was at a Dreadful Dead concert with a couple friends, excused himself to go to the bathroom, and just vanished." He paused to let his words sink in, to let the personal connection to *them* sink in. "Like you, I wasted the first few precious days trying to get help from the police, which turned up nothing. I spent the next six months trying to find him myself."

There was an audible gasp across the table from Kari, but the other women remained deathly silent.

"Did you ever find him?" Anne finally asked, her voice more of a croak than an inflection.

"Yeah," Jax said. "Two years later. But by then, he was already caught up in the sect. They had kept him...groomed him...indoctrinated him." He shook his head as if dismissing an extremely painful memory. "That's how I know so much about it."

"I'm so sorry," Kari whispered.

"Me too," Nicky said.

Anne furrowed her brows in sympathy, and Jax felt like shit. But what Lord Dragos demanded, Lord Dragos got, and this was the story the diamond lord had given him.

"Then you finally got him out?" Joy asked, her expression eager.

"Eventually, but it took three years, a whole lotta patience, and a shit ton of therapy," Jax said. "That's why I was trolling the web on Halloween night. Checking up on Jonas, I guess. Making sure he wasn't on Community Social Circle, making contact with any of his old Cult of Hades' buddies or jumping into suspicious chat rooms. That's how I came across your post, and it's why I had to respond. You don't want to walk down the same road I've been on. I lost my little brother—at least the guy I knew—on that awful Halloween night, and I still don't know if there was something I could've done...something I might have found...someplace different I could have looked, but I do regret wasting so much time with the police and not following my instincts."

"What instincts?" Kari asked, leaning in Jax's direction.

"The seven sins. I felt it. It was like the words were drifting all over the room, hovering above me, beneath the ceiling. I know it doesn't make any sense—hell, it probably sounds batshit crazy—but the night Jonas disappeared, that was all I could think of. Lust, gluttony, greed, and sloth. Wrath, envy, and pride." He paused to let the weight of his words sink in. "Look, when I saw Kari's post on Community Social Circle, I almost closed the window, but something inside me buzzed...practically hummed... took notice. I don't know Beth from Adam, and there are a million things that could've happened to your friend, but what I did know—what I do know—is that if the Cult of Hades got her, if the Cult of Hades has her, then mentioning the seven sins would resonate. If it didn't, great! Even better. But if it did, then maybe I could save someone else the pain and heartache I went through. Maybe I could tell this girl's companions that she's probably alive, that yeah, go to the police, see if they can help you, but put some feelers out with the Cult of Hades too. See what turns up. Maybe you will be luckier than I was. Maybe it's not too late to find your friend, while she still is...your friend."

Anne pinched the bridge of her nose, clearly overwhelmed, and maybe a little bit dubious. "None of this makes sense," she argued. "I mean, you still didn't explain what kind of rituals, at least not in detail. And how could they take her without leaving a trace? Why was there no sign of a struggle? And if they have her...then where? I mean, where the hell are they keeping her? And how? Put some feelers out with the Cult of Hades—what does that even mean! We're single women—a massage therapist, a real estate agent, a waitress, and a paralegal—not private detectives or superheroes. What the actual fuck, Bryce?"

Joy reached out her hand, placed it on Anne's shoulder, and

gave her a little squeeze. "I think we need to trust him, Anne." She blinked two times, then stared into space as if trying to access a buried memory. "Something in my gut just says...yeah, gotta take him at his word."

Kari and Nicky nodded in agreement, and Jax leaned back in the booth.

Yep, they got it.

And Joy's compulsion didn't hurt.

The whole sordid tale was littered with holes, about as plausible as telling the females Beth had been abducted by King Kong or taken to the Planet of the Apes. And no, none of it made any sense, except to some degree, if one really thought about it, it *was* all true: Beth *had* been taken from a haunted house by monstrous beings, intimately, if not indirectly, tied to the Cult of Hades, and one way or another, the seven sins had *everything* to do with it. The pagans had easily abducted Beth from the fairgrounds without leaving a trace, and there had not been any signs of struggle.

Truth.

All truth...

The human police didn't stand a snowball's chance in hell of finding her—they would inevitably run into one dead end after another—and yeah, she was probably still alive. So, all and all, Jax had woven the farfetched tale in and out of a whole lotta truth.

And honestly, none of that mattered.

Not the lie about Jonas.

Not the shock, fear, hope, or disappointment Jax had tossed out there.

Not the fact that a massage therapist, waitress, paralegal, and real estate agent were not only in way over their heads but being used as human bait. And not the fact that he was about to send them straight into the lion's den, so to speak, to see if they could flush out the enemy.

It didn't matter because the underlying justification was solid: Wherever Lord Drakkar's human worshipers were to be found, demons and soul eaters were not far away, watching over their faithful sheep, monitoring their words, cataloguing their prayers, and influencing their thoughts and behavior. And wasn't that just it?

The whole game, the real ploy, the entire reasoning in a nutshell?

Jax's directive was to make sure Lord Dragos and the remaining six dragon deities had psychic eyeballs on Lord Drakkar's minions, and at the end of the day, these women could go where the Dragyr could not. The human females could get up close and personal, leaving the Dragyr undetected, and whatever they heard, whatever they saw—whomever or whatever they met —the Seven could watch through the women's eyes and hear through their ears, as if they were standing in the females' skin. And maybe—just maybe—they would draw out a pagan, not just a human sycophant, and the moment they did? Game on! The dragon lords, feeling through the human females' senses, would be able to read that pagan's thoughts, scan his memories, probe his impressions, and maybe—just maybe—they might catch a glimpse of Ghost.

Ghost!

Ghostaniaz Dragos, firstborn hatchling to the most depraved dragon lord.

Jax's lair mate, his Diamond brother, and a fearsome kinsman who had always taken the brunt of their common sire's abuse— the one who was stranded in Lord Drakkar's hell!

Yeah, that's what all of this was about...

So let the chips fall where they may.

"Look at me," he said, adding a thick measure of compulsion to his voice, then waiting until all eyes at the table were firmly fixed on his. "Whenever you search, do it in pairs. There's more safety in numbers. I want you to go to the King Castle Credit Union in lower downtown and tell them you want to open a sacred account. Then go to Fred's Pawn Shop, off Colfax and Vine, and tell them you're looking for a particular piece of rare, antique jewelry, an ancient emblem on a ring or a necklace, perhaps a brooch or a breastpin, a witch's pentacle on the pommel of a sword, with a reversed numerical seven just below the cross guard. Go to the small Wizards Witches & Ancient Theologies Bookstore on the corner of East 17th and Krameria—it's a shabby little hovel with an old green barn door that opens from the alley—and tell them you've been searching everywhere for a rare, ancient text, a fifty-page, leather-bound tome transliterated into Greek around 1100 AD from old Egyptian papyrus scrolls: *A Treatise on the Seven Sins*. That's what I mean by putting out feelers, so be sure to leave your business cards and cell phone numbers; then just sit back and wait." His eyes began to glow—he could tell because he could feel the heat rising as the compulsion deepened. "You are not going to question the story I gave you. You are going to steer clear of Beth's family, boss, and coworkers. As in zero contact. You are not going to bother any further with the Denver Police, and they are not going to bother with you, Beth's family, or her place of employment, either. No one outside of this table is going to question her absence, and you're...settled with that. Okay with that. You do believe Beth was taken by the Cult of Hades, you do believe you may yet still find her, and you will not share this information with anyone outside this table. No more social media."

The tabletop began to glow with a pale orange light in reaction to the supernatural energy Jax was manipulating as he imparted, set, and sealed each compulsion so deep into the females' minds as to obliterate any possible objection or sense of confusion. They would not process the information on a conscious level; rather, it would remain burrowed deep within the well of the subconscious, not so much that its power disturbed them, but just enough to command obedience.

He exhaled slowly and released the coercion.

Kari stared at him blankly.

Joy looked at him cross-eyed.

Nicky clutched her sacred necklace, and Anne, well, she stared right through him.

Shiiit.

Jax folded his hands in his lap.

It was done.

He had executed Lord Dragos' orders, exactly as instructed: He had stopped by Beth's place of employment to convince her boss and coworkers that the female was on extended leave. He had located her mother and father in Elizabeth, Colorado—she didn't have any siblings—and implanted fresh memories of phone calls and visits, enough to last for the next thirty days. And he had slipped inside the local police precinct, hacked the computer database, and closed Beth's case. No one was going to contact Kari, Joy, Nicky, or Anne. No one was going to bother Beth's family or her employer—there would be no follow-up questions or requests for cooperation. And now—*just now*—Jax had set the stage for Lord Dragos' play.

Act One...

The overwhelming impression of the seven sins permeating Nicky's small living room.

Act Two...

Bryce M's little foray at the coffee shop, leaving specific hints and instructions.

And as for Act Three...

Well, that remained to be seen.

So be it.

As a male of at least a little integrity, Jax couldn't help but feel...something...about putting these bright, beautiful, loving women in so much hideous danger. But as a son of the Diamond Lair, beholden to Lord Dragos, Keeper of the Diamond, and ruler of the same, his duty was inviolable. As a lair brother to Ghostaniaz Dragos, a soul who had suffered more torture, humiliation, and pain than any living creature had a right to, Jax just couldn't bring himself to regret the manipulation: These women were in their late twenties, maybe early thirties—Ghost had lived for a thousand brutal years. These women had known kindness and friendship and family—Ghost had only known cruelty, isolation, and the tutelage of a merciless sire who had reared him in blood, sweat, tears, and sadism. These women had each other. Hell, these women had Beth. They were sitting in this booth because they had each other's backs. But who did Ghost have?

After all the times he'd had Jaxtapherion's back—Chance's back, Romani's back, the entire Diamond Lair's backs—the fact that he was now trapped in the underworld because he had gone through the portal against the Seven's orders and leaped into a pit of mystical quicksand in order to get Axeviathon back, a male from another lair who Ghost rarely even fraternized with...

No, Jax didn't have any regrets.

Jax was a son of the same sadistic sire, and he had obeyed his master's consummate orders. He was the lair mate of a powerful, dragyri brother, and he would do all he could to save him. If Jax could help the women, protect the women, save even one of them from harm, then of course he would try to do so—he was a male of at least a little integrity—but fuck it in the end. When all was said and done, if even one word, one suggestion, or one compulsion resulted in bringing Ghostaniaz home, then Jax would do it again.

"We good?" he asked, eyeing each female in turn to make sure the compulsion had set like cement.

"Yeah," Joy said, her voice thick with conviction.

"Sure," Kari said, glancing around the table to get a read from her friends.

"No problem," Nicky agreed, the pad of her thumb absently brushing the top of her crucifix.

Her deep, dark eyes fixed on Jax like a pair of silent daggers, Anne nodded politely, but she didn't speak. Her stare never faltered, and her lips never parted.

CHAPTER TWELVE

THE PAGAN UNDERWORLD ~ 6:00 P.M.

At the rear of the superior, yet still quite lowly, dungeon-level dorms, Felicity Payne stared into an ancient full-length mirror constructed of polished bronze, and appraised her perfectly curled, platinum blonde hair. She shook her head from side to side to make sure the thick, waist-length locks were flawless, fluffy from root to ends, and silky as velvet, not a cluster out of place, and then she fluffed the crown with her fingers. She checked her blood-red lipstick next, made sure her dark, metallic eyeshadow was the exact same shade as her hunter-green eyes, then appraised her elaborate, strapless red dress with appreciation.

The gown was sexy, provocative, and much too tight.

Her matching five-inch heels were spiked and festooned with garnets.

And her nail polish practically sparkled in the torchlight.

The shit mattered.

A lot.

Tonight, as any other night she was allowed to venture into the castle's interior, was another rare opportunity, a long shot to be sure, but perhaps if fate was on her side, this night would be different...

At 340 years old, Felicity Payne did not look a day over eighteen.

Black magic, as well as having one's life prolonged by pagan blood, had that effect on an ancient woman, especially a female witch born in colonial Massachusetts in the late 1600s. Now to be sure, the Salem Witch Trials were a misogynistic joke: pure, innocent, kind-hearted women were tortured and executed for no legitimate reason whatsoever, outside the fact that a bunch of old, crotchety, sexually repressed men desired their youthful bodies, resented their intelligent minds, and could not deal with a single independent thought they did not possess or could not control. And the women tied to these vile men—their daughters, wives, and pious parishioner sisters of faith—were equally wretched, jealous, and perverted by fear. It was a ghastly time to live through. All that was holy had become wholly depraved. And while yes, it was true, there were witches in that time—alas, there have been witches throughout all time and place, whether in Salem, Hartford, or anywhere else—*true* pagans believed that nature was sacred. They found spiritual meaning along paths of healing, restoration, love, light, and rebirth. There was—and still is—nothing evil about them.

In truth, an authentic dark sorceress such as Felicity Payne was a very rare oddity, indeed, and perhaps that was why her spellcasting and abhorrent behavior had attracted the attention of Lord Drakkar and his evil horde, several centuries gone by. Perhaps that was why Felicity had been abducted from Salem, Massachusetts, on her sixteenth birthday and had lived in the underworld ever since—

But who really cared...

The past was in the past.

And opportunity, though scarce and unlikely, was potentially knocking today.

Felicity sidestepped around the polished bronze mirror and exhaled a white plume of vapor, formed from the cold, even as she traced an uneven stone in the wall with the tip of a painted nail. The stone rolled over, and the mortar slithered away like a giant pill bug retreating within a circle of restless clay worms. The Pagan Palace was a living thing. It listened. It spoke. It breathed and shared secrets, and Felicity had learned how to hear, translate, and interpret its mysteries.

She had spent the last 324 years doing exactly that, whilst being traded back and forth between the soul eaters and the demons. For half of each year, she resided on one of the far left, lower levels of the gothic castle in a dormitory for the soul eaters' slaves. Connected to the shadow-walkers' upper residential wing by a winding stone staircase that traversed the main castle floor, she had become easy access for Bale Oberon and Nefario Rage, the shadows who used her most often. During the second half of each year, Felicity resided on one of the far right, lower levels of that same castle floor in the dormitory reserved for the demons' favorite human toys, and she considered the entire season *winter* due to the crazed, imaginative, beastly torture and attention she received from Kyryn Sable, Salyn Stryke, and Mongryn Time, three of Lord Drakkar's most insidious sin eaters.

Back and forth...

Back and forth.

Bounced between dormitories, demons, and shadow-walkers.

Wishing all the while, craving all the while, hoping and praying for the day when she might reside in the middle hall instead, the dormitory reserved for Lord Drakkar's favored, private consorts. Slaves? Yes. But seven flawless, stunning human males and females who spent the majority of their days at the foot of his red velvet throne, naked except for a simple animal-skin loincloth, their perfect bodies admired, desired, and slathered in oil.

Their perfect bodies *off-limits* to others!

No one was allowed to touch Drak's slaves.

The bottom line: There were seven of them and only one of him, and he couldn't use them all at once. Thus, hands off in the meantime.

Oh, how Felicity had lusted after such a simple pleasure, to be owned and used by Lord Drakkar, alone, to say nothing of the lavish living quarters she would be granted, the elevation in station she would obtain, the beautiful gowns she might wear for pagan rituals and necromancy festivities, or the decadent food she would be served each day in order to nourish her perfect body.

And Felicity's body was perfect.

Felicity's face and her features were perfect.

According to the rolling stones and the moving mortar, the ice-cold pitch, and the hot, dancing flames, the rats that scurried about the castle's lower levels, and the spiders that spun their webs in the eaves, Felicity's rare, exquisite beauty was the only reason she still lived. Lord Drakkar had long ago forbidden his horde to kill her on account of the fact he enjoyed the view: He wanted to pass her on occasion in the castle halls, he wanted to listen to tales of Kyryn and Nefario's exploits, and he wanted to reserve the right to use her, himself, should the rare, inexplicable mood ever strike him.

Oh, dark lords...

Felicity bit the tip of her nail.

If only...

Lord Drakkar did not typically partake of sloppy seconds— slaves from the lower, left and right wings were never moved to the center, and the king did not populate his sacred harem of seven from the ranks of the castle's gallows.

But...

She sighed.

Yet and still...

She sniffed.

There was always a chance.

A girl could hope.

Just one erotic encounter, one violently deviant tryst, one chance opportunity to win the king's favor, and her life might be changed forever. That is, as long as Lord Drakkar Hades did not take that new human bitch back! The one Wraith had captured on All Hallows' Eve, the one whose beauty rivaled Felicity's, the one whom Ghostaniaz Dragos had claimed for himself, usurped from Lord Drakkar no less than six hours hence. As long as Lord Drakkar did not change his mind, Felicity still had a chance.

Oh yes, the walls could talk, and the floors could whisper.

The limestone and the creaking oak, as well as the ether, could divulge much knowledge to a true Salem witch, and Felicity had, long ago, learned how to listen.

Now, she just needed to improve her odds, to make damn sure Lord Drakkar did not ask for Bethany back. Felicity needed to eliminate the competition before the human woman gained a foothold in the emblematic castle door—such were the human-and-pagan politics at play in the underworld. Sooner or later, the wretchedly beautiful newbie would have to join the other slaves in service to the castle, and at some point, her drudgework...her abysmal, dreary duties...would overlap with Felicity's. It was unavoidable, not a matter of *if* but *when*.

Felicity filed the tantalizing thoughts away, curbed her anticipation...for later.

This night was about Felicity, not Bethany.

Salyn Stryke had requested the witch's carnal company, two points after vespers in the Sinners' Cave, which meant Felicity would be allowed to enter the inner castle sanctum. Pray tell, it was only a hope—the odds of seeing or running into Lord Drakkar were almost as daunting as the odds of the dark, powerful, ghastly king taking the witch back to his private chambers—but still, a woman could wish...and scheme...and hope.

* * *

Well, shit...

Ghost cursed beneath his breath, even as he turned on a heavy-booted heel and headed in the direction of the firelit cavern that housed the pagans' Sinners' Cave.

It was already 6:15 in the evening.

All night and all day had come and gone since he had left Beth alone in that cold, oppressive bedchamber, and he wasn't any closer to returning to the vulnerable female with some food, clothes, and blankets than he had been at 6:15 that morning.

Just shit!

First, he had run into Killian Kross in the main castle foyer, and just why the creepy chief counselor to Lord Drakkar was roaming the halls at 3:00 A.M. was a mystery to Ghost, except he figured the evil bastard had probably followed him the night before, tried to spy from a distance, and was hoping to catch him in...something...somehow trip Ghost up. As it stood, Ghost had come up with some lame excuse as to why he had left the chamber in the middle of the night, himself: He needed to retrieve his belongings from the upper residential wing and move them to the lower castle floor; after all, he would be staying in the main-level bedchamber with Beth for the duration.

And that had gone over like a ton of bricks.

Ghost had spent the next two and a half hours swearing his fake fealty to Lord Drakkar, coming up with every debased excuse he could think of as to why he had asked for the human woman, and trying to prove to Killian that he was now on Team

Drak—team Uncle Drakkar to be more exact—and in no way politically threatening. He had tossed out every false, insignificant, and misleading detail he could conjure about the Pantheon and its Dragyr inhabitants, stopping just short of claiming that the Dragyr kept pet unicorns in a secret fortress.

One hour had turned into two.

Two had begun to morph into three, and before Ghost knew it, that damn hawk-eyed chief counselor to the king of the underworld had insisted Ghost accompany him to the castle's undercroft to retrieve some particularly strong mead and sour wine.

Who the hell drank sour wine?

Then on the way to the damnable cellar, several additional high-ranking demons had joined them.

Truly, one couldn't make this shit up.

Again, Ghost had no illusions...

No way were all these demons up at three in the morn, randomly perusing the palace halls long past the last reasonable witching hour, and heading for the castle's undercroft to imbibe in some post-midnight spirits, perhaps to aid with sleep. No doubt, Killian had called out to his demon brethren, woken them up, and told them to get their freaky asses to the cellar, posthaste.

The shit was staged as fuck.

Yet another test for Ghost.

Yet another slippery slope and unforeseeable danger: One false word, one questionable reply, one reckless sin eater or pissed-off shadow-walker, and Ghost could've been killed whilst drunk as a skunk in the castle's underbelly.

But he could play poker as well as the next bastard.

Thing was: He could *not* handle that putrid, toxic, pagan mead.

There was something in it, something rotten and unnatural, and whatever it was, it was not meant for beings who had anything resembling a soul. It had to have been one part honey, one part water, one part yeast, and three parts black magic...dark spellcast...and death.

Whatever it was, it knocked Ghost out, and by the time he came to, almost twelve hours later, he apparently had a date—well, another imminent, non-optional appointment—with Salyn Stryke in the Sinners' Cave, ostensibly to check out the cavern, the demon technology, and some witchy monitors the sin eaters used to spy on their human followers. Oh, and also to join in on some...carnal recreation...with some notorious female slave named Felicity.

A witch.

Nah...

Ghost would pass on the foul, unclean, group orgy shit. He'd find some way to get out of that nasty nonsense. Yes, he still had to prove his sudden familial loyalty to the liege of the lepers, aka king of the underworld, but even Ghost had higher standards than some three-way tryst with a profane, black magic princess, whilst pretending to betray his Pantheon lineage.

He had zero shits to give about Salyn Stryke or the soul eater's technology, even less to give about human sycophants, as seen on cavern monitors, and whether or not they indulged frequently enough in the seven sins, but he did have a *fated* to get back to—and Beth did need food and water...some clothes. So yeah, Ghost would play the game just a little longer. Then hopefully he could get back to his dragyra, say, before next year.

Shit.

Just "fuck-my-life" level shit.

CHAPTER THIRTEEN

Bethany sat on the edge of the clean but naked mattress, rubbing the outside of her arms with her hands and rocking back and forth for warmth. The massive stone fireplace was filled with fresh wood and roaring with flames, but she couldn't ease the bone-deep chill. Her stomach was growling, her body felt weak, and her tongue kept sticking to the roof of her mouth.

She was so hungry.

So thirsty.

Where was Ghost?

She tilted her head to the side and stared longingly at the raised tin tub curtained inside a three-stepped private alcove, imagining it filled with clear, crystal water, visualizing new age plumbing and clean copper pipes, picturing her cold, shivering body slowly slipping into warm, soothing liquid and drawing a thirst-quenching drink from the imaginary tap.

But no such luck.

As it stood, she was alone and freezing, hungry and scared.

Lost...

And Ghost had not returned with anything.

As worry seized a foothold in her heart, and fear raised the rent in her head, she clasped her hands together and bent her head to pray, even as she did her best to focus her prayers, the mental images and her creative powers, on a vivid, cherished memory, a happier time from her childhood: Bethany was sitting on the edge of a big brass bed in her maternal grandparents' small white farmhouse on the eastern plains of Colorado. The fresh smell of old, hand-sewn fabric was thick in the air, emanating from the pale rose and green quilt beneath her, and her small stomach was filled to the brim with biscuits, gravy, and farm fresh eggs, leftovers from the morning's ample breakfast.

Grandma's aged brown hands were soft and tender, resting gently on Bethany's tiny shoulders as the beautiful elderly woman leaned against her granddaughter's back and nuzzled Bethany's hair with her chin: "It is such a blessing to have you here, Bethy. I so enjoy your company...such a peaceful spirit." She twirled a lock of Bethany's thick, wavy hair. "Just the other day, I was talking to your grandpa, telling him how sweet you are, and do you know what he said?"

Bethany looked into her grandma's bright brown eyes with eager anticipation and smiled.

"He said, 'That little one has a chorus of angels surrounding her; I'm certain she is never alone.'" Then Grandma had squeezed Bethany's hand and asked if she would like to have her hair braided before bed.

Bethany absently fingered her tangled hair, even as the memory faded.

Arms still shivering...

Stomach still aching...

Feeling alone, afraid, and increasingly hopeless, she tried hard to block out her current predicament and focus on her late grandma's words instead. "Angels," she whispered softly, "if

113

you're still all around me"—*I can only hope*—"I pray you're surrounding Ghost as well. Please give me the strength to endure this nightmare; please give Ghost wisdom as he navigates his way through this terrible castle; and please bring him back to this chamber safely. No matter what happens, please help me believe that I'm never truly alone."

For just a moment, the subtlest of heartbeats, Bethany could almost sense her grandma's presence; the faintest sigh disturbed her ear, and a loving smile warmed her spirit.

* * *

The circular cavern containing the Sinners' Cave was just east of the Great Hall, which held Lord Drakkar's infamous red velvet throne, although admittedly, it was next to impossible to tell directions in the lower world. Without the aid of a distinct sun or a moon, the regular ebb and flow of tides, whether earthbound or in the Pantheon, knowing north from south and east from west was kind of a crapshoot at best. The underworld's dense atmosphere was a thick, murky haze, largely permeated by infinite shades of black and gray. That said, the Pagan Horde considered Lord Drakkar Hades' throne *true north*, possibly because things could go south very quickly if you crossed him. No matter. Ghost was learning to gauge his bearings by the same macabre polarity, and he had no trouble at all finding the firelit cavern.

He held his head high, shoulders back, as he sauntered beneath the high, stony archway, entered the way-too-hot grotto, and instantly appraised the dark, spherical interior. The ghoulish chamber resembled a cheesy human lounge that possibly doubled as a gaudy office: three blood-red leather sofas positioned in a semicircle facing a floor-to-ceiling fireplace, the stones slathered in pitch; multiple liquid screens that appeared more like aquariums, each screen bordered by archaic swords with witches' pentacles carved into the pommels; and a very strange kind of twisty coffee table that gave Ghost the willies, even though he couldn't quite make out its elements. The smell of sulfur assailed his senses, and as expected, Salyn Stryke was already there...waiting...perched like an overeager gremlin on the edge of one sofa. And damn, if that large, muscle-bound soul eater didn't have a tattoo of some kind inked into every square inch of his flesh, his neck, his arms, his shiny bald head, even around his witchy yellow eyes, and snaking along his forehead.

Ghost drew back and grimaced.

The fuckin' ink was moving.

Shifting...

Lines slithering; black magic symbols scurrying; shapes morphing into other shapes, forming new patterns and symbols.

What the alchemic hell...

Salyn flashed a wide, sinister grin, and his dark goatee, which trailed into a long, pointed beard, followed the curve of his sinister lips. "Like the ink?" he grunted. "Mongryn carves it, then Requiem brings the shit to life."

Requiem, Ghost thought. *King Drakkar's chief sorcerer.* Made sense. But nah, he didn't like the ink. "Whatever," he grumbled, and just like that, Salyn shot to his feet, his bare toes twitching beneath the hem of his sweatpants, his massive biceps pulsing beneath the straps of his tank top.

A fucking barefoot soul eater in sweats and a tank...

The shit just got stranger and stranger.

But Ghost didn't have time to worry about etiquette or contemplate pagan wardrobes. Out of pure instinctive self-preservation, he dropped into a defensive posture, spread his legs a shoulder's width apart, balled his fists at his sides, and shifted his weight onto the balls of his feet. Salyn could not be trusted. None of the shadow-walkers or demons were Ghost's friends, and he was pretty damn sure they resented the hell out of the latest news from their leader: First, Wraith Sylvester was dead, and as far as they knew, Ghost may or may not have had a devious hand in the soul eater's passing. Second, at least for the interim, and until Drak said otherwise, they were to pull back on the overt hostility and give Ghost more space. Lord Drakkar's dragyri *nephew* was interested in power, position, maybe making himself at home in a new, more well-suited environs, and the king of the underworld had adopted a new *Wait and See* posture...

Wait and see.

Watch, but be wary.

Ghost would either prove himself useful—and faithful—or they would make up for the hiatus on hostility and torture later... and in spades.

Salyn jerked his head in Ghost's direction, throwing his chin like a fist to make Ghost flinch. When Ghost held steady, just stared him down, the soul eater withdrew just as quickly, tossed his head back, and laughed. "Fucking *nephew*," he snarled. "Dear Uncle Drak..." His words trailed off, and his laughter grew more raucous. "You're a ballsy little son of a bitch, aren't you?" He took three giant strides across the cavern floor and sauntered up to one of the liquid screens. "We can see into the hearts and souls...the lives of our human sycophants...through these windows," he said casually. "Also, don't kid yourself. Lord Drakkar can see right through you—better believe it! And so can Requiem Pyre." He stepped back and assessed Ghost from head to toe. "I'll give you this much: You've got some kind of strange, low-key magic, some sorcery or alchemy you hide behind like armor, but you're way, way out of your league, Ghostaniaz Dragos. Our king will eventually peel your skin from your bones, extract your soul from your body, like he did that day with your spine in the throne room, and play with it like a gob of silly putty until he grows bored or tired. And then you will know what pain really is, the consequences of lies and treachery."

So much for pulling back on the hostilities...

"Then you will know how badly you fucked up," Salyn continued, "when you chose to play the nephew card." He rolled his massive shoulders and gestured toward the screen. "Check out this whore." He pointed at a beautiful African American woman, a mirage inside the aquarium, and Ghost's eyes followed as the two of them watched her naturally curly, blonde-and-black twists bounce above shoulders which were hunched from the cold, as she reached for an iron doorknob on an old, rustic barn door and entered an establishment from the alley. "Wizards Witches & Ancient Theologies," Salyn grumbled. "It's a bookstore owned by Mitch Moretti, one of the most prolific human sinners in the Cult of Hades."

The Black woman held the door open with a perfectly manicured hand, and another, much smaller Asian female ducked inside the shop, her keen eyes darting nervously around the entrance.

"Joy Green and Anne Liu," Salyn said. Then he placed the pad of his finger against the glass of the aquarium, the front of the mystical screen, and slowly dragged the image from left to right, as if fast-forwarding a digital movie. The scene sped up. "Look. Here. She's about to ask the guy behind the counter if he's ever heard of an ancient text: *A Treatise on the Seven Sins.*" He paused to play the interaction for Ghost, complete with sound and a 360-degree, immersive field of vision. Then he drew a circle with his finger around an object, and the witchy monitor zoomed in on the same. "That shit was written around 3000 BC in Ancient Egypt, then later translated into Greek. And just out of a clear blue sky, these two sexy bitches stroll into a bona fide Cult of Hades storefront as if they just got the sudden itch to do some light occultic reading." He gestured toward the entire bank of screens. "Lit this shit up like the Aurora Borealis."

Ancient Egypt...

The Aurora Borealis.

So what?

These demons read books—they were educated?

Ghost grunted.

Salyn dragged his finger over the taller woman's breasts and groaned. "I'd like to suck those creamy titties into the back of my throat," he said, "before carving her heart out...slowly...with my teeth."

Ghost ignored the crass, infantile comment. "So, is this what you wanted to show me?"

"Fuck you," Salyn snarled, spinning around to face him. "I wanted to show you the mystic technology, make sure you're good and familiar before Requiem Pyre and Killian Kross start fishing around in your hippocampus, using our own powerful brand of alchemy to hook your fucking memories up to these same omniscient monitors." He stared intently at Ghost, trying to gauge a reaction. "Yeah, *nephew*, Uncle Dearest is gonna make you put your money where your mouth is, see if you're ready to display every damn thing you know about the Pantheon on the Sinners' Cave's newest cinema, a private viewing for your pagan brethren." His necromantic yellow eyes narrowed in contempt, practically glowing in their sockets.

Ghost didn't move a muscle.

His face held no expression.

Just then, the sound of sharp, crisp heels clopping atop the natural limestone flooring interrupted the tense, testosterone-laden standoff. "Salyn?" A female voice. A human voice. Dark, sultry, and cunning. "You requested my company?"

Ghost stared at the platinum blonde, human slave with arrant curiosity: flawless curls, hair like silk, not a single strand out of place; hunter-green eyes like two crystal jewels sparkling with desire and *ambition*; long, sexy legs, a dress that hugged her curves, and lips so red they could've been dipped in crimson ink. This female had spent a lot of time preparing for this interlude.

For Salyn Stryke?

Nah, that didn't jibe.

She was after something loftier.

"Ghostaniaz Dragos, this is Felicity Payne," Salyn grunted in greeting. Then he moved so fast, the motion was a blur as he crossed the cavern, snatched the slave by her hair, and dragged her in front of the monitors. He pushed her down onto her knees, then forced her face into his groin. "Get busy, bitch," he snarled. "You weren't invited for your company."

Ghost did his best to ignore all the moaning, slurping, and gagging as Felicity, the ambitious actress, went to work on Salyn's...privates...and the soul eater turned his divided attention back to the Sinners' Cave's monitors. "The way Requiem Pyre sees it"—Salyn paused to groan and clench his fist in Felicity's hair—"the alchemy picks up...mmm...*fuuuck*....the alchemy picks up images and impressions from..." He lost his train of thought and cleared his throat. "From the host spirit's thoughts and intentions. So, you should...*ahh, shit*. You should—" He yanked Felicity's face away from his groin, turned her head in a violent, fisted twist of her curls, then booted her in the ass, sending her sprawling in Ghost's direction. "Him too," he snarled. "Both of us. Same time. Two-handed, and don't get sloppy."

Felicity rose higher on her knees, reached for the fly on Ghost's jeans, and gaped in confusion when he slapped her hand away and took a rapid stutter step backward. "Nah, I'll pass."

Salyn bristled. "What the hell is wrong with you? Too good for the best damn piece of ass we possess? This whore is a 340-year-old witch straight from Salem, Massachusetts, and she'll suck you inside out if you let her. Besides"—he licked his bottom lip like he was relishing a delicacy—"she likes it when you pluck her eyeballs out of their sockets while you...unload...then put them back in, slowly, later."

Ghost stared at Felicity like she had dung on her chin, one part pity, one part disgust. "Eyeballs notwithstanding, looks like yesterday's trash to me. *I'll pass.*"

Salem's jawbones literally dislodged from their sockets, and the upper maxilla scraped, side to side, against the lower mandible, even as his tattoos scurried away from his cruel, angry grimace. "From where I'm standing, that new bitch you bartered away from the king didn't look like a virgin, either. Maybe we can both trade sloppy seconds."

Ghost didn't take the bait, but then he didn't have to.

Apparently, his hesitation must have pushed the soul eater over the edge because Ghost never saw the right cross coming, and damn, if that fucker didn't land like a battering ram, crashing into Ghost's lower jaw with a fury.

Ghost sucked in air and staggered backward.

Well, hell, the violence was inevitable...

Everything was a test.

No one trusted or wanted him there—Ghost shared the sentiment—but he wasn't gonna stand there like a punk or make any inroads by acting like a pansy.

If Salyn wanted to dance, so be it!

Ghost caught his bearings, lunged at the soul eater, and snatched the tattooed freak by the throat, even as Felicity, who was still on her knees, scampered out of the way like a cockroach. He head-butted Salyn into the back, center monitor, then kneed him in the thick, erect appendage still jutting out of his sweatpants.

Salyn grunted.

Then chuckled.

Before unloading a shit ton of wicked-fast, ungodly powerful jabs—right and left crosses, lead and rear hooks—followed by an ever more vicious series of short, crisp uppercuts.

Ghost blocked that shit like a side-to-side, up-and-down windmill.

He balled his fist and threw a nasty, potent right jab of his own, determined to knock Salyn's teeth out, but the soul eater bobbed, weaved, and swept Ghost's feet out from under him with a low, roundhouse kick, sending the dragyri to the limestone floor like a stack of heavy dumbbells wrapped around a stiff iron bar. Ghost started to jackknife back onto his feet, when something in his peripheral vision caught his attention—stole his momentum ——and froze his gaze in place.

What the fuck was that?

A crude, ancient coffee table fashioned with human leg bones.

Annnd, so the fuck what!

Did it really matter?

Ghost tried to steer his attention back to Salyn, but something about those leg bones continued to hold him captive, rattled...frozen...and shaking like a leaf, his heart pounding a harsh, macabre symphony in his chest, like his ticker was about to break free from the cavity.

Where had he seen that shit before?

In a dream...

A fucking nightmare.

A flash of...something...he still couldn't place.

Salyn was kicking him now, stomping at his jaw, booting the back of his head, and twisting the ball of his foot into Ghost's exposed throat, trying to cut off the dragyri's airway, yet all Ghost could do was lie there like a paralyzed dolt, staring mindlessly at a two-foot-high bench crafted of calcified marrow.

He felt like his head was gonna split in two.

Flashes of light, like flickering strobes, began to assail his retinas.

What the devil was happening?

A coffee table.

Made of bones...

Sitting amongst a semicircle of blood-red sofas—

So the fuck what!

A coffee table.

Made of bones...

Sitting in Lord Dragos' private boudoir, in the upper residential quarters of the Temple of Seven—*what the devil?*

When.

Why.

What!?

Bile rose from Ghost's stomach, lodged in his throat, and he nearly choked on the bitter, alkaline fluid before spitting it out on the cavern floor and finally, mercifully, breaking free from the... from the...from the what?

The image...

The flash...

The memory?

The paralysis.

And just like that, Ghost was back in the Sinners' Cave, getting the shit stomped out of him by Salyn Strike. He grasped the soul eater's ankle, twisted until he heard bone snap, then scurried out of the way as the soul eater toppled over. He was just about to pummel the pagan son of a bitch, using his massive fist as a jackhammer, when Lord Drakkar Hades' deep, discordant voice pierced the inner sanctum of the cavern and ricocheted off the granular floor. "Not in here!" the king of the underworld thundered. "Damage this equipment, and I will murder both of you."

Salyn scrambled to attention, favoring his broken left foot as he swiftly stood upright and bowed his head in deference. "My liege."

Lord Drakkar Hades snarled.

Ghost spit out a second spew of bile on the cavern floor and slowly hefted his heavy frame upward. He rolled his shoulders and clambered to one knee. "Lord Drakkar."

"Not even gonna say *Uncle*?" the pagan king taunted.

Ghost snorted, ambled onto both feet, and rose to his full, imposing height. But he didn't make eye contact, and he didn't answer the smart-ass, rhetorical question.

The king turned his attention to the sad, compromised female, who was still on her knees, swiping moisture from her mouth with the back of her hand, and his voice dropped to a sultry croon. "Can you really suck it inside out? You enjoy having your eyes plucked out of their sockets?"

The woman—Felicity—scampered to her feet and curtsied so low she could've kissed her own kneecaps. "For you, milord, I would suck until I hyperventilated and bid you remove my eyes— and my beating heart—if either gave you pleasure. Whether you put them back or not, I would live...or die...in ecstasy, having given my all to the greatest being in the universe. My liege, I have waited 324 years for the privilege."

"Huh," Lord Drakkar harrumphed, seemingly surprised by her words. "Have you now?" He paced a contemplative finger over his thin, pursed lips and paused while mulling it over. "Like Ghost, I don't usually dumpster dive, nor take my meals from the trash. But you—you do intrigue me, witch—I think I shall remove your eyes, your tongue, and your heart, but not before you have pleased me thoroughly. Whether we put some of them back, none of them back, or rearrange the order...*yesss*, that will be a novel game indeed, even if it falls just shy of ecstasy, on my end." He took a come-hither step backward, crooked his pointer finger, and Felicity followed like a little lost lamb, only too eager for the shear or the slaughter. On his way out the cavern, Lord Drakkar turned around and glared at the dragyri and the soul eater. "Clean this shit up, and next time, roughhouse elsewhere."

Salyn snorted with indifference, still favoring his broken foot, even as Ghost swallowed an ill-bred retort. The soul eater no longer seemed as keen to tussle. And as for Ghost? Well, he'd also had enough adventure for one evening. Not to mention, he still needed to get some supplies back to Beth.

Besides, his usual amped-up, mercenary heart wasn't in it.

Something deep in his soul was still floundering...

Lurching.

Recoiling.

Reeling.

And it had nothing whatsoever to do with the pagan king's presence, nor his hard-hitting, heavily tattooed lackey. It had nothing to do with the scandalous witch and her soon-to-be sexual torture.

No...

Deep inside, somewhere Ghost couldn't pinpoint or name, he wanted to scream until his lungs caught fire and his soul was burned to ash.

Something...

That had *everything*...

To do with that creepy coffee table.

CHAPTER FOURTEEN

"Can you believe this freaky shit?" Joy said to Anne as she held up the ancient, tattered tome in her left hand and pinched her nose with her right, just beneath her furrowed brows. She leaned back against the stiff, cool fabric seat in Anne's compact SUV and exhaled slowly. "*A Treatise on the Seven Sins.*" She bristled at the name of the book. "This shit actually exists, and it's written in Greek!"

Anne leaned into the steering wheel, crossed her arms at the wrists, and rested against the two-toned leather, while slowly shaking her head. "I still can't get over the fact that the creepy *bookstore* exists: Wizards Witches & Ancient Theologies—what the actual hell?"

"Right!" Joy exclaimed. She could not have agreed more. "And that guy behind the counter—*what was his name, Mitch?*—that boy gave me the willies." She visibly shivered. "I tried to get a look at his neck. You know, check for that witch's pentacle on the pommel of a sword, but between his turtleneck and his hairline, I couldn't see his skin."

"Ditto," Anne said. "And yeah, I think he said his name was

Mitch Moretti, but who knows—that guy looked about as Italian as I do." She rolled her eyes and shook her head. "So, what now?" She shrugged her slender shoulders. "I mean, now that we have this bizarre book? Should we go back to Nicole's, show it to her and Kari, or should we call Bryce M and let him know we found it?"

Joy felt like her brain was perpetually stuffed with cotton, and every now and then, particularly in moments just like this, the cotton filled up with water and grew denser...heavier...the fluff expanding. "I don't know," she whispered softly, feeling so incredibly lost. "It's not like any of us can read it. Bryce told us to put out feelers, which we did. He said we should leave our business cards or cell phone numbers everywhere we go. Did that too. In fact, I wrote my cell number, work number, and Nicole's landline on the back of the card I left with that creepy Mitch-not-Italian-Moretti, but the entire time I was doing it—walking into that shop, asking about and buying the book, leaving my number and my business card—it was like something in my brain was shouting, *Stop! What the hell are you doing, Joy? How is any of this gonna help you find Beth?* But then as quickly as the thoughts... the questions...enter my mind, they vanish, and then something stronger says, *Trust Bryce. Keep at it. You are going to see Beth again.* And none of this damn shit makes any sense."

Anne stared at Joy blankly before finally blinking two times. "I feel like that too," she said. "Not only like we're being led down a wild, pointless rabbit hole, but also like we're being watched. My logical brain tells me this doesn't make sense, go back to the police, and stop talking to this Bryce guy. All this crazy Cult of Hades stuff doesn't exist, and if it does? Well, we don't want any part of it. But then, it's like when a professor writes a math formula on a chalkboard, and you're still trying to copy it...study it...but he erases it too soon. Whatever doubts I have...yeah, they just vanish before I have a chance to take a closer look."

Joy centered her body in the narrow bucket seat, laid the creepy book squarely in the center of her lap, and crossed her arms over her stomach, slowly shutting her eyes. She took several deep breaths, inhaling through her nose and exhaling through her mouth, to try to calm the perpetual unease. She opened her eyes once more and gazed out the lightly tinted window, watching as several cold, wet, brittle flakes of snow swirled about in a haphazard oval, before slowly drifting to the ground. In truth, it was a beautiful night.

Dark.

Quiet.

And oddly serene.

The cast of snow, illuminated beneath the high, arched, iron streetlight, almost gave off the feeling that all was exactly as it was meant to be, nature carrying on as usual, seasons gently turning, night destined to give way to day, like this thing with Beth—and Bryce—would come to a peaceful, if not positive, conclusion.

But it wouldn't.

Despite herself, Joy knew better.

She sniffed. "Six in one hand, half a dozen in the other. Whether we take the book back to Nicole's or give Bryce M a call, not sure it really matters. What was it Shakespeare said in *Macbeth*? Maybe 'it's all sound and fury, signifying nothing.'"

* * *

Okaaay...

So, Joy was quoting Shakespeare now.

They had all truly fallen further down the rabbit hole than Anne first thought.

Still, Anne understood Joy's disconnect as well as her cynical outlook: On one hand, Anne also felt virtually compelled to keep pressing forward, to follow all of Bryce M's instructions, yet on the other hand, every action she took felt incredibly futile...point-less...like they were all just spinning around in prescribed, useless circles for no apparent reason. Her brain, maybe even her heart, believed Bryce's words, but her eyes, which were the seat of her soul, they saw straight through him. They saw something else. They saw *someone else*. But for the life of her, she couldn't place it. And above all else, Beth was still missing.

Anne followed Joy's wistful gaze up to a glowing streetlamp and watched as large, crystalline snowflakes danced in the lamp-light. She wondered if Joy was watching them too, wondering what all of this meant—

"How long have you been a Seer, child?"

Anne jerked upright in her seat and stared blankly at Joy, who was still gazing out the window, almost as if she were lost in a trance.

"A seeker of knowledge, a conduit for truth? How long, sweet girl?"

Anne leaned toward her friend and gawked, even as she studied Joy's features. Nothing. Her lips weren't moving. Joy hadn't said a word!

"Since childhood?" the persistent voice queried.

Anne gasped.

This was freaky as hell!

She glanced in the rearview mirror, half expecting to find an elderly woman nestled in the confined, narrow space, but once again...nothing. There was no one there. She craned her neck and twisted her shoulders in an effort to survey every nook and cranny, the farthest corners by the backseat doors, the floor mats, the tiny space behind the center console, even as she knew nothing could hide in an area that small. "Joy?!" she exclaimed, twisting back around and leaning heavily toward her friend. "Do you hear that! What the hell is it?"

Joy didn't even turn her head.

It was like time had stopped, all matter was standing still, and Anne's beautiful passenger-seat companion was just...somewhere else. Distant. Unaware. Lost in a motionless vortex, wholly captivated by the streetlamp and the snow. It was like Anne and Joy were living in two separate, alternate dimensions, even as they sat side by side in the SUV, less than three feet apart from each other.

"Not Joy," the disembodied voice said softly. "Betsy Davis, but you can call me Grandma."

Anne's eyes grew wide with equal parts trepidation and wonder—she could've sworn she had heard that name before, but she couldn't place when or where—and then the entire back seat of the car filled with a soft yet brilliant otherworldly light: an incandescent silver-white glow with pink around the edges, blue and purple radiating outward from the center, each lumen pulsing in a subtle, soothing vibration like living beats from a lucent, animated heart.

The disembodied voice was part and parcel of the lumens: "I can't stay long, child. Making contact like this isn't easy. So, I need you to listen. Listen...and absorb...all I am saying."

Anne parted her mouth to speak, but no sound came out.

"My sweet, darling Bethy is still alive, yet she is in the gravest of danger. There are many souls at play, many dimensions, many motivations, many *deities*, but you, dear Anne, have both a gift and a role to play. You are indeed a Seer, and your eyes will become the window of the soul for many. You are correct to feel like you're chasing shadows, spinning around in circles, but I am asking you to keep trusting Ja—keep trusting *Bryce*." Her voice hitched at the unusual stutter. "Like the steps on a ladder that lead to the top, so will your actions and your eyes lead to strange persons, whose actions and eyes will lead to strange creatures, whose actions and eyes will lead to powerful beings, like brilliant gemstones shimmering in the sun, and once all have seen through the step above them, the one who *must see* the whole picture will be able to view Beth and her troubled companion. Keep doing what you're doing, Anne. Have faith."

Anne was utterly gobsmacked.

First and foremost, not one word of that made sense.

Second, that stutter: "Keep trusting Ja—keep trusting Bryce."

Third, and more important, Grandma Betsy had said Beth was still alive, but she was in a lot of danger—and what the heck, who the heck, was this mysterious, troubled companion? "I don't understand."

The elderly spirit chuckled. "You don't need to, nor will you. Just follow your heart. Let your eyes be the windows through which *others* will see."

"See what?"

The incandescent light pulsed brightly, then began to flicker.

"What others?"

"I cannot stay long, for there is one steeped in darkness who has been viewing you and Joy this day, through his own malevolent screen...or window. And at least this far, I have managed to hide my essence from his awareness. Pray for my sweet Bethy. All of you. Pray in whatever manner has the most meaning, and know she is never truly alone." The light began to fade, growing ever more faint.

"Wait," Anne contended. "Don't go! I still don't understand. Who the heck is watching me and Joy through a screen of malevolence...darkness...and what does that even mean?"

"Angels. Demons. Light. Shadow, darkness...or love. There are many souls, many mysteries, but in the end, hold fast to the knowledge that across all dimension, beyond all time, transcending both station and place, the greatest of these still remains love." With that, the light fully vanished, Grandma Betsy was gone, and Joy snapped out of her stupor.

CHAPTER FIFTEEN

THE PAGAN UNDERWORLD

Exhausted, drained, and feeling profoundly antisocial, Ghost cranked the heavy iron handle on the thick wooden door of what was now his and Beth's bedchamber and silently strode in. He crossed the annular grotto, without glancing left or right, on his way to the barred, stained glass window at the back of the room.

He needed to open that window.

He needed to get some air.

As he passed the stark, naked mattress and the girl sitting atop it, he kept his eyes forward, bent to place two large baskets at the foot of the bed, then continued along the same trajectory, until at last he reached the stained glass window, cranked the lever beneath the black iron bars, and waited for that first, desperately needed gust of fresh air.

Gust of fresh air...

What the hell was he thinking?

This was King Drakkar's castle in the dense, inky underworld —ever gray, ever foul—there was no fresh air to be had.

He glanced over his shoulder, at last making eye contact with

Beth, and nearly winced: She was sitting on the edge of the mattress, bare feet on the floor, shoulders curled inward, still wearing nothing but Ghost's black, classic crew neck, and she was practically wringing the skin off her hands. And damnit all to hell if she didn't look one part desperate and two parts...*pissed*.

What the hell to say?

Ghost had been gone for a protracted minute, and Beth had not had anything to eat or drink in, well, forever and a fucking day.

He watched as his fated dragyra—and he still couldn't get over that shit, that crazy twist of fate—reached for the first of the two baskets, in spite of her distress, and snatched a large loaf of dry, seedy bread. She tore off a sizeable chunk and shoved it in her mouth. She reached for the jug of ale and downed at least six ounces before she had even chewed or swallowed the bread, and then she devoured three or four mouthfuls of stale, moldy cheese, one right after the other, without stopping to scrape off the mold.

Damn.

It was the best Ghost could find in the anemic, human slaves' kitchen, yet the bread was stale, the cheese was growing fungi, and the ham was at least three days old. Drak clearly couldn't care less about his servants' nutrition, and the fruit, if you could call it fruit, came from some sort of tree, some foreign species even Ghost could not identify after living for over a thousand years. Yet Beth ate every morsel of that refuse too. "Slow down, girl, you're gonna choke on that shit, or at least get a really bad stomachache."

She glared at him behind thick, leveled lashes, then turned her attention back to the cache of food, searching for something else to eat. Finally, when she had consumed enough calories to make up for her famine, she washed down the rest of the ale, sat back on the mattress, and crossed her arms over her now-swollen stomach. "What happened to you?" Her tone was more despondent than angry. "You've been gone for over seventeen hours." She glanced at the thin silver watch on her left wrist for emphasis.

"Long-ass story," Ghost grunted.

"Yeah, well?"

"Well, what?"

"Seventeen hours, five minutes, and thirty-seven seconds to be exact, Ghost. *What happened?*"

Ghost leaned back against the open bars of the window now hanging to the left of the arch, and rested his forearm against the open sill. "Damn. A lot of shit, Beth. I got tangled up with Killian Kross, Lord Drakkar's chief counselor, for a long-ass time, ended up in the castle's undercroft, downing some mead and putrid, soul-tainting wine with Kross and three other demons...drank until I finally passed out. I made a trip to the Sinners' Cave— *don't even ask*—where I got into a little scrap with a pagan named Salyn, and then finally made my way to the human slave quarters, where I came by all the food and shit in those baskets." He left out the part about completely freaking out at the sight of a coffee table made from human bones. Rather, he pointed at the second cluster of items in the yet untouched basket. "Threadbare sheets, some toiletries, and a new cotton T-shirt. Some sweats, plain cotton underwear, well, at least the bottoms." He held up one hand in apology. "And beneath that small pack of hand towels, there's two washcloths and a single bar of lye soap—gonna have to double as shampoo or...whatever. Sorry I couldn't score any pillow slips, blankets, or another bedcover. I'll try again in the morning."

"Water?" she asked, sounding exceedingly weary. "For washing and stuff?"

Ghost shrugged one shoulder. "Yeah. It would seem there's modern plumbing in the upper and lower dorms, but in the main floor chambers, it's hit or miss. I guess"—shit, this was gonna fall like a ton of bricks—"guess the slaves empty the chamber pots daily and drop off buckets of water outside the doors in the early mornings."

"Slaves?"

He grunted.

"As in human slaves, like me?"

He acknowledged the remark with silence; no need to belabor the obvious.

Beth sighed, shook her head, then glanced at the second basket.

As she leaned over to thumb through the items, clearly cataloguing each in her mind, her eyes, her delicate hands...the simple despondent motion made her look so incredibly fragile, and in that unguarded moment, the truth of her predicament struck him like a sledge against an anvil: She may as well have been an innocent, newborn rabbit thrust into a wild, savage jungle. He knew the truth, and so did she. Beth was at the bottom of a very nasty, unforgiving food chain.

She licked her bottom lip. "Thank you." She pointed toward the bedchamber door. "For going out there and...and for whatever you had to go through to bring all this back. I was just..." Her voice trailed off, and she covered her face with her hands. "Just waiting here for all that time. Like a sitting duck. Not knowing who was going to come through that door: you, or one of a hundred bloodthirsty hunters, each with a loaded shotgun."

Ghost searched for a gentle reply but came up short.

He had nothing.

No words of encouragement, no demonstrative empathy, not even an obvious *You're welcome*.

She seemed to grasp that fact, or at least she read the silence. Absently tucking a thick lock of wavy, dark brown hair behind her ear, she locked eyes with Ghost and forced a paltry smile. "Were you in a lot of danger? I mean, out there?"

He raised his brows, indifferent. "Always, but it's the same in here. As long as we are in this castle—"

"We?" she interrupted, and this time, her voice sounded vacant and far away. "*We* are not both human." She frowned in demonstration. "*We* are not both female. I think... Ghost, we need to have a plan B, just in case we don't make it out of here. Just in case something happens to you. I've had seventeen hours to think about what that looks like. For me. And if only for my sanity, I need a plan B."

Ghost furrowed his brow. "What kind of plan B?"

This time it was Beth who shrugged a much smaller shoulder, before taking a deep breath for courage. "The kind that involves a bottle of poison or swallowing some toxic herbs." She paused as if to steady her resolve. "The kind where, maybe, you use your supernatural strength, your paranormal abilities, or even your dragon's fire to do something—*merciful* and *quick*. Something I can't do on my own, yet something I may need if push comes to shove, bad goes to worse, and there's no other way out of an... inevitable...situation."

As if sucked out by a giant vacuum, the air in Ghost's lungs left his body.

Shit.

Fuck.

Talk about a heavy dose of reality, blunt and to the point.

The newborn rabbit had surveyed the jungle—clearly, succinctly, and with chilling accuracy—and now she was seeking a way out if necessary: a way out of the castle, a way out of the stifling bedchamber, a way out of *her life* if things got too desperate. If Ghost could not protect her...save her...ultimately get Beth out of there, then she still needed a way out of a potential doomsday nightmare. And she was asking Ghost for help, to provide her with a means to take her own life, or to promise to take it himself, should push come to shove.

Shit, he thought.

That was one heavy request.

Thing was: The rabbit quaking beneath the oppression of such a wicked-harsh jungle still did not have all the facts. Ghost had left out some important details about the Pantheon, the Temple of Seven, and the true nature of their time-sensitive predicament.

When Ghost had explained to Beth that they only had eight days to make it back through the portal for conversion, he had purposefully omitted the potential end result should they fail to pull it off. If the Seven did not convert Beth in the temple, on or before Wednesday, one week from tomorrow, if they didn't show up in time, Beth was already as good as dead, and Lord Dragos would remove Ghost's amulet.

Yeah, she wouldn't make it through the night.

She would die in her sleep, and Ghost would become a permanent feature in the Garden of Grace: no more sentience, no more life.

That was that...

For both of them.

The difference was: Beth still had a choice.

Ghost could not force her to enter the temple, and neither could, nor would, the dragon lords. She still had free will. She still had to consent. She still had to agree to both the mating and the rebirth by fire. So, all things considered, the dragyra's request was a bit premature, if not incomplete. From Ghost's point of view, the Pantheon was every bit as lethal, just as dangerous, as the underworld jungle, and the "little rabbit" was just as likely to die from some consequence related to the ten-day claiming as at the hands of a shadow-walker or demon.

Than at the hands of Lord Drakkar.

Selfishly, Ghost also understood that Lord Dragos could hardly remove his amulet while he was stuck in the Pagan

Underworld, worlds away, in an unknown, parallel dimension, safely—or unsafely—sequestered in Lord Drakkar Hades' wicked domain.

Nope...

Between the two of them, Beth's days were literally numbered, while Ghost's were still up for debate. And for a fleeting second, the image of that coffee table—*the second coffee table, the one in Lord Dragos' private boudoir*—once again creeped into Ghost's thoughts. And *hells bells* if it didn't complicate everything. Confuse everything. Make Ghost feel like he wanted to hurt Lord Dragos, almost more than he wanted to survive, almost more than he wanted to save Beth.

For reasons he couldn't pin down or make sense of, Ghost was rethinking his entire approach: If he resigned himself to stay in the underworld, to actually form a true alliance with Lord Drakkar, he would never have to claim a female, he would not have to risk life and limb to escape, and more important—more tempting, soothing, and inviting—he could hurt Lord Dragos, all the way down to the bastard's black-hearted core. Knowing Ghost was gone, knowing he had lost a Genesis Son, and knowing Ghost had switched his allegiance to the Seven's original enemy?

Yeah.

Fuck yeah...

That would do the trick.

But then there was Romani, Chance, and Jax to think of...

In truth, Ghost rarely exchanged more than a couple of sentences with any of his lair mates, but they were still his diamond brothers, and he still owed his fealty to each and every one of them. His allegiance. His honor. And that was to say nothing of the other GIs, the firstborn hatchlings of the remaining dragon lords: Blaise, Brass, Jagyr, Nuri, Zane, and Tiberius. The seven of them had existed, together, as a fraternity of firstborn hatchlings for at least a millennium, and that was a helluva lot of common memories and joint survival to just toss out the window...flush down the drain.

And, well...shit.

As much as the thought of caring for another sentient being, let alone a vulnerable human female, curdled Ghost's stomach, he also had to think of Bethany Reid, his *fated*. She hadn't asked for any of this shit, and the fact that such a decision—to switch his loyalty and bat for the other team—would certainly seal her fate and demand her death; well, that would be hard to swallow.

Beth's demise would be Ghost's decision, and her blood would be on his hands.

Selfish?

Definitely.

Black-hearted?

Sure.

A true chip off the old Dragos' block!

Ghost sought Beth's vivid, dark brown eyes to recognize her question, at least acknowledge her presence; then he lowered his head in shame: Her brows were creased with worry, her gaze was shrouded in shadows, and in that moment, he thanked the Seven that humans couldn't read the Dragyrs' thoughts.

Shiiit.

What was he thinking?

Never.

Not in a million years.

Ghost might not be a paragon of virtue, and while sticking it to Lord Dragos once and for all, with both brutality and finality, might be the most rewarding act of his long, pointless life, killing the woman in front of him—or at least sanctioning her death— was beneath him.

Too far beneath him.

He was not his father's son.

His heart might be cold, empty, even lacking compassion, but Ghostaniaz Dragos was not Lord Dragos Junior—*aka, Lord Dipshit, the second*—he was not cut from the same soulless cloth.

"Ghost?" Beth whispered, tilting her head to the side. "Where'd you go? You still here?"

Ghost blinked a couple of times. Yeah, he was here. And it was time to double down on getting both of them out of the blasted castle. It was time to pick a date, hatch a plan, and get working on a final exodus. Although he didn't possess enough charm or tenderness to influence his *fated* romantically, he could at least try harder to explain her options, do a better job at leading, if not influencing, the female's decisions, make sure Beth understood what would happen if she refused to enter the Temple of Seven of her own volition. Hell, just put all the cards on the table, so if anyone died unnecessarily, it wouldn't be this innocent female.

Another unbidden memory flashed through Ghost's mind: himself, as a five-year-old child, hunting with his sire, being reared, trained, broken, and *scorched* by his pitiless father for trying to spare a pregnant woman's unborn child. The lesson Lord Dragos had sought to impart: no mercy, no conscience, never consider the life of a human, never pity your prey. Ghost shut that shit down with a sniff and a nod, locked the door on the flashback, and tossed the key.

Beth wasn't human prey.

She was his chosen dragyra.

And Lord Dragos wasn't teaching the lessons anymore— Ghost was in charge of his own treacherous destiny. "Yeah," he mumbled. "I'm still here." He pushed off the windowsill and took several long, determined strides in his *fated's* direction. "Doesn't matter where I went. I'm still here." He kept moving forward, drawing closer to Beth, ignoring the mounting, stark reflection of fear brimming in her dark, vivid eyes, and the closer he came, the more her shoulders tightened, the more she visibly drew her body away, and the more he pretended not to notice.

Didn't matter.

Ghost might not be the epitome of compassion, but he wasn't a brain-dead idiot, either. He could mimic emotion if he had to. He could provide a semblance of...comfort...even if he was just going through the motions. At the least, he could give Beth the same raw honesty, directness, and respect she was bravely giving him.

He stopped short in front of her.

He knelt on the floor between her now trembling legs and cupped her face in two determined hands. "Don't be afraid of me," he rasped, hating that his voice was more gruff than soothing. "I already told you; I have no desire to hurt you. But yes, I promise—*I give you my word*—I don't know if I can score any poison in this castle, but I think I can score a dagger once I win a little more trust. And I will show you how to use it in a swift and lethal manner, should shit hit the fan...go too far south. And yeah, no doubt, if something unthinkable is about to happen to the two of us, if something even worse is about to happen to you—if death or torture are ever imminent, and there's no way I can stop it— then yes, Beth, I will do everything in my power to make sure you don't suffer, even if that means taking your life."

She shivered at the force of his words, or maybe she just shivered because the subject was so grave, her body had to expel some of the morbid energy. Either way, she raised her chin, placed her hands over his, and nodded with incredible bravery. "Thank you."

Uncomfortable with the contact, Ghost drew back, causing Beth's hands to fall away, yet he managed to hold her stare unerringly. "Welcome." And then he truly, intently, studied her face, scrutinizing each feature unabashedly: her high, almost angular cheekbones, the regal slope of her nose...soft cast of her jaw...her flawless, baby-fine skin overlaying so much beauty, masking so much turmoil, and the inescapable resolve in otherwise uncertain eyes. "Strong," he murmured.

"Excuse me?"

"You really are strong."

She let out a nervous chortle. "No. Not strong. Especially not as a child." She sniffed and shook her head. "Maybe just desperate...determined." When he didn't reply, she went on. "At one point in my life, I worked hard to...toughen up...become more assertive, maybe even brave when I had to be, but this, all of this?" She waved her hand in a wide, encompassing arc, gesturing toward the cold, dark castle bedchamber. "I'm scared to death, Ghost. And I'm trying really, *really* hard not to let it get the best of me."

Ghost allowed her words to linger. *True that*, he thought. "Yeah, well, you made it through seventeen hours, five minutes, and thirty-seven seconds, *to be exact*, so I'm sure that counts for something."

She smiled then, and her beauty was undeniable. "Thing is," she said, "I don't know what's scarier: this place, its inhabitants, or knowing that my only chance of survival is you." She quickly held up the same elegant hand. "No offense, but it's a lot to take in. All of it. Everything you've told me. Everything that's happened. And everything I've seen...in you."

"Seen in me?"

"Yes," she said softly, "everything I see in you."

He wasn't sure he wanted to go there, but honesty, directness, respect, and all that. "Like what?"

"Your eyes."

He smirked. "What about them?"

She shrugged her slender shoulders. "So many things..."

"Like?"

"Like when you first got back to this dungeon of a bedroom

and walked through that hideous, oppressive wooden door, your eyes, they were haunted, like all the way to the depths of your soul."

This time, it was Ghost who sniffed at his dragyra's words. "Nah," he argued. "That's just my look. Been told that my eyes, all the colors, those ice-cold shades of silver and blue...they can be a bit disconcerting."

"True," Beth said, forcing a faint, acquiescent smile. "Your eyes are different for sure, but the haunted part—the pain, the rage, the dozens of hidden shadows behind them—that's got nothing to do with the color of your pupils."

Ghost measured her words in silence.

He turned them over on his tongue and tasted each one in turn.

So, she was both strong and intuitive.

Perceptive.

Good to know.

Yet, he wasn't about to touch that subject with a fifty-foot pole. "I tell you what," he said brusquely, "you don't worry about my inner demons, and I won't worry about your inner fears, including the fact that you're already contemplating a way to commit suicide." He tried to force a facetious smile, but it really didn't suit him. Came off more like a genetic tic in his upper lip than a gesture of friendly banter. "Seriously," he said, "we've got bigger fish to fry, don't you think?"

Beth bit her bottom lip, then nodded, and the awkward silence that ensued didn't suit her any better than Ghost's unnatural twitch of a smile.

"Look," he finally relented, "cards on the table—'cause I know you're not interested in my hellish past or my psychological makeup—so what is it that you're really asking me, Beth?"

As if contemplating whether to jump into a pool of frigid water, Beth took a deep breath, held it, then leaped, headfirst.

"Can you really get us out of here?" she asked, pointedly. "I mean, the very first time we talked, before you left to find clothes and food, I asked you to explain everything, all of it...*specifics*... and not to leave anything out. Did you?" Must have been a rhetorical question because she didn't give him a chance to respond. The moment he opened his mouth to speak, she leaned forward and held up both hands. "For whatever it's worth, I know the last thing you ever wanted, expected, or needed was a human woman, a female...dragana...or whatever you call it, making your life, your predicament, even more complicated than it already was. But—"

"Dragyra."

"What?"

"Dragyra, not dragana."

"Dragyra." She paused to let the correct word linger. "And I know that the odds are against us. I'm not stupid. But I guess what I'm really asking, what I'm really wanting to have and to know is"—she lowered her voice to a whisper—"can I trust you, Ghost? I mean, in spite of your demons? Are you open enough... unreserved enough...to trust me with the truth? Because I don't think anyone, anywhere, has ever been your ally. You're a one-man show. Still, I need to know that I'm not alone, that we're at least in this nightmare together. Getting out of here, I mean. No bullshit. No hidden motivations. And no secrets. Can I really trust you, Ghost?" She folded her hands in her lap and sat there...waiting.

So...

Beth had just called him out on being too closed off, holding things back, and maybe not being altogether trustworthy in the process. So be it. She had also just opened the door, given him the segue he needed to broach the full subject of conversion in the temple.

Good.

He waited for the space of two or three seconds, rose from his squat, rocked forward onto the balls of his feet, and anchored his arms on either side of his *fated*, his palms pressing flat against the naked mattress. Then he looked deep into his dragyra's eyes, acutely aware that he was, unintentionally, towering over her—didn't mean it, but oh well. Trust went two ways. "You're not wrong about my demons, Beth." He leaned in even closer. "And you're not wrong about the secrets, or the fact that I'm a loner. Just like I'm not wrong in guessing the only reason you're even speaking to me, trying to push through your fear...coming clean with me...is because you're desperate to get the hell out of this castle, and you need me to make that happen. No harm, no foul. That's just smart, clear thinking. Self-preservation. But I'm also guessing that you plan on bolting the second that happens. *If* it happens. So, as long as we're sharing the uncut version, getting everything out in the open, then truth is—you can't. Bolt, that is. If we do make it out of here, and you decide not to go through with the ceremony...the conversion...to enter the Temple of Seven, you won't live to tell about it, dragyra. And that's a lot of shit you're gonna have to unpack in fairly short order without me, a lotta pros and cons, heavy decisions I can't weigh or make for you. So yeah, I withheld that morsel of info when I first explained who I am...*what I am*...and who and what you are to me: my *fated*, my dragyra, a reciprocal lifeline."

Her face grew ashen, and she pursed her full lips, the wheels in her mind turning in silence.

"Figured you had more than enough to terrify you already," he said by way of paltry explanation. "And no, I wasn't looking for an added complication, any more than you were looking to be dependent on a son of a dragon for your protection, but here we are in this shitstorm, together, mutually dependent on each other for survival. So yes, Beth, you can trust me. And I need to know I can trust you too. No bullshit. No hidden motivations or agendas.

And no more secrets on either end of the equation, except for one non-negotiable caveat." He furrowed his brows and narrowed his gaze. "My past, my demons, whatever the hell haunts me? That shit is off limits; are we clear? Just gotta trust me anyway."

Beth inhaled sharply.

She rubbed her temples.

She closed her eyes and noticeably relaxed her mouth, her jaw, then her tense, tightly drawn shoulders. Finally, when the silence had become too uncomfortable, she opened her eyes, tilted her chin upward to meet his gaze, and stared at him, unflinching. "The temple thing: You said I wouldn't live to tell about it. Why not? Would you harm me?"

"Never." He shook his head emphatically.

"Would someone else in the Pantheon harm me?"

"The other dragyri? The mercenaries? No."

"Then why...how...I don't understand."

"It's the way the gods created our world, Beth. Once a fated human female has been found, and the ten-day window has closed for good, the dragyra can no longer survive without her dragyri. No one would have to harm you. You would die in your sleep."

Beth gulped, her eyes grew wide, and she fisted the hem of her oversized crew neck—*Ghost's crew neck*—with pale-knuckled fingers. She drew in several harsh gulps of air, then let the last one out, slowly, methodically. "Okaaay..." She took another deep breath, held it for several seconds, then resolutely relaxed her fists as she released it, visibly willing calm into her mind and body. "So, we can unpack that later as you say. But right here and now, there's only one agenda, finding a way out of this underworld together. I trust you, and you trust me—one hundred."

"One hundred," Ghost echoed.

Beth nodded decisively, forced a faint, miserable smile, and slowly lifted her hand, extending her little finger.

Ghost stared blankly at the curved, slender digit.

She toggled it in the air.

"The fuck?" Ghost asked.

Her smile brightened. "Pinky swear; it's a human thing."

Ghost lowered his body until he was half standing, half squatting, at perfect eye level in front of her. He circled her pinky with the tip of his own, drew her hand forward, and turned it over, leaving her wrist exposed. Then he dipped his head and punctured her vein, utilizing two sharp, dragonese canines, siphoned some heat from her essence, and swirled the tip of his tongue over the resulting drops of blood. "Sworn and sealed," he said gruffly. "It's a Dragyr thing. And Beth, we will escape together, or we will die together. And that goes for both planes of existence, in the Pantheon or here in the underworld. When it comes to conversion...the Temple of Seven...the call is yours, and yours alone, to make: If you choose *not* to go through with the ceremony, it will be the end of my existence too. But if that happens, then it happens. No pressure, no persuasion. You have to be true to you. And should you choose to go through with conversion, assuming we actually make it out of here, that doesn't mean..." His voice trailed off. "That doesn't mean...you still don't need...we still don't have to be anything...do anything...or commit to anything we both don't choose. Far as I'm concerned: Fuck the dragon lords on both spheres of creation. We decide; they don't. No bullshit. No secrets. No hidden motivations."

Beth stared at Ghost like he was an alien species. Her eyebrows furrowed, and her mouth gaped open. She licked her lips and cleared her throat. "You...you would be willing to die rather than force me to go through with conversion?"

"I would die with you, yes."

She shook her head in wonder. "Ghost, do you value your life? I mean, apart from this predicament. Before you were captured, did you value your life?"

He cocked one heavy shoulder. "I value...yours...*enough*."

She shivered.

"Don't sweat it, Beth. Not your burden to carry."

She nodded slowly. "That shit is off limits, right?"

He winked at her.

"Got it," she said softly. "And Ghost, just for the record, I wasn't judging you. Thank you for your honesty, no matter how...unsettling."

It was his turn to nod.

This female really was strong.

Different.

Practical.

And wasn't that just a novel concept, or at least the start of a whole new paradigm—neither one *owed* the other a damn thing. They would do what they did with their eyes wide open, because they chose an allegiance for the sake of freedom.

Freedom.

Not oppression.

And not duty.

Nothing more and nothing less.

Beth needed Ghost to live, and Ghost needed Beth to live. Beyond that, it was anyone's guess and *nobody's* solitary call.

To hell with all the extraneous bullshit.

CHAPTER SIXTEEN

THREE HOURS LATER

L ord Drakkar Hades strolled through the twin, ornate blood-red doors leading out onto his bedchamber's private balcony, and swayed his shoulders to the erotic, serpentine motion of all the pet snakes slithering around his naked ankles, the glorious feel of their slippery scales and rough, wet tongues greeting their lord and master.

He briefly thought of Felicity Payne.

The fellatio had been good, the actual sex exquisite, but the witch had lied about enjoying the extraction of her eyeballs...and heart. In fact, she had screamed like a virgin sacrifice, rather than moaning like a seasoned harlot, the entire time Lord Drakkar had carved out her still-beating heart with the tip of a curved, extended fingernail. And while he had placed the organ back in her body and restored its beating for obvious reasons, he had alas enjoyed the hilarious game of *Go Fetch* with her eyeballs: tossing them about his massive bedchamber, watching as she scrambled naked on her hands and knees, trying to find them, feeling around while blind as a bat, bumping into furniture, cutting open her scalp on a heavy brass amphora, then finally retrieving them and bringing them back...just to repeat the entire challenge, not once, not twice, but half a dozen times hence.

Having finally grown weary of the woman and the game, Lord Drakkar had folded her eyeballs neatly in the palm of her trembling hand, given her a sound scolding about lying to her king—*"never let your mouth write a check your ass can't cash"*— and sent her on her way, still plagued with empty sockets to make her way blindly through the castle and back to the lower dormitory where she truly belonged. Kyryn, Salyn, or Mongryn Time would surely replace the eyeballs; she was much too beautiful to leave as they would find her. No matter. If she survived, so be it. If she perished, so what. If she was scarred for life, then she would learn a valuable lesson.

As it stood, Felicity had always been far too ambitious. There was no way in hell, no chance in the underworld, Lord Drakkar would have ever made her one of his delectable seven. Her body had been known by too many—human men on Earth and pagans in the gothic castle.

Sadly, Bethany Reid was no longer viable either.

Wraith Sylvester had seen to that when he had placed his duplicitous hands on her perfect body. Lord Drakkar would need to find another to serve in the venerable throne room and complete his private harem. No, he did not necessarily require a virgin, but to elevate one who had been touched by a member of his horde? Unthinkable. Not going to happen. Ghost would enjoy this newest human female, at least for a time, and then, when the king of the underworld was ready, he would command his duplicitous *nephew* to offer the slave as a sacrifice of fealty, proof of his desire to serve Lord Drakkar. Her perfect body would still serve the king as an exquisite, erotic offering— oiled, carved open, and set on fire—on the throne room's golden altar before all the Pagan Horde. If, at that time, the shadow-walkers and the demons wanted to mount her as she burned, then, well, that would be more entertaining than the recent game of *Go Fetch*. Either way, the point would be made before all Lord Drakkar's adoring sycophants—no one *demanded* anything from the ancient king of the underworld and actually got to keep it.

Not Requiem Pyre, Drakkar's chief sorcerer.

Not Killian Kross, chief counselor to the same.

And not even the members of Drakkar's venerable congress: Aegis Hawk, Gemini Stone, Lithos Black, or Prism Archer.

All knew Salem Thorne had lost his penis, the fact that Trader Vice now had a tiger snake in the place of a missing left hand, and soon, all would know what had happened to Wraith Sylvester. Lord Drakkar did not suffer insolence, and neither did those who stood closest beside him.

He let out a long, drawn-out sigh, reached down to stroke the head of a particularly restless copperhead, then stood back to his full, imposing, masculine height of six feet, eight inches, before raising his arms to embrace the thick, sulfuric, dense night air.

In truth, his heart was troubled.

What to do with his duplicitous nephew, indeed, the son of a lifelong archenemy.

The copperhead slithered up his leg, wrapped around his forearm, and sank its fangs deep into Lord Drakkar's heavily veined neck. Drakkar reveled in the feel of the mild venom, even as he allowed his thoughts of Ghostaniaz to wander...

I despise Lord Dragos, and that is the truth.

Lord Drakkar believed Ghost's words.

I have zero shits to give, whether I live in the Pantheon or this soul-forsaken cauldron of an underworld, as long as I'm reasonably comfortable.

Mmm, not so much; Ghost was disseminating here.

What I'm after is clemency...I'm superior to your horde...what I want is the girl, the one on the bed. What have I got to lose? What

*do you have to lose? And I am flesh of your flesh and blood of your
blood, the only blood kin in this palace.*

Now these things gave Lord Drakkar pause.

Yes, Ghost desired clemency—what fool would want to
endure endless torture? And yes, he was arrogant, ballsy, and far
too cocksure, but he was in fact superior to Drakkar's soul and sin
eaters, if only by measure of his divine hatchling birth. And
yes...*maybe*...he wanted to screw the human woman, especially
after realizing she was no longer fit for the throne room, but ass
was ass, and slaves were plentiful; why barter with what could be
certain death for the pleasure of one particularly pretty maiden?
No, this did not ring true with Lord Drakkar; there was something deeper beneath Ghost's forked-tongue explanation.

What did Ghost have to lose?

Absolutely nothing.

What did Lord Drakkar have to lose?

Only his pride...

But wait, that wasn't entirely honest—Ghostaniaz had spelled
out exactly what Lord Drakkar had to lose: the flesh of his flesh
and the blood of his blood. Lord Drakkar's first and only chance,
since time immemorial, to share his eternal existence with one of
his own DNA. The thought was positively mind-blowing...unex-
pected...something the king had never considered as even a
possible conundrum.

And a conundrum it was.

On one hand, Lord Drakkar knew he could not turn his back
on the offspring of Lord Dragos, first of the Seven—the wily,
heathen dragyri was lying through his teeth, and Lord Drakkar
could likely trust Ghostaniaz Dragos as far as he could throw
him. Well, that wasn't entirely true. As an original creator, an all-
powerful deity, Lord Drakkar could toss Ghost through the time-
space continuum if he chose. Hell, he could send him back to the
mid-thirteenth century's Ming Dynasty with nothing more than a

flick of his wrist, but the point remained: Ghost was trying to play Lord Drakkar like an ebony fiddle. The king just didn't know to what purpose, to what ends.

And ultimately, it didn't matter.

He had already spoken to his chief sorcerer, Requiem Pyre. He had already made plans with Salyn Stryke. The moment Ghost's mind, his heart, and yea, his soul were hooked up to the scrying screens in the Sinners' Cave, the truth of his memories, the dragyri's thoughts, and his hidden motivations would be on full display for all to see. So, duplicity was not really the issue.

The issue was Lord Drakkar Hades' true desire.

To make that ballsy bastard his true follower, his true blood kin.

And to do so would require a level of cunning and a practice of evil that neither pure nor wounded souls would ever see coming: darkness concealed as light, hatred disguised as love, honesty masking duplicity, and loyalty served up on a platter of betrayal.

Ghostaniaz Dragos hated his sire.

It was the only true declaration that had left his lying lips.

And that meant the dragyri had a hole in his soul the size of the underworld—filled with pain and confusion, hatred and rage, vengeance and recklessness—that Lord Dragos had carved with his merciless talons…slowly, indelibly, cruelly…over the span of a thousand years. If Lord Drakkar Hades chose to fill that hole with hope and promise, acknowledgment and belonging, the novel sensation of simply being alive and worthy, however false and conscripted, even a cutthroat such as Ghost might soften…a little. The hard-hearted bastard may yet be "brought into the light," which of course was only and truly utter darkness in disguise.

Yes, it was a crapshoot, but also a worthy game.

A greater challenge than playing fetch with Felicity's eyes or sacrificing Bethany Reid on an altar of fealty for the fuck of the festival, though he still intended to follow through with the latter, whenever the time was right or the passing mood hit him.

Converting Ghost, however, would be a far more serious scheme.

The stakes were higher, the payoff potentially greater, and that meant Lord Drakkar would need to bring his A-game to the auspicious challenge.

"Mm, yes," he murmured, dislodging the copperhead's fangs from his neck, then uncoiling the serpent from his arm. He planted a kiss on the snake's scaly head, lowered it gently to the ground, then took two large strides forward in order to lean against an iron baluster anchored between two tall, ornate stone pillars. This would have to be thought through carefully—a ceremony worthy of a regent or a prince—a royal robe? A ruling scepter? Just how much power was Lord Drakkar willing to give his enemy's offspring, and would Ghost be willing to trade a thousand years of fealty to the Seven in exchange for a trial elevation...his ascension to the role of privileged regent, if not underworld prince? Would he be willing to acquiesce, to willingly consent without discord or objection, to displaying his thoughts on the Sinners' Cave screens?

What would the Pagan Horde think of the unlikely coronation?

The king waved his hand over the thigh-high baluster, shrugged his shoulders, and harumphed.

Who cared...

It didn't matter if Ghost went willingly, nor what the king's loyal servants thought.

Ghost would do as he was bid, the demons knew their monarch, and the shadow-walkers trusted Lord Drakkar's bottomless guile.

His pagans would know he had something more delicious

planned, something more devious and diabolical than they could ever hope to fathom. They would go along for the wild, duplicitous ride, and should Ghost prove...worthy...well, then Lord Drakkar Hades, king of the underworld, would let his servants know what's what.

Obedience was never an option.

He had made each and every soul in the abyss, and he could destroy any soul at will.

What had been created once could be created again.

The whole damn lot was replaceable!

Ah, but Ghost had not been created—he had been born. No Genesis Son was so easily replaceable, and neither was a genesis nephew. Content with his decision and eager to get on with his plan, Lord Drakkar Hades pushed away from the balustrade and strolled back into his royal, sex-scented bedchamber.

CHAPTER SEVENTEEN

G host reclined atop the threadbare sheets, even as Beth curled up beneath them. Despite the raging fire in the bedchamber hearth, the poor human female had shivered for an hour before finally falling asleep. At last, Ghost had been forced to warm her with a film of dragon-heat, a faint yellow flame, neither orange nor red, to raise the temperature above the bed, without conjuring the latter's maiming and murderous powers. It had been a delicate tightrope to walk, and now, an hour later, sleep still eluded him.

He couldn't really blame it all on Beth.

Ghost's mind had been turning, nonstop, like the inner workings of a mechanical timepiece: trying to manufacture a systematic plan to escape, weighing the consequences of various actions and outcomes, and if truth be told, avoiding slumber for an entirely different reason...

The Deep.

The three-inch brass keys fashioned in the shape of swords with witches' pentacles on the pommels and reversed numerical sevens just below the cross guards, the ones that unlocked the door to the gothic castle's undercroft cistern, a spherical tank Ghost believed was really a tunnel, if not some sort of interstellar vortex.

Wednesday, November ninth, eight days out, the day he and Beth had to present themselves in the Temple of Seven.

Ghost had spent the last hour braiding the strands of all three facts, over and over, with his mental fingers. If he was counting the night he had been snatched from quicksand, dragged across a fog-encased drawbridge above an antiquated castle moat, and taken into Lord Drakkar's throne room, then Ghost had been in the underworld for 127 days. And he had seen and heard a lot since then, especially late that first spine-chilling night when the pagans had taken him below to the castle's dungeon to torture their newest hostage, again and again. Between bouts of consciousness and continual cycles of mind-numbing pain, Ghost had overheard various demons and shades refer to a cordoned-off section of that same castle underbelly as *The Deep*, even as Requiem Pyre had gestured casually toward the same. Moreover, Ghost had catalogued and stored various slang in the back of his mind as the weeks and months dragged on: "Going deep... heading down under...he isn't here—just went south...meet me in The Deep at midnight." At first, the phrases had just seemed cagey...sophomoric. Who the hell understood the thoughts, let alone the jargon, of cannibalistic creatures who ingested sins and souls for sustenance?

But then slowly, over time, Ghost had also noticed numerous distinctive brass keys, and they were always associated with whomever was using the peculiar vernacular: Nefario Rage was *heading south*, and he just happened to have a brass key clipped to his belt loop. Raptor Wormwood was *going deep*, while twirling a key around his twitchy forefinger. And Salyn Stryke needed to *head down under* to hunt for a ripened soul—or three— while clutching a dagger in one hand and a brass key in the shape of a sword in the other. Nah, too much for coincidence. A pattern was emerging: The Pagan Horde seemed to exit the castle with the use of a key—nay, they appeared to actually exit the underworld from a place they referred to as The Deep—and that same Pagan Horde seemed to always return atop the outer castle drawbridge.

In addition to those not-so-random occasions, there was also Ghost's recent drunken adventure with Killian Kross—the chief counselor had insisted Ghost accompany him to the castle undercroft to imbibe some nasty mead and sour wine, along with several high-ranking demons, who were all just magically suffering from insomnia at the time, and as they had headed for the musty wine cellar, they had passed by a stone archway framing a thick wooden door, both to the right of the stone staircase and cordoned off by a rope. The door had been securely locked, and directly above, below, and all around the keyhole had been an artist's rendition of a sword with a witch's pentacle on the pommel and a reversed numerical seven beneath the cross guard, another strange coincidence to file along with the rest. In fact, Ghost had made an offhanded comment at the time—he had asked about the doorway, the lock, and the keyhole, yet each unobtrusive query had been met with a curt, sarcastic dismissal, followed by a period of tight-lipped silence.

"Nothing in there but a cistern," Gemini Stone had told him.

"Yeah, that and a really *deep* shitter," Aegis Hawk had nearly snarled.

"Go in there, and you'd better have a nose plug." Ghost could still hear Gemini's laughter, but he was no longer buying any of it. Who the hell locked up a shitter, a trivial castle outhouse, and painted the door with a sacred, albeit maleficent, symbol? And even though Ghost's memory was hazy from the night he had been abducted, he still had bits and pieces, passing visual flashes of being dragged along that undercroft floor and up the stony stairway. He couldn't swear by it, but if he just got still and zoomed in on the picture, he could almost see some paint in his peripheral vision, paint around a large brass keyhole, and the whole damn thing smacked of otherworldly design and original gateway construction.

Fourteen billion years before the universe as Ghost knew it existed, Lord Drakkar Hades' essence had been there with that of the Seven, part of the swirling mass of evolving kinetic energy present in the black hole full of burning, thick gas. Drakkar had been there when All had expanded, then exploded, and just like the gods of the Pantheon, his separate consciousness had come out of the same divided mass and eventually taken form. Lord Drakkar Hades had taken part in the initial creation, utilizing the same power of Thought and the same universal energies.

The same elemental principles.

And the same quantum physics.

While his soul had cleaved to darkness, even as the Seven's had embraced myriad gradations of light and shadow, they were all working with the same universal precepts. If the lords of the Pantheon had fashioned a portal, an energetic vortex that could transcend worlds, common sense would imply that Drakkar had done the same. One world held hope, promise, at least some light and positive potential, the other, pure darkness and evil, but all were bound by the same principal laws of nature: a portal...a vortex...a *deep* hidden tunnel concealed beneath a gothic castle?

Why not.

The Pagan Horde had to travel between worlds somehow, and those keys did not unlock the basic bedchambers.

Nope.

The way Ghost saw it his ticket out of this gods-forsaken underworld was straight through that "really deep shitter," and what he would likely find, if he could get a key, was not a latrine but a passage, a portal that would lead to Earth.

So, there it was...

November sixth through the eighth was his general target, though the eighth would be cutting it close. Not only would he need to choose a moment when no one was watching either him or his dragyra, but somehow, someway, he had to either ply another pagan with enough spirits to give up his key or find one... somewhere...that Ghost or Beth could steal. And then he had to trust in his magic, his hidden alchemic powers, to be able to play things by ear: Clearly, the Pagan Horde did not clutch an amulet to evoke the powers of their mystical gateway, so what would it take to activate the vortex?

TBD...

Still to be determined.

Beth sighed in her sleep, just a soft, gentle exhale, and then she rolled over onto her other side, taking the threadbare sheets with her. Ghost watched as her thick, wavy hair fanned out along the bare, grimy pillow and wondered at how she could sleep, how her inner peace was still so prevalent in the midst of a category-five, never-ending shitstorm.

He had never known that kind of tranquility.

Not even for a minute.

And that brought him back, front and center, to the third reason he was still awake: avoiding sleep at any cost: Again, he had been in the castle for 127 days—126 nights, if he was yet to count this one—and whether it was something in the ether, the taint of the vile souls all around him, or just Lord Drakkar's all-pervasive presence—a purely evil aura that spread out in the night like billowing incense, filling every nook and cranny of the castle—Ghost's dreams had become...abominable.

Unbearable.

At first, they had just been strange...

Every night for his first thirty days, he had dreamed of a simple cardboard egg carton, empty except for two lone eggs. At first the eggs had been sitting on opposite sides of the carton, like two boxers in a ring, sequestered in diametrical corners, but then every night, the eggs had moved, coming ever so slightly closer together, until at last they were side by side and touching in the middle of the carton.

Yeah, weird as hell...

Only, for the next seven nights, the dream had progressed: Ghost was back in the Pantheon in the Diamond Lair, about to cook some breakfast, and the carton of eggs was sitting on the counter, nothing-to-see-here, right beside him. He would crack the first one and drop it in the pan, add a little salt and pepper as it started frying, but when he reached for the second and tapped the shell, a gooey, bloody embryo would fall into the skillet, and the half-formed chick would start screeching...crying...wailing in a little boy's voice, causing Ghost to jump back and shiver.

Stupid dream, really...

But it would not let up!

The same damn scene played over and over, every night for a week.

And that's when things started to become more sinister. That's when the screeching, bloody heap of a chick leaped out of the pan, grew two child-sized legs, both anchored in old-fashioned wooden braces, and scurried across the kitchen floor. It limped through the living room to the nearest balcony, then crawled...clawed...climbed its way over the communal railing, before dropping to the private veranda below. That's when the frantic, panicked, two-legged hatchling continued to scale one private terrace after another, story after story of the high, beachside home, until it...*until he*...finally dropped onto the sand and buried himself beneath the smooth, pure white granules.

Thing was, Ghost could feel the child's terror inside the bloody heap, and for reasons only explained by the nonsensical nature of dreaming, he would inevitably follow the chickling's vertical trek and try to dig the embryonic boy out. And that's when the sand would close in on him, swallowing the screeching mass, much like the quicksand that had swallowed Ghost the night he had been captured by the Dragyr's enemies. The night he had been brought to the Pagan Palace. And frankly, that's what he'd believed the dream was about, some macabre, disturbing recreation of losing his freedom to the Pagan Horde, replaying that reckless, gods-forsaken, hellish event.

But no...

Couldn't be that simple.

Just earlier, this very night, somewhere between 6 A.M. and 6 P.M., while Ghost was sleeping in the castle's undercroft, drunk as a skunk on putrid mead and wine, the dream had picked up again, replayed...taunted...rolled the same sinister reel for the umpteenth time in Ghost's head, only there had been one distinct and terrible difference: The embryonic boy had not buried himself in the sand outside the Diamond Lair. He had transported himself to the Temple of Seven, scampered up the long, elegant, curved staircase to Lord Dragos' private chambers, and climbed beneath a twisted, garish coffee table...a table fashioned from leg bones.

And fuck if that hadn't rocked Ghost's world...

Twice!

The first time, when he had seen the table in the dream, and the second time, when he had seen an eerily similar replica smack-dab in the middle of the blasted Sinners' Cave. What was it his dragyra had said? "When you first got back to this dungeon of a bedroom and walked through that hideous, oppressive wooden door, your eyes, they were haunted, like all the way to the depths of your soul."

The girl didn't know the half of it.

Ghost had always been haunted.

Ghost had always been broken.

He had been raised by the devil and reared in his own private hell, but he had never been plagued by nightmares—and he had never been rattled all the way to the depths of his soul by a piece of fucking furniture. And now, here he was, all six-feet-five of a heavy, muscle-bound mercenary, too wary and weary to fall asleep.

Maybe Lord Drakkar was playing tricks on him.

Maybe Requiem Pyre was fucking with his head.

Or maybe his own tainted soul, his seven-times-seventy life-time of sin, was finally catching up to him.

He ran his hand through his hair, and then he rubbed the back of his neck. He stared at the woman lying so quietly beside him, and bent closer to study her face: placid eyelids, angel's cheeks, such soft, perfect lips, just barely parted. Hell, if she only knew: Ghost would've traded all his power, dragon's fire, and supernatural strength for just a hint of the vibe she was putting out, the aura that surrounded her, the ability to rest while in the eye of a storm.

Shiiit...

The ability to exist, to reside, in an unblemished temple, instead of six feet, five inches of tarnished flesh and bone.

He scrubbed his hand over his face, then shook it out, dismissing both thought and emotion. He linked his fingers behind his head, stretched his neck, then settled in. He couldn't hope to get the two of them out of the castle—come what may on the other side—if he didn't catch some shut-eye. Time to man the fuck up, recognize that dreams were only dreams, and venture back into the nightscape.

CHAPTER EIGHTEEN

THE NEXT MORNING ~ 6 A.M.

"Gideon!"

Ghost's harsh, plaintive shout jolted Bethany out of her slumber. It pierced through both the fog of sleep and the never-ending cold.

"*Gideon!*"

She bolted upright, flailed her arms, then twisted on the bed in the direction of the noise. "What! *What?* What is it?"

"Get his arm. Grab his hand! He's under the table! Gideon-Gideon-*Gideon!*"

Bethany's brain could not latch on...

The table—

What table?

She spun around in the dark, stony bedchamber, eyeing the antique nightstands, velvet footstools, and gawdy chests of drawers.

Grab his hand—

Whose hand?

She rubbed her eyes, glanced down absently at the thin, clean white cotton T-shirt she was wearing, a shirt that did nothing to hide her mocha breasts, then lumbered unsteadily onto her knees to face the shaken, husky male beside her. "Ghost!"

"Don't let go!"

"*Ghost*! Wake up!"

"Gideon—"

"You're dreaming." She reached out to nudge him by the top of his shoulder, and he shot up like a rocket, his eyes blazing red. She dropped her hand and jerked back. "Ghost! Wake up!" Fear swelled in her chest like a sudden surge of turbulent water, causing her adrenaline to spike—dear God, for a second, she thought he might just strike her. "Ghost, wake up! You're having a nightmare!"

The dragyri male blinked two times. He whipped his head to the left, then the right, his tongue swiping over a dry bottom lip, and then he braced both palms against the ragged sheet beneath him and inhaled a long, harsh gasp of air. "Beth?"

She let out an audible sigh of relief. "Yes, it's Bethany. I think you were dreaming."

His eyes latched onto hers, and for a moment they were still vacant...haunted...desperate.

Angry.

"Ghost?"

He shook his head briskly.

"You okay?"

He shook his head again, angrily, shifted his weight forward, raised his hands, and balled his fingers into fists. "What the... what was I doing...saying?"

Bethany swallowed her hesitance with a nervous gulp. "You were shouting the name Gideon. Over and over."

He frowned. "I was?" His eyebrows creased, and he stared at her blankly. "What do you mean, 'shouting the name'? Like I was chasing...fighting...who the hell is Gabriel?"

"Gideon," Bethany corrected, but his eyes were still blank.

This time, he shook his head more softly. "Don't remember."

Her jaw dropped open in surprise. "You don't remember your dream?"

His phantom-blue peepers, rimmed with crystal contours like marquise diamonds, turned upward as if scanning his memory, searching for missing stimuli that had just been so...disturbing.

"You said, 'Grab his hand; he's under the table. Don't let go.'"

Ghost's nostrils flared as he sucked in air, filling, expanding, then evacuating his lungs. "Fuuuck." He pinched the bridge of his nose. "Grab his hand, he's under the table? Damn. Wonder what that was." His eyes shot down to her breasts, but not in a lurid manner, more like when a contrasting color reflects light off the eye and automatically draws the brain, like a sudden, reflexive motion. He immediately looked away.

"You really don't remember?" Bethany asked, trying to hide the fact that she was cringing inwardly.

Ghost cocked his brows and shrugged his shoulders.

"Do you have a lot of nightmares?"

"Never." He spoke too quickly. "Well, at least not before I came to this castle."

"And you don't know anyone named Gideon?"

The hairs on his arms stood up, and they were surrounded by rising goose bumps, even as he unconsciously shivered. Still, his answer remained the same: "Nope." He paused as if thinking it over, just to be certain. "Nah. Not that I know of, but who knows —there's so many damn demons and shadow-walkers in this castle, could be anyone."

At this, Bethany nodded, but in her heart, she knew better: Ghostaniaz Dragos, "firstborn hatchling to Lord Dragos, first of the seven dragon gods," a creature akin to "part human, part vampire, part...dragon...and all savage male" had not just been rattled all the way down to his core, while screaming a meaningless name. "Well," she said softly, "you may not remember at this moment, but I think—"

"Don't worry about it." Ghost flicked his wrist in a dismissive gesture, bounded off the bed, stretched his shoulders, and started to stroll toward the raised, private alcove that contained the tin bathtub and an empty bucket for water.

So, other than getting away from her, what was his point? she wondered. "Ghost," she called after him.

"I said, *Drop it*," he snapped, before turning to face her. "Sorry if I woke you up."

Whoa...

Okaaay.

Bethany wasn't altogether sure how she wanted to handle this. On one hand, the male had been rattled, and nightmares could be brutal—if he didn't want to go there, that was his business. But on the other hand, the unsettling behaviors were starting to add up: that time he had slapped her to shake her out of her...unhinged episode, the fact that he had told her to calm the hell down *and* shut the fuck up, and now, *Drop it?* She didn't think so. It was no longer about the nightmare, but navigating this harsh, broken male and this God-forsaken castle.

Bethany was afraid of everything and everyone, and rightly so.

She was helpless, defenseless, and completely dependent on this shattered being for even the slightest chance at survival. She never knew, from moment to moment, what was going to come through the door or what horrific scenario might unfold next.

Neither did Ghost.

She got that.

No wonder he was having nightmares.

But still, she was not his enemy, she was not his bitch, and she was not his expendable sex slave, regardless of what he had told King Drakkar. And if Bethany let Ghost treat her like anything other than what she was—supposedly his *fated*, his dragyra, his spirit's other half—then there was nowhere, no time, no space, where she could breathe, not even for an illusory moment. The Pagan Horde had taken her freedom, her life, her family, her job, and her friends—hell, they had even taken her clothes and her dignity—she had nothing left but the stillness in her mind, a stolen private moment here or there as she waited for death...or worse.

As she waited for Ghost to save them both.

He could not be her oppressor too.

He could not treat Bethany like she was...nothing.

She stood up quietly and walked straight toward him, trying her darndest not to tremble. Head up, shoulders back—she could not care less that her feet were bare, her thighs were exposed, and her nipples were probably showing like two glowing headlamps beneath the stupid white T-shirt. "Ghost." She said his name with both strength and purpose.

He eyed her warily.

"I didn't have to wake you up. I could've just left you in that nightmare."

He snorted, a bit surprised, a bit indifferent.

"You said, *Don't worry about it*. Well, guess what? I'm not. I'm not your mother, and I'm not your therapist. I'm not even trying to be some kind of friend. Just civil. Just...honest. Just *real* with you, Ghost. Do you get that? *Can you get that?*" She didn't wait for a reply. Rather, she held up a slender hand to prevent one. "And yeah, if we're keeping this *one hundred*, then I also get that you're being real with me, too, when you say you don't remember and ask me to back off. But for the record, you're also being real cocky, real nasty, and *real* condescending. And none of that shit is acceptable by me. I'm not your lackey. I'm not your dog. I'm just a woman who is trapped here with you."

Ghost studied her carefully, maybe too carefully, and then he finally let out a sigh. "You can't care about me, Beth."

She pursed her lips, incredulous. Surely, that was not what he'd garnered from that reprimand.

"It's not in your best interest...or mine."

She closed her eyes and shook her head, and then she linked her hands in front of her. "Is that what you think I'm saying?"

"Just keeping it *one hundred*," he quipped. "Words are one thing. All that emotion? That's another."

Well, shit. *Huh.* Was there some truth behind his rudeness? She suddenly felt both defensive and annoyed. "So, you don't care...about me...not even a little?"

He tilted his head to the side. "I care *enough* to keep you alive."

"Because you need me to survive?"

"And you need me to survive. We both need each other, Bethany. It's a two-way street."

"*Bethany*? I usually refer to myself as Bethany, even though my friends mostly call me Beth, and my family calls me Bethy. But you—you never asked—and you've always called me Beth."

He shrugged a surly shoulder. "And you didn't ask, either. Ghost or Ghostaniaz."

She smiled and shook her head. "Not true. The very first time I said Ghostaniaz out loud, you corrected me by saying, 'Ghost.'"

"True," he conceded. "Beth."

She chuckled beneath her breath. "Okay," she whispered. "Then how about this: Yesterday, you brought me bread, ale, cheese, and those scruffy, tattered linens, which I appreciate. Very much. Still, I *needed* the food and water. I didn't need the sheets. You said you were gonna go back out today to try to find a pillow slip, a blanket, even a bedcover—again, those are wants, not needs."

"*Beth*," he groaned, sounding exasperated. "You don't—"

"Wait," she said. "You apologized for not bringing everything. In fact, you apologized five minutes ago for waking me up. You healed my wounds, you brought me new clothes, and you spent nearly an hour last night warming the room, keeping me from getting too cold with that...*mystical* fire. My wounds weren't fatal. Being naked was not going to kill me, and while the chill gets really uncomfortable, I don't think it's cold enough to freeze to death. You did all those things to make me more comfortable, Ghost. You're even going out of your way to spare my dignity by not staring at my see-through shirt. That's called caring."

"It's called courtesy. Having manners. I wasn't raised by a pack of wolves."

"No," Bethany countered. "You were raised by a pantheon of fire-breathing dragons."

Ghost stiffened.

And his sudden discomfort prompted Bethany to do something unexpected: She reached out and took his hand, just the tips of her fingers brushing his. "Ghostaniaz, you said, *You can't care about me, Beth.* Thing is, I can." She withdrew her fingers and placed her hand on the left side of her chest. "It's called a heart. And I hate to break it to you, but you have one too. Being cold, being hungry, being trapped in this place doesn't make me weak; it just makes me vulnerable in that moment. And so does having a nightmare. I needed that food, and you needed me to wake you. It doesn't have to be about love or catching feelings, but it's not about just having manners either. I *can* care about you, Ghost, and you *can* care about me too. The real truth, if we're keeping it one hundred, is you can't care about yourself. You don't. And *that's* the only real difference between us."

Ghost lowered his head and rubbed the back of his neck, looking irritated, strained, and exhausted. "What do you want from me, Beth?"

She shrugged. "Honesty. Equity. And respect. 'Child of fire;

daughter of flames. More than a woman; more than a name. Born from the soul of the Pantheon.' Doesn't matter what happens or where we end up, but while we're in this prison, this hellhole of a chamber, alone...together...you act like that saying is real. Speak to me with respect."

Ghost licked his lips and just stared at her.

"*Gideon.*" She breathed the word softly, and he flinched.

"Don't."

"Gideon."

"*Please...*"

"Do you remember who that is, Ghost?"

He shook his head. "I really don't."

"And you really don't remember your dream?"

He shook his head in earnest.

"Then I'm sorry I pushed you, and I'm sorry if I upset you—I didn't mean any harm."

He scrunched up his face like he was in physical pain.

"It's just that...it's hard to explain...but when you woke up shouting, I think I *felt* it before I heard it. We are connected in some inexplicable, mysterious way, and your words, your tone... shouldn't have mattered, but they hurt me."

"Ah, fuuuck. Just...no. Seriously?" He held up both hands. "You don't wanna go there, you really don't. I'm not gonna tell you not to care about me, but this shit"—he circled his sternum in the air with his hands—"it's all a wasteland, Beth. Nothing to see here but random, broken, jagged glass. There's no heart. Probably not even a soul. My bad if I hurt you, but you can't come in. You don't want to come in, and I need *you* to respect that."

Bethany studied his eyes—they were stark, staunch, and brutally transparent—and she took a slow step back and nodded. "I do respect that, Ghost. We'll figure it out...together." She cocked one shoulder in a playful lilt, but there was nothing joyful about it. "I mean, if we live to see tomorrow, that is."

At that, Ghost's jaw stiffened, and his rugged, masculine features hardened like granite.

He reached out a hand, snatched her off balance, then tugged her beneath him, locking a rigid, bent elbow around her slender shoulders—it felt more like a misplaced headlock than an embrace. "I might not be the most respectful or compassionate bastard," he whispered in her ear, "but I would kill for you, Beth. Consider that respect." He pulled back just as suddenly. "Not to mention, I am working on a plan, so don't lose hope just yet."

CHAPTER NINETEEN

―――――――

Anne Liu woke before sunrise.

She stirred in her comfy, queen-sized bed, raised her arms above her head to stretch, then peered at the fluffy white Persian cat, Queenie, still sleeping at the foot of the bed.

Peaceful.

Her simple but modern, understated bedroom was clean, quiet, and unusually tranquil: the trickling water flowing through the clay and stone waterfall sitting atop her small black vanity, the soft, warm sheets caressing her back, and the scent of lavender wafting from a matching purple gem votive perched on the nightstand—they each added to the feel of serenity.

Safety.

A momentary respite from all the chaos since Halloween.

She fluffed two large feather pillows behind her shoulders, rested her arms at her sides, palms up and open, and welcomed the brand-new morning with a familiar routine: a prayer of thanksgiving, a series of deep, diaphragm breathing, and a conscious focus inward to awaken, align, and circulate her energy...activate her chakras. And then she quietly, subtly, allowed her attention to drift to a much heavier subject, while trying to maintain a counterbalancing feeling of lightness...

The ancient leather-bound tome she and Joy had purchased at the eerie bookstore on 17th and Krameria, *A Treatise on the Seven Sins.*

The appearance of "Grandma Betsy" in the back seat of Anne's SUV.

And the elder woman's—the *spirit's*—cryptic words: "I cannot stay long, for there is one steeped in darkness who has been viewing you and Joy this day through his own malevolent screen...or window, and at least this far, I have managed to hide my essence from his awareness."

Anne took another slow, deep breath, careful to let the disturbing thought-energy pass through without getting stuck.

One steeped in darkness...

Viewing Anne and Joy...

Who was this person, this man or woman, and were they following, stalking, or watching...*how?*

Queenie arched her back and stretched her paws, and Anne made note of the transferred energy before returning to her point of focus. And then just like that, she had a strong, sentient impression, not quite as clear as an actual vision, yet not nearly as vague as a passing thought. Her hackles began to rise, as did Queenie's, and she slowly...gently...backed off, holding the impression from a distance, rather than zooming in. Studying the *sense* as a passive observer, she allowed the details to move in and out.

A man, covered in tattoos from his head to his toes—

No, not a man.

His energy felt more like that of a malevolent spirit than a human man from any known walk of life or familiar ethnicity, and he was standing, gazing, into some sort of screen, perhaps a computer monitor or a large flat-screen TV. Anne couldn't make out the detail. Only, what she could make out almost jolted her out of her deep, half-conscious state: The tattooed man was touching the screen, moving images from the left to the right, and the figures commanding his attention were that of Anne and Joy!

She gasped, and the image left her.

Darn it...

She took another deep breath.

Nothing.

She closed her eyes, shook out her hands, then laid them softly atop the coverlet again, returning to her deep, rhythmic breathing.

In and out...

In and out...

Nearly fifteen or twenty minutes of focused relaxation.

Still nothing.

The image did not come back, but something far more intuitive and important did: a sudden realization of how such energy worked. Whoever this male was, he could see Anne and Joy by looking through a device like a two-way mirror, and that meant the connection, whatever it was, contained two distinctly separate axis points, an alpha and an omega. Vitality didn't flow in a frozen void; what streamed north must also stream south. The vortex was either open or closed, but never restricted to one-way transmission.

Anne shook her head, knowing she could not make sense of *the knowing* with limited, inadequate words, but she could make use of the knowledge with action. Turning on her side, she stretched her arm toward the drawer of her nightstand, pulled it open, and fumbled for a familiar object, her small, ivory, compact powder case with a tiny, circular mirror on the top. She rolled onto her back, opened the lid, and stared at the powder-smudged glass. Light. White traveled fastest. Gold had more power. Purple and blue invited the higher vibrations of spirit, so she swirled all four colors into a rainbow of sorts, holding the image in her mind's eye; then she sent the light into the mirror, out into the cosmic void, and into the space she had seen in her impression. She circled it around and around the tattooed male before bringing it back, and then she did it again...

And again.

Over and over.

Imagining the colors—growing finer, faster, buzzing and humming—as they swirled back and forth, in and out like a cosmic lasso, until at last she was casting the light with expert dexterity.

And then it happened.

The two-way channel opened.

What one male could see through a mirrored screen, another female could see from its opposite gateway, and Anne could see the bald, tattooed male, the one who had been tracking herself and Joy: his bright yellow eyes, a long, pointed goatee, and the cavern he was standing in, filled with three red velvet sofas.

"Bethy."

The audible word shook her.

She dropped the compact and shot up straight on the bed, instantly breaking the mirror's connection.

Grandma Betsy's voice?

Why had she just said *Bethy?*

Anne closed her eyes and repeated a mantra for protection: This guy, this malevolent being, was not just watching Joy and Anne—he was also, somehow, connected to Beth.

The connection broken, Anne's serenity gone, she had no idea what to do with the information. She wasn't even sure whether she should try to explain what had happened to the girls, Beth's band of besties, or if she should just keep the whole...incident...to herself.

"No," she said sharply, eyeing Queenie as if the cat was a witness. "Can't keep it to myself. At least not entirely." Ignoring the pit that rose in her stomach, Anne resolved to do what she must—it was time to call Bryce M.

* * *

Still hovering above a tranquil stone waterfall—the elemental energy both enabling and expanding her presence in the room—Grandma Betsy let out a sigh of relief.

She had done what she had come to do.

The gods of the Pantheon would be waiting forever to make a connection between Bethy's friends, a cult worshiper, and those horrific beings on the other side of the equation, in order to glimpse Ghost's plight...

Bethy's plight.

And Betsy's sweet granddaughter did not have much time.

Wicked plots were springing up like weeds in an already dark, twisted garden.

Anne Liu was a Seer—she had a rare gift—though not nearly as strong on her own.

So be it.

While Grandma Betsy could not step in, interfere with free will, or change the course of fate—she could not alter the cause-and-effect trajectory born of thoughts, actions, and intentions—she could amplify what was already there. Strengthen another spirit's perceptions. And she had done just that with Anne Liu: "Relax, draw inward, and focus. *Listen.* Try to see the male who is watching from afar. A mirror has two sides—look into it. Yes. *Yes...* The one watching is not human, and yes...*yes*...my sweet Bethy is nearby."

CHAPTER TWENTY

Bethany gathered her thick, wavy hair and braided it loosely behind her neck, even as she shuffled rapidly on bare feet in the wake of the tall, gaunt human servant who had come to the bedchamber she shared with Ghost, to take her to the castle laundry.

Shit.

Things were happening too fast.

She hadn't even had time to eat some breakfast, even if it consisted of stale bread and water, to slip a second T-shirt over the first—two layers would provide more privacy than one—or to slip into the shoes she had been wearing the night Wrath Sylvester had abducted her from the haunted house. Hell, she hadn't had a chance to ask Ghost about his escape plan, to question him about the layout of the castle, or to inquire about the human-pagan politics: What was her best chance of staying safe? Was there anything she could do—or not do—to increase the odds of keeping her head on her shoulders?

Now, as she followed the sullen, taciturn human man along a series of long, dark passages, down a steep, stony staircase, and around a torchlit corner, her mind did not fixate on the danger, all the *what ifs*, or even the impending slave labor. It did what minds so often do when current circumstances are simply too overwhelming to process; it took Bethany somewhere else, to another memory. Only, the associated flashback was in many ways far, far worse.

Bethany was seven years old, in second grade, and even though she was a bright, gifted student, she was also horribly shy, helplessly gangly, and more prone to stutter than to speak her mind. She had not really come into her own until her late teenage years, and if someone had told her she would one day be both confident and beautiful, she would've laughed at the joke...or cried from the torment.

No, Bethany had been anything but lovely at seven years old, and consequently, she'd had a hard time making friends. At least until Kimberly Johansson had moved in, a few blocks away, with her cherry-red bicycle, her mouth full of braces, and her large, quirky, floppy hats with flowers that always matched her bedazzling outfits.

Kim had taken to Bethany right away, almost as if she hadn't noticed Bethany's awkwardness or her stutter. The peculiar, eccentric, redheaded girl had made fun of the school bullies and passed notes to Bethany in class, notes that always contained warm, cozy secrets; sweet, heartfelt compliments; and bright, colorful smiley faces. Kim had surrounded Bethany like an itty-bitty, exuberant shield of armor, sheltering Bethany from the other children at recess, during gym, and whenever the two of them were alone at their own table in the lunchroom. And weekends had been one adventure after another: Bethany following Kimberly's bright red bike on her own pale blue Schwinn, wading in a nearby creek behind the park, and packing their own sack lunches—the girls had laughed and played and gossiped for hours. They were truly the best of friends.

Until one summer break, on an especially rainy Monday in June, Kimberly had not shown up in a flowery hat or with her cherry-red bicycle. She had not shown up at all. At seven years, five months old, Kimberly had been diagnosed with a rare, extremely progressive form of child leukemia, and two months later, Bethany's world had been gone.

Everything that had been bad before grew ten times worse overnight, because now it was coupled with the knowledge of friendship, the memory of laughter, and the absence of warmth and light. Bethany still had her parents, Grandma Betsy, and Grandpa John, but Kimberly had been like a bright, blazing comet lighting up the sky of Bethany's life. Nothing could replace her or the friendship they had shared, and watching another little girl suffer like that...well, it had broken Bethany's heart for a decade.

It really wasn't until college that she had formed any friendships as strong.

And now, as she made her way along the lower level of Lord Drakkar's cruel, gothic castle, her mind bounced back and forth, like a fitful Ping-Pong ball, between memories of Kimberly Johansson, Bethany's present-day besties—Kari, Joy, Nicole, and Anne—her parents, and what those still living, those who still loved her, must be going through as a result of her sudden, inexplicable disappearance.

It was all too much.

Just...too much to comprehend or process.

And just why this long walk to the castle laundry had reminded Bethany of losing Kim, she couldn't quite say, except for, maybe, being snatched from a world of light, hope, and camaraderie, only to be thrust into darkness, pain, and loss felt eerily the same.

"The laundry is on the other side of that doorway," the tall, gangly guide said brusquely. He pointed at a tall, arched stone entry and took a broad step to the side, ushering Bethany forward with a curt wave of his hand.

She blinked rapidly, trying to shift back into the present moment, and then she leaned forward to peer inside—what if it wasn't a laundry, but a trap? Another Wraith-Sylvester-in-the-bedroom moment, or worse, a dungeon full of serpents and rats?

"You'd better get in there," he warned. "Believe me, you don't wanna get caught hesitating in this castle, not even for a second. When you're asked to do something, do it quickly. And if you're told to be somewhere, show up early. Never hesitate, and never let them smell your fear."

Bethany started.

Good Lord.

She forced her feet to shuffle forward, beyond the threshold of the archway, took two long strides ahead, then stopped dead in her tracks. "You have got to be kidding me," she murmured absently, as alarm bells went off in her head.

The castle laundry was a joke.

A chamber of hazards in its own pathetic right.

The damn bowl-shaped cavity was cluttered from one end to the next with large, round wooden buckets, several filled with scalding-hot water, and the wafting scent of lye permeated the thick, damp, pungent air. There were old-fashioned, heavily worn washboards strewn about the floor, and multiple flat, antique irons, like relics from the 1700s, warming atop two ancient woodburning stoves.

No, not warming...

Glowing like iron in a sweltering fire.

Piles and piles of dirty clothes, soiled sheets, and grimy linens were scattered about the uneven stone floor, and there was some sort of mystical, archaic clothesline circling the perimeter of the room, following the trajectory of a subordinate firepit that spewed unnatural blue-and-white flames without

GHOSTANIAZ

the aid of kindling, ostensibly to act as some kind of demonic dryer.

Bethany knew the pagans had heard of electricity!

Hell, according to Ghost, half the trappings in the castle were high-end, luxurious, and modern to excess, even as they were surrounded or encased in medieval architecture and furnishings.

This was a joke!

No, it was another form of cruelty and degradation, just as she had surmised—the pagans kept the castle laundry in the Dark Ages to further demean their human pets, and now Bethany was just one more expendable toy to play with.

She licked her lips and fought back tears of anger and frustration.

This was just like that first day, back at school, after Kimberly had passed, facing all those bullies and heartless children, once again on her own: the cruel, insecure "mean girls" who fed on Bethany's grief and insecurities, the so-called adults, teachers, and authorities who looked the other way, and the angry young hooligans who likely lived their own private hells at home, who went so far as to taunt Bethany about the "poor sick girl" who had left her all alone.

Only this time, it was Ghost who was missing, and the cruel, inhuman children were actual monsters.

Demons.

Shadow-walkers and soul eaters.

Supernatural heathens.

As she studied the sundry piles of clothes, towels, and filthy bedding, Bethany had to remind herself she was no longer a child. She was no longer in grade school, and she was no longer insecure, at least not as a person or a woman. Bethany Reid had healed from great loss. She had matured, found her agency, and discovered her voice. And it had taken a lot of self-awareness and inner work to do so. If anything, her greatest hurdle going

181

forward—besides the obvious challenge of staying alive—would be to show the obedience her guide had spoken of, to hold her tongue when her temper was flaring, and to hang onto hope, keep faith in Ghost, and suffer through all the humiliation, knowing it was only temporary.

Should there still be angels surrounding her, as Grandma Betsy had always said and Kimberly Johansson had once embodied, then maybe, just maybe, Bethany still had a chance of surviving even this.

* * *

Felicity Payne held her breath as she held the spell that enabled her to blend into the stones and mortar flanking her back. She had been waiting in the castle laundry since 6 A.M., plotting, seething, fuming, much like the plumes of steam rising from the wooden buckets filled with hot, scalding water.

The mere idea of Bethany Reid, Lord Drakkar Hades' newest acquisition, made Felicity's blood boil. True, there had been some sort of kerfuffle between the king and Wraith Sylvester, one that had cost the soul eater his life, and as the wicked, whispering winds would have it, the king had ultimately discarded the female, while the dragyri heartthrob had claimed the newbie's body as his own—*private property*—even as he had scorned and dismissed Felicity as "yesterday's trash," unworthy of defiling in a decadent, three-way act of oral...gratification...alongside Salyn Stryke.

The audacity of the cocky Dragyr bastard.

The unmitigated gall!

He was a slave of sorts, like any other, even if he was the king's chiliad-distant, blood nephew.

Pshaw.

What a crock of absolute shit.

The Dragyr was playing the Pagan Horde for all they were worth, trying to vie for some sort of power or position, himself, in the eye of the storm, play on Lord Drakkar Hades' vanity, self-interest, and narcissism, whilst hiding behind the throne.

Whatever.

Didn't matter...

Felicity couldn't really care less about Ghostaniaz Dragos—what she did care about, deeply, intimately, and with her whole, vengeful witch's heart, was the outcome of the brief, nearly unbearable time she had spent with the king of the underworld in his private boudoir...and all to no avail.

Lord Drakkar Hades had discarded Felicity more easily than Bethany.

He had used her, maimed her, carved out her eyeballs as well as her heart, and sent her scrambling, naked, along his bedchamber floor to fetch the dislodged orbs like a flea-ridden dog: Felicity had endured unspeakable agony in the hopes of winning a carnal position of some standing with the dark, craven king, even if she wasn't placed in the throne room, and the king had mocked her, much like Ghost, and written her off like so much garbage.

Her nostrils flared as she sucked in air and glared at the dark-haired beauty. While no longer a threat for Lord Drakkar's affections, the woman was still an unacceptable rival, just in general, and now, she was also an unwelcome reminder of how Felicity was cast aside by the mongrel female's unworthy Dragyr handler. Nay, the mocha-skinned woman before her, with a set of really nice tits, was still far too valued...much too desired...and way too attractive for Felicity's liking—Bethany Reid would not receive a witch's welcome, nor any measure of mercy.

As pride, envy, and disdain left an ever more bitter taste on Felicity's tongue, she narrowed her contemptuous gaze on the half-breed bitch and studied her...prey...in earnest: thin, elegant shoulders framing a delicate, enticing collarbone—Felicity would break those bones in half. Vivid, dark brown eyes—haunting, mysterious, and absent of guile—Felicity would carve them out of the human slave's head. Flawless, imperial features, like a lost Egyptian princess—her face would no longer be recognizable when Felicity got through with her craft.

No...

Bethany would not be worthy of use by Ghostaniaz Dragos, the least important members of the Pagan Horde, or as second-hand table scraps by a bored or curious king, should Lord Drakkar be desperate enough to summon her. She wouldn't even be worthy of the monarch's faithful hellhounds—Felicity would see to that.

Watching as Bethany stood so stupidly in the middle of the launderette, eyeing the various piles of soiled threads with visible self-pity, so forlorn she had no idea where to start, Felicity stepped out of the shadows, flashed a huge, beguiling grin, and extended a perfectly manicured, traitorous hand. "Bethany—may I call you by your given name? So nice to finally meet our latest human arrival, a fellow bitch for the horde, and a sojourning slave." She dipped into an infinitesimal curtsy. "I'm Felicity Payne, another of Lord Drakkar's acquirements—he brought me here in 1692 from Salem, Massachusetts, and I've been serving His Majesty and the members of his court ever since."

CHAPTER TWENTY-ONE

As requested, not ordered, Ghost arrived outside the Great Hall's entry around 7:30 A.M., about a half hour after he and Beth had received a surprise visit from one of the castle's rare, male human slaves, a gaunt, somber messenger who had come to escort Beth to the castle laundry.

They had not had time to prepare for Beth's sudden departure.

And Ghost had no power—no means—to stop it.

Lord Drakkar had been crystal clear the night Ghost had asked for the human female: "Just see to it that as long as she is breathing, she joins the other slaves in service to the castle and unerring obedience to my whims." No room for confusion or argument in that statement—Ghost had agreed because he'd had no other choice—and now, Beth was somewhere in the castle on her own and vulnerable, not just to the whims of Lord Drakkar but to any other pagan who passed by and took an errant fancy...

Ghost shook his head to dismiss the thought.

He had to focus on the highly suspicious, unusual state of

affairs before him, lest he be the one to lose his life and leave Beth to the Pagan Horde's nonexistent mercy before he could get her out of the palace: *King Drakkar Hades, The Chosen One, Father of the Pagan Realm, Sire of the Pagan Horde, and Dark Lord of the Underworld requests your humble presence in the Great Hall at six points past Prime.* That's what the cryptic missive had said, the hastily scrawled, calligraphic dispatch the skinny human messenger had handed to Ghost...on his way out the door with the dragyri's female.

And just what kind of demonic tomfoolery was this?

Requests your humble presence...

Since when did Lord Drakkar *request* anything?

And what was with all the vain, ceremonial titles—was this a formal meeting of some sort, and if so, who all would be there?

Ghost glanced down at his basic, casual attire. He was wearing a dark gray crew neck, a pair of light gray, stone-washed jeans, and a pair of flat, ankle-high, black- and white-checkered Vans over bare feet, in lieu of his preferred sleeveless black tee and customary military boots—*what the hell; he wore what the pagans gave him.* If Lord Drakkar wanted him in something more formal or...pretentious, he should've left a suit with the slave.

As for the *"six points past Prime"* bullshit, Ghost absently scratched the back of his head. Was this some sort of trick or a test? Get Ghost to show up too early or too late, then behead him and remove his amulet for insubordination? Was Lord Drakkar rethinking their last encounter, or had one of Lord Drakkar's counselors whispered something in his ear?

No telling...

What Ghost did have was the extensive, exhaustive, and frankly overbearing tutelage of his father, Lord Dragos, during the first ten to fifteen years of his life. He could speak three languages, fluently, by the tender age of five, and he also had a pretty strong command of history, both early Pantheon and Earth's three basic time spans: *Prime* was a medieval term, and while not exact, it referred in general to about 6 A.M., and a *point* was typically fifteen minutes. So, Ghost would either be on time, or he wouldn't—either way, he would at least come close.

Now, as he stared at two enormous, arched wooden doors— one fifty feet to the left and another fifty feet to the right of what Ghost knew was a towering, floor-to-ceiling, pure obsidian stone fireplace inside the inner sanctum—he wondered at two immediate questions: Which door was he supposed to use—*was there any formal protocol?*—and why the hell weren't there any sentries positioned outside the Great Hall, the king's throne room, waiting to receive and direct him?

He shrugged his shoulders, popped his neck, and strolled purposefully toward the door on the left—it was what it was, and it would be what it would be.

What-the-fuck-ever.

Just get it over with.

He tugged so hard on the large, ornate handle, he could've ripped it off the frame; then he flung it open and strolled in boldly. He took four or five steps forward and stopped—*what the hell?* As expected, the huge obsidian fireplace was blazing with mystical fire, flames popping, crackling, and roaring with echoes of demonic laughter, and the eerie light from the macabre flames danced in haunted reflections off the four looming obsidian pillars situated equal distances apart in the hall, but outside the elemental presence of fire, the throne room was virtually empty: no congress consisting of ten demons and shades, each perched behind the cathedra in blood-red robes; no Killian Kross to the left, in the place of royal dignitary, chief counselor to the Chosen One; and no Requiem Pyre to the right, also as royal dignitary, chief sorcerer to the same.

No seven humans, four stunning men and three breathtaking women—well, absent the one Beth would have made—prostrate before the throne naked, with the exception of animal-skin loincloths, their bodies slathered in oil.

And most important, no king with long, ghoulish, spindly arms or sharp, pointed nails gleaming pitch black.

Okaaay...

What gives?

And then the two raised torches on either side of the red velvet throne suddenly blazed with firelight, and Lord Drakkar Hades came fully into view.

Fuuuck, Ghost thought.

The king of the underworld had not been invisible, nor had he been hiding in the darkness whilst seated in the exact geometrical center of the gallery. No, Lord Drakkar Hades *was* the darkness, and the firelight had simply provided contrast.

Ghost lowered his head, linked his hands in front of him, and waited.

"Come forward." The king's voice resounded, then vibrated throughout the hall, as if his diaphragm was part and parcel of the raw materials: Sound was everywhere...and nowhere...at once, even as the dark lord's presence was all-consuming.

Yeah, this shit was meant to be very formal.

Ghost strode forward, head up, shoulders back, but he left the cocky swagger out of his movement. "You asked for me?"

"I did." The king stood up, and his kaleidoscope eyes revolved with heated color like two otherworldly windmills surrounding occultic pupils. "Kneel at the foot of my throne."

Now this caught Ghost off guard, but he didn't figure this was the right time for rebellion. He took one additional giant stride forward, stopped at the base of the dais, and bent to one knee, hoping it was sufficient.

Lord Drakkar Hades chuckled.

The king held out an empty hand, and a heavy, thick, gold and blood-red robe suddenly appeared, draped over his wrist, the garment emblazoned along the left breast with a witch's pentacle etched into the pommel of a sword; a reversed numerical seven inscribed below the cross guard; and the tail of the geometric seven, outlined in permanent blood, extending along the length of the blade. He held out his other hand, and a heavy, solid gold scepter appeared in his palm, similarly embossed with the same wicked emblem, the head of the scepter carved into the shape of an imperial dragon. "Stand up, Ghost."

Ghost rose slowly...warily...with extreme mistrust and judicious caution.

"Look at me, Ghost."

Ghost squared his jaw, his teeth on edge, and met the king's brazen glare head-on.

"Good. I do not want there to be any confusion, and for this, I need to see those witchy blue eyes."

Ghost furrowed his brows, and then his tongue got the best of him. "If we're keeping it real, my liege, then we both know you can read my thoughts, am I right? So, there can't be any confusion."

The king flicked his wrist, studied his nails, and shook his head in annoyance. "Ghostaniaz," he said, derisively, "if I had spent the last four months and six days reading your thoughts, I would have removed your head and your amulet already. Your carcass would be fodder for the crows and the ravens, scattered about the underworld." He stroked his jaw in contemplation, causing the imperial robe to sway back and forth. "Think of it like this: A lion is already king of the jungle, and he sleeps a lot because he has no equal, no challenge...no threat...no true stimulation. Nothing and no one can best him, so why bother patrolling. I do not typically read the minds of my followers, nor my human servants. I don't eavesdrop on their conversations or waste my time with their petty whims and motivations." He leaned forward, and his eyes glowed so deep within the centers, Ghost could glimpse infinite galaxies beyond the shadows. "It would be too easy, too simple," the king continued. "I would walk around this palace, pointing in varied directions, accusing viola-tors with every pace forward, and incinerating the guilty as freely as I breathe. No, Ghostaniaz, I want to catch my prey unaware. I want them to run and hide and, occasionally, provide a challenge: I want to outwit them, catch them, devour them with my claws, and tear their hearts out with my canines as sport, not as a matter of such inherent superiority. No, Ghost, you shall never know if or when I am reading your thoughts or checking up on you, but trust me, such occasions are rare, for I have lived for millennia and prefer to assuage my boredom as opposed to displaying my power. I am a lion, king of the jungle. You are a mouse—*who really cares what you're thinking?* At least give me something to toy with."

Ghost licked his bottom lip.

All riiight.

Talk about traveling from Las Vegas to California by route of China—*methinks thou doth protest too much*—so, Lord Drakkar *rarely* read his subjects' thoughts.

True or false?

Who knew.

"Now then," Lord Drakkar persisted, "I want you to hear what I say very clearly." He lifted the arm with the robe draped over it, narrowed his planetary gaze, and lowered his voice to a deep, placid tone. "Flesh of my flesh and blood of my blood, I have thought your words over, quite carefully, and it is my inten-tion to anoint you prince of this realm, second only to myself. Family. Blood. A general to one day lead my legions in war against the Pantheon of Dragons, but that is a tale...a plot...for a future discussion. On Wednesday next, seven days hence, I will present you to the Pagan Horde during a special feast day. On Friday, thus, two days hence, you will repay me for this honor by willingly, humbly, and openly entering the Sinners' Cave and sharing all your knowledge and private memories of the world you come from, the dragon lords, and the Temple of Seven, on a public broadcast scrying screen. And there will be no more separation between us. You will forever change your allegiance." The king closed his eyes, stretched out his royal, object-laden arms, and breathed in deeply. When he exhaled, a frigid, pitch-black wind tunneled out of his mouth and encased the dais in a dense, dark mist. Two giant beasts, like midnight-black rottweilers, the size and shape of bullmastiffs, appeared at the dark lord's sides. Each beast had two heads, with two horns and four sets of canines, the teeth filed down into points like knives, and before Ghost could truly take in the vision or react to the presence of the mongrels, the hellhounds lunged forward and ripped off his arms.

Ghost recoiled in shock, shouted in agony, and dropped to the throne room floor.

Snarling, gnashing its teeth, and foaming at the mouth, the first hellhound slathered Ghost's face with a long, thick, slimy tongue, leaving putrid bile on Ghost's lips in its wake, and then he regurgitated spittle like burning lava into Ghost's mouth and down his throat, even as the second hound began to gorge on Ghost's midriff, dispatching his intestines, consuming his organs, and rending his heart from his breastbone.

Ghost arched his back and shouted in agony, trying to protect his torso with hands and arms he no longer possessed, and then just like that, the hellhounds were gone, Ghost was once again standing upright before the dark king's dais, and Lord Drakkar Hades was staring him down. "Your future, should you cross me," the king whispered softly, growing quiet to allow his words to sink in.

Ghost gasped for air, patted his chest and his stomach, then eyed the room warily, searching for the hounds. Nothing there. He shivered, licked his lips, and met the king's cold, intimidating stare. "Point taken," he rasped. *Holy fuck.*

"Good." Lord Drakkar smiled. "Now then, where were we?" He held up the golden scepter and waved it through the air. "Ah, yes, prince of the abyss, blood kin to King Drakkar Hades, the Chosen One, Father of the Pagan Realm, Sire of the Pagan Horde, and Dark Lord of the Underworld. A privilege previously bestowed on no other. An opportunity beyond your wildest imaginings. A position of power you do not deserve, but one that appeals to my blackened heart. You shall possess both robe and scepter, and you are free to wield the latter as you choose or see fit, as long as it is done in the following manner." The king lowered the head of the scepter and touched the arm of his throne. The red velvet melted, the arm crumbled, and the broken pieces from beneath the manchette scattered across the throne room floor, morphed into dozens of hissing black beetles, which then dropped dead a few yards out, vanishing in a plume of smoke. "I'll have to get Cyprus Blade to fix that rail and fabric; the soul eater is quite proficient with his hands. Still, I assume you get the gist—whenever you lower this scepter, whatever you touch with the mouth of this dragon will disintegrate to dust in true, dark fashion, whether man, beast, demon, or shade...object, element, or spirit. It, he, she...will be no more."

He raised the golden dragon-head scepter along with his narrow, pointy chin, and Ghost fell to the ground in a prostrate position, his face pressed into the granite. "When *raised* before my Pagan Horde, the sin eater or soul eater shall cease whatever he is doing and lie prostrate before you. Stop talking. Stop moving. Stop challenging or...resisting. A raised scepter is akin to my very own presence and command. Obedience, subservience, complete and absolute submission shall be yours for the taking from all those who fall beneath its control. Power over my horde. Obedience from human servants. Utter authority over the elements and the beasts that roam the underworld. Do you understand what I am offering you, Ghost? What I am freely *giving* in exchange for your secrets, secrets I could simply take if I wished?"

Ghost didn't answer.

"Get up!" Lord Drakkar snarled.

Ghost crawled to his knees and tried to rise with dignity, though he wasn't quite sure he pulled the last part off. *Son of a bitch*; the king was offering him a Get Out of Jail Free card on a silver platter, but yeah, he understood—it was a Faustian bargain. He thought he had sold his soul to the devil back in the bedchamber, when he had helped to orchestrate Wraith Sylvester's demise and asked the king for Beth, but he hadn't even come close to bartering with his soul, his fate, or his future...not like this.

King Drakkar Hades was asking for everything.

All of him.

Complete allegiance.

And the king was offering something Ghost could hardly refuse, not if he still hoped to—

He cut the thought short.

One never knew...

The king had said he didn't listen, eavesdrop, read his servants' minds, but this could be one of those rare times; Ghost could never be too careful.

"I understand," he said succinctly.

"Good," Drakkar said, "then you will also understand this: I am neither a sucker, a fool, nor a charitable shadow-demon-dragon...monarch. Quite the contrary, as I'm sure I've made clear. But I do enjoy a challenge, a break from all the boredom, empowering my quarry, and playing wicked games. Therefore, this elevation...this ascension...this anointing to just a heartbeat beneath my own throne shall be limited, a test, a three-month probation to see how you use your newfound privilege. To see if you exalt, elevate, and venerate your liege with every lift or descent of this scepter and with every step you take in this robe. To that end, you may only wield the scepter thrice, whether upward or downward, to force obeisance, or to destroy: once for each symbolic month of the trial period. I care not if you wield it thrice in one day, in one hour, or per plenus tribus mensibus"—*over the full three months*. "But know that its power is limited to only three uses, so choose your indulgences wisely. And if, after three months' time, you are yet my loyal servant, a true blood relative, and a worthy prince, then all the ordainments I have this day issued as my *nephew's* birthright shall forever remain yours, without limit nor end."

Ghost's jaw dropped open.

What the actual fuck had just happened?

He closed it in order to catch his breath and gather his thoughts, without looking like an unworthy simpleton: Lord Drakkar Hades wasn't yanking Ghost's chain; the king of the underworld was as serious as a heart attack, and he was about to make Ghost a prince.

His prince...

Second in command of the underworld.

Shiiit.

He was just about to follow up with a few no-nonsense questions, like wouldn't the Pagan Horde be murderously pissed and try to take Ghost out the second he had used up the scepter; would Lord Drakkar stop him or try to limit his powers if the king did not agree with his choices; and would the scepter work on Lord Drakkar too—okay, so he wasn't actually bold enough or dumb enough to ask that last question—when King Drakkar

Hades stepped back, tossed both royal implements high in the air, and shouted the words: "Think fast!"

Through a din of echoing, disembodied laughter, the blood-red robe landed perfectly about Ghost's shoulder and fastened in the front, just above his collarbone, even as the heavy royal scepter landed in his hand. And then the duo of two-headed hell-hounds reappeared on the top of the dais and lunged at Ghost again.

He dropped the scepter, balled up both fists, and smashed the mongrels' snarling faces into bloody pulp the moment they went for his arms—yes, this time he was ready, but two more hounds just as quickly appeared. Ghost dropped down low, released his own claws, and waited until they launched from the platform; then the moment they hit the air, he shot upward like an exploding geyser, spun around in dizzying-fast, supernatural circles, and shredded the barbaric canines like a high-powered blender with a vertical row of razor-sharp blades.

Ten more hounds appeared on the dais.

At least one hundred filled the throne room.

"Fuck!" Ghost bellowed as he reached for the scepter and slowly raised it over his head. He didn't know if lowering it would destroy all 110 hellhounds or only the one he could touch with the dragon's mouth, and he couldn't afford to take that chance. As desired, the hellhounds dropped to the floor with a whimper, rolled onto their backs, and exposed their bellies.

Then the roaring flames in the towering obsidian fireplace behind him, flanked by the two arched entries to the throne room, popped and crackled with demonic laughter, before bellowing in a thunderous voice: "Prince Ghostaniaz Dragos, nephew to the king of the underworld, father of sin eaters and sire of shades. Heel, sit, and bow before him!" The hounds rolled over, sat on their haunches, and lowered their heads to the unholy ground.

Ghost gawked at Lord Drakkar, who just smiled wanly.

"Wicked games, indeed," the king jeered. "I thought I could provoke you to waste all three advantages, drain all the scepter's uses in one fell swoop. Well played, Ghostaniaz; you may prove worthy yet. I shall see you at matins on Friday in the Sinners' Cave, where we shall all partake in your...public revelations, and then again at vespers, next Wednesday, for the *Feast of Coronation*. Until we meet again, remember, you only have two uses of the scepter left."

Ghost held his tongue.

He just wanted to get the hell out of dodge before Lord Drakkar could think of something else to conjure and throw at him. *Matins* referred to extremely late at night, midnight, maybe even later, and *vespers* meant dinnertime, around 6 P.M.

Whatever.

He had more than enough to process as it stood.

Like could he use the mouth of the scepter to open The Deep without the need of a cryptic brass key? Just how badly would shit hit the fan if he and Beth could not make tracks before Friday? And could he raise the scepter on their way out the door if they were being pursued by—

Cut it, Ghost! he said to himself. *Don't you dare take stock in the word of a demon monarch.*

Never mind the fact that he could be listening...

Ghost met Lord Drakkar's amused, evil gaze as he slowly backed out of the hall, all the while trying to take the king's true measure. Lord Drakkar was playing a game with Ghost, for sure —the lion and the mouse, times infinity—but no, the wicked ruler of the underworld was not listening to Ghost's thoughts or eavesdropping inside his private chambers, any more than he had eavesdropped on Wraith Sylvester prior to finding the soul eater on top of Beth and killing the pagan for the insult.

The king, indeed, preferred his vindictive games.

He liked to chase and outwit his inferior prey.

Only this time, Ghost would have to stay several steps ahead of the powerful, Machiavellian deity and pray his efforts would not be in vain when the deepest recesses of his mind—his own deceitful plans and stark duplicity—were exposed to the entire underworld, come Friday.

CHAPTER TWENTY-TWO

W here had the woman come from?

The absolutely stunning creature with platinum blonde hair that fell to her waist in perfectly symmetrical curls, framing large, hunter-green eyes, such nearly flawless features, as if set from a plastic mold, and beguiling, feminine curves, ideal in every dimension?

She was breathtaking, yet her presence was hair raising.

Chilling.

Disturbing.

On the deepest level of the soul, this unnatural beauty's energy came off as base, sinister...

Nearly suffocating.

And she had stepped right out of the ether, like she was part and parcel of the chamber itself—the stones, the walls, the dark, gothic architecture—before flashing a lethal smile and extending a duplicitous hand: "Bethany—may I call you by your given name? So nice to finally meet our latest human arrival... I'm Felicity Payne, another of Lord Drakkar's acquirements. He brought me here in 1692 from Salem, Massachusetts, and I've been serving His Majesty and the members of his court ever since."

Bethany shuffled back so quickly, she almost tripped over a pile of dirty clothes. She tucked one hand against her lower belly and covered it with the other in a defensive posture. No, she did not want this woman to use her given name. She did not want any variation of her name to cross this woman's lips...not ever... not for any reason, and she did not want to touch this woman's hand. She had been in the castle since 1692! How was that even possible? And why had she emphasized *Salem* with so much pride and loosely veiled suggestion? Everyone knew the Salem Witch Trials had been a crime against innocent women, perpetrated by crazed, religious zealots—had she thrown that out just to make Bethany squirm?

"So are you saying you're—"

"A witch. Yes, that's exactly what I'm saying." Felicity took a lithe, threatening step forward, and shifted her hand up and down once more. "You don't wish to take my hand?" She laughed, but there was nothing light-hearted about the jeer or the sound.

Bethany shook her head. "Where did you come from? Just now?"

The dark red lipstick on Felicity's heart-shaped mouth appeared to slide...or trickle...like wine pooling over the top of a goblet, only it slid from side to side over the fleshiest portion of her lips. *What the heck?* And then her eyes flashed with an instant certainty, the way eyes do when someone has come to a sudden decision or resolved some inner question in their mind. She licked her repulsive, watery mouth.

"From hell, Bethany." Her tone had changed, just that fast, from dripping with bitter honey to chilling as frigid ice. "I came from hell, and I lied when I said it was nice to finally meet you. It wasn't nice. *I* am not nice. It was fortuitous...opportunistic...in truth, it was planned. I've been here since lauds, just waiting to see you, to behold the woman Lord Drakkar would have made his own, the woman the Dragyr prisoner opposed the king to claim... just waiting to get you alone."

Bethany's heart skipped a beat in her chest.

And in the space of that missing pulse, her body released a surge of adrenaline, causing her airway to dilate, filling her muscles with oxygen, and triggering an overwhelming sense of fight or flight.

She turned on bare heels to run.

She dodged a full wooden tub and leaped over a pile of dirty linens as she sprinted like a startled gazelle for the shadowy, arched threshold that would take her out of the castle laundry.

Thwack.

Clang.

Boom!

Her lungs burned from a sudden, deep gasp of air as one of the large wooden washtubs struck the peak of the stony arch; the wooden crank and wringer pinged off the unyielding rocks; the washboard splintered into pieces; and boiling water gushed from the laundry ceiling, pooling toward Bethany's feet.

How the hell had Felicity picked that up and tossed it?

Without moving, twitching, or lunging, the witch suddenly appeared in the doorway, framed by the gothic arch, blocking the only path of escape, and giving Bethany her answer: Felicity had not picked up anything, at least not with her hands; she had used magic to hurl the washtub across the room, and she had used witchcraft to transport her body.

Oh shit, oh shit, oh shit!

Bethany danced on her tippy toes, trying to avoid the scorching water, even as she backpedaled rapidly to the rear of the launderette, dodging several obstacles as she scurried. "No!" she cried out, instinctively. "*Please...*" Then, "God, help me." She pressed her back against the farthest wall, palms braced rigidly against the warm, moist stones, and her eyes darted frantically, backward and forward, then side to side: a hot cast-iron press sitting atop a woodburning stove, maybe three or four feet away, in the corner of the room! Bethany made note of the potential weapon yet fixed her eyes on Felicity.

The foul woman smiled.

Her shoulders creeped upward, and her chest rocked forward —*the witch was about to take flight!*

Bethany took her hands off the wall, lunged forward, and sprinted toward the woodburning stove. She dove for the iron, grasped its wooden handle, and snatched it off the antique burner with a desperate, fevered grasp.

Felicity shot into the air like a rocket exploding on the Fourth of July, cursing, screeching, erupting with rage. She flew across the room and descended just as Bethany spun around and thrust the tip of the iron upward, trying to scorch the witch's chin.

She missed.

Felicity jerked backward, let out a bestial snarl, and landed squarely on her feet. She raised both hands in the air and began to draw some cryptic diagram with her forefinger. Bethany's heart nearly burst in her chest.

Fuck that!

She couldn't let the witch complete some deadly spell.

Bethany braced her left hand over her right, so that both fists were firmly controlling the hot iron's handle, and then she rotated her wrists, lunged again, and thrust the scorching base of the iron into Felicity's face, pressing it upward into the witch's eyes.

Felicity screamed like a pig being slaughtered, and the inhuman sound sent rivers of terror surging through Bethany's spine. She couldn't stand the horrific noise, and she couldn't remain where she was: an arm's length away from the crazed, wounded witch, a stone's throw from such dark, vile energy—it was like being surrounded by a chorus of swine.

Bethany dropped the iron and tried to run, but Felicity reached out and caught her by a narrow fistful of her cotton T-shirt, the hem sewn into the collar. She dug her nails into Felicity's hands, but the witch's palm melted beneath them, and then her fingers turned into centipedes.

Bethany tried to flick the venomous creatures away.

She brushed them frantically off her shirt, even as she shoved at Felicity's chest, but the witch didn't budge—she sucked in air, released a deep, ragged breath, reclaimed her mortal fingers, then exhaled a plume of blood-red vapor. Bethany ducked and lost her balance. She fell to her knees and tried to crawl away, and that's when the witch mounted her back...and Bethany nearly fainted.

"Get off me!" Bethany clawed at Felicity's neck. She twisted this way and that, trying to pitch her off, then finally threw several sharp elbows, aiming at the witch's rib cage.

"Blood and bone; flesh and stone." Felicity cackled like she was mad. "Water, heat, and fire. Earth and stain; fear and pain—grant my heart's desire. Deliver this woman into my hands: body, mind, and soul." With that, she seemed to grow a thousand times stronger. She stood up straight, grasped Bethany by her thick, threaded braid, and dragged her, face down, kicking and shouting, to the nearest boiling cauldron, a wooden tub in the middle of the laundry, filled with scorching-hot water. She flipped her over, straddled her waist, and glared into Bethany's eyes.

Bethany stiffened, blinked rapidly, and sucked in air, trying to regain her bearings.

She punched, slammed her knee upward, and grasped at Felicity's wrists, trying to get the witch off her. She tried to break her little fingers, like Ghost had taught her, but the long, elegant digits wouldn't snap.

Nothing worked.

Nothing hurt her.

Nothing cut through the witch's madness.

Bethany could not overpower this sixteenth-century sorceress. She could not break free, and she could not snap her out of it. In a last-ditch effort, she reached frantically for a block of old-fashioned lye sitting on the floor beside the antique washtub—Felicity kicked it away. The welts in her face from the hot, antique iron were still steaming in charred, bloody rivulets seared into the witch's features. Yet Felicity didn't seem to feel it, and the ghastly wounds did not hinder her sight, nor did they lessen her power.

Desperate, confused, and all out of options, Bethany held her breath and closed her eyes as Felicity's overbearing, murderous presence—her black heart, her iniquitous soul, and her wicked, murderous intention—swelled with the energy of triumph and power. "How dare you disfigure a face so incomparable! You shall die by the same curse you wrought." She wrapped her hands around Bethany's neck and squeezed with all her might, hefting her by the throat and dragging her, headfirst, to the basin of the wash bucket.

Bethany braced her shoulders and moaned aloud, her mind struggling mightily to shift its focus, to find a purchase, to grasp onto something...*anything*...that might take her away from the hellish laundry and allow her to endure the unimaginable, withstand her final moments.

She couldn't do it...

The moment the steam from the basin licked the back of Bethany's neck, scorching her skin like fire, every survival instinct in her body awakened with renewed, fevered earnest, and she strained against her captor's feral grip.

Felicity pressed down on Bethany's forehead.

Bethany strained against Felicity's hands.

"Lower," the fevered witch snarled. "*Lower.*"

"No. *No!* Nooooo."

A gruesome blast!

A crackling explosion, the most revolting sound Bethany had ever heard, filled the castle laundry, echoing from every direction at once: flesh rending, blood spurting, and bone blasting like a hundred splintering fragments of detonated rock, bursting, shooting...scattering...ricocheting, and landing all over the medieval laundry's stony walls and cobbled floors.

Bethany's eyes shot open, and she sucked in a ragged breath. "Ghost!"

The fearsome dragyri was standing in the laundry at the edge of the scalding bucket, his shoulders draped in a thick red-and-gold cloak, a heavy, ornate scepter clutched in one hand, and what was left of Felicity's skull oozing between his hard, fisted fingers...falling from his other palm.

His eyes were ablaze like twin molten coals.

His chest was heaving, his biceps contracting, and his perfect, supernatural complexion was coated in leathery, reptilian scales. *Holy dragons of the Pantheon,* he was an awesome sight to behold.

"Fuckin' bitch," he snarled as he caught the witch's torso just as it slumped to the floor.

He tossed the carcass across the chamber, watched as Felicity's spine slammed into the granite wall and shattered into a dozen fresh pieces, and then he leaped the distance, caught the corpse again, and wrenched what was left of the witch's once-beautiful, perfect head from her shoulders.

He bent over the gory pile of pulp.

He dipped his hands in the blood.

And then one by one, piece by piece, he began to toss the gruesome remains across the launderette and into the same scalding wash bin she had come *this close* to drowning Bethany in.

Bethany scooted away from the wooden barrel. She crawled

to an unmarred section of floor, buried her head in her hands, and wept.

"Beth." His voice was softer than usual. *"Dragyra?"*

She shook her head from side to side, the tears continuing to flow.

He squatted down beside her, wrapped a tight, muscular arm around her quaking shoulders, and tunneled his large, blood-soaked fingers inside the top of her loose, disheveled braid. "I got you, girl. It's over."

Uncaring about the blood in her hair or the putrid stench now filling the laundry, Bethany grasped Ghost's forearm with two trembling hands and lowered her head to his arm. And then she washed his blood-streaked skin in rivers, gullies...oceans of tears...until his stained flesh was clean, and all the pain, fear, and frustration she had held back since the moment she'd been taken on All Hallows' Eve had washed down the laundry's ancient drain. Finally, when her soul was spent, she sniffed, backed away, and looked up at him. "What...when...*how* did you find me?"

He shrugged and shook his head. "This morning, when that sketchy human slave came to get you..." He turned up his lip and scowled. "Not much I could do at the moment, but I had every intention of circling back...checking up...as soon as I was free to do it."

She let out a sigh of relief, still too rattled to find coherent words. "And you walked in on—"

"That crazy-ass bitch about to boil your head in a cauldron."

Bethany grasped both shoulders in an unconscious, self-protective gesture and shivered. "Lord Drakkar is going to kill us, isn't he? Or at least turn us over to his Pagan Horde?"

Ghost grit his teeth and shook his head. He raised the golden scepter still resting in his left hand, and thumbed the edge of the red-and-gold cloak to indicate both objects. "Nah," he said resolutely. "Trust me; the king is not gonna do a thing. The witch was mine to kill. And as for the rest of those black-hearted bastards—they won't say a word. At least for now, they wouldn't dare."

Bethany stared at him like he had just grown two heads. "Ghost, what the hell are you talking about?"

He whistled low, beneath his breath, brushing the underside of her chin with his second and third fingers. "Long story, dragyra, but suffice to say: You're looking at the new prince of the underworld, at least for the next three months."

Her jaw dropped open. "Prince of the underworld?"

"Trial period. I'll tell you more later. But trust me when I say we have a lot to talk about and even more to get done before this whole insane, royal blasphemy of a train wreck comes crashing into the station like a runaway engine on Tinkertoy tracks. For now, we just need to get the hell out of this laundry."

Bethany nodded in agreement, as her mind went rolling down those same toy tracks. "I can wait. Believe me, I'm ready to get out of here. I just hope"—she glanced around the gory, disheveled, *train wreck* of a laundry—"that all this shit doesn't come back to haunt us. Killing the witch. Skirting my duties. Leaving this...mess...for someone else to clean up."

Ghost smirked. "Trust me, this thing with Felicity ain't shit compared to what Lord Drakkar has planned. The king is orchestrating the World Series, while this"—he waved his hand to indicate the bloody room—"this is a Little League game. We'll live through the night, dragyra, but after that? Hard to say. All future bets are off."

CHAPTER TWENTY-THREE

Bethany sank deep into the antique tin tub in the private, curtained alcove in her and Ghost's bedchamber, reveling in the feel of the fresh, lukewarm, not boiling hot, lavender-scented water. She tried not to feel self-conscious about being naked this close to Ghost, despite the fact that he was seated less than five feet away on a high-backed, blue velvet chair, his back turned to the basin.

Bethany really did not have the words to thank him.

He had saved her life, spared her from Felicity's worst, and just in the nick of time.

He had healed her bruises, the scalding on the back of her neck, and even the sore, stinging roots on her scalp with his mystical silver fire, and he hadn't made her feel as helpless or weak as she knew she was after the completely one-sided struggle with the ancient witch. Felicity had wiped the floor with Bethany, and despite Bethany's repeated attempts to fight back, she had been no match for the supernatural female—the thought was beyond disturbing.

It was terrifying.

Sobering.

And as if all Ghost had done in the castle laundry had not been enough—protective enough, defiant enough, generous enough—Ghost had also lifted an embroidered satin duvet, a half-dozen matching pillow slips, and three warm wool blankets from the storage cabinet just outside the laundry's foyer, and made a quick, emboldened trip to the dungeon level, center hall, which housed Lord Drakkar's personal human slaves, on their way back to the bedchamber, just to grab an additional bundle of undergarments, gowns, and modern, upscale toiletries for Bethany.

Thus, the lavender-infused water she was now enjoying...

She scooped a dollop of vanilla-and-chamomile shampoo from an ornately decorated mason jar and worked it into her hair, before submerging one last time in the clean, invigorating water to rinse it out of her strands. She sat up straight and smoothed the drenched locks behind her ears. "Are you sure there isn't going to be hell to pay for this...all of this?"

Ghost grunted and shifted in the too-small chair. "Nah. The way I see it, you're no longer just a regular slave. The pagans will regard you as some sort of carnal consort, maybe even a concubine to the castle's prince. And if I'm asked about it, I'll justify it in purely selfish—and equally carnal—terms." He shrugged his heavy shoulders. "Besides, Lord Drakkar did say, 'It is my intention to anoint you prince of this realm, second only to myself.' If I can't put a fresh pair of knickers on my lady's ass, then what the hell was the point of that statement?"

Bethany opened her mouth to protest, then closed it.

Ghost was...

Well, *Ghost*.

And she caught his meaning.

"But the feast day is not until next Wednesday, still one week away," she said.

"Tomato, *tomahto*," Ghost groused. "Now you're splitting hairs."

Bethany bit her bottom lip, paused, then pressed on with a much more sensitive subject: "And Friday is the Sinners' Cave..." She let the words linger until the sound trailed off. They both understood the gravity of this particular upcoming event: For all intents and purposes, it would likely lead to the dragyri's demise, and Bethany's would follow in short order. When he didn't respond right away, she spoke his name in a whisper. "Ghost?" Sill nothing. "You can tell me, dragyri, so at least I'm prepared. What will they find when they expose your thoughts and memories?" She quickly turned the delicate question into a more concrete, manageable plan of action. "I mean, do we realistically need to try to get out of here by Thursday?"

Ghost shook his head and grumbled, "Dunno. I'm hoping all the king is after is more information about the Pantheon, and while that shit feels traitorous—doesn't sit well with me, either— it's better than the alternative. If the Pagan Horde can use my mind to see directly beyond the portal, well, there's a lifetime of memories and intel to recover—don't want to put my dragyri brothers at risk. At the same time, if the horde reads my thoughts, as in every last one, then you and I are fucked six ways to Sunday, or Friday to be more exact. Can't hide subterfuge. Can't fake disgust. Can't pretend I'm all onboard and suddenly loyal if the jackasses can see my true heart. But getting out...when we go...a lot of things have to come together before then: I still need to figure out the vortex, get hold of a brass key, and try to make our exodus line up with the pagans' schedule."

He turned around to face her, and she blanched, sank down into the water, pressed her knees together, and covered both breasts with the palms of her hands.

"Beth," he said frankly, his eyes fixed on hers. "I've turned this over, again and again, in my head, and I honestly think that

Feast Day is our very best, if not only, chance. The entire horde will be in once place, together, the Great Hall. No doubt, Lord Drakkar will provide various forms of...entertainment...for his demons and shades. A distraction. A chance to get up or slip away. Maybe even some cover. Not to mention, there'll be plenty of wine and mead to be had." He cocked one shoulder in an exaggerated, happy-go-lucky fashion. "If we can get enough belladonna from the castle apothecary before Wednesday night—"

"Belladonna?"

"*Atropa belladonna*, also called deadly nightshade. It's an herb scavenged from a tall, bushy, earthside plant. Dull green leaves, violet or greenish flowers, and sweet, shiny, blackened berries about the size of cherries in the axils of the leaves...forks of the branches. Poisonous as hell, even in low doses. If we can get enough, we can mix it with the spirits. We only need five minutes or less to make our—"

"Are you crazy?" Bethany interrupted a second time. "Ghost, we'll get caught. They'll catch us, torture us, and execute us both —and not in some quick, painless fashion—no, they'll really make us suffer, maybe for eons. How in the hell could we steal that much belladonna in just seven days, let alone poison an entire feast of supernatural savages without being discovered?"

Ghost leaned forward in the chair, and his phantom-blue pupils were stark with conviction. "It's our best shot, Beth. There are no good options or easy outs, should anything we try fail to succeed, but we've already talked about a Plan B—remember? If we go with the belladonna, we can at least hold a large enough dose back for ourselves. You know, just in case." He paused for the space of two or three heartbeats. "Go big or go home, right? I mean, the way I see it, we're down to *Go big, or never make it home*. Got one shot to get this shit right—fortune favors the brave."

Bethany shivered and closed her eyes.

Yeah, fortune favored the brave, but failure, ruin, and, in this case, catastrophe could just as easily annihilate the foolish, to say nothing of the unspoken truth behind Ghost's bold statement. She reopened her eyes and stared right through him. "What you really mean is we can hold a large enough dose back for *me*, not you." There. She had said it. "Poison won't kill a dragyri, will it?" She watched as the powerful, preternatural mercenary cocked his head to the side in a subtle consenting gesture, and she knew. "And it can't actually kill demons or shadow-walkers, either...can it?"

This time, he shook his head more forcefully. "No. But it might slow 'em down. It *will* slow 'em down. If nothing else, it'll get 'em a helluva lot more drunk, and if that makes even half of them slower, less alert...if it makes even a dozen of our enemies pause for sixty seconds..." He didn't finish the comparison. He didn't have to. "Beth, I get the stakes. All of them. Trust me, I have no intention of playing ranger games with our lives. I wish I could give you something more, a stronger assurance, but at some point, words become redundant. All I can give you is my pledge: to get us out or die trying."

Bethany let out a slow, deep breath and studied the random crystal-and-gray patterns of steam as it settled atop a nearby antique cheval glass, before turning her attention back to the son of a dragon. "And you think you can get the brass key...*a* brass key...figure out how to manipulate and get us through the vortex?"

Ghost sighed with barely concealed frustration. "Just more words, Beth. Said I was gonna try, and if not, I'll still have the scepter."

"Yeah," she snipped, her own irritation beginning to rise, "if everything doesn't go south on Friday."

"True."

Damn...

Just one word...

True.

Nothing ever fazed him, did it?

Bethany continued to shield her breasts with her forearms, even as she lowered her head and pinched the bridge of her nose. There was no point in asking any more questions. Ghost had his plan, and it would either work or it wouldn't—but she wasn't going to get what she was truly seeking out of such a cool and collected, no-nonsense companion.

She wanted a sense of camaraderie.

Or at least a false sense of safety.

Not in terms of having a foolproof plan, but of having another soul, so close and connected, that whatever they went through, at least they were in it together. She wanted to feel like she was being...sheltered...beneath someone else's superior strength. Hell, she wanted an intangible awareness, akin to... asylum, and she knew it was an unrealistic yearning. Maybe what Bethany really wanted was just a make-believe friend, someone who could manufacture a sense of well-being, no matter how untrue, the same kind of security Kimberly Johansson had given her in grade school. But that false dream had gone up in smoke as well.

As tears of frustration, or maybe helplessness, stung the corners of her eyes, Bethany tried to erase the slate of her mind by staring into the water, and that's when something...strange and unexpected...happened: That's when she felt a tender, aged hand, with the gentleness of Grandma Betsy's, subtly tugging at the door of her heart, opening something that had been closed for —well, forever—even though Bethany hadn't known the barrier was there. That's when she felt a surge of peace, like palpable, physical light, fill all four of those wounded chambers, and that's when she saw Ghost, not his face or his persona, but a sense or a vision of his original soul, through that same illuminated, inward prism.

Chains.

Thorns.

Scattered, broken pieces, like shards of razor-edged glass, all encapsulated in strength and control—his own lifelong protective barrier.

That's when she saw him through the eyes of Spirit, all judgment and condemnation aside, and she was able to recognize the inner warrior, what creation had made, before time and hardship had dismantled the blueprint.

As if drawn like a moth to an enigmatic flame, Ghost rose from his seat on the blue velvet chair and approached the tin tub with caution. "C'mon," he rasped. "Don't do that; don't cry."

Bethany hadn't realized she was crying.

He closed the distance between them, dropped into a squat beside her, and wrapped one large, powerful hand around the rim of the tub, his eyes more intense than usual. "Dragyra," he said softly, the word like cotton candy, "I don't...I wish you wouldn't... please don't cry."

Bethany forced a fragile smile and turned to look at him, studying every intense, haunted attribute, as if she had never noticed his cast before now: short, dark black hair, the shade of moonlight hidden behind a lunar eclipse; phantom-blue pupils, yes, but the eyes of a Siberian husky, curious, fiercely loyal, and pure as glass; strong, angular cheekbones, a jaw cut from granite, and a brow so stunning, skin so smooth, he could almost be mistaken for an ancient marble statue.

His eyes were nearly glowing as he watched her...watching him.

She opened her mouth to say something, but nothing came out but a sigh.

There were no words to describe what she was seeing—

studying, noticing, *feeling?*—as she gazed at the enigmatic male before her and, for the first time, saw so clearly beyond the surface.

"That witch," he whispered, in a voice so hushed it was barely audible. "The one in the castle laundry."

"Felicity?" Bethany raised her brows, listening intently.

"She could've killed you. She almost...killed you."

Bethany wasn't sure she grasped his meaning, but her heart nearly froze in her chest as she reached for more...tried to process his words...and waited.

He released the rim of the tub, placed the palm of his hand along the frame of her jaw, then brushed each of her high, arched cheekbones with the pad of his thumb, drying her tears in two soft, slow sweeps.

Bethany didn't blink.

She couldn't look away...

As his thumb drifted lower from the crest of one cheek, swept along the soft indentation, toward her mouth, then outlined the silhouette of her upper lip. He traced it like an artist, panning his thumb back and forth, before inadvertently withdrawing his finger, bringing it to his own parted mouth, and biting down on the tip...to taste her...while closing his eyes for the space of a heartbeat.

Bethany inhaled sharply.

Holy shit.

His tongue followed where his teeth had been, he opened his eyes, and then he stared straight through her, as if every sentient part of him had left the room, and all that was left was instinct.

"Ghost?"

He answered with a primitive growl.

"Ghost!" Bethany shot backward in the tub, sloshed water over the rim, and then scrambled to her feet, straddled the basin, and tiptoed in reverse along the wet, stony floor. With the breadth of the tub standing as a barrier between them, she covered what she could of her exposed, naked body.

"Don't," he snarled, but the word wasn't angry.

It was haunted.

Parched.

Hungry.

Against her better judgment and whatever was left of her common sense, Bethany stared at Ghost in morbid fascination, gulped, shivered, and summoned her courage. She allowed her arms to fall to her side, ignoring the cool, crystallizing water running down her chest, pooling over her stomach, and dripping softly, rhythmically, onto her thighs before falling in random, scattered droplets to the floor.

Ghost studied every contour, curve, and line she exposed, as if he had never seen a naked woman before, and then he lowered his haunted gaze, ever so slowly, along the seam of her ribs, down to the flat of her belly, then lower still—

"Ghost!"

She couldn't take a moment more.

His stare was so...hypnotic.

His soul was so alive and *present*.

His *species* was so distinctly different.

Not human!

That undeniable truth was as apparent as it was overwhelming.

Yet and still, what chilled Bethany the most was the fact that the male was almost...vulnerable.

Almost.

As if snapping out of a distant reverie, or an unconscious, thirst-induced trance, he jerked back, stood up, and reached for a nearby cotton towel, his glorious eyes now averted, downward. "Put this on." He tossed it at Bethany and backed away from the basin. "I'll get you something to wear." He turned on his lithe, animalistic heel and headed out of the alcove.

Bethany let out the breath she didn't know she was holding.

She shivered, shook her head, and gently cleared her throat. *What the hell had just happened?*

Almost happened.

"I'm gonna make tracks," he called from the other cavity, completely dismissing the entire scene as if nothing...awkward or intimate...had just happened. "Scour the castle, try to survey the apothecary, maybe see if I can locate a brass key."

"Ghost..."

"Goes without saying, but keep the door bolted. Now that I'm prince, don't answer it for anyone. If Lord Drakkar shows up, then...well, scream. I won't be gone long."

"*Ghost.*"

"Beth, not gonna tell you to drop it, but I'm *asking*...let it go."

Recalling the soft, aged hand that had pried her heart open, Bethany pursed her lips together, swallowed her pride, and wrapped her body firmly inside the soft cotton towel. Peace. Light. Revelation. The absence of judgment—zero condemnation. Was this what Grandma Betsy was trying to show her... teach her...*give to her*? A way to make it through this harsh situation.

She would let it go.

She *could* let it go because it wasn't about being heard, being right, or asserting her agency as an equal partner in this unimaginable battle for survival, life over death, at least not right now, in this singular moment.

No...

That had been Bethany's truth, according to her human mind, what she saw with her mortal eyes and heard with her corporal ears, but just for a moment, however fleeting, she had seen through the eyes of Spirit: chains, thorns, and scattered pieces, like broken shards of glass.

Bethany had seen...all of Ghost.

And for the first time, she had understood.

Yet and still, the way the carnal male, the flesh-and-blood dragyri, had looked at her, touched her, admired her body, the undeniable current that had flowed between them—there was something still living inside those ruins. And unless all four chambers of Bethany's heart remained open, unless she could substitute light and acceptance for fear, judgment, and personal wanting, she and the dragyri did not stand a chance in hell of making it out of the underworld.

She didn't know how she knew.

She just did.

She didn't understand all that had happened.

But something in her heart had lifted...changed.

Opened.

And whether Ghost wanted it or not, saw it or not, the connection between them was no longer superficial. In truth and spirit, it likely never had been.

* * *

Lord Drakkar Hades strolled along the upper castle battlements with his favorite hellhound, Plague, at his side, staring out at the infinite gradations of black, gray, and thick, dark blue, whilst reveling in the dense, oppressive haze permeating the stifling, hot air.

Morning.

Afternoon.

Evening...

It really made no difference.

The underworld remained a grim, inhospitable land, filled

with dead grass, gnarled tree limbs, and rotten, spoiling vegetation as far as the eyes could see—exactly as Lord Drakkar preferred it.

He stopped pacing long enough to lean against a dark gray parapet and scratch both of Plague's thick, box-shaped heads. "Ghost," he whispered in a fetid exhale of breath, shaking his head. Things had gone well with the barbaric, mercenary, first-born hatchling to a savage dragon lord. Well, things had gone as well as could be expected, considering the state of Ghost's character, the condition of his soul.

And wasn't that just the entire situation in a nutshell?

The condition of Ghostaniaz Dragos' soul!

Lord Drakkar was certainly banking on that mired wasteland to be the doorway through which all manner of evil could ultimately enter, to be the true opening to Ghost's ascension as prince of the underworld and Drakkar's faithful blood kin. A servant unlike any other before him. A male who would choose his fealty with his own free will.

Lord Drakkar waved a long, spindly hand through the air—he was getting ahead of himself again. He was imagining the future, following the certain revelation in the Sinners' Cave, and dreaming, waxing poetic, about the day after Ghost's true ascension, following the feast of coronation: Oh, yes, Ghost would ascend to his metaphoric, princely throne, both eagerly and willingly, though his devious, treacherous mind and his hardened, recalcitrant heart were currently unaware of this.

It really didn't matter.

Lord Drakkar knew the truth.

Being omniscient was a useful schtick, even for a dark lord who refused to listen to his *nephew's* thoughts, to eavesdrop over his traitorous conversations, to follow him around like a baby duckling, trying to discern his quackery and deceit. The woman, however, the female slave—now that had been a delightful twist.

Little surprised an original deity, but the fact that Bethany Reid was Ghost's fated female, his singular and promised *dragyra*? Lord Drakkar had to admit—he had not seen that shit coming. Nonetheless, he had felt...something...scented something the moment he had bent over her delectable, quivering body in that bedchamber, the moment his scorpion's tongue had hovered above her naked breasts and her creamy, concave stomach. He had *suspected* something when Ghost had chosen to barter for the pleasure of one particularly pretty yet insignificant maiden. But he hadn't *divined* it, put two and two together, until Ghost had dismembered Felicity earlier that morning—so much vengeance, bloodletting, and ferocity! Such *overkill* was simply over the top.

He tossed back his head, clapped his hands, and cackled.

What were the fucking odds!

That Wraith Sylvester would search an entire planet to bring back a beautiful, near-perfect slave to complete Drakkar's private seven and snatch Ghost's promised woman from a blasted haunted house.

Zero.

The odds were simply...zero.

And that meant the Seven had their royal, dragon-god, interloper hands—or talons, as it were—in the proverbial pot.

Delightful, indeed!

Twisted.

Magnificent.

A true game of imperial, inter-celestial, and underworld poker.

Plague snarled from his left mouth, gnashed his teeth with his right, and Lord Drakkar concurred with the sentiment: Yes, Ghost had asked for the female—under the circumstances, he could have done none other. And yes, he had just murdered the ancient Salem witch in the castle laundry; again, his balls were in a bit of a vise. After all, he only had ten days from All Hallows' Eve to somehow...someway...get the wench to the Temple of Seven. That is, if he wanted her to live. If he wanted to avoid becoming a permanent statue in that bizarrely stupid Garden of Grace, a factual morsel Drakkar had not been privy to until Ghost had drawn it on Killian's map.

Splendid.

Interesting.

Just one more layer on this decadent cake.

Oh, but it was a mired and multilayered conundrum as well, was it not?

Only Lord Dragos could remove Ghost's amulet—another delightfully fresh revelation discovered when Lord Drakkar had tried it himself—so if the Dragyr failed to show up at the temple, beautiful bitch in tow, then his life would be forfeit, along with hers, unless...yes, *unless*...Ghost remained in the underworld.

Lord Dragos could not remove what he could not get his claws around.

And the life of the female was moot at best, whether she died in her sleep or—well, something else. Ghost's eternal life was all that mattered, and it would remain sustained, just so long as he never ventured beyond the vortex.

Beyond The Deep.

And how could he?

Lord Drakkar would be watching his protégé like a hawk.

Though, truly, after Friday's revelation and next Wednesday's feast of coronation, the surveillance would not be necessary.

Ghost was not in love with the human woman.

Hell, the bastard couldn't love at all.

Lord Drakkar would not fuck with the human slave girl again, nor would he insist upon her working. There was no point. Her existence was irrelevant, her consideration beneath him, and no matter how one turned the various scenarios over, her insignificant human life would be fleeting.

Requiem Pyre or Killian Kross could still find the king another consort, a replacement to fulfill his throne-room seven, and Ghost would swiftly get over Bethany's...passing...once he understood that her life was no longer connected or vital to sustaining his own.

Yes.

"*Yesssss*," Lord Drakkar Hades hissed, even as Plague tossed back both heads and howled in unison. "Once broken, once exposed, once the dragyri is choking on his sire's original sin— once he recalls such unforgiveable betrayal—Ghost will change his allegiance and accept his new fate. He has to."

Ghost was teetering on the edge of oblivion, even now.

He was suffocating beneath the weight of the unconscionable chains that bound him.

The chains that had *always* bound him.

The coming ceremonies would tip him over the edge—Lord Drakkar was 99.99 percent sure of it.

CHAPTER TWENTY-FOUR

nne Liu shifted uncomfortably on the stiff wooden picnic bench, placing her body half in, half out of the meager sunshine filtering through the leafless, November branches of a red maple tree in Riverside Park, trying to make sense of Bryce M's words—

Correction!

Trying to make sense of *Jax's* words.

Jaxtapherion Dragos, to be exact.

She clutched the collar of her Nordic-blue down parka, raised the zipper to meet her chin, then curled her shoulders forward to try to conserve some heat.

"You sure you wouldn't rather be inside?" Jax asked. "I'm sure we can find a coffee shop or a—"

"No," Anne insisted. "I'm fine. *I'm fine.*" It was forty-six degrees, Anne's fingertips were numb, and the wind had not stopped blowing since Anne and Jax had sat down. Anne was not fine. But the thought of going anywhere else with this Bryce M guy, who was really not a *guy* but some sort of primordial species, *and not named Bryce*, was more than her mind could handle at the moment, to say nothing of being stuck with him—*with it?*—in a closed-in space.

Jax measured her thoughtfully, and his light green pupils seemed to warm with empathy. "At least let me help." He cupped his hands over his mouth, breathed into them slowly, then extended them outward and to the side in a circular motion, encompassing the adjacent section of the picnic table, and just like that, the air filled with warmth. Anne's fingers thawed like they were hovering above a campfire. The temperature rose as if they were seated inside a protective bubble. And the wind, just above and below where the two of them were gathered, stopped blowing.

Anne raised her eyebrows and gawked at the table.

"Better?" Jax asked.

Um, yeah, Anne thought. "Much," she said. She linked her gloved fingers together and ruminated inwardly: The temperature was decisively better. The weird, freaky, none-of-this-was-happening-or-possibly-true factor just jacked up about a hundred notches. She shook her head and cleared her throat. "So, um, why are you telling me all of this now? I mean, you obviously went to great lengths to hide your real identity, to sell me and the other girls on the whole Bryce M, who lost his little brother to the Cult of Hades five years ago story. Why would you come clean now? And why with me?" She wanted to ask him if they were all in danger, if she, in particular, was going to be... eliminated...now that she knew this earth-shattering secret, but she wasn't ready to hear the answers. Especially if the answers were *yes,* affirmative.

"*Anne...*" He leaned forward and placed his hand over hers, which literally caused her to shiver: Not only was Bryce—*Jax*—the most breathtakingly beautiful *anything* Anne had ever seen, but his supernatural presence was overwhelming. It always had been. She just hadn't understood the *why of it* before, all the heat, energy, and power she had been picking up on. "Everything changed when you called me," he said frankly.

She gulped.

"What you saw in your mirror? What you were able to channel. My sire thought it was best that we meet and speak candidly."

Anne pressed her eyelids together like a child watching a scary movie. Maybe if she held them shut for a couple of seconds, the terrifying scene playing out in front of her would be gone when she reopened them.

No such luck.

"So," she whispered sheepishly. "You spoke to your dad about me?"

Jax chuckled. "My *sire*. My...creator. The first of the seven dragon lords."

Anne jerked her hand from beneath his and held it up in the air to stop him from elaborating. *Nope. TMI. Way too much supernatural information.* "I get the gist," she murmured.

He smiled brightly. "I'm not sure you do." And then his voice became somber, his silken tone far more serious. "Anne, you were able to see something...to see someplace...none of us have been able to glimpse, despite jumping through hoops to try to make that happen." He sat back and crossed his arms over his rock-hard chest. "The whole reason I responded to you, Kari, Nicky, and Joy on Social Circle was to, hopefully, open some kind of back-end channel to the very place you just conjured so easily in a three-inch, circular mirror atop a compact of makeup."

Anne swallowed convulsively. "Powder."

"Excuse me?"

"You said *makeup*. Loose powder is different than..." She didn't complete the asinine sentence.

"A three-inch mirror atop a compact of powder," he corrected.

She nodded, feeling foolish, then quickly refocused on the original subject: "You thought if we could attract some members of the Cult of Hades, and they could attract some...pagans...then you could look through our eyes, maybe hear through our ears, get a glimpse at some underworld, using us as your looking glass?"

"Exactly like that," Jax said.

She shook her head. "I still don't get it."

He sighed, bit his lower lip, then leaned in toward her. "Imagine the first three planets in the Milky Way, the way they line up: Mercury, Venus, then Earth. Now imagine the world I come from being much like the sun in that same solar system. We are the sun, you and your friends are like Mercury, and the Cult of Hades is Venus. The underworld, where Beth and my compatriot are trapped, is like Earth, the place where the pagans reside. We wanted to look straight through the lineup—from the sun, through Mercury; farther, through Venus; then into Earth—by using your mortal senses, but now?" He held up both hands in the air. "We no longer need to go through all three planets because you, Anne, can link us directly."

"No, I can't!" Anne gestured emphatically. "*Seriously*. I mean, I'm not clairvoyant or psychic, and I can't just look into some other world whenever I feel like it. It was just early this morning, after a lot of meditation and trying. It was just some sort of fluke—I'm sure of it."

"The woman," Jax said, "the one who spoke to you—she said you were a Seer, didn't she?"

Anne shook her head slowly. "Not like what you think. Honestly, I'm just—"

"You're just sensitive, intuitive, aware of energies, beyond the obvious. It's subtle, but it's instinctive." He quickly changed tack. "Tell me this, honestly: Yesterday morning, when we all met at the coffee shop...the way you looked at me, the way you stared right through me...you felt something, didn't you? Despite the compulsion, something still felt off."

Anne licked her bottom lip, preferring not to answer. She was grasping at straws, and she knew it. This guy—this *Drag-gear-eee* —he already knew everything, so what was the point? He came from some fantastical world, beyond a freakin' portal, some other dimension, where dragons were gods and could fly around on wings and breathe fire. He lived in a lair, but the lair was beside a beach, and some massive hunter or mercenary—*whatever*— named Ghost, yeah, *Ghost* of all things, was trapped in some underworld, along with Beth. Beth had been snatched from a haunted house and taken to hell by some really bad creatures, *the pagans*. And now, this dragon-guy wanted Anne to help him and his dragon gods find—no, not find but *see*—Beth. See Ghost! They wanted their roommate back.

It wasn't sane.

It wasn't even possible.

So why did every instinct in Anne's body confirm it? Why did her soul believe it was true?

Why did this explanation make more sense than everything else they had entertained, until now, and why did Jax's story check so many boxes: Beth had disappeared, without even a hint of a struggle or a trace of foul play. *Check!* That had to be supernatural. The Cult of Hades had been real, the Wizards Witches & Ancient Theologies Bookstore had been real, and so had the ancient tome, *A Treatise on the Seven Sins*. To say nothing of the fact that Bryce M was *truly* a supernatural creature named Jax, who had just about sealed that narrative when he'd altered the weather and changed the temperature over a plain, everyday picnic table.

Check. Check. Check.

And check again!

Jax was not wrong when he said Anne had sensed something.

Grandma Betsy *had* appeared in the back seat of Anne's car, and she had said, "There are many souls at play, many dimensions, many motivations, many *deities*, but you, sweet Anne, have both a gift and a role to play. You are indeed a Seer, and your eyes will become the window of the soul for many." And the creepy, inhuman male with the bald head, bright yellow eyes, and long, pointed goatee—the one who had been tracking Joy and Anne —*had* appeared in Anne's compact mirror. She had seen him as clear as day. And she had known, intuitively, that he was somehow connected to Beth.

Check...

Check.

Damnit all to hell, but *check.*

"Your eyes will become the window of the soul for many." As if he knew exactly what Anne was thinking, Jax spoke Grandma Betsy's words aloud. "That's what she told you, right?"

Anne nodded slowly.

She had told Jax everything.

It was a little too late to take it all back.

And besides—*Beth, Beth, Beth!*—if everything was true, then Anne needed Jax every bit as much as he needed her. Jax wanted Ghost back. Anne needed Beth back. She couldn't just leave one of her best friends in hell. "So, how does this work," she said softly. "I mean, going forward? What's next? Do you still want me, Kari, Nicole, and Joy to go to King's Castle Credit Union and try to open a 'Sacred Account'? Should we still try to find a rare piece of jewelry with all that witchy stuff on it at Fred's Pawn Shop, or should we just let that go? And what about the book, *A Treatise on the Seven Sins*; what do you want us to do with it? What if these cult guys, these human worshippers, still come after me and my friends?"

Jax stood up, stepped over the bench, and sauntered to where Anne was seated. Without speaking a word, he placed two strong hands on each of her petite, narrow shoulders, and a stream of calm, tranquil energy flowed through the Nordic-blue parka, Anne's thin cashmere sweater, and down her chest, through the heart chakra, the solar plexus, the sacral, and finally, the root chakras.

Anne released a breath she didn't even know she was holding.

"First," Jax said gently, "you and your friends are in no more danger than you were before—just like before, we are close by... watching. And no, you will not be *eliminated* because you know my secret, my true identity. Your memories can be altered, erased. They *will* be altered when all of this is over, regardless of the outcome. No, you do not need to proceed to the credit union or the pawn shop at this juncture—let's wait and see what happens first. My sire would like the ancient book, so I will be taking it with me when I return to the Pantheon. As for what happens next, you need to listen carefully: Say nothing to your girlfriends—they are safer not knowing. Simply tell them that Bryce M called you directly, asked for the *Treatise on the Seven Sins*, and told you to lay low for a minute. Then don't worry about the bank or the pawn shop, unless and until you receive further notice. Do not tell them about the male you saw in your mirror. If possible, don't mention the underworld or Ghost. As for your prayers, your soulful interventions on Beth's behalf, I have nothing but respect and reverence. Clearly, the apparition, this Grandma Betsy, is working toward the same ends as we are, and I would never interfere with any soul's connection to its Creator."

He took a deep breath, ostensibly to allow all he had said to settle before pressing on: "At some point in the not-too-distant future, I may call on you for that same intercession. That said, should any human member of the Cult of Hades try to harm you or one of your girlfriends, know that you are now under the Diamond Lair's protection—your assistance is not without reward and acknowledgment. Such human miscreants are quite easy for us to dispatch, and as I said, we *will* be watching, Miss Liu."

With that, he brushed the palm of his hand over her hair and filled her entire being with a fresh infusion of peaceful energy. Then he bent to her ear and whispered, "Lord Dragos requires your presence, beyond the portal, in the Temple of Seven, prior to next Wednesday at midnight. That's an inflexible deadline, if you get my meaning, at least if we hope to rescue Ghost and Beth from their...untenable circumstances...in time to save them. There is an oracle pool in the temple, and the Seven believe it will magnify your special abilities. The dragon lords will be able to see all that you see and so much more, should your spirit be immersed in its waters. Shh," he added, as she started to murmur an objection. "Anne, don't worry. We need you. The dragon lords need you. Lord Dragos needs you to find his son, and I will take you through the portal myself and stay with you. I promise."

Anne felt her stomach lurch and her breakfast rise, heading in the wrong direction. She swallowed hard, pushed it back down, and waited while her stomach settled. "Wh—when?" she muttered weakly. "I mean, the Temple of Seven, traveling through the portal?"

"Not sure yet. Definitely before midnight next Wednesday, but likely not today. Lord Dragos wants to pore through the ancient tome first. The Seven still need to discuss this latest development in greater detail. But be ready, anytime, night or day, because I will probably come get you on a moment's notice."

Anne was too shocked to speak.

Too scared to reply or ask further questions, even about the so-called "inflexible deadline." What in the world did that mean —*if we hope to reach Ghost and Beth in time to save them?*—and what in the world had just happened?

All of it...

Any of it.

What had Anne done, and was it too late to get out of it? How would she hide any of this from the others? And the book... the tome...as far as Anne knew, Joy still had it! She had never taken it to Nicole's or had a chance to show it to Kari. So how the heck did that work?

Anne was about to hyperventilate!

"Look beneath your purse."

Anne shot up straight. *That wasn't Jax speaking!* The voice belonged to Grandma Betsy.

Anne twisted around to peer beyond her shoulders; her eyes darted around the park; then she looked up at Jax to gauge his reaction—but the supernatural being had not heard it. Not a single word. And he had not felt a preternatural presence.

Holy shit.

Could this get any stranger?

Jax took a reflexive step back in response to Anne's sudden movement, her strange behavior, but he seemed none the wiser as she lifted her purse from the distressed wooden bench and gawked at the ancient leather tome lying beneath it.

A Treatise on the Seven Sins!

She gulped.

Fear is the main cause of suffering...

She reminded herself of Buddha's words.

Then, "Here," she said, her voice lightly croaking. She was going to need some Xanax or Valium before this whole supernatural encounter was over. As if on cue, the cold wind, once again, started blowing. Some sort of rodent scampered across the worn, grassy path that led to the picnic table, and a rare crack of winter's thunder retorted in the heavens.

Anne shivered and clutched the lapel of her parka, as Jax bent forward, grabbed the book, and tucked it beneath his black leather duster. "I'll be in touch," he said softly. "If you need me before then, use the phone number I gave you."

Anne sighed. "The phone number you gave us for Bryce."

Jax smiled, and despite the gravity of the situation, Anne's nerves, her spine, and a significant portion of her reticent heart melted.

"Jax," she said plainly, "tell me the truth: Do you really think we can get Beth and your friend back?"

The supernatural male shrugged his powerful shoulders, his features hardened like clay in the sunlight, and his voice cast a hint of fierce determination: "I don't know, Anne, but we're gonna try like hell. Remember what we talked about, and try to take some comfort in the knowledge that we're watching... working day and night on the same mutual problem...not gonna stop 'til we find a solution." Before Anne could reply, he nodded, then winked, grasped an odd diamond amulet hanging from his neck, and simply vanished.

CHAPTER TWENTY-FIVE

D espite the obvious importance of his newfound status as prince of the Pagan Shit Post, Ghost couldn't find it in his heart to parade around in the heavy, opulent, gold and blood-red robe. He did, however, find the golden scepter necessary for obvious reasons.

Carrying the gawdy stick was proof of his status, new rank, and authority should someone in the castle try to challenge any of the three. Who knew if Lord Drakkar had loosed an entire legion of those damnable, two-headed hellhounds wandering like a pack of wild wolves through the halls of the castle with one inviolable command in their twofold, odious brains: *Eat Ghost!* Not to mention, Ghost had recently murdered that witch, Felicity, so any number of demons or shades might be pissed, especially Salyn Stryke, who appeared to deeply appreciate the witch's oral talents. The scepter could be used to halt an ambush, best an enemy, or buy a few more days with Ghost's head and amulet still intact, should some wayward pagan try to prematurely end Ghost's sudden and ridiculous, unwarranted reign.

Yeah, the scepter was definitely necessary. Although, as it

stood, Ghost had only encountered one pagan thus far, Psion Ripclaw, a gnarly sin eater who had passed Ghost in the basement hallway, nodded, and promptly averted his eyes.

The shit was eerie.

Ghost shook off the memory—he needed to stay grounded in the present moment.

He tucked the golden wand beneath his left armpit, pressed his upper arm against his side, and continued through the castle's cellar on his way to the apothecary to scope things out before making a crucial visit to the dungeon-level slave quarters: The way Ghost figured, there was no way he or Beth could venture in and out of the medieval dispensary a dozen times a day for the next forty-eight hours—collect as much of the herb as they needed, as early as they must. They still had to brew and extract the desired medicine from the plants, store or collect it in airtight vessels, and figure out a way to get it into the feast day's wine and mead.

But one step at a time.

For now, Ghost would use a combination of his position as prince of the underworld and his metaphysical powers of mind control to sear an absolute and overriding command into the minds of a dozen different human servants: *Enter the castle apothecary at the hour I give you, fetch a bushel of belladonna and an airtight amphora, and wrap both in an ordinary gray blanket. Place the blanket in the plain wooden trunk situated at the bottom of the staircase at the end of the hall leading to the main castle, first-floor bedchambers. Take any vessels or blankets found in the same back to the apothecary with you—rinse and repeat.*

Rinse and repeat.

The compulsion would have to be laced with an automatic *Delete* and *Reinstall* command, plus a highly dangerous false confession, should any of the servants get caught.

Each hourly compulsion would be automatically deleted

from the servant's memory the moment he or she carried out the command, then spontaneously reinstalled the next time their shift came up. Should the servant get caught, they would confess to a duplicitous plot, concocted with the help of several other servants, to destroy the highest-ranking member of their own ilk. In other words, human politics. Human treachery. They would confess to wanting to see a fellow human slave slowly poisoned and eventually killed. Ghost hoped no one in the castle would give two shits about powerless humans plotting to destroy one another. If anything, the pagans or the king would find the whole thing amusing, industrious, and possibly worth rewarding.

Regardless, it was the best Ghost could do under the circumstances.

And to pull something that intricate and difficult off, he would likely have to feed from each and every one of them, extract a modicum of their blood, heat, and essence, which in truth, he had to do anyway. It had been three months and four days since he had been forced to drain one of Lord Drakkar's personal slaves, one of his favored seven, to the point of exsanguination in the throne room. Ghost needed to reanimate his inner dragon—he needed to regenerate his serpent's fire.

And so here he was, moving cautiously but freely in and out of various castle passageways, trying to avoid both hellhounds and pagans, while setting his and Beth's escape plan in motion.

His and Beth's...

That wasn't exactly accurate.

The plan itself had been strictly one-sided and top-down dictatorial—my way or the highway, if Ghost was being frank—but that wasn't the part that was wreaking havoc on his equilibrium.

Not even close.

Bethany Kayla Reid, his dragyra...

That tin tub, his *fated's* tears, and the way she had drawn him, like a moth to a flame, with her eyes, her innocence...her body. What the actual hell had happened back in that bedchamber?

Ghost shook his head, trying to untangle the miry cobwebs, and refocused his attention on the path and plot ahead of him. He did not want to explore that particular shadowy territory, anything to do with confusion...*feelings?*...or Beth. Any one of three could derail him.

As it stood, it was probably best to spend the next forty-eight hours as far away from the bedchamber as possible, at least leading up to the potentially explosive, impending interlude: exposing his mind, thoughts, and psyche to the whole damn pagan underworld via the mystical Sinners' Cave.

In truth, if Ghost was being smart...strategic...he needed to spend the next two days in as close proximity to Requiem Pyre, Killian Kross, and the whole damn underworld congress as possible: learning castle politics, asking questions about the court's inner workings, showing a deep and abiding interest in the *future* of the government, the palace's long-term objectives. He needed to convince his new pagan brethren that he planned on hanging around for a while.

A long, long while.

Definitely beyond this coming weekend.

And he needed to sell the whole princely prospect as something he was buying into, hook, line, and sinker.

Even more important, he needed to lead all eyes, ears, and devious minds as far away from Beth as possible: keep the pagans' attention off his female. It could not look like Ghost and the human slave, consort—whatever they were calling her since Ghost's elevation—were conspiring together, sequestered alone, all day and night, whispering, plotting, scheming, whilst hiding away from the others.

No, not if Ghost was truly Lord Drakkar's ambitious nephew.

Not if Ghost was to be remotely trusted, moderately believed, and eventually accepted.

Yes...

He would have to pop in and out of the bedchamber, both to get some sleep and to help with the preparation of the belladonna.

And yes...

If he were being honest, manufactured absence would also soothe his own beleaguered spirit—there were way too many nightmares, unseen spirits, and ancient if not deeply entombed secrets provoked by the castle's unseen powers.

Nope!

He wanted no part of that dark, paranormal shit to stir his own internal demons.

And yes, his dragyra would be upset, if not angry. Beth wouldn't like Ghost's absence one bit—but she would be safer for it. Ultimately, it would be in Beth's best interest for Ghost to maintain a clear head and vacant heart, to keep his eyes on the prize, so to speak. If and when the two of them ever got free of the underworld, if and when they were back in the Pantheon, all the power would shift back to Beth: Ghost's dragyra would choose conversion by fire, or death as a consequence of refusal. His dragyra would choose to accept—or shun—what the dragons lords had forced upon both of them. And even if the female consented to the fiery ritual, she would be free to choose what happened thereafter: whether she and Ghost would remain in the Pantheon, as some semblance of a couple; live separate lives—one earthside, the other beyond the portal—or whether they ever interacted or spoke again.

Yeah, not exactly what his sire intended when he undoubt-edly chose to force this premature mating, but *fuck Lord Dragos and the wings he flew in on*—Ghost was prepared to violate the Fourth Principal Law if it came down to it. And as long as his dragyra was changed, immortal...safe...when he did so, then let the chips fall where they may.

Even if they fell along with his head.

Along with his amulet.

And along with his last breath of life.

Even if they fell—and landed—as a statue in the Garden of Grace.

So be it.

CHAPTER TWENTY-SIX

I t was rare indeed, though not unheard of, for a primordial deity to spare a bit of its essence in order to travel, intervene, or just...look. Yet at this point, Lord Dragos would have done so thrice: First, when his hatchling, Ghost, had prayed for intercession in order to leave his physical body, deep in the bowels of the underworld; next, when the lord had sent a piece of his own formidable spirit, in the form of an icy wind, into Nicole Perez's apartment to seal the influence of the Seven Sins into each human female's psyche; and now, again, as he exhaled anima from his own sacred breath and sent it tunneling through the interstellar portal to look upon those same four souls as they went about their paltry human lives on Earth.

He spied on Kari Baker first, observing the human female as she waited tables in a high-end Italian restaurant, odd selection for such a rare Irish beauty. No matter. There was nothing to see or garner here. No wicked human sycophants with pentacles and swords etched along the napes of their necks, dining on pasta, risotto, or chicken Parmesan, no evidence that the female was defying Anne's request to lie low for a while and abort any excursions to the pawn shop or the clandestine Cult of Hades' King's Castle Credit Union. Unlike Anne, Kari didn't appear to have a single clairvoyant bone in her body.

Lord Dragos inhaled, drawing his essence back from the restaurant, then turned his attention to the small, three-person law office where Nicole Perez worked as a paralegal. He exhaled slowly, yet again, and a fragment of his essence was there, an eerie breeze, more like a waft of moist, frosty air settling behind a light blue partition, perhaps five or six feet from Ms. Perez's leather chair.

Nicole stiffened and spun around, staring blankly into the air.

She inhaled sharply and grasped the cross nestled above her blouse.

Well, well, kudos to you, my lovely Latina lackey. At least you know power when you feel it, even as you remain blind as a bat.

Once again, there was nothing to be gained by the visit: no energetic evidence of Cult of Hades' interactions, no deep, sudden insights that might shed light on Bethany or Ghost, and no cause for concern, alarm, or correction, should any of Jaxtapherion's compulsions have lifted.

As if.

Jax was a son of the Diamond Lair.

His compulsions were as solid as spiritual tungsten, greater than titanium, chromium, or steel, and Nicole Perez was a nonentity, at best—the one Dragos needed was Anne.

He sighed, a cross between frustration and impatience, for surely, Anne would be in the Temple of Seven soon. And once she was immersed in the sacred waters of the powerful Oracle Pool, they would *all* see through the eyes of this prophetess and discern many secrets through her sensitive soul. Much like Lord Dragos had already discerned from the ancient tome she had given Jaxtapherion...

Ah yes, the cryptic book.

A Treatise on the Seven Sins.

Lord Dragos had been scouring the text from multiple angles since earlier that morning, from the moment Jax had brought it back to the temple, and unlike the human women, who couldn't read it anyway—the 1100 AD transliteration was in Greek—Lord Dragos had not only read the ancient manuscript but scanned beneath the pages to intuit and visualize the original logographic, syllabic, and alphabetic elements within the 3000 BC hieroglyphs.

If there had been anything hidden within the transcript, anything to be discerned or divined that might provide further insight into Ghost's unholy predicament, Lord Dragos would have uncovered it, firsthand.

But alas, no...

While interesting and insightful, the fact that Lord Drakkar had been worshipped by both human priests and ordinary Egyptians, even in 3000 BC, did nothing to help Lord Dragos now. There was no unexpected, fortuitous drawing of the secret pagan underworld tucked within the ancient pages, nor was there any description of dungeons, torture, slave and servile practices, all things Lord Dragos might extrapolate to potentially apply to his son. There were just three random references that gave the dragon lord...pause...references that sent electrical currents up his tail, along his spine, and into his serpentine skull.

First, within the treatise on pride, the book spoke about the majesty and utmost superiority of the deity secretly worshipped by the cult and the priest, and within that elaborate description, there were many references made to the colors black, gold, and red—but not just red—*blood-red*, which had obvious implications. While none of that should have been of any interest to Lord Dragos, Keeper of Diamonds and ruler of the same, the literal word *gold* as well as the words *blood-red* continued to jump from the page. They practically glowed with emphasis as if outlined in a yellow highlighting pen. And second, within the treatise on *envy*, something altogether different had occurred— every time Lord Dragos had read the actual word, he had heard the echo of a female's laughter. He had heard the word *Salem*, and he had heard the word *witch*. And while his vast omniscience might allow him to search the annals of history as far back as he wished—nay, to search the energy, the lives, and the very minds of long-deceased souls—he could not pierce the veil of the pagan underworld, for his ancient brother's power was equal to his own.

Still, he had divined the realms of which he had access, and nothing of practical value had come to him, save the name of a sixteen-year-old, true Salem witch who had disappeared from Earth in the late 1600s...

Felicity Rebecca Payne.

So what.

As far as Lord Dragos could conjecture, the Cult of Hades, or Lord Drakkar himself, may have had something to do with her disappearance: yet again, so what!

The third random divination had to do with the treatise on *wrath*, and this one had shaken Lord Dragos to his core, even as it had shown him nothing tangible. He simply knew that all in the underworld was not as it seemed: What appeared benevolent was malevolent indeed; what appeared generous was a means to an end; and what appeared as an occasion to share honor and union was an opportunity—coated, steeped, and baked in *wrath*—to strip Ghostaniaz of his last vestige of hope...or resistance.

What in the name of all that was unholy did any of that foresight mean!

What was happening with Ghost right now, and what was Lord Drakkar Hades up to?

Lord Dragos shook his head and snorted as he withdrew in

entirety from the paralegal's office and streamed the scant trail of his essence to a real estate agency instead.

Joy Green.

Columbine Home & Hearth...

How quaint.

Before he could pass through the wall of the three-story brick building, he spotted the voluptuous female outdoors, in the agency's parking lot, fumbling with her keys whilst trying to get into her car. No, not fumbling with the cumbersome keys—too unsteady to properly use them.

She dropped them.

She squatted down to pick them up.

And an angry human male hovered over her.

Well, well...

It didn't take a deity to divine what was happening—in an instant, Lord Dragos knew everything. Joy was being harassed—nay, assaulted—by a male named Mitch Moretti, a human syco-phant whom Joy had met briefly in the Wizards Witches & Ancient Theologies Bookstore. Mitch was a Swede, not an Ital-ian, who was using a fake moniker to hide a series of nefarious actions committed on behalf of the Cult of Hades. The male was indeed under the current influence of a sin eater named Psion Ripclaw, and although Psion had influenced Mitch to "follow up with the ladies who purchased the ancient book, see if they may be potential converts," Mitch's own pride, greed, and lust had clearly gotten the best of him.

Pride...

He wanted a woman such as Joy on his arm: her physical beauty, her monetary accomplishments, her ample, voluptuous bosom.

Greed...

He saw Columbine Home & Hearth as a personal wealth- and cult-building opportunity, a chance to set up a franchise of companies that could all double as recruitment, meeting, and ceremonial facilities. Only, Mitch's *lust* had gotten the best of him. He had propositioned Joy Green several times, and she had promptly turned him down. She had rejected him, plain and simple, and now he was doing all his thinking with another, less intelligent organ.

Perhaps Lord Dragos had left out *wrath*.

Either way, it was clear that Psion Ripclaw had tremendous and longstanding influence over the prideful, horny human, and it was equally clear that things were about to get incredibly nasty, which would not do, as Jax had already promised Anne Liu—and thus, her human girlfriends by association—the full protection of the Diamond Lair.

To be sure, Lord Dragos couldn't care less about the human female or Jaxtapherion's noble promise, but he wanted Anne Liu to be trusting, willing, and open when she entered the sacred Temple of Seven and was immersed in the oracle waters. Lord Dragos could not afford to allow resistance or resentment to take seed in Anne's psyche. He could not allow such a wound to Anne's psychic soul...at least not now.

The female was just too gifted.

And at least for the present moment, her *gifted* spirit was wide open.

As if that fact was not important enough, Miss Liu was also being influenced by a deceased angelic presence—*go figure!*

No, Anne's energy did not need to be disturbed by yet another friend's sudden, tragic circumstances, and not when Lord Dragos could simply peer, right here and now, into Mitch Moretti's mind—Michael Svenson's mind—and see what he could see regarding Psion Ripclaw and any potential interactions between the demon host...and Ghostaniaz. If Psion's imprint on the human male was as strong as it seemed, then any recent connections might still remain in the aura.

Done.

And done.

Yes, Mitch was under Psion's influence, but the two had never met in person. Thus, Psion's residual imprint was faint at best, yet and still—the sin eater had spiked blue-black hair, glowing obsidian eyes with snow-white pupils, and Nordic bronze beads festooned in his beard. Psion had passed Ghost recently, in some sort of dark, sunken, narrow hall, which meant Ghostaniaz was still alive, and when they had traversed like ships in the night, Psion had nodded his head and averted his eyes in some sort of show of...obedience...or deference?

What the devil?

The demon had felt only contempt, yet he had treated Ghostaniaz in a submissive manner.

Interesting...

Very interesting.

But that was all Lord Dragos could perceive: There was nothing more to discern, just the faint hint of two large bodies passing in a hollow shaft, a whiff of deference, and an almost forced sense of regard, if not obeisance, on the sin eater's part. According to the dimmest projection of Psion's psychic energy, transferred through the aura of this human male, the demon's behavior had not been genuine, but rather based on protocol and good sense.

Very well.

Lord Dragos' ethereal outing had not been in vain. And as for Joy Green and the savage encounter about to take place in the parking lot—in front of her very own office, no less? Well, the matter did need tending, but it was beneath Lord Dragos' station. Saving humans who had not prayed—nay, begged—for interces- sion from a dragon lord was a level just too low for the diamond deity to stoop to. That was why mercenaries had been created.

Lord Dragos chuckled inwardly; then he exhaled slowly. He

fashioned the ensuing breath into the shape of a column and began to turn it counterclockwise.

Round and round.

Faster and faster.

He spun the column into a gyrating funnel, rotating backward, until time in the parking lot nearly stood still.

Jax! He sent the telepathic call beyond Earth's boundaries, across the portal, and into the Pantheon, using only a scintilla of his spirit to do so. *I assume you and your brethren are keeping track of the four human females and the goings-on surrounding them.*

Yes, sire, Jax immediately shot back.

Then why aren't you doing your job?

Already on my way.

No! Lord Dragos thundered. *The female already knows you as Bryce. Send Romani in your stead.*

Yes, sire.

And do not kill the worthless human—we don't need a pack of pagans earthside, investigating or interfering, before we have a chance to meet with Anne. With that, Lord Dragos withdrew the funnel as well as his partitioned anima from the earth, coalescing his full essence, once more, inside the Temple of Seven.

CHAPTER TWENTY-SEVEN

J oy's hand was shaking so violently, she couldn't work the key fob to unlock the door of her Honda Accord. She pressed the wrong button twice, and then she dropped her keys.

"Nooo!"

Shit.

She dropped down to scoop them up and gasped in alarm as the toe of her black high heel butted against the tip of the fob and sent the entire key chain scattering beneath the Honda's undercarriage.

What the hell was happening?

One minute, that creepy guy from the Wizards Witches & Ancient Theologies Bookstore had strolled boldly into the first-floor lobby of Joy's real estate agency, catching Joy off guard. The next, he had barraged her with a series of bizarre, disturbing questions: Why had she and her friend purchased the ancient book? What was her interest in sin and the occult? Could she interpret the ancient Greek, or did she need someone to assist her?

Someone like him.

Joy had taken several startled steps back, and each time, the creepy guy—Mitch Moretti—had taken an equal, bold step forward.

What the fuck?

And in truth, Joy didn't have the book anymore. It had vanished like a puff of smoke earlier that morning—either that, or Joy was losing her mind, and she had placed it somewhere she couldn't remember. She had almost told Mitch exactly that, but he had changed the subject too quickly. While crowding her into the narrow glass doorway of her agency's foyer, he had bombarded her with a second series of even more disturbing questions: Do you find me attractive? Can I take you to dinner? How about we get away for the weekend and study the book together?

Was he kidding?

No.

Just...no.

Hell would freeze over, and pigs would fly before Joy would go anywhere with a guy like Moretti—the level of *ewww* and the extent of *yuck* were too mind-numbing to even contemplate. And she had tried, in much more tactful, subtle language, of course, to relay that very sentiment.

Never.

Ever...

Not gonna happen.

And that's when Mitch Moretti had lost his shit, snatched her by the throat, and pressed his groin against Joy's stomach. That's when Joy had kneed him in the nuts, shoved at his chest, and punched the delusional fool in the esophagus. She had spun around like a bat fleeing hell, dashed through the heavy glass doors, and fumbled for her keys as she sprinted to her car.

Only, the crazy, amorous idiot had chased after her, shouting curses so vile and obscenities so profane that Joy had lost her concentration, her coordination, and her ability to operate her key fob. Having dropped the entire key chain, she had tried to bend over and pick it up, only to boot the entire jumbled ensemble farther out of reach. And now, as she swept the ground beneath her car, frantically sliding her hand back and forth across the concrete, an icy wind began to swirl behind her, the stone and pitch inside the dark gray asphalt widened into 3D focus, and time felt like it was slowing down, until it was nearly standing still.

Joy could hear her own heart beating in suspended animation.

Then, "Where do you think you're going, bitch!" Mitch was standing right above her, slurring his words, panting, grunting, and breathing in sluggish, drawn-out inhales and exhales. "Get up!"

Joy's head was spinning, and she couldn't think. It was as if her thoughts were mired in quicksand, and she was trying to reason her way through sludge. Still, she had to come up with a way out of the predicament, and she needed to do something fast.

Maybe...

If she could just reach her keys...

She could stand up, turn around, and gouge Mitch's eyes out.

Or maybe...

If she could just get to her cell phone, she could bypass the login and call 911.

But then what?

It would take too long for the police to arrive—the operator would become a witness to whatever Mitch did next, to whatever Joy was about to experience.

The operator...

The police...

Nine...one...one...

The brain fog was too heavy, and Joy began to croon in fear.

Mitch Moretti was going to kill her—or possibly worse—and there was nothing she could do to stop it...change it...because her brain no longer worked. She felt a hard, slow, heavy weight slam into the back of her head, and on some distant level, she understood that the violent, unhinged asshole had just punched her.

"I said get up!"

Get up...

Get up?

She wasn't sure she knew how.

She covered her head with her arms and ducked down, staring blankly at the asphalt and the key chain just inches away from her well-manicured hand. And then, just as curiously as the icy wind had appeared, a sudden gust of heat swept in, taking its place, and time sped up, immeasurably.

Joy snatched her key chain.

She lodged the blade of the largest key between the knuckles of her second and third fingers, and then she spun around, leaped to her feet, and raised her arm to Mitch's eye level. She was just about to throw a violent jab when she inhaled sharply, took a stutter step back, and dropped the keys, this time on purpose. She braced both palms against the door of the Honda, her mouth dropped open, and she gawked in silence.

What in the name of Sam Hill was that!

There was a circular black hole in the shape of a windmill, maybe ten feet tall, five feet wide, spinning, whirling, turning, like a giant fan in front of her, and flames the color of diamond, emeralds, sapphires...topaz were shooting out the center of the cavity. Joy sucked in air, then exhaled slowly, muttering a string of broken, unintelligible syllables as a giant Adonis stepped out of the whirling, rainbow-colored...gateway.

Holy.

Shit.

The guy had to be at least six-foot-four, strapped with muscles from his neck to his ankles, and the most powerful...*anything*...Joy had ever encountered: flaming diamond irises, surrounding saffron pupils; thick, silky, golden-wheat hair tied back in some sort of leather fastener; a clean-shaven face with perfectly symmetrical features; and a flawless, bow-shaped mouth, the upper lip sculpted like the riser and the limbs, the bottom fashioned like a thick, taut string.

"Oh, my Lord," Joy whispered beneath bated breath, "I think those are actual wings." Had a guardian angel come to save her? But...but, come from where?

Before she could ponder the questions any further, the angel, Adonis, retrieved a shiny silver dagger from a sash around his waist, twirled it in his fingers, inverting the blade and the pommel, and then he grasped the cross guard in his fist, lunged forward, and struck Mitch Moretti in the back of the head with one clean, crisp *thwack!*

The greasy-haired bastard dropped like a stone.

The angel, Adonis, booted his body into a thick patch of grass at least ten feet away, before twirling the dagger once more in his fingers and dropping the blade back into the sash. "I apologize for any discomfort," he said casually. "I got here as soon as I could."

Joy gawked like a ninny.

She licked her lips, cleared her throat, and leaned forward for reasons she could not quite articulate. "Oh, um...yeah. Okay." *Well, that was intelligent.* She bent her elbow, raised her arm, and tried to lean casually against the hood of the car; only her elbow slipped, and she almost fell down. The angel, Adonis, caught her by the arm, and she felt light-headed. "Thank you."

His smile could have rivaled the sun. "You're welcome. You okay?"

Joy smiled back.

He raised his perfect eyebrows.

She smiled some more.

"*You okay?*" he repeated, in that million-dollar voice.

"Nope," she finally said. Then, "Can I get you some...water... or, um, maybe some water?" She flicked her wrist in the direction of the building. "My office is just right inside, and, uh, there's a kitchen...with, um, lots of...water."

This time, he chuckled, a deep, low, sensual sound, before taking a gentle step forward, tunneling his hand in the back of her curly, blonde-and-black twists, and feeling her scalp with the pads of his fingers. He withdrew his hand and checked his fingers for blood. "I don't think he did any damage."

Joy exhaled softly, fanned her face with her hand, and then her eyes grew wide with alarm. Her knees were failing—she was going to pass out. She couldn't control it, and she couldn't reel it in. "I think...I'm sorry, but I don't feel well."

The angel, Adonis, wrapped his powerful arm around her waist and tugged her forward with his forearm, the palm of his hand pressing their bodies together. "Not angel...or Adonis," he rasped in her ear. "Romani Dragos. *Roman.* And I'm sorry, but I'll have to pass on the water, though I hate to leave so soon." He brushed his finger along the side of her jaw, and the corner of his mouth quirked up in a smile. "Another time and place...another world or species...you are truly a breathtaking woman, Joy Green." Then he bent his mouth to hers and kissed her, exhaling a mist that felt like flame, smelled like sandalwood, and tasted like honey.

Joy reached for his jaw.

She wanted to touch him, but...*but*...what the hell was she doing?

She was standing in the parking lot, posing beside her car with one arm raised up in the air like a ridiculous Grecian statue! She glanced around the parking lot: Her keys were on the ground, her dress was ruffled, and the back of her head was kind of...tingling. She cleared her throat and furrowed her brows.

What the actual hell?

Last she remembered, she had been in her office, thumbing through a file; then she had headed out to the lobby to get her mail. And now...*now*...she was standing in the parking lot beside her car, posing like some idiotic human statue. "Oh man," she whispered, feeling more than a little concerned. "You need to start eating breakfast, Joy." She thought back to earlier that morning: She had not taken any medication, she had slept fine the night before, and while there may have been something bothering her—*maybe something missing, like an earring or a book?*—that didn't explain her odd behavior.

An earring...

Or a book.

Hmm.

Joy had not had time to read a novel in ages, and Anne still had that creepy tome from the witchy bookstore, so...so what could be missing, other than Joy's good sense?

Yeah, Joy had lost her right mind.

That's what had happened.

She shivered, tucked her arm to her side, then bent down to pick up her keys, which she promptly placed in her purse. Heading back to the building, she turned around and stared blankly at a tall, ruffled, empty patch of grass. She squinted, scrunched up her nose, and tried to reach for an image—*retrieve a memory?*—something just outside her awareness.

Nope.

Nada...

There was nothing there.

Shaking her head, she resolved to set an appointment for an annual physical, posthaste, accompanied with comprehensive bloodwork.

Too much stress.

Poor eating.

Yeah, that's what this was.

And Joy would have to do better, starting right away, before her current condition got any worse.

CHAPTER TWENTY-EIGHT

THE PAGAN UNDERWORLD ~ LATER THAT NIGHT

S leep was an amazing thing.

A remarkable state of renewal, at least when there were no nightmares present.

Even a lion or a grizzly bear looked innocent when sleeping. As did a mercenary. A son of a dragon. A broken but compassionate—reckless yet pragmatic—soul, a male who was bound by chains, mired in thorns, and formed like a statue from broken shards of glass.

Bethany gathered the heavy wool blanket tighter around her shoulders, even as she tucked her knees to her chest and continued to stare at Ghost through the dim, banked light of the bedchamber's archaic stone fireplace.

He was actually sleeping.

Not tossing or turning.

His features weren't strained, and he wasn't calling out in terror or shouting a mysterious name. As her eyes traced his hard but classical jawline, much like she had done earlier, while in the tin tub, she could almost hear his voice in her head, repeating all he had said when he had returned from his foray in the castle apothecary, the slave quarter dorms, and every hidden nook and cranny—every dark cavern, winding passageway, and recessed alcove—in the Pagan Palace. "Not gonna be able to snag a brass key. Not even possible—we'll need another plan."

Ghost had explained that the pagans kept their brass keys secured on their physical bodies twenty-four-seven. They wore them as amulets around their necks. They had special pouches or pockets sewn into belt loops. And some even had flesh-and-blood compartments carved into their skin to carry the valuable implements as surgically imbedded implants, like microchips of sorts. Still others had them inked into their epidermis, like brass-colored tattoos, which they could manipulate or retrieve through the general use of sorcery. Either way, stealing a brass key to unlock The Deep was "dead upon arrival, no pun intended."

Ghost had said he would use the scepter, instead, to get through the keyhole on the outside of the cellar door—he would either break it with the golden dragon's mouth or wield it against another pagan to steal his key on Ghost and Bethany's way out the door.

Bethany shivered beneath the otherwise warm wool blanket.

There were so many miracles Ghost had to pull off.

Perhaps too many...

And maybe that was why she hadn't completely panicked or become angry as hell when he had told her he planned to keep his distance—or at least as much as possible—until after the public "shit show" in the Sinners' Cave. Ghost planned to spend as much time as possible during the day with Requiem Pyre and Killian Kross. He needed to try to convince Drakkar's congress that he was truly with them, long term, and he wanted to keep all eyes, ears, and dangerous, lustful minds as far away from Bethany as possible.

Maybe that was why she had taken him seriously when he'd told her she needed to use the time wisely, think about what she wanted to do, going forward, if they did manage to get out of the underworld: whether she felt brave enough to go through with the conversion in the temple, or whether she was truly ready—and defiant enough—to trade her life and his for freedom, autonomy, and one final, glorious chance to give the ultimate fourth finger to anyone who would assume to dictate her destiny or prescribe her future.

He had said the decision was *hers* to make.

And the very idea of it had blown her mind.

Maybe that was why she had trusted him to continue to stop in, if only to help collect and extract the belladonna—they had already received eight batches of the deadly herb, via the trunk at the end of the hallway, since Ghost had made her the promise. The fact that he had circled back at least three times to drop it off and get it steeping in the tin tub by way of several buckets of water and mystical, hot red fire had gone a long way to ease her anxiety and build her trust. The fact that he had *fed* on no less than a dozen human slaves to set the feast day plan into motion—he had sucked their blood, expunged their heat, and drawn from their very life essence in order to control their minds—yeah, well, that had made her want to take off running and screaming until her legs gave way beneath her, and her lungs collapsed from exhaustion.

Who had the power to do such a thing?

What kind of being could control another's thoughts, behaviors, and memories...

Ghost could—that's who.

And if Bethany was being perfectly honest, none of that had anything to do with the reason she was up this late, huddled beneath a woolen blanket, or staring at the dragyri like an artist who had been commissioned to paint an exact replica of his body and features. None of that had anything to do with the urgency in her heart or the breathlessness in her lungs. No, Bethany was still reeling from what had happened that morning in the tub, when she had seen Ghost's spirit, the statuesque soul of a timeless warrior, before the bust of his being had splintered into so many shards of glass. She unwittingly reached out with a tentative finger and lightly traced the arch of one brow, the deep, high angle of a rugged cheekbone, and the linear plane of his hard-set jaw.

His phantom-blue pupils flew open, and his hand shot to her wrist. "Don't."

She drew back her arm, but her wrist didn't budge.

He tightened his fist around it. "Beth, you're playing with fire. Just...don't."

She gasped and studied his heavily muscled forearm, her heart beating a tempo faster. "Not playing, Ghost." The words came out through whispered breath.

His dark brows narrowed. "What are you doing? Why are you up so late?"

She gulped.

"Beth?"

"I was watching you sleep."

He exhaled slowly. "*Beth...*"

"When you aren't tossing or turning, when you aren't... having a nightmare...your chest rises and falls in such smooth, even valleys and crests."

"*Ah, shiiit.*"

"But the cast of your jaw—it never slackens. It always stays in that hard, stubborn line."

He released her wrist, sat straight up, and grasped her larynx with the same taut hand, applying pressure with his thumb and the side of his forefinger to her now quivering throat. "It never slackens because I'm not a yielding man."

Despite her trepidation, Bethany grasped Ghost's forearm, and she did not try to force his hand away from her neck. "You aren't a man at all, Ghost. You're a hired soldier, an instrument of war, a rebellious son, and a defiant loner. A Dragyr. A supernatural creature. But no, never a man." With a boldness she didn't know she possessed, she released his forearm, raised her hand, and began to trace the same curious outline of his tense, angular jaw. "In your own hard, unforgiving way, at least when you sleep, you're—"

"Hateful," he supplied, "purely, entirely...*always* hateful."

She shook her head.

His eyes flashed with warning. "Damaged, Beth. Hateful, damaged, and far, *far* more dangerous than you realize. *Stop*."

"Beautiful," she whispered.

His eyes flashed like sparks shooting out from a flame, and his hand tightened around her larynx. "You're insane."

"You weren't always like this."

"What the fuck!" he bellowed.

"I don't believe you were born full of hate."

"My past is off-limits—remember, Beth?"

"I know, but I think you were taught—"

"You're like a baby fuckin' moth just flittin' around a bonfire!" he stormed. "Too young to know shit about the world around you, too fragile to survive beyond this one reckless flight, and too ignorant to recognize that the flames right in front of you promise nothing but pain, torture, or death."

"Death?" Bethany said softly. "No. Not death. Maybe...passion."

Ghost's lip turned up in a parody of a smile, and he chuckled, low in his throat. "*Ah, Beth*...I almost feel sorry for you."

With that, she snatched his arm and tried to wrench it away from her throat, all the while holding his severe, witchy eyes in an unyielding stare of her own. "Ditto," she lashed out.

He blanched.

And then he released his grip, grasped a fistful of her hair, just below the crown of her head, and pulled her forward, before sealing his mouth halfway between her clavicle and the mandible on her neck.

Razor-sharp, elongating teeth...

He scored her skin, then sank his fangs slowly...cleanly...into her flesh.

She gasped in both surprise and pain, but she didn't jerk back or pull away as he drew from her essence with a ravenous gulp, tasted her blood, then swirled a rough, calloused tongue around the wound he had just created.

He released her with a sudden backward jerk, his phantom-blue eyes blazing like two molten coals. "Go!" he said, flipping the blanket off her like an angry matador directing a bull. He pointed toward the other side of the chamber. "Give me a minute to collect my—"

"No." She leaned forward, cupped his face in both hands, and met his fiery gaze beneath steely, lowered lashes. She refused to blink or turn away.

He stared at her with incredulity, his chest rising and falling in harsh, ragged breaths, and then he grasped her by both slender shoulders, pressed her against the flat of the bed, and rolled on top of her, groin against groin, his enormous weight anchoring Bethany to the mattress. "Is this what you wanted, dragyra?"

She gasped in alarm and shuddered.

She hadn't thought this through.

In fact, she hadn't *thought* at all...

She had just wanted to look at him, to really *see* him, to study the male who haunted her every waking thought, her figurative dreams, her metaphoric nightmares...her heart. "I...I...I wasn't trying to provoke you. I was just—"

He covered her mouth with a huge, rugged hand. "Too late, Beth." He traced her lips, harshly, with the pad of his thumb. "Too late." And then he seized her mouth with his, ravaged her lips with his tongue, and tasted, explored—overpowered any protests—with wild, untamed lust.

He drew her bottom lip into his.

He bit, then devoured her tongue.

He explored every fleshy crest, taut plane, and soft, moist curve of her full, sculpted mouth with his thick bottom lip like a frenzied animal—or a savage master—until she was gasping for breath.

He raked his fingers along her sides, from the crests of her shoulders to beneath her arms, to the slender hollow along her waist, kneading each rib with his thumb and his fingers, then following the assault with his mouth.

His teeth.

His tongue.

His wild hunger.

Then he reared back onto his knees and stared at her, shamelessly taking in her feminine form with devastating thirst and feral desire—he palmed her hips, stroked her stomach, then kneaded her breasts, as if testing all three for pliancy, strength, and stability.

He moaned—or growled—maybe both at once, and then he buried his face in her abdomen; once again, using his wicked mouth to taste, explore, outline her belly button, to gnaw at trembling flesh through plain white cotton, until at last he grasped the T-shirt in two angry fists and shredded the fabric like paper.

The night air teased Bethany's breasts, and she shivered from the sudden sensation.

Her face flushed, her throat constricted, and her breath grew rapid and shallow as he cupped both breasts in his powerful, mercenary hands and slowly bent to her nipples.

Devastation.

Fierce, bearish, and primal—Bethany could hardly comprehend what the fearsome male was doing, how anyone could be so harsh yet sensuous, coarse yet passionate, brutal yet delicate with two lips, a divinely appointed tongue, and the sharp, untamed canines of a dragon.

Yet and still, he was magical...*masterful*...mind-numbing and terrifying at once.

She fisted the sheet beneath her, arched her body, then grasped at his biceps, desperate to find something to hold onto. *What the hell was happening?*

Had she meant to trigger such a primal reaction?

She didn't know how she felt about Ghost, let alone consummating their union, but she was swept up in a turbulent flood, and the waters were carrying her swiftly...mercilessly...unwittingly forward.

Ghost abandoned the sensitive peaks of her nipples and began to lavish the underside of each breast, instead, dragging his tongue along the thick of each crescent, down the center of her chest, to the soft, concave floor of her belly. He raked his fingers along the crease of her pelvis, kneaded her thighs in earnest, then grasped her hips, snarled like an alpha wolf, and dipped his head...much lower.

Lower...

Lower still, until Bethany's entire core caught fire.

She grasped his hair in her hands.

She tried to raise his head and object.

She opened her mouth to say his name in reproach—to beg him to stop—but nothing escaped but a tormented sigh: The storm was raging, the flood was rising, the waves were cresting...crashing...in violent swells.

Bethany tossed and turned and flailed in the current, not knowing which way was up—his hands, his mouth, his teeth, his tongue...his scent, his passion, and his power—each dragged Bethany below the surface like a mighty, relentless undertow, and she was helpless to protest or resist.

She did not *want* to protest or resist.

Not when he brought her to climax, then held her down until she cried out for mercy.

Not when he crawled above her, yanked her panties over her hips, and slid out of his own commando gray sweats.

Not when he strained his neck, arched his back, and fisted his enormous sex in his hand. Not when he pressed against her—just to tease her—then pulled back, time and again.

Not when he finally thrust inside her, waited until she began to writhe, then toyed with her mind and tortured her body, alternating quick, shallow prods with slow, deep thrusts.

He explored her from every conceivable angle, tempo, and depth.

He rolled his pelvis against her core until she feverishly scored his back.

And then he withdrew the pleasure that was driving her mad, raised her hips with one hand, parted her intimate flesh with the other, and pressed slowly, agonizingly, deep into her body, again and again...and again.

He flipped her onto her stomach and repeated the torture.

He set her in his lap and thrust upward, while holding, pressing...pulling her down.

He forced climax after climax out of Bethany's untested body, until finally, she could take no more.

And then he laid her down beneath him, held her wrists above her head, and locked his blazing, phantom-blue eyes with hers. "Beth," he moaned, his thick bottom lip still moist with passion. "I want to—"

"Yes," she breathed, intimately understanding the question, the fact that he was asking for permission.

His eyelids closed like two heavy curtains, the muscles in his lower stomach tightened against her belly, and he found her core again. Only, this time, his thrusts were uniform and steady—deep, rhythmic, and languid.

His breath captured hers in a matching, reciprocal cycle of inhales and exhales—yin and yang—and he slowly reopened his eyes, those stunning, haunting, unearthly orbs...

He locked them unerringly with hers.

Two vast, glowing windows to the soul, clashing...shining... drawing her in, commanding Bethany's submission, yet giving more than Ghost could afford to give.

Female clung to male as the storm rose, then suddenly abated, and the waves crashed into the shore. Ghost stiffened. Shuddered. Released his seed. Then slowly hung his head in...

Shame?

Bethany bit her bottom lip and welcomed the silence—the stillness—struggling to collect her thoughts. There's no way he could have known—*why would anyone just assume?*—that a twenty-nine-year-old woman was saving herself for marriage. That Bethany was still a virgin. Or, at least, she had been. And there was certainly no way Ghost could've understood that her brazen attention, her awkward, dangerous...insistent...staring, touching, and rousing—a "baby freakin' moth flittin' around a fire"—had been clumsy inexperience, perhaps a lack of sexual maturity, more than it had been seduction.

But none of that mattered, not anymore.

Because the truth was too stark and undeniable.

Virgin?

Yes.

Stupid?

No.

Bethany had known she was playing with a dragon's fire.

She had known she did not give her heart lightly, and she would never, ever give her body recklessly...or carelessly.

Unwillingly.

On some terrifying, hidden, subconscious level, Bethany had known exactly what she was doing, and now it was too late to take it back.

Any of it...

The act.

The decision.

Or the burgeoning promise—the covenant and vow—that went along with it.

Bethany had ceded much more than passion to Ghost, the moment he had entered her body.

* * *

Ghost rolled onto his back, braced his arm against his forehead, and groaned.

Fuuuck...

Just what kind of heathen animal was he?

He had known the instant he had entered Beth's body that the female was still a virgin...inexperienced...yet he had been unable to control his arousal.

His primal, savage hunger.

Yes, he had used more than just a little of his supernatural power to ease her discomfort, and yes, he had worked to give her at least a half-dozen orgasms, all to assuage his guilt. Yet he had carried on—*and on*—like a fevered, rabid animal, and that was only the half of it.

Ghost had done something he had never done before.

He had given something he had sworn he would never relinquish—and he couldn't blame that on primal instinct.

Not on hunger.

Not on lust.

And not on being a barbaric savage.

In his own harsh, if not rote, distant, and mechanical way, he had more or less touched her, caressed her, divided her body into familiar, objective quadrants in order to please her, until he had slipped-the-fuck-up and gotten...involved.

Hell, he had given a shit.

And moreover, he had looked her in the eyes while he was inside her.

He had looked her in the eyes as he'd released his seed.

And that shit—*all of it*—had his head spinning and his chest tightening, his entire foundation and world order shaking...

Flipping!

Upside down.

What the hell had just happened?

CHAPTER TWENTY-NINE

Anne Liu gasped, flailed her arms, and grasped wildly for Jax's hand, even as she staggered atop a magnificent glass floor, the refracted light from its brilliance temporarily blinding her gaze.

Just five minutes earlier, the preternatural male had appeared like a ghostly mirage, without ceremony or warning, in her living room. "Lord Dragos is ready to receive you now." He had held out his hand as if she were actually bold enough to take it. "It's time."

Yes, Anne had known Jax was planning to take her to the Pantheon, prior to midnight on Wednesday, November ninth—he had told her as much in Riverside Park—but in her deluded, optimistic mind, she'd still had five days to go, and a girl could hope. She had not been prepared to simply stop what she was doing, grab her purse on a moment's notice, and follow Jax outside to the vacant courtyard and watch, wide-eyed, as the supernatural male encircled her waist with one hand and lifted the tether of an ancient necklace with the other. He had flashed the face of a diamond amulet. "The portal is not a literal place," he had said, matter-of-factly. "It's more or less inside this gemstone. As long as I'm touching you, all I have to do is touch this amulet, visualize the temple, and draw on the powers of my sire, Lord Dragos, first of the Seven. The portal will open through his power."

Anne had blinked several times, wanting clarification, but before she could part her lips to request it, Jax had fisted the stone, a bright light had flickered, and her body had experienced an overwhelming sense of vertigo. Then just like that, they were there—*she was here!*—staggering to catch her balance, reaching for Jax's hand, needing courage, and shielding her eyes from a near-blinding glare.

"Relax," Jax whispered, taking the outstretched offering. "Your eyes will adjust."

Anne squeezed his fingers so hard, she could have cut off his circulation, as she stared more intently at the glass beneath her feet and the bright prisms of light illuminating upward from its smooth, specular surface. She turned her attention to the high, coffered ceiling, which was plated in multiple layers of gold and jewels—diamonds, emeralds, sapphires, and amethysts; onyx, citrines, and topaz—each gilded layer also refracting light, as if from within its very essence. No wonder the upward and downward reflections culminated in a dazzling optical prism.

She squeezed her eyes shut, then slowly reopened them.

In the center of the room, facing an eastern wall of thrones, she saw a raised dais on top of an octagon platform, the platform constructed of the same, identical gemstone tiles, and outside of the thrones, which were magnificent, giant, and radiating both heat and light, the dais clearly the focal point of the sanctuary.

And then her attention was drawn, like a boat being steered by a rudder, to the northern side of the inner temple and a brilliant pool of pearlescent liquid, all seven gemstones undulating in what could only be described as *living* waters.

She gasped and pressed closer to Jax.

There were seven gemstone pillars lining the western wall, each pillar mirroring an opposite, jeweled throne, and even the pillars nearly pulsed with swelling energy.

"Anne." Jax's hushed but urgent voice interrupted her reverie and awe. "I need you to pay attention to my words, do everything I instruct you to do."

She gulped, and her knees knocked together. "Jax, I can't do this."

"You can."

"No," she argued emphatically. "I really can't." She searched his stunning, light green pupils amidst a sea of diamond irises, and licked her chapped, quivering lips. "I'm not whatever you think I am. A Seer or some kind of sage. I'm just a girl who lost a best friend, and everything else is...accidental."

"Shh." The vibration of his breath whispered over her cold, clammy skin like a warm summer's breeze, and she took an unwitting deep breath. "Face the Oracle Pool and kneel."

Kneel? she thought.

Why kneel?

But before she could whisper the question audibly, the sanctuary filled up with an amorphous fog—a white, smoky, glowing film—and the scents of cedarwood, cypress, neroli, and sandalwood, along with three other fragrances she could not identify, filled the enormous, opulent shrine, even as seven shadowy beings appeared and gathered around the pool.

Anne almost screamed, but her throat constricted, and her stomach tightened into knots—she could not have produced a significant sound even if she had tried.

Kneel, Jax repeated, this time speaking inside her mind.

Anne turned counterclockwise, away from the thrones, and followed Jax tentatively across the floor, toward the pool of living waters. They stopped maybe fifteen or twenty feet out, where the son of a dragon took one knee, and just to be safe, Anne followed suit, descending onto *both* knees and folding her hands in her lap.

Dragons...

But not fully formed.

Giant, resplendent, imposing creatures standing like seven hulking prisms of gemstone light, the outlines and ethos of terrifying men flanked by the silhouettes of fantastical beasts, the subjects of legends, the heroes and villains of countless science fiction novels come to life right before her eyes.

"Come forward." A mighty being of pure diamond light spoke like thunder, his voice and his presence filling the temple with eerie kinetic energy, and Anne couldn't help but peek at the ferocious dragon in the background, the mirrored soul hovering in, around, and atop the semi-human form.

His energy was...angry.

His countenance was cruel.

And the temperature in the temple rose by several degrees.

Jax tugged on Anne's hand and hoisted her off the floor, even as he rose with the grace of a gazelle and the stealth of a leopard. He spoke in her mind again. *Say nothing unless spoken to, and keep your eyes averted.*

Ten steps felt like fifty.

Six breaths felt like one as Anne gasped for air while following Jax forward, growing closer and closer to the terrifying dragon lords.

When at last they stopped, just a few feet shy of the glowering diamond dragon, Jax bent to one knee a second time, and once again, Anne followed suit—in truth, her legs were growing too weak to hold her much longer anyway.

"Son," the diamond dragon thundered.

"Father, may I present Miss Anne Liu, a Seer and lifelong friend of Bethany Reid, who is daughter to my lord through his genesis offspring, Ghostaniaz. We have come at your behest. How may we serve you?"

Lord Dragos snorted, and the smell of sulfur wafted from his thick, scaly nostrils. "Rise. Both of you," he replied in an imperial tone.

Anne's heart nearly leaped from her chest, her eyes rolled back in her head, and she felt an overwhelming surge of nausea sweep through her. *Shit!* She was going to be sick. She could not stand up. And she was pretty darn sure this dragon was going to kill her.

"For fuck's sake!" the dragon lord bellowed, shocking Anne out of her queasiness. "I have neither the time nor the patience to deal with this human's fear and reticence. My Genesis Son is being held in the underworld! Purify her flesh and place her in the water. *Now*."

Everything happened at once.

Jax stood up, taking Anne with him. He took a measured step back and bathed her, from the top of her head to the tips of her toes, in an onslaught of glistening silver fire. And then Anne screamed, covered her head with her hands, and tried to run.

Only, just as she had feared, her wobbly, unsteady legs would not cooperate.

Jax held out his hand, and her entire body was instantly paralyzed, frozen in place like a frightened hare in the arctic tundra. Just as swiftly, her mid-length black skirt and her rose-colored blouse fell away, along with her tights, boots, and undergarments, and she was suddenly wearing a billowing white robe. Without notice or preamble, Jax raised the same hand, and Anne's feet left the ground. She rose into the air and floated above the glassy, iridescent floor, until she was standing dead center in the now churning pool of pearlescent water.

The living, undulating waves rose upward.

They cocooned her body in a swirling funnel, then rained

down pure, polished ribbons of color, moisture, and glistening, cool crescents, until she was drenched in the mystical fluid.

Liquid, disembodied hands seized her ankles, tugged, and pulled her under.

In an attempt to take one last, life-saving breath, Anne gulped a river of water, yet her lungs did not burn, and her body did not struggle. Rather, she drifted down...down...down into the pool, allowing the weightlessness, tossing, and turning to overcome her.

There was nothing but color and mind-blowing light, nothing but water swirling all around her, through her...within her... nothing but stars, moonlight, and an infinite number of planets, galaxies of time, and universes of information.

Anne saw...and smelled...and tasted.

And knew.

She felt and conceived and breathed in truth, taking it in through her nostrils and all six senses, like a lucid dream in which she saw, felt, and heard five distinct, mysterious...symbols... taking each one in from a 360-degree view.

A pair of eggshells.

A table made of bone.

An antique brass key and a golden scepter.

A ring of fire exploding upward, as if from the core of the earth.

The ring surrounded...scorched...blazed like molten lava as it enveloped the familiar Arapahoe County Fairgrounds, the location of the haunted house on Halloween from which Beth had first gone missing. And then, just like that, Anne shot out of the water, both hands linked in Jax's, fresh vertigo assailing her.

The sense of a portal.

The sensation of traveling.

A seamless, easy...*landing?*

Staggering, yet again, to regain her footing, she gawked at her living room furniture and appraised her familiar surroundings—

Anne was back home. She was dressed, once more, in her mid-length black skirt and rose-colored tunic, and there were no dragon lords hovering above her, no mercenary dragyri manipulating her body with the wave of his fingers or giving her orders.

Perhaps it had all been a dream!

She placed her hand over her heart, took several deep breaths, and stared blankly at her clean, dry, unwrinkled clothing. And then her stomach clenched, her heart skipped a beat, and the hand on her heart grew sweaty.

Drip, drip, drip...

Drip-drop.

Her long black hair was soaking wet, the scent of cypress, neroli, and sandalwood permeated her outfit, and droplets of rainbow-colored water fell to the carpet.

* * *

Lord Dragos dismissed his son Jax, turned his back on his brother deities, and paced wildly in front of the Oracle Pool as the remaining lords stood watching.

"A bit hasty, don't you think?" Lord Onyhanzian queried, glaring at Lord Dragos like he had dung on his muzzle.

"Perhaps we could have debriefed her, asked her a few questions, then sent her home with her memories...lessened," said the annoying Lord Topenzi, with his endless, damnable, self-righteous musings.

Lord Dragos snorted and averted his eyes.

He would not be questioned by his fellow deities!

The First Law of Harmony, a primordial covenant amongst the eternal dragon creators, was inviolable: Absolute Liberty! That meant Lord Dragos was free from reproach or tyranny. He could think, choose, create, and act as a sovereign, independent, supreme being without the consent or knowledge of his brethren.

Indeed, his lair and his mercenary sons were his to command as he saw fit, and the Second Law of Harmony was like unto it: Sanctity in Privacy. This was self-explanatory. The dragon lords neither had a right to use their omniscience to divine what another dragon lord was doing, nor to discern what he was thinking. They could not look, listen, or eavesdrop within their brethren's private chambers, be such lodgings, external buildings, or internal landscapes. Privacy—nay, secrecy—was sacrosanct.

But it was the Third Law of Harmony that was giving Lord Dragos severe indigestion.

Preservation of the Species via reverence for all Dragyr offspring.

Damnit all to hell!

Wasn't that why they were here?

All of them!

Why Anne Liu had been brought to the temple and immersed in the soothsaying waters?

A desperate, yet necessary attempt to save Ghostaniaz's life!

As if reading Lord Dragos' thoughts, Lord Ethyron cleared his mighty throat. "Brother..." He allowed the word to linger, ostensibly understanding that Lord Dragos was in another of his dark, brooding tantrums. "Do you take meaning from anything the waters revealed? A pair of eggs, a table made from bone, an antique brass key, and a golden scepter...a ring of fire exploding upward, as if from the core of the earth?"

Lord Dragos spun around on a three-clawed heel, his divine and mortal forms morphing in and out. A plume of smoke escaped his nostrils, and he stomped a foot against the brilliant glass foundation, shaking the sanctuary's columns. "We move in and out of the heavenly realms by means of our own sacred portal, the primeval gemstones of our own sacred birth—our cosmic and divinely inspired eruption—being part and parcel of the stones' sacred powers. Yet the eighth at creation split apart from the remainder! In his search for darkness and absolute dominion, Drakkar descended into the deepest of evolving, dark energy. It is my thought—nay, my wisdom and divine intuition— that the antique brass key in Miss Liu's projected vision has everything to do with that deep, dark evolution."

"Ah," Lord Ethyron mused, "a key that unlocks a deep, dark passage—*The Deep*—if you will. Then perhaps Ghost now has such an object in his possession?"

Lord Dragos shrugged his hulking shoulders, and Lord Saphyrius took a giant step forward, his silhouetted hand rubbing the outline of his dragon's scaly muzzle like a man might stroke his chin. "Speaking of keys, the reference to the golden scepter seemed quite apparent, a rod to rule as a lord or king. Perhaps our fallen sibling Lord Drakkar Hades has offered Ghostaniaz some measure of his kingdom?"

"Aye," Lord Cytarius concurred. "While the human girl only saw a golden scepter, I had a shadowed, yet strong impression of a gold and blood-red robe. I believe Ghostaniaz has played his hand well in the underworld thus far, perhaps appealing to Lord Drakkar's most masculine instincts, the innate impulse we all possess to reproduce and rear our own biological offspring, an impulse Lord Drakkar chose hastily against when he separated Self from his blooded seven kinsmen."

Lord Dragos waved a clawed hand through the air.

Yes, yes...yes.

His indigestion was quickly becoming a dynastic headache.

Must they revisit Creation 101?

Fourteen billion years ago, the swirling mass, a black hole full of scorching, dense gas, the mass containing *All Thought* of light and shadow...love, hate, desire, and sin...joy, purity, hope, and destruction.

Yada, yada, yada...

During the critical moment, the quantum fluctuation—nay,

the cosmic explosion—when the pulses gained consciousness, developed minds, and separated out from the ether, Lord Drakkar Hades had reviled even the faintest hint of light, and thus, he had split from the pack.

Ah, but he had reviled more than a trace of hope, or the necessity of sharing divinity with seven others...

He had reviled the *female* energy, the *yin* alongside the yang, the dual energies that swirled together in that ancient magma, and he had singularly chosen the hard, logical, masculine forces, at the exclusion of anything else.

Indeed, whether knowingly or out of pure, blind ignorance, Drakkar had denied his own divinity the ability to procreate. For while it was true the Seven had tried unsuccessfully for centuries to procreate with human women, none of the offspring had lived. Yet and still, they had been able to harness *both* male and female energy, to splice and clone their own reptilian genes, and to create over a thousand original eggs, of which only forty-nine eventually hatched.

Randomly, and across epochs of time, the forty-nine had become the seven Genesis Sons of the seven sacred lairs, and each of those precious, irreplaceable hatchlings had also become capable of producing his own future offspring with a living human mate, a chosen dragyra.

One thousand eggs, whittled down to forty-nine hatchlings...

Forty-nine hatchlings, survived by only seven.

But—and wasn't this truly the long and the short of it—that was seven more than Lord Drakkar had begotten! The powerful pagan had castrated his own genetic procreative energy eons past, because the short-sighted fool had never had any original female energy to work with.

Nay, he had created his minions—his followers and his Pagan Horde—from the works of his hands and the Thought of his mind, but his own biological seed had been, and still was, absent from the equation.

So, yes...

Indeed...

Ghostaniaz would be the closest thing to DNA Lord Drakkar had ever encountered.

Why hadn't Lord Dragos thought of this before?

"I agree with Lord Cytarius," Lord Amarkyus said dryly. "But what of the ring of fire exploding upward, as if from the core of the earth?"

The sanctuary fell silent, and Lord Dragos wanted to scream just to punctuate the absurdity of the silly question. *A ring of fire could be anything!* Hell, they were all dragon lords. They released rings of fire at night when they snored! "Anyone?" he bellowed, spinning around to face each of his brethren, one by one. "Someone?"

No one answered back.

Finally, when the silence had grown deafening, Lord Onyhanzian offered a stab in the dark: "This Wednesday, hence, shall be the tenth day of Ghostaniaz's mating, and he must bring the female, Bethany, into this very temple to be consecrated by fire, before his seven lords. Perhaps the ring of fire is an omen of sorts, a good and hopeful portent that the male will make it back, that all of us, indeed, will have the opportunity to usher her into the Pantheon of Dragons."

Lord Dragos turned up his nose in derision. "Maybe," he snorted. "Maybe not."

"Let us think on it," Lord Onyhanzian offered.

"Pray on it," Lord Topenzi said.

Now this chapped Lord Dragos' hide. "Pray on it?" he mocked, licking his leather lips. "Pray to whom, dear brother? Each other? Ourselves?"

Lord Topenzi rolled his topaz eyes. "You understood my

meaning. Prayer as a form of meditation...divination...let us go inside to the sacred place of Thought and ponder this ring of fire." His voice became a bit more abrupt, something rare and uncharacteristic for the lighter deity. "And while we are *praying* on the meaning of the ring of fire, mayhap we should meditate on the remaining two symbols—the pair of eggs and a table made from bone—because as odd as it feels for a divine, all-knowing being to suddenly embrace the absence of *knowing*, I must confess, I've got absolutely...nothing."

"Neither have I," Lord Cytarius offered.

The other four dragons grunted in agreement, and Lord Dragos knew exactly what they were implying: For an oracle to be completely blacked out, as if sequestered behind a psychic wall, perhaps that oracle was being blinded by the second harmonic covenant, Sanctity in Privacy.

Perhaps *Lord Dragos* was keeping his own private cards too close to his duplicitous chest.

"I resent you, Lord Topenzi," he snarled, "as well as the insinuation. Am I not the grieving father who has lost his beloved Genesis Son?"

"*Beloved?*" Lord Cytarius nearly choked on the word.

Lord Onyhanzian coughed in his half-human, half-dragon amalgamated hand.

"You know what I mean!" Lord Dragos bellowed. "Ghost is my own flesh and blood, and if I had knowledge of something...anything...that might aid him, that might bring him back into our fold, I would certainly share it with the likes of my divine, all-powerful brethren, if only to further my own selfish cause."

This shut them up for the moment.

But Lord Dragos felt sick from his innards.

The table made of bone...

Fuck it all!

Lord Dragos had Absolute Liberty to do as he liked with

Ghostaniaz, to torture the recalcitrant mercenary as he saw fit, even if that torture had spanned a near millennia, and the table of bone resting in Lord Dragos' opulent bedchamber was also shrouded by sacred covenant, Sanctity in Privacy.

As for a pair of eggshells?

What the actual fuck!

This made no sense, though it felt like the cosmos was exploding afresh.

There were *never* a pair of *eggshells*.

"Out of Sanctity in Privacy, I shall not speak of the table, but I shall make this vow to my brethren, here and now: Should my time in prayer, offered to my...*self*, unveil any pertinent revelations, those I will share freely and gladly."

This time, Lord Topenzi, the most enlightened of the Seven, snorted in derision—*was the entire world going mad?*

"That said," Lord Dragos continued, "I know not of any duo of eggshells. Perhaps Lord Drakkar has decided to try his hand at creating an heir of his own, harnessing Ghost's divine DNA. Or perhaps he is feeding the muscular mercenary a pair of farm fresh, free-range, non-GMO-fed eggs, harnessed earthside, every hour of the day, to keep up his Dragyr strength. Or maybe—*I know!*—it's a symbolic, visionary pun of sorts. Ghost or the king have egg on their face. Do let me know if your own prayers prove more fruitful than my current divination, but I have no more to offer or to say on the subject."

Telepathy was never used between the sacred Seven.

Well, it was *rarely* used, as they already shared one ancient celestial mind and a sacred temple body, yet the words of Lord Ethyron, the second-darkest dragon, floated through the sanctuary's ether, assailed Lord Dragos' stubborn mind, and lingered long after the meeting was over, reverberating like soft, roiling thunder: *Your tirade is juvenile, even for you. Your protestations are...over the top. Brother, what have you done?*

CHAPTER THIRTY

THE PAGAN UNDERWORLD

Bethany ran her hands through her thick, wavy hair, pulling it away from her face, and secured it in a low, loose ponytail using a torn strip of cloth from a pillow slip as a tether. She made her way to the barred, stained glass window, turned the crank to prop it open, and stared at the wretched, barren landscape, only what she saw in her mind's eye was entirely different: lush, living, and vibrant. Her grandparents' farmhouse on the eastern plains of Colorado, luxurious green grass in the summer, and golden, honey-hued fields in early spring and autumn.

She saw Grandpa John's black, gray, and tan blue heeler running through the fields, chasing rabbits, the litter of kittens born to a stray, wild cat the winter of Bethany's tenth birthday, and the row of cottonwoods that lined the creek just beyond the old, inoperable tractor.

If she closed her eyes and focused hard enough, she could almost smell the dew as it mixed with the grass—she could almost feel the sunshine on her forehead, cheeks, and shoulders. She sighed, wishing for times gone by, wishing to be anywhere but in this present moment.

Matins...

Midnight.

In the Pagan Underworld.

Friday night and Ghost's impending, defenseless, public exposure about to take place in the Sinners' Cave.

What in the name of heaven would happen?

Bethany had tried all day to wrestle her thoughts and fears like a toddler facing off with an alligator, but now that the moment of truth was here, the alligator was clearly winning. There weren't enough childhood memories in the universe to subdue her dread or redirect her terror. She absently turned toward the raised, curtained enclave that encased the tin tub, and the high-backed, blue velvet chair about five feet away from the tub's antique clawed feet. Her eyes fixed unerringly on a tiny, dark blue vial resting on the chair and filled with a measured, potent dose of liquid belladonna, and she chastised herself inwardly for not having it on her person. From now until Wednesday, she needed to carry it with her, keep it close at hand in case of emergency.

She shuddered at the thought, recoiled at the reality, but truth was truth—and there was no more denying it. Over the next several hours—or perhaps only minutes—every second of Bethany's life was tenuous. Ghost could walk back through the chamber door, having bought the couple more time, or any number of demons, shades, or human servants could break it down with the intent to torture, main, or execute...

She let the thought trail off.

The point was: Anything could happen at any moment, and Bethany needed to be ready.

Like the sharp, piercing discord of a cell phone ringing in the middle of a funeral service, Bethany suddenly laughed out loud, and the sound echoed throughout the chamber—*having bought the couple more time!*

Was she batshit crazy?

Bethany and Ghost were *not* a couple.

Hell, the male had been distant at best, and standoffish at worst, ever since they had made love two nights ago. As promised, he had kept up with the deliveries of belladonna, provided the blue vial of...readily available self-destruction...and helped Bethany hide every drop of poison they made for feast night in the bedchamber's floorboards. As planned, he had spent the lion's share of his time intermingling with Lord Drakkar's congress, while trying to convince the evil monsters of his heartfelt fealty. But every time Bethany had tried to broach the subject of what had happened between them, or what it might mean going forward, he had either changed the subject or become his name-sake—he had ghosted right out of the conversation.

Still...

Bethany had noticed several subtle nuances, things the dragyri was likely unaware of: the fact that his stark, phantom-blue pupils softened whenever he looked at her; the fact that he moved his body in a protective, almost predatory manner, positioning his heavy, muscle-bound carcass between Bethany and the bedchamber door nearly every second he was with her; and the fact that he stared...*and stared*...studied her like a watching hawk, whenever he thought she wasn't looking.

The wheels in his head were turning.

And the blood in his heart was not only pumping—it was stirring.

Something in the male had changed, however subtle or insignificant.

And at least to Bethany, it no longer mattered, because she

had made her final decision: If Ghost could get them out of the underworld in time to make it to the Temple of Seven, she would go through with the conversion, and she would alter her universe, at least as much as feasible, to forge a path forward, both on Earth and in the Pantheon, *with* him.

She couldn't explain it.

There was no explanation, outside of those four closed chambers of her heart, the chambers Grandma Betsy had opened, outside of the constant prayers and the endless hours Bethany spent alone in the stifling bedchamber...alone and in silence. There was no explanation outside of one wild, ferocious, passionate interlude—a virgin and the son of a dragon thrown together in a time of bondage, fighting for survival, and finding the eye of the storm together, if only for one rare, soul-shattering encounter.

The look in his eyes.

The way he had spoken her name.

The fact that he had asked Bethany for permission to climax inside her body...

Anything was possible!

Spirit and Grandma Betsy had been right—the male still had a soul.

And for a woman who was neither submissive, codependent, nor inclined to try to rescue a "broken" man from his inner demons, a woman who would describe herself as a solid feminist, who had learned, early on, to both protect herself and cherish her independence, her decision was as grandiose as it was contrary.

Bethany and Ghost were *not* a couple!

And maybe they never would be.

But life had taught Bethany patience.

And in spite of loss, she had been reared with love.

"Child of fire; daughter of flames. More than a woman; more than a name. Born from the soul of The Pantheon..."

Yes.

Sometimes faith was more than an utterance, hope was more than a trite expression, and one's light was actually meant to illuminate another's darkness.

Yes, yes, and yes.

Now Ghost just had to live through the night's ordeal.

CHAPTER THIRTY-ONE

G host drew back his massive shoulders, held his head high, and braced himself for all the sarcastic smirks, self-satisfied glares, and downright evil side-eyes the sin eaters were about to give him as he entered the infernal Sinners' Cave. Not that he gave a shit about what these heathen bastards thought of him—or even the fact that the entire Pagan Horde would be watching on either legit or mystical screens throughout the castle—but he understood, quite well, the potential fallout, the consequences, what could potentially go down, depending on what the whole sordid affair revealed.

So be it.

Ride or die.

The moment of reckoning was here, and Ghost had no illusions whatsoever that he would come through the hazardous ordeal unscathed or even alive. He knew his inner thoughts, he was well acquainted with the huge, miry, tangled web that consisted of a millennium of his darkest memories, and he also understood he was about to betray every last one of the Pantheon's deeply guarded secrets, albeit against his will and without his permission. Hopefully, the Dragyr as a whole could withstand the betrayal.

As usual, the floor-to-ceiling fireplace, constructed of huge, uneven stones slathered in black pitch, was blazing and illuminating the otherwise dark, creepy cavern, but what halted Ghost's breath and brought him up short was the unexpected visage of Lord Drakkar Hades—*and Lord Drakkar, alone*—sprawled like a lazy, carefree lion atop the center blood-red sofa, wearing an elaborate black-and-gold surcoat embroidered with actual jewels. His thin, reedy lips were curved upward in a sanctimonious smile, and his long, bony fingers rested peacefully atop his lap.

"Ghostaniaz...*nephew*...welcome."

Ghost regarded the king warily. "Where is everyone?"

Lord Drakkar raised his brows and smirked, but he didn't speak.

Ghost waited, holding his ground, even as he glanced around the cavern, trying to make sense of what he was seeing: No Salyn Stryke, with his shifting, slithering, alchemic tattoos; no Requiem Pyre, with his awesome powers of sorcery and dark necromancy; no Aegis Hawk, Gemini Stone, or even Trader Vice, with that freaky tiger snake filling in for a missing left hand. In other words, no sin eaters from congress or the general horde crowded inside the cave of iniquity. There were no sneering pagans lurking, jeering, or eager to consume Ghost's deepest, darkest secrets.

So, what the hell was happening?

Ghost took a deep breath, strode a cautious step forward, and laid his golden scepter on the repugnant, gnarled coffee table, ignoring the fact that the legs were clearly made from human bones. "My liege, what gives?"

This time, Lord Drakkar did not smirk. His deep-set, kaleidoscope eyes narrowed with solemn intensity, the striations in his neck grew taut, and he stood to his full six-foot, eight-inch height, allowing his terrible, mighty presence to envelop the space between them. "Change of plans."

Ghost winced and sucked in air.

Change of plans...

What kind of change?

Had Lord Drakkar changed his mind about the scrying screen observance? Was the Pagan Horde gathered somewhere else, perhaps in the Great Hall or some unknown, communal auditorium, watching from afar? Or had the mendacious, scheming king decided to execute Ghost after all, right here and now?

"Tsk, tsk, tsk." Lord Drakkar flicked his slimy tongue three times, and Ghost couldn't help but remember the scorpion that had once come out of that same vile mouth and hovered over Beth's trembling body. "None of the above," the king drawled on a hiss, obviously reading Ghost's thoughts—so much for rarely reading the minds of his followers.

Apparently, this was a special occasion.

Okaaay...

So, the shit show hadn't even started, and the king was already playing mind games.

"If you're planning to behead me and remove my amulet, I would just as soon you get on with it, my liege." *I'll see your double-tongued hedging and raise you a direct, in-your-face confrontation,* he thought, not caring if the king was—or was not—listening. "I'm not really one for guessing...waiting...or prevaricating with my life. Just say what you're gonna say and do what you're gonna do."

"Mm," King Drakkar vocalized, "a spine of steel, I see." He waved a spindly hand through the air. "Well, not really steel. It was flexible enough to remove from your back, with ease, the first time you defied me in my throne room." He allowed the words, as well as the horrific, agonizing memory, to linger. Then he splayed those same lanky fingers, pointed the tips of his nails at Ghost, and an unseen force, like the blunt end of a battering ram, struck the dragyri in the center of his chest. It stole Ghost's breath, knocked him off his feet, and planted his ass on the first of the three blood-red sofas. "Sit down!" the king ordered. "And listen carefully. Yes, Ghostaniaz, my plans have changed. *Several plans have changed.* Yet all you need focus upon right now is your present obligation in this Sinners' Cave and the life-or-death choice you will be given, fresh and anew, the moment the obligatory production is over."

Ghost locked his jaw and summoned fresh courage, wrapped it in a shell of stiff resolve.

What the actual fuck was happening?

Yeah, Lord Drakkar was right, at least partially...

Ghost's spine was both flexible and made of steel—it could bend, bleed, and break, especially when a demon king yanked it out of his body, but what Lord Drakkar may or may not fully realize was the fact that Ghost had spent a dozen lifetimes under the dominion of another cruel and sadistic dragon, his sire, Lord Dragos. And being broken, burned, threatened, or lashed...being starved, beaten, punished, or rebuked...hell, it was just a day in the life of an ongoing epic tragedy, so Ghost didn't really care one way or the other. "I'm listening," he grunted.

Lord Drakkar cocked his head to the side, his kaleidoscope eyes spinning in their sockets, and then he smiled. "Good. *Good.* Your stubborn hatred, your practiced defiance, the fact that you have zero shits to give about anything—*is that the correct vernacular?*—either way, all will serve you well this night." He linked his hands behind his back and began to walk in slow, predatory circles around and around the semicircle of garish sofas.

"Yes, we are going to go forward with the scrying screen exhibition, but no, the Pagan Horde will not be viewing your...cerebral dissection...at least not yet. The *shit show,* as you like to refer to it, shall be for an audience of one. *Me.* Your king and eternal master, Father of the Pagan Realm, Sire of the Pagan Horde, Dark Lord of the Underworld, and author of your fate, going forward. Requiem Pyre has made it possible for me and my minions to save each and every memory you reveal on these hallowed, liquid screens inside a set of ancient obsidian, stone-point crystals so that we might store, shelve, and retrieve them like ancient scrolls in a bibliotheca, to study and utilize at our willful discretion. But your more personal memories, the more *intimate* revelations, I, and I alone, shall decide what is recorded for posterity versus what is discarded. Knowledge of the Pantheon shall become a permanent part of the underworld's vast, eternal library, but your deepest, darkest, inner secrets may yet be kept private, at least from your new pagan brethren, depending upon my preference. Time will tell."

He stopped pacing, spun around to face Ghost, and his huge, imposing frame practically loomed like a tower of doom directly over him. "There is more about this night, much, *much* more, that I shall soon reveal to you, but first, the *shit show* we both were promised—time to get on with the skull-fucking drama."

* * *

Before Ghost could blink or react, the Sinners' Cave grew dark as midnight. Lord Drakkar slithered behind the first sofa, stood behind Ghost, and placed both hands on his shoulders; then the undulating liquid screens illuminated, and their firelit depictions came to life.

Every thought, plot, and recent conversation Ghost had shared with Beth appeared on the screens in dizzying, lifelike representations and pictographs, including the numerous hidden amphoras filled with poison belladonna. Wednesday's love-making flashed as a series of sounds, fevered energy, and chaotic gasps for breath, but before Ghost could cringe—or get up and run—the screen sped backward through his time in the under-world, his capture in the quicksand, and back through the portal into the Pantheon of Dragons.

The mountainous region, the white, sandy beaches, the desert, the grasslands, and the purple-blue lake. The flatlands and tropics, the Garden of Grace, the seven gemstone lairs, and the Temple of Seven. Every square inch of the Pantheon was displayed in a swift, accelerated, moving picture.

And then the true, insidious shit show began to play...

First, century by century, then year by year, going back in time, from the present day to Ghost's horrific Dragyr origins: adulthood, puberty, childhood, and infancy. Every significant encounter, every consequential word—every substantial decision and monumental event—the scrying screens zoomed in and out, sped up or slowed down, then circled back, depending on the import of the occurrence.

Ghost's skull felt like a watermelon being chopped open by a machete.

His forehead was pounding, his temples were pulsing, and the crown of his head was going to explode any minute, detonate into a thousand sticky, watery pieces.

And then his breath caught in his throat as the scrying screens practically catapulted him back into a ghastly memory: five years old, hunting with his sire, an alley in London filled with thick, snaking fog, a pregnant woman and her adoring husband meandering down the cobblestone path...

Ghost closed his eyes and turned away.

He covered his ears in an effort to silence the familiar *pitter-patter, pitter-patter* of the unborn child's heartbeat: He did not care to see or relive the brutal attack, his own futile attempt to save both mother and fetus while feeding upon the former's blood, heat, and essence at his merciless sire's command. He didn't need a scrying screen to remind him of how the entire grievous event had turned out: "You are an immortal Dragyr, Ghostaniaz, the first-generation offspring of a dragon god, and more prominently, you are my son...my youngling...my own flesh and blood. Dragons do not show mercy, nor do we consider the plight, fate, or well-being of human prey. Kill the male, Ghostaniaz. Drain the female. And if you hold back on the woman, you will be severely punished."

Ghostaniaz *had* held back.

Lord Dragos had cremated the survivors while still alive.

And then he had scorched his own Genesis Son, forbidding Ghost to call him *Father* again, not until his eighteenth birthday.

Lord Drakkar Hades bent over the sofa, removed Ghost's hands from his ears, and whispered, "You will watch, and you will listen. Every word. Every scene. Every impression, going forward. Do not turn away again." His fetid breath assailed Ghost's nostrils as the scrying screens zoomed in again; this time on an enormous lizard, then a female tortoise, both from the Mesozoic Era, the time in which the dinosaurs lived.

What the hell did this have to do with Ghost?

This was long, long before he was born.

"Parthenogenetic species," Lord Drakkar said, "lizards, Komodo dragons, even hammerhead sharks. Asexual reproduction—each can reproduce with twice the number of their own chromosomes, eliminating the need for a partner or a mate. Ah, but the process can get tricky. Unless they recombine their existing DNA *just so*, they risk creating an offspring with an identical group of chromosomes, thus allowing all manner of genetic weakness, mutations, and disease to sneak in."

The scrying screens zoomed in on the turtle. "Did you know, dear nephew, that a female tortoise can have twins? When her egg is fortified with protein, minerals, and water—and calcium carbonate, alas, forms the shell—the yolks will occasionally stick together. And when the tortoises hatch, they are still combined, unless and until one slices the yolk sac, very carefully, without breaking it open."

Ghost shot up straight, twisted around on the couch, and glared violently at Lord Drakkar, behind his right shoulder. The hair on the back of his neck stood up, and his stomach lurched in his belly. "No!" he thundered, not knowing where the sudden emotion was coming from. "I've seen enough. Shut that shit off!"

"Oh," Lord Drakkar said softly. "No, dear nephew, you have not. Not nearly enough. We have just begun to watch the true story of your life." His eyes flashed molten red, and his hushed voice hardened. "Turn back around. Fix your eyes on the screen. And do not look away, lest I remove both your head and your amulet, right here, right now, on this sofa."

Ghost grimaced and turned around, more afraid of the screen than Lord Drakkar's threat of execution, yet drawn by some latent, morbid fascination...or curiosity...a moth to a flame, much like Beth Wednesday night in the bedchamber. From this point forward, he could not have looked away if he had wanted to.

The scrying screen returned to the Pantheon of Dragons, the white, sandy beach, and the cove filled with dragon's fire, to several deep, hidden caves beyond the Diamond Lair, places Ghost hardly remembered.

Then a dark, musty cavern...

Many, many millenniums past.

Lord Dragos harnessing his latent female energy and splicing, dividing, his own divine genes.

Of the thousand original eggs begotten of the Seven, the dragon gods produced 143 each, while Lord Dragos produced 142 of his own, not knowing how many would come to fruition, but taking all he had created to the Temple of Seven to incubate in power and eventually hatch over epochs of time.

The scrying screens sped up, showing the wasting away of

numerous ova, until only forty-nine of the original thousand remained, seven still belonging to each dragon lord, including the ruler of the Diamond Lair. One by one, the ova hatched, revealing ancient dragyri mercenaries and Genesis Sons, bygone siblings, and brothers of the lair Ghost had never met or known. They had lived and died before his time. Their eggs had ripened first.

And then his own precious ovum—perfectly oblong, shiny, and still—resting for eons in a mystical petri dish, began to break open on the scrying screen, and Ghost leaned forward to watch, his eyes wide with wonder, his heart filled with dread.

The fissures were small at first.

The egg glowed, a diamond hue.

And then the center crack widened, Ghost peered in, and shock stole his breath from his lungs: two hatchlings, not one! Both yolks had been coated in their own slimy albumen, the gelatinous substance fused together, and a twin pair of fledgling dragyri were struggling mightily to break free. Only, the one on the left was robust and strong, emerging with a mighty shout like a trumpet, whereas the one on the right was sickly and weak, became tangled in the albumen, and fell out of the sac with a whimper.

The one on the left pumped his fists and kicked his legs.

The one on the right was gnarled and bloody, his hands hung limp, and his leg bones were twisted.

Ghost shot back on the couch, his own legs kicking at the stony ground of the cavern, like he was trying to backpedal through the blood-red sofa.

No-no-no.

His head was spinning.

The fucking dream!

His chest was aching.

That terrifying, never-ending nightmare—Ghost felt like he was about to vomit—*a simple cardboard carton filled with two lone eggs: first, on opposite sides, then coming ever closer together, until they were side by side.*

The depiction from the dream progressed.

Ghost, in the kitchen of the Diamond Lair, about to cook some breakfast. He cracked the first egg, then the second, and a gooey, bloody embryo fell into the pan: a half-formed chick screeching, crying...wailing with the voice of a masculine child.

The boy jumped out of the pan.

The boy grew two gnarled, child-sized legs.

The boy limped and struggled against tight, restrictive braces, before leaping over the nearby balcony, scaling each veranda in turn, and finally dropping like a sodden weight into the hot, unforgiving sand.

The boy tried to bury himself beneath the granules, even as Ghost tried feverishly to dig him out—the mire closed in like a cascading mudslide, and the boy disappeared beneath the sand.

The scrying screens crackled like liquid thunder, shifting from the nightmare to cold, hard facts, and electric fingers emerged like lightning from the tempest and began to sketch images atop the now molten monitors: exquisite pictorials, detailed portraits, a magnificent replica of a sweet, handsome boy.

Ghost narrowed his eyes on a single screen, a molten pictorial directly in front of the sofa he sat upon, and he studied the portrait like an ancient pantheist sun worshipper beholding his first solar eclipse. And then he sank back in the leather couch.

"Gideon..."

He breathed the word with equal measures of pain and reverence; then he rocked forward on the leather cushions, his stomach spasmed, and he retched and retched—*and retched*—spewing vomit all over his boots and his lap.

The scrying screen trundled back like a scroll, and lost,

buried memories rushed in like a freight train, every lovely, agonizing, or forgotten recollection displayed one by one inside the desolate walls of a foreign Sinners' Cave...

The snout of a diamond dragon testing the strength of each newborn son.

The same diamond dragon breathing pure, silver fire over the first perfect offspring, to sanitize, heal, and cleanse, while he ignored the plaintive whimpers coming from the second hatchling.

Lord Dragos' claws, his magnificent wings transporting the crippled infant dragyri back to the white, sandy beach where the deity had first laid his eggs, then hiding him deep inside a cold, obscure cavern, a cave without fresh air, water, or light.

Lord Dragos shackled the weak, helpless offspring to a stone, and Ghost clawed at his hair as he watched. Who the fuck *shackled* a newborn baby, a boy who could barely move his limbs on his own, inside a living crypt, a certain grave, just to hide the evidence of his...flawed...existence? Lord Dragos had left his own flesh and blood to die—slowly and in agony—because his own perfection had been called into question, his divine, supernatural powers had proved inadequate, and his supposedly superior, omnipotent chromosomes had mutated, revealing a genetic defect.

And Ghost had borne the brunt of that decision for six long, unholy years.

Because original hatchlings grew so quickly, Ghost did not have long to wait before he could return. In the absence of having a human mother, whether mortal or dragyra in form, there was no Homo sapien DNA in Ghost's blood, and thus, he had matured from infancy to early childhood within a matter of days—and he had immediately returned to the cave to loosen Gideon's shackles and look after his twin.

He had fed his brother.

He had bathed his brother.

He had given him water and applied ointment to his fresh abrasions and wounds.

He had tried like hell to heal Gideon's afflictions, but either Ghost's fire was too weak, or Gideon's infirmities were too elemental, a result of hard-cast, genetic permutations resistant to outward manipulation or change: The best Ghost could do was recast Gideon's wrists, build him a pair of crude metal braces, massage his frail muscles with an analgesic ointment, and over time, teach his twin to walk—or hobble—as best as he could.

Ghost had also taught Gideon to read and write, arithmetic, geography, and astronomy.

Dragonese, English, and Latin.

Creation, philosophy, and history of the planets.

He had read to him. He had told him stories. And he had promised to one day find a way to set him free...to set them *both* free from their evil sire.

Yes, Lord Dragos had known exactly what Ghost was doing, but as long as Ghost kept his sire's secret, completed his chores, and attended his lessons, Lord Dragos had allowed the clandestine, charitable sessions to go on. In some sick, sadistic way, Ghost's stark desperation and Gideon's never-ending suffering had almost given the diamond deity pleasure.

Still, Ghost had waited...

He had honed his powers, studied more magick, and absorbed more alchemy than his sire knew. By all that was holy, he had made a pact with his twin—someday, somehow, the two would flee the Pantheon together, and if fate ever allowed for anything that even resembled revenge or justice, Ghost would put Lord Dragos in his own gruesome grave.

The scrying screen shuddered, the scrolled sequence of the twin birth was expunged, and Ghost drew several ragged breaths —how had he forgotten *all* of this? Every memory, every heart-wrenching moment, and every prayer for Gideon? Every desperate longing for revenge? The screen before him began to change once more, as if depicting Ghost's soul instead of his memories, painting a portrait of his inner mind rather than Gideon's outer features. And the agony of what appeared before him was almost more than Ghost could bear.

Ghost saw, felt, and remembered...love.

He tasted it on his tongue, felt its pulse on the tips of his fingers. He smelled it in the air and saw it in Gideon's bright, diamond eyes and guileless, hope-filled smile. He heard it in his twin's pure, golden laughter and the suffering child's kind, adoring voice.

"*Ghost!*"

The way Gideon said Ghost's name whenever Ghost appeared in the dark.

"*You came to see me again today!*"

Ghost came to see him *every* day—every morning, every afternoon, and every night—yet Gideon always greeted him with that same pleasantly surprised, grateful welcome. And now, Ghost was seeing it all—the friendship, the loyalty, and the trust between them—in a gods-forsaken cavern in the bowels of hell.

How?

What...

Why?

The Sinners' Cave grew eerily dark, as if the fireplace had just gone out, and the scrying screen before him began to creak and moan.

"Stop this!" Ghost barked, not even knowing what *this* was, only that every fiber of his being was screaming, *No more!*

"Do not look away," Lord Drakkar commanded in a merciless voice, even as the screen once again brightened, and a fresh, new memory slowly came into focus.

The winter of Ghost and Gideon's sixth year.

Mystical snow falling in the Pantheon, as the sea in the cove glistened with gemstone-colored dragon's fire.

Ghost entering the cave just after midnight, bringing fresh bread, roasted pheasant, and boiled potatoes, left over from dinner—only Gideon wasn't there! Ghost searched the cave. He combed the shore. He spent the next two hours flying in systematic grids and organized patterns from one end of the Pantheon to the other.

Still, no Gideon.

Finally, fueled by fear and abject panic, he approached the Temple of Seven the next morning, seeking an audience with his cruel, heartless sire, and Lord Dragos let him in, not just into the venerable sanctuary, and not just into one of the pristine rear drawing rooms, but up the long, winding staircase, beyond the hall of thrones, and into Lord Dragos' private chambers.

"Have I displeased you again, Lord Dragos?" Ghost had asked him, after taking a seat on a satin gold ottoman. He knew better than to call him Father, at least not until his eighteenth birthday. "Is that why you moved my brother, Gideon, somewhere I can't find him?"

Lord Dragos chuckled, a foul, disharmonic sound. "Did you know that Jagyr Ethyron almost followed you to the cave in the dark of night when you last went to attend to your brother, to bring your favorite pet some scraps left over from supper?"

Ghost had gulped, hugged his stomach, and bowed his head. No way Jagyr could have followed him—Ghost was always *very* careful. "I circled around twice, Lord Dragos."

"You were ten minutes late to mercenary training."

"I...I...I won't let it happen again."

"Ah," Lord Dragos snorted. "I see. Let me ask you then: Have you ever been late to one of your private alchemy sessions with Lord Ethyron or one of your spell-weaving tutorials with Lord Topenzi? *Lord Topenzi!*" he repeated in disgust.

Ghost's eyes grew wide, and his hands began to tremble—*how did his sire know?*

"Private classes in magick and sorcery; did you think I would never find out?"

"No," Ghost muttered, rushing the words. "I just...I just thought...if I learned even more than is required, you would be pleased with your Genesis—"

"Do not say *Son!*" Lord Dragos barked. "Perhaps *Betrayal* or *Treason*, or even *Treachery*, but do not form your tongue to say Son."

Ghost knew his goose was cooked. Lord Dragos was so harsh, so punitive, so unforgiving—he had not forgotten the scorching he had endured that morning in the London alley—still, this was not about Ghost and his extracurricular activities. It was about protecting his brother, Gideon. "Forgive me, Lord Dragos. I will accept your punishment, but please know that none of my choices...none of my disobedience...had anything to do with Gideon."

"You stupid wretch," Lord Dragos snarled. "You don't even have the good sense to keep his name from your tongue, whilst we whisper in this temple. You can no longer be trusted to keep this secret, nor to show the proper discretion or deference."

"Father, please..."

"*Father?*"

"Lord Dragos, please. I'm your last living original Genesis Son. Whatever you've done with Gideon, I beg you: Show him mercy and turn your ire on me instead. I promise—no, I swear—from this day forward, I will—"

"It's already done," Lord Dragos snorted.

Ghost's bottom lip quivered. "What's already done?"

"Your brother is no more, and further, he has been dismembered, one body part for each of your sins. His arms are buried in the grasslands, his torso is at the bottom of the purple lake, his head is in the high, rocky mountains, and those piteous, twisted, bony legs, well, they're right in this room, in front of you." He reached behind a broad, heavy chest of drawers, retrieved a pile of metal braces, and gestured toward the bottom of the coffee table in front of the ottoman.

Ghost took one look, froze like a startled animal caught in a predator's crosshairs, and then he screamed...and screamed...as if his body was being devoured. He fell to the floor of the opulent chamber and ripped out two handfuls of his dark black hair, his chest heaving in violent sobs of rage, anger, and raw, feral agony. "No! *Noooooooooo*! What have you done!? *Oh gods, oh gods, oh gods*—why? *Whyyyy*!"

Lord Dragos swept a carefree, indifferent hand over the top of Ghost's head, and the room, as well as the memory, fell silent. The six-year-old child rose from his perch on the flamboyant, sparkling floor, declined his head in reverent obedience, and slowly backed out of the private apartment, his face as placid as a still mountain lake.

"He removed your memory." Lord Drakkar Hades' dark, satin voice shattered the silence. "And he did more than just place those bones in the table. He trapped Gideon's spirit inside the wood—sentient, still feeling, suspended in eternal suffering— so it would never rest peacefully in the Garden of Grace. He placed your twin's bones beneath his feet, and trapped his soul in suspended animation, in order to torture and degrade him for all eternity, even as he mocked you in perpetuity."

Ghost balled his hands into fists.

Then he extended and splayed his fingers.

He repeated the same exercise, again and again, trying to divorce his soul from his body. He would not cry in front of the king of the underworld. He. Would. Not. Cry. In front of Lord Drakkar Hades.

His shoulders shook, and the smell of his own vomit wafted

to his nostrils like fresh, pungent urine; still, he opened and closed his fists, staring straight ahead into nothing.

At nothing.

Through nothing.

Then the scrying screen zoomed in on Lord Dragos' bedchamber table, the outline of a six-year-old's knee attached to a femur, and Ghostaniaz Dragos leaped to his feet. "Turn that shit off! Turn it off now!" He turned his back on the monitor, but the image, oddly, followed him. "I said, *Turn it off*!" he shouted, his voice shaking the stony rafters. He tried to spin around, shield his eyes with his arm, but no matter what he did—or didn't do— the ghastly image followed him: long, shiny shinbones, the remains of a beloved twin brother.

Ghost lunged toward the Sinners' Cave coffee table, scooped up his scepter with one hand to keep it safely out of the way, and lifted the heavy, wooden, defiled piece of furniture with the other. "What the fuck is this shit!" he bellowed. "Some sort of demonic replica! Are these legs...these bones...did you somehow retrieve something of Gideon's from the Pantheon?" He sounded utterly unhinged as he smashed the table against the ancient stone floor and pummeled it repeatedly with his trembling free hand, over and over, until the tabletop and the bones were mere fragments, scattered pieces, and the small, scattered pieces became piles of ground ash.

Yet and still...

The image on the scrying screens followed Ghost around, hovering in the air at eye level, growing larger and larger and more insistent, every minute detail of Lord Dragos' abomination flashing like a suspended neon sign.

Ghost raised his scepter and shouted like a crazed, primitive warrior: "Turn. That. Fucking. Shit. Off!" The monitors exploded outward; the fire went out in the cavern; and Ghostaniaz Dragos sank to his knees and grasped his head in his hands.

I will not cry in front of this devil.

I will not lose my shit in this fucking castle.

I will not...I will not...

I won't!

I can't...

As Ghostaniaz Dragos kneeled on the floor, still covered in his own snot and vomit, his shoulders shook like a seismic avalanche, and the groan that escaped his lips sounded bestial and inhuman. He didn't just cry—he keened, and he wept—he raked his nails against the stones beneath him until his fingers were bleeding, and he choked on his own drizzling mucous.

And still, he could not stop.

Why...

Why!

How could anyone—

Not Gideon!

Not Gideon. Not Gideon. Not Gideon.

Finally, when he felt like he might just drown in his tears—or die from the depths of his anguish—Lord Drakkar Hades, king of the underworld, knelt on the ground in front of him. "Our table had nothing to do with your brother...an unfortunate, untimely coincidence. The bones belong to a mere disobedient human servant who was deeply disliked by my pagans. But, alas, I believe we understand one another: Ghostaniaz Dragos, nephew of my lineage, should you choose to serve me, willingly and with true, heartfelt fealty, together we will be unstoppable. You can open a portal to the Pantheon of Dragons, and I and my legions can avenge your brother. Yes, Ghost, I—and I alone—have the power to destroy your father. And further, I possess both the ability and the sorcery required to locate your brother's remains and release his soul from that inanimate object, to free him from his eternal agony.

"Am I a deity of death and destruction? Absolutely and

unerringly. Yet, in exchange for your eternal oath and everlasting devotion, I would give Gideon Dragos eternal rest, and I will still make you prince of the underworld. No more plots. No more hedging, and no more piteous harvesting of useless herbal poison. No searching for brass keys, and no counting down the days until the Temple of Seven. No waiting. No prevarication. Just bold, decisive action. The decision of a Genesis Son who was bred to be a fearsome warrior, choosing instead to become a mighty pagan. The throne room is ready, and my horde is waiting—all has been converted and prepared for your Feast of Coronation. *Yes, this night.* Right now, not on Wednesday. I told you much had changed, and now you understand me. Bethany, your dragyra, is being bathed, dressed, and shall be exalted as a princess, to both sit beside you at the ceremony and reign beside you, for all eternity.

"Yes, I have the power to override her inevitable demise, should she fail to appear in the Pantheon for conversion. Am I not equal to the Seven in every manner of divinity, aspect of authority, and facet of creation? And what took place in this cave, this night—what I saw on those scrying screens, outside of information about the Dragyr and the Pantheon, what *you* saw on those scrying screens with regard to your sire, your upbringing, and your twin hatchling—shall remain our secret forever. Come to me, Ghost, of your own free volition, and I will give you savage, pitiless, diabolical vengeance."

CHAPTER THIRTY-TWO

Anne Liu shot straight up in bed, her eyes fixing instantly on the bedside alarm clock.

It was 1:30, late Friday night.

Well, technically, it was now Saturday morning, and something was wrong—horribly, alarmingly, terribly *wrong*—something that had everything to do with Beth and the dragyri male Jax had told Anne about. Ghostaniaz Dragos. The son of a dragon Beth's fate and her future were intrinsically tied to.

Anne hugged her lower stomach, grasped the silky pink fabric of her nightgown with her fingertips, and stared blankly at Queenie, her Persian cat. The feline was standing alongside Anne's ankles, spine arched, the fur on her back sticking straight up. "I feel it too," Anne murmured, petting the cat on the head to calm her. "What the heck is happening, kitty?"

Queenie hissed and rubbed against Anne's ankles, and in a flash, one of the images Anne had seen in the Oracle Pool during her terrifying ordeal in the Temple of Seven—*the experience had not been a dream!*—instantly appeared in the air above her...

The ring of fire exploding upward, as if from the core of the earth.

Surrounding, scorching, and blazing like molten lava as it engulfed the Arapahoe County Fairgrounds.

"What the hell?"

Queenie growled and swiped a claw through the air, causing Anne to shiver.

"Oh my gosh, not again," Anne murmured anxiously. "Why do these visions keep coming to me?" She took a deep breath and closed her eyes, but she couldn't conjure a fresh revelation—and she couldn't shake the heebie-jeebies. *Oh, hell*, she thought. It was nearly two in the morning, and despite her desire to remain sequestered, perhaps hide beneath her bedsheets until the next millennium, she knew she was going to have to reach out to Jax. Maybe text him or call him? She had no idea how any of that worked—cell signals getting through to another world, transcending spiritual, celestial, and cosmic dimensions—but Jax had never had a problem getting a message through to Anne, and "Bryce M" had replied to her last phone call like a human who lived next door.

A push...

A nudge...

A sudden sense of peace, like a cool breath of fresh air sweeping along the back of Anne's neck, then a sudden *impression* of Grandma Betsy: "Send a message to Jax, then awaken your girlfriends. Return as one in spiritual harmony to the Arapahoe County Fairgrounds and pray for Bethy. As least on this planet, the imprint of her energy still remains strongest in the place she last stood."

Anne spun around.

She looked left, then right, up, then down.

She snatched Queenie and dragged her onto her lap.

What in the world was happening?

She gulped and tried to focus, reaching toward her night-stand to retrieve her cell phone. She opened her contacts, hit the dictation icon, and began to compose a crazy, late-night text to a supernatural creature a parallel galaxy away.

* * *

Lord Dragos, Ruler of the Diamond Lair, was positively apoplectic.

It was 1:45 in the morning, he hadn't had an ounce of sleep, and his humongous dragon heart was racing like a jackhammer, nearly pounding out of his scaly chest.

Lord Drakkar Hades still had his son.

His son!

The only remaining original hatchling from Lord Dragos' superior bloodline, his genesis lineage, his own flesh and bone! And whatever the crazed, evil, self-serving bastard of a pagan king was doing to Ghostaniaz, it was causing a rift in the entire collective cosmos.

Lord Dragos could feel it from here!

To say nothing of Anne Liu's nearly ruinous revelations—a pair of eggs, a table made from bone, a powerful brass key, a golden scepter, and a ring of fire exploding upward—*poppycock*!

That crazy bitch was dangerous.

Yet and still, if Lord Dragos tolerated the girl just a little bit longer, Anne might just lead them all to Ghostaniaz. She *had* to lead them all to Ghost. The Seven had managed to decipher their own sacred divinations out of the human female's gibberish, at least enough to devise a tentative game plan going forward, but Lord Dragos would have to tread carefully from now on.

Very, *very* carefully.

Lest his own dastardly deeds inadvertently rise to the surface.

"So what the fuck if they do!" he snarled.

He strolled across his expansive, private apartment, plopped down on a giant, gawdy, cream-and-gold sofa, and stared at the gold satin ottoman across from him. Smiling, he slammed his feet against the wood-and-bone coffee table and reveled in the feel of the skeleton beneath him, just as a faint psychic query swirled in the air all around him. "Yes?" he spoke aloud.

"Father, it's Jax. Forgive me for waking you."

Waking me? Ha! "What the fuck do you want?"

"My lord, I just received a message from Miss Liu, and I think you will want to hear it, posthaste."

"Very well," Lord Dragos grumbled. Then he closed the telepathic connection with the equivalent force of slamming a door in one's face. He did not need Jaxtapherion to dictate the message —he was a primordial, omniscient, all-powerful deity. Had he not been distracted with his own meritorious thoughts, he would have already intercepted the message himself.

Alas...

The divine lord of the Diamond Lair did not waste his time or his mental energy spying on mortals or constantly watching his dragyri children, at least not unless and until it was imminently warranted: The question was not *Could a preternatural god see, hear, or know everything if he chose to?* but rather, *Should he bother?* And since, clearly, he should, in this one onerous and portentous instance, he simply rolled back time, focused on Anne Liu—sneered at the sight of her fat, ugly cat—and absorbed each and every thought, fear, hope, and sensation she'd had in her bedroom whilst composing the text. And he made special note of the angelic presence, the unseen, aged, spiritual visitor who had woken Anne up and fed her the information.

Interesting...

Very interesting.

CHAPTER THIRTY-THREE

Ghost entered his bedchamber like a walking slab of petrified lava, in order to wash and prepare for his own coronation. He was nothing but hard, unfeeling stone. His huge, bulky muscles expanded and contracted almost robotically, as his steady, even, predatory gait moved him mindlessly across the stony floor.

He knew in an instant that Beth wasn't there.

She had already been bathed, dressed, and escorted to the throne room, more than likely by an assembly of human maid-servants.

So be it.

It was better that way.

Ghost didn't have to repeat, explain, or tell her anything—he didn't have to excuse his decision or justify why the two of them would live out their remaining eternal existence in the bowels of hell: *"Come to me, Ghost, of your own free volition, and I will give you savage, pitiless, diabolical vengeance."*

Ghost didn't just want vengeance.

He wanted pain...prolonged agony...and utter obliteration.

He wanted living hatred; inhuman, pitiless, tyrannical slaughter; and everlasting dominion over Lord Dragos' futile, castrated, insufferable incarnation. And he would have it, if it cost him...everything...if it killed him, if it killed Beth, if it killed every dragyri in the Pantheon of Dragons.

He passed by a gilded, ornate mirror hanging toward the entrance to the curtained platform, and turned his head to appraise his profile—he no longer recognized the male in front of him. Short, dark hair may as well have been an arcane, pitch-black halo hovering above a skull filled with magick, alchemy, and sinister intentions. Diamond irises and phantom-blue pupils may as well have been the eyes of a shark: empty, bloodthirsty, and swimming in cold, vacant circles, waiting for someone to toss carrion in the water. As he passed the familiar high-backed, blue velvet chair, he couldn't help but notice the tiny, dark blue vial filled with belladonna, still resting on the upholstery—Beth must have forgotten to take it with her, or perhaps she had not had time to retrieve it.

No matter.

Whether Lord Drakkar had broken his word, *after promising not to spy on Ghostaniaz—the forked-tongue monarch had said,* "Rarely"—heard it from another source, or simply caught notice of all the strange comings and goings, human servants shuffling between the lower apothecary and the dimly lit main floor stair-case, stuffing odd, bulky gray blankets into a wooden trunk, Lord Drakkar had already known all about the hidden poison, and Ghost and Beth would no longer need it.

Ghost was just about to strip out of his vomit-soaked jeans and his sweat-drenched T-shirt, grab a bucket of water and a bar of lye soap to scrub away all the filth and degradation, when he noticed something else by the chair, a piece of ancient papyrus that had fallen to the ground, with fresh, undried ink leaching through the parchment, and he bent to pick it up.

He held it beneath his eyes and winced: *Dear Ghost...*

What the fuck?

He almost tossed it across the chamber and into the fire, but curiosity got the best of him.

Dear Ghost, please forgive me for putting these words on actual paper, but I have no idea what might happen before this night is over or if I'll ever see you again. If everything we've said, done, and...considered...is somehow revealed on the Sinners' Cave screens, then even if you make it out alive, I may have to resort to another option. The blue vial. And if that happens, you will never know the decision I wrestled with as I waited in this chamber.

Ghost, I will never understand why all of this happened, why I was taken from my friends, thrust into a nightmare, or why the two of us were thrown together. Even now, we hardly know each other, yet that doesn't change my decision. If only you could see what I see: the male inside of the mercenary, the warrior beyond the dragyri, and the kindness beneath the armor of indifference, so many layers of scars formed by such inhumanity... Yes, I have heard your warnings and felt your detachment, but I have also heard you breathe my name and felt the passion beneath your fingertips. I have experienced your concern and known your fierce protection, and I have learned through it all that, above all else, you are a "man" of your word and a being of honor.

Ghost, you are brave, strong, and incredibly faithful.

And more than that, you are worthy, even if you don't know it.

Moreover, I know, without doubt, that I can learn to love you, that I will come to love you, and that I already both adore and respect you (as a woman, I am lost, shattered, and hopelessly enchanted every time I look in your eyes). So, my decision is yes, to all of it, Ghost. Today. Tomorrow. And forever. And until I see you again—if I never see you again—know that you had both my heart and my fealty.

Love is a choice. It's not just a feeling.

And I choose you, Ghost. I choose you!

Child of fire, daughter of flames, more than a woman, more than a name, born from the soul of The Pantheon ~ "Beth."

Ghost's mouth dropped open.

He tilted his head to the side.

And for a fleeting moment, he was truly...*bewildered.*

Then the pitch-black halo atop his vacant skull tightened in the form of a thought-piercing headache, driving all but blind rage out of his mind. The shark circled forward, flicked its menacing fins, and sniffed for the bloody carrion in the water. And the soulless slab of petrified lava tightened its fist around the paper, crumpled Beth's letter into a ball of wrath, and stood, silent, while the dragon inside the lost, pitiless mercenary breathed a single blood-red flame and scorched the letter to ash.

CHAPTER THIRTY-FOUR

I n the elaborate gold, opal, and magnesite anteroom just north of the Great Hall, which typically exalted Lord Drakkar's legendary red velvet throne, the solemn king of the underworld sat back behind his heavy baroque desk, flicked his wrist to shoo a gargantuan python away from the tabletop, and watched in keen fascination as the serpent swallowed one of his two-headed hellhounds.

The scent of incense billowing in the waiting gallery, just 200 feet south of the sequestered chamber on the other side of the thick, decorative panels, wafted beneath the cracks near the floor and filled the king's nostrils with anticipation: *Ghost's imminent coronation and the endless possibilities!*

Lord Drakkar could only hope all would go as planned.

Requiem Pyre, the king's chief sorcerer, knocked softly on one of the side panels, waited three seconds, then entered somberly, his broad but bony shoulders draped beneath a heavy gothic robe literally dipped in blood, as was customary formal attire for the king's illustrious dignitaries during sacred events and hallowed ceremonies. "My liege."

Lord Drakkar crooked two fingers, ushering the dark-blue-eyed demon closer to the desk. "Is everything in order?"

Requiem strode forward, his long, plaited braids, festooned with bone and ancient fox shells, swaying as he walked, and for a moment, Lord Drakkar couldn't help but wonder—*why have I not yet had sex with him?* "Indeed. All has been made ready," the chief sorcerer said.

The king shrugged an absent shoulder. "Did you find an acceptable human slave, perform the necessary spellcast, and set up the pit and the skewer, exactly as I instructed?"

Requiem stepped over a second python, careful to keep his ankles a safe distance from the giant serpent's dual upper jawbones as he leaned against the desk. "The female slave I chose is the same height as Bethany, she has the same hair color and the same bewitching skin tone, and the spell I cast was impeccable... flawless. Ghost will never detect the difference."

Lord Drakkar nodded with appreciation. "So then, Ghost will not know that the woman who sits beside him is an imposter, and Bethany will in turn appear as the slave girl when we fasten her to the spike and roast her body atop the molten pyre? Ghost will not detect Bethany's...*chosen*...DNA when he feasts on her flesh and devours her unique *fated* anima?"

"No, my liege. He will not."

"Good. *Good*. And if she cries out in agony as she's dying... burning...roasting alive—nay, *when* she cries out in agony—her voice will not give her away?"

At this, Requiem Pyre declined his head in both deference and a bit of annoyance. "I have been your chief sorcerer for nearly eight hundred years, my liege, and my alchemy is unassailable. The spell is impermeable. Neither her voice, nor her whimpers, nor any infinitesimal marker that distinguishes her distinctive eternal spirit will give her true identity away to Ghostaniaz." He paused as if considering his next words carefully. "But if I may ask, and only to learn from your infinite knowledge and expert tutelage; what difference would it make if he did? Is this male's fealty to you still in question? Is his desire for power and vengeance not solid, even after all that was revealed on the scrying screens?"

Lord Drakkar's brow heated with anger, and he narrowed his kaleidoscope eyes. "Who are you to question me!"

Requiem took a cautious step back, bowed his head in exaggerated deference, and then raised it again in rare defiance. "I have many questions, lord. I am a numen of the ages, and I only wish to imbibe your wisdom. I am no one to question my sovereign king, nor do my queries hold any weight against your temporal desires or immaculate preferences, but if my liege would indulge me—"

Lord Drakkar drummed his long, pointed nails against the tabletop to shut his chief sorcerer up. He glanced at his hellhounds and then the twin snakes slithering about the ornate, golden, broadloom rugs and considered feeding Requiem to the latter—but then he thought better of it. There was too much at stake this night...this early morning...and Drakkar needed all his servants to play their required roles. What harm could there be in an ancient demon sorcerer increasing his vast wealth of knowledge? "Speak freely but quickly. Ghost's coronation must not wait."

Requiem bowed again, this time with full sincerity. "The male's loyalty, my liege?"

At this, Lord Drakkar had to smile. "You were not there. You did not see his eyes, you did not feel his rage, nor did you behold the darkness that eclipsed his already-bitter soul. His lust for vengeance is...*absolute*...and I have counted his hatred as fealty. Next?"

"Your decision to feed the dragyra's flesh to Ghostaniaz is equal parts wicked, wise, and lawful: You deceived him when you said you could sustain her life beyond the tenth day of her claiming, should she fail to appear in the Temple of Seven. Consuming her flesh will seal Ghost's blasphemy once and for all against the seven dragon lords of the Pantheon, thus consummating his final, irrevocable descent into darkness. And of course, there is the matter of Salyn Stryke, your loyal and obedient soul eater: a life for a life, Bethany for Felicity, reprisal for what Ghost took from both demons and shadow-walkers without your sovereign permission. But"—he prevaricated—"if it would please my king, could you expand on the first two reasons, if only to enlighten my understanding? The third is self-explanatory."

Lord Drakkar took a deep breath, rolled his eyes, then attempted to proceed as judiciously as possible. "Yes, I lied to Ghost about exalting his dragyra as some sort of pagan princess to rule at his side for all eternity—it was a necessary falsehood to procure his compliance. Perhaps, if I could, I would. But I cannot. The reason? The number seven is greater than the number one. Think about it and get back to me if it still perplexes you."

Requiem did not have to think about it. "You are a sovereign, all-powerful deity, but so are the Seven who came out of the original swirling mass along with you. You cannot undo their collective will or revoke the supremacy of their laws, any more than they could undo your own?"

"Bully for you, chief sorcerer," Lord Drakkar sneered. "Your powers of reasoning astound me. Now then, *yes*—the female's death will solidify Ghost's darkness and appease my servant Salyn, but that is not the only reason her consumption is imperative. There is the matter of both light and darkness, good and evil, as well as male and female energy. I do not have time to revisit creation, but suffice it to say: When I chose utter darkness, without even the hint or possibility of light, I knew that the errant, destructive, and divisive vibrations would serve my purpose and please my soul more than any *living* energy could. I chose death over life. The Seven chose differently. And Ghost was begotten from one of those seven, despite the fact that Lord Dragos was three parts corrupt to begin with. That said, Bethany's goodness, her hope, her ability to love would always be a threat to Ghost's darkness—even a pinprick of light in the form of a single candle can illuminate a vast, lightless cavern. That flame must be extinguished in its entirety."

"And the female energy?" Requiem asked.

"We both know I chose to abort all things feminine when I emerged from the original cosmos, in spite of the fact that the timeless ether contained equal parts, both feminine and masculine. It was balanced, just as Bethany would always threaten to balance Ghost's anima. A gentle stream can wear down an enormous, prehistoric rock, given enough time and patience. No!" He slammed his fist against the desk. "My own extolment depends upon his full devotion. The sooner the female is removed from the equation, the better."

Requiem Pyre nodded in understanding and rolled his wrist to signify his appreciation. "Just one more question?"

"What is it?"

"Why did Lord Dragos do it?"

Lord Drakkar cocked his dark, thinly arched eyebrows. "Why did he create a rare egg containing twin yolks, a perfect, powerful offspring and a weak, sickly brood? Or why did he profane his own Genesis Son, torture Ghostaniaz for amusement, then erase his own faithful child's memories?"

"Any of it. All of it. If Lord Dragos' soul contained even a pinprick of light, as you infer, then why did he hate Ghostaniaz so much?"

Lord Drakkar shook his head and waved his hand in condescension. "You really don't get it, do you? You really can't grasp the whole sordid chronicle?"

Requiem remained silent.

"Ah, dear sorcerer! If only you could see the same intricacies I do, then like me, you might have a small, burgeoning respect for Lord Dragos—for he is truly more devious and duplicitous than first imagined. When the Seven decided to create their own genesis offspring, without the aid of women, they drew lots to see which of the six would produce one hundred and forty-three eggs, and which remaining lord would only produce one hundred and forty-two. Lord Dragos lost the draw, so he chose to secretly even the odds with alchemy—he always knew one of his eggs would contain twin yolks, but he did not understand that the very deception he introduced into the process would also taint the albumen, causing one of the yolks to wither. Magick always has a price. As for why he hated Ghost that much?"

Lord Drakkar threw back his head and laughed. "He did not hate Ghost! He has *never* hated Ghost. The dragon god *feared* his own supernatural offspring. Once again, do the math: Just as seven is greater than one, sixty-six is greater than thirty-three. Chromosomes, that is. Ghost's spirit combined with Gideon's would equal the very number of their Father-Creator. Together, and if they had wielded their alchemy correctly, the twins would have possessed power nearly equal to a god. Unbeknownst at the time, Lord Dragos had created his own supreme, metaphysical double, and he had to correct that...control it...rein it in before it backfired."

"Shiiit," Requiem whispered.

"Yes. *Shit*," Lord Drakkar echoed.

"And in doing so, he did you a favor."

"Oh," Lord Drakkar droned thoughtfully, "indeed he did. *Indeed he did.* Lord Dragos did the one thing, the only thing, that would have caused Ghostaniaz to turn wholly to darkness and betray his Pantheon brethren. And one day in the not-so-distant future, should luck and superiority be on my side, I shall rule both the barren underworld and the pristine, mystical territories beyond the Dragyr portal because of it." A fresh eddy of incense wafted to the king's nostrils, and he turned his attention to the anteroom doors. "Alas, it is time to get on with our own decadent genesis...Ghost's glorious pagan beginning."

CHAPTER THIRTY-FIVE

On the northwest end of the throne room, behind one of four obsidian pillars, Bethany gasped, writhed, and tugged at the bindings on her wrists, as a soul eater named Salyn Stryke and a one-handed demon named Trader Vice slathered her near-naked body in oil, affixed her arms to a tall, vertical, birchwood column, and pressed her bare back against a rough, unfinished post.

Her thick, wavy, dark brown hair looked fine, straight, and white.

Her smooth mocha skin was ghostly pale and covered in random pink blotches.

And her tall, slender frame, with modest curves, was buxom, curvaceous, and at least five inches...shorter.

What the hell had the pagans done to her?

Her breath caught in her throat as they raised the column, anchored it into the center of a circular pit filled with lava rock and charcoal, and affixed her wrists and ankles to two notched platforms carved into the birchwood.

Oh, no-no-no...

This wasn't happening!

Why hadn't she consumed the vial of belladonna the moment three maidservants, a demon, and a shadow-walker had used a skeleton key to enter the bedchamber?

She had known right away that something was wrong.

Terribly, terribly wrong!

Perhaps the pagans had read Ghost's thoughts and sentenced both him and Bethany to death as punishment for their treachery...treason...plotting. Lord Drakkar had probably found out about the apothecary, the servants, and the belladonna, and now he was going to make a public example of Bethany in the throne room.

But where was Ghost?

What had they done with the dragyri?

Salyn dipped his fingers into a deep silver bowl, swirled his hand around in a circle, then scooped a palm-sized portion of strange, unknown elements out of the container before squeezing Bethany's cheeks to force her mouth open and violently shoving the scoop in her mouth.

She gagged and choked on her tongue.

What the hell was—

Flavors.

Textures.

Not strange, unknown elements, but seasonings and spices!

Two sticks of cinnamon, a bundle of oregano, a sprig of thyme, and a clump of salt. Before Bethany could retch and try to spit it out, he wedged a small red apple between her teeth and forced her to clamp down on the fruit.

Dear angels in heaven, this could not be happening!

Panic enveloped her senses, and terror became a living entity, even as the one-handed demon pointed his stump at the coals; a turquoise-and-black tiger snake shot out of the stump and flicked its tongue over the pit; and the lava rock...the coals...caught fire, burning a hot, deep, burnished red.

Bethany's eyes rolled back in her head.

They were going to cook her alive and eat her!

What in the name of heaven had she ever done to deserve such a hideous, painful, and merciless ending? Her eyes shot absently across the throne room, and for the first time, she noticed it had been set for an elaborate banquet—*what the hell?*—Ghost's coronation!

But what...

When?

How!

Her eyes fixed unerringly on a long, elegant table set with gold and ivory platters and multiple layers of silver cutlery atop a rich, deep, blood-red, spider-spun silk cloth, and then they narrowed in on an elegant woman sitting in one of two plush armchairs clearly reserved for the guests of honor: The woman could've been Bethany's doppelganger, only she was adorned like a Roman empress.

Realization struck Bethany like a sinister bolt of lightning.

Her eyes filled with tears, and her head lolled back.

And then, at least for this one blessed moment, she passed out, and the whole wicked world went black.

CHAPTER THIRTY-SIX

FEAST OF CORONATION

The Great Hall, which Ghost had always regarded as a dark, garish throne room, was now an elaborate if not ostentatious banquet hall fit for a medieval monarch. The banquet table was front and center, where Lord Drakkar Hades' throne usually sat, and it was festooned with multiple candelabras, the numerous individual flames merging with surrounding torchlight, and bedecked with every manner of gluttonous fare: platters upon platters of unidentifiable, roasted meat; large wooden troughs, deep enough to feed a passel of hogs, filled with fruits, vegetables, and seeded breads; diamond, obsidian, and emerald vessels replete with marmalade, broth, and strange-looking, bubbling gruel. The desserts were endless, the puddings were plentiful, and the tabletops were laden with huge barrel-sized jugs of wine and ale.

Ghost could have never poisoned so many containers.

In addition to the banquet table, the opulent feast, there was another tall bench made of wormwood, and it was piled high with medieval axes, every manner and era of daggers, crossbows, and swords, as well as enough gold, silver, and jeweled trinkets to fill a hundred ancient treasure chests. Ghost instinctively knew these were gifts for him—alms for the new prince of the underworld.

The incense was thick.

The main towering fireplace was crackling.

And Ghost was more than eager to get on with it—the sooner the better—the sooner he was elevated to second in command, the sooner he and Lord Drakkar Hades could begin to plot against his soulless sire.

He loosened two of the five leather buckles on the silver-and-scarlet Blacktide vest he was wearing beneath his gold and blood-red robe, tightened his fist around the golden scepter, and strolled purposely toward the table of honor, where Beth was already waiting.

Ghost felt nothing.

If it were not for the fact that he could hear his heart beating and feel the rise and fall of his chest, he would not have been certain he was still living, nor would he have cared.

And then the hairs on the back of his neck stood up.

Something was amiss.

Something just felt...off.

Beth looked beautiful. In fact, her outward appearance was both striking and impeccable: She was dressed in a pure white gown resembling a Roman toga. The draped stola was tied loosely about her open back and shoulders, and the golden pallium hung over her forearms, just below her elbows, the hue a perfect match to several shiny, untarnished hairpins. About half of her tresses were plaited into braids, then coiled into knots at the crown of her head, while the remaining thick, dark brown waves cascaded loosely over her slender left shoulder.

But her eyes were different.

Blank.

Empty.

She didn't even turn around to acknowledge Ghost as he approached.

Odd...

Especially when one considered she had just left him such a revealing, intimate letter in their private chambers.

Very odd...

Considering the fact that it was Friday night, five days prior to Wednesday's promised ceremony, and the Feast of Coronation was happening right now.

No heads-up.

No alternate planning.

No opportunity to harvest and utilize the poison, belladonna...

The complete upending of all their plans.

For all intents and purposes, Beth should have been angry and confused, desperate and scared—hell, she should've been trying frantically to find a way to speak to Ghost alone, if only for a stolen moment, in order to figure out what the hell was going on —but nothing. Not a care in the world. Perhaps the pagans or the human maidservants had given her some sort of sedative, something to settle or calm her nerves. Anything was possible at this point.

As if reading his thoughts, she shifted languidly in her chair, angled her shoulder, and met his dubious stare: "Well, hello, Prince; you look...gorgeous."

He blinked several times, then winced: Yeah, the female was definitely three sheets to the wind—*they had undeniably plied her with something*—but before Ghost had a chance to process that information, the flames in the towering, pure obsidian fireplace began to groan and creak, hiss...and speak: *Behold, the blooded nephew of your sovereign king, a stranger made brother, a Dragyr made pagan, an adversary made ally. Witness his oath, anointing, and resumption.*

The Great Hall fell silent, and Ghost remained standing as every blasted soul eater and sin eater in the underworld turned to gawk at him...hiss at him...glare at him. Yeah, this was going over like a rotten ton of bricks made of feces, fire, and brimstone, but Ghost didn't really give a shit.

"Raise your right hand and repeat after me!" Lord Drakkar Hades' voice echoed through the Great Hall like thunder, ricocheting off the floors, walls, and ceiling, yet Ghost couldn't make out where the king was standing...or sitting. It *felt* like he was everywhere at once. "I, Ghostaniaz Hades," Lord Drakkar continued, "do solemnly swear to govern the pagans of this kingdom and the Dominions thereto belonging, according to the Carnal Statutes of Congress, the Archaic Laws of Iniquity, and each and every depraved, irreverent custom, as begotten or desired of Lord Drakkar Hades."

Ghost's breath caught in his throat, his tongue began to swell in his mouth, and his lips grew uncharacteristically dry.

Fuuuck.

He knew the oath was going to be foul, but changing his name from Dragos to Hades and swearing allegiance to every depraved whim Lord Drak might ever conceive of, desire, or command? Ghost's hackles rose and his stomach clenched—but then he remembered Gideon, the horrific coffee table in Lord Dragos' private chambers, and a lifetime of having to obey a slew of wicked desires and commands, courtesy of his dragon sire. He raised his right hand and drew back his shoulders. "I, Ghostaniaz...*Hades*...do solemnly swear to govern the pagans of this kingdom—"

"*Nooo!*"

A muffled, plaintive female whimper rose from somewhere along the far northwest end of the throne room, piercing through the din of hot pagan breaths and crackling, hissing fire, as the image of Beth's face that night in their bedchamber—her flawless skin, trusting eyes, and thick, dark hair fanned out atop the pillow beneath her—suddenly flashed through his mind.

What the hell?

He cleared his throat and pressed onward: "To govern the pagans of this kingdom and the Dominions thereto belonging, according to the Carnal Statutes of Congress—"

"*Ghost! You came to see me again today!*" Gideon's bright, diamond eyes and guileless, hope-filled voice, punctuated by the most innocent smile.

Ghost popped his neck, rolled his shoulders, and stared outward at the Pagan Horde. "According to the Carnal Statutes of Congress, the Archaic Laws of Iniquity, and each and every depraved, irreverent custom—"

Moreover, I know, without doubt, that I can learn to love you, that I will come to love you, and that I already both adore and respect you.

Beth's letter!

Shit.

No!

Shake it off.

"And each and every depraved, irreverent custom," Ghost repeated, "as begotten or desired of Lord—"

Love is a choice. It's not just a feeling.

"Begotten or desired of Lord Drakkar Hades."

No sooner had Ghost spat the last words than the large, opulent gothic hall went black, flickered red, then illuminated once more in eerie shades of orange, yellow, and oscillating obsidian.

"Do it again!" Lord Drakkar bellowed, as if from a disembodied state. Ghost still couldn't place him. "And this time, do it without any hesitation." *Shiiit*, the pagan king sounded angry.

Ghost licked his lips and steadied his resolve. He glanced down at Beth, just because—*just because*—she was sitting so serenely, hands folded in her lap, and she actually nodded in encouragement.

Something was so, *so* incredibly wrong.

Ghost's eyes shot absently back and forth between the northwest end of the throne room, down to Beth, then once again to the corner, beyond a lone obsidian post: nothing but dark, slimy energy...orange, yellow, and obsidian light. And shadows. So many species, signa, and gradations of inky, odious shadows, each filling the hall, consuming the oxygen, poisoning Ghost's bloodstream, and claiming his soul.

It was as if he were being immersed in an unseen tar pit.

His head anointed with a foul, unclean oil.

His very cells drowning on a molecular level, submerged in maleficent pitch and changing with each spoken word.

This was supposed to be easy!

Simple.

Necessary.

And if only for Gideon, if only for revenge, it was time...

"Beth." He didn't know where her name came from, yet he spoke it with reverence, like a prayer or a plea, before cocking his head to the side one last time, and locking his gaze with hers.

In the space of a heartbeat, less than that really—a glint, an instant, a fleeting portent—Beth's vivid, dark brown irises glowed neon yellow, and a deep, blood-red orb eclipsed her pupils, glowing like the earth's inner core.

Ghost flinched.

He followed the arc of that strange, menacing glow back to the northwest corner of the throne room, and for the first time, he noticed the hot, glowing coals, the birchwood spit, and the female slave, half naked and trussed like an animal, slathered in oil. For the first time, he smelled the cinnamon, oregano, thyme, and apple, amidst all the other scents in the hall, and it struck him like a freight train—of course! *Of course,* Lord Drakkar would include the most profane of unholy rites in Ghost's formal induction, his *Feast* of Coronation...

The king did not just want Ghost's ascension and fealty—he wanted his immortal soul.

Ghost's mind flashed back to the Sinners' Cave, replaying the dark king's final recitation: "He removed your memory, and he did more than just place those bones in the table: He trapped Gideon's spirit inside the wood...sentient, still feeling, suspended in eternal suffering...yes, Ghost, I—and I alone—have the power to destroy your father....in exchange for your eternal oath and everlasting devotion. I would give Gideon Dragos eternal rest. Come to me, Ghost, of your own free volition, and I will give you savage, pitiless, diabolical vengeance."

Ghost cringed at the recollection.

He wanted that vengeance.

He *needed* that vengeance!

Yet he knew, on a level he had previously failed to comprehend, that the price was indeed his eternal soul.

Gideon...

An eternal oath.

Gideon!

Everlasting devotion!

Gideon, Gideon...*Gideon*.

There was nothing more to consider: no time, no second-guessing, and no room for mercy.

The darkness closed in all around him.

Above him, below him, inside of him...

And for a fleeting moment, Ghost realized something that sucked what was left of his soul right out of him—his deepest, darkest, lifelong fear had just come true: After all the years, the decades and centuries, rebelling, resisting, and defying his wicked sire, in the end, when all was said and done, he had become the thing he most detested, Lord Dragos' true Genesis Son.

Ghost was now the mirror image of his father.

He swallowed that truth like a bitter pill and forced his vocal cords to vibrate: "I, Ghostaniaz Hades, do solemnly swear to govern the pagans of this kingdom and the Dominions thereto belonging, according to the Carnal Statutes of Congress, the Archaic Laws of Iniquity, and each and every depraved, irreverent custom, as begotten or desired of—"

Yellow eyes!

Red pupils...

Hot, baking coals and a female sacrifice.

Oh shit...oh shit...oh shit!

The woman roasting over the coals was not a random slave, and the beautiful female beside Ghost was not Beth!

Ghost's temples pounded, and the back of his head felt like it had been pierced by an axe. Like two ancient, bloodthirsty gladiators pinned inside the Colosseum of his flesh-and-bone skull, each savage, opposing force warred for dominion, prepared to fight to the death.

Ghost sucked in air.

His body began to tremble.

He fisted his hair in his hands, then pressed the heels against his temples.

And that's when he heard Lord Drakkar's voice ringing in his ears like twin clashing symbols: "You are clever, Ghost, but not as clever as me. Alas, you comprehend the full picture. Did you really think I would give you a human woman—nay, your chosen dragyra—as some sort of exquisite princess bride, to claim and enjoy, throughout all time, even as she threatened your lost, condemned soul with living fissures of light? Did you truly not realize I would avenge the death of Felicity on behalf of my servant Salyn? That I would avenge the witch's death, if only to honor my shadow-walkers Bale and Nefario, on behalf of the sin eaters Kyryn and Mongryn, and to appease any and all other loyal servants who have used and enjoyed her for over three centuries past? Could you really be that arrogant!" The king's voice rang out like a clap of thunder, and Ghost's vision blurred, he staggered sideways, and his stomach turned over in a violent wave of nausea. "Am I not even-handed as well as gracious? Lenient as well as wicked? Do you not understand that everything I have done for you—offered you—is only and always for my own exultation? Consuming your *fated's* flesh shall be the final and full measure of blasphemy against the Pantheon and your biological sire, the moment your name is truly changed, both in symbol and in substance, and the moment your oath is sealed and your soul becomes eternally pagan...forever my own." He appeared to try to soften his tone, yet it sounded a thousand times more wicked. "Lest you forget, Gideon's soul is waiting."

Ghost glanced at the lavishly adorned woman seated to his left, and the human female immediately became a plain, shrinking violet, just a random pawn on Lord Drakkar Hades' chessboard, who had obviously been used—and bewitched—to pass as Beth, because she clearly shared the same height, hair color, and skin tone. He glanced, yet again, toward the northwest corner of the throne room, and saw that the guise had lifted from his dragyra as well: The short, white-haired, buxom slave who was about to be roasted over a circular firepit had wavy, dark brown hair, a smooth mocha complexion, and a tall, slender, modestly curved form...a body Ghost recognized because it had once lain beneath him.

A tempering voice of light echoed in Ghost's memory, slicing through the chaos like a soft blade through butter: clean, straightforward, and concise. *I choose you, Ghost. I choose you!*

Ghost fell into his opulent chair and grasped the ornate arms with strained, trembling knuckles—he could not bear the weight of the moment standing, yet he knew he was helpless to change it. Ghost was a warrior. A hardened mercenary. He had been reared and trained to give his body in service and to yield his will for the greater good, and it was a deep-seated mindset—nay, an unalterable reality—bred into every fiber of his being. Yes, Beth would suffer unconscionably—*but it would be over soon!*—and her soul, unlike Gideon's, would return to her Creator. Ghost's twin, on the other hand, was truly damned—his soul would suffer forever.

There was no choice before Ghostaniaz.

No pros and cons to consider...

No room for compassion, no place for pity, and no liberty to act out some fairy-tale hero bullshit. The war raging in his skull grew silent, and Ghost mumbled, "Forgive me." Then he kept his full attention fixed on the northwest corner of the throne room, because he did not deserve to look away, and he watched as Salyn Stryke, followed by Trader Vice, stepped out of the black, haunting shadows. The latter released a turquoise-and-black tiger snake from the stump at the end of his left wrist and pointed the head of the serpent at the hot, glowing coals, setting the sacrificial pit on fire.

CHAPTER THIRTY-SEVEN

D espite the obstruction of an apple muffling her voice, Beth shrieked in agony, and Ghost's throat constricted. As his dragyra began to writhe, twist, and jerk, pulling against the birchwood spit, trying to stay out of reach of the fire, her screams grew louder, she bit through the fruit, and every cell in Ghost's body recoiled in anguish.

He closed his eyes and tried to hold his breath.

He clenched his fists and tried to relinquish his sanity, divorce his mind from his body, as he had done so many horrific times when his own sire, Lord Dragos, had scorched the dragyri as punishment...or for amusement.

Beth screamed again, and Ghost's eyes shot open—a tall, thin, dancing flame had licked the bottom of her feet, and her panic, her torment, had turned to sheer, unadulterated terror.

He couldn't do this shit, but Gideon...Gideon...*Gideon*!

The scepter!

He could use it to end Beth's suffering, raise it and command her heart to stop beating.

He still had one application left, and Lord Drakkar could not hold it against him. If Ghost used the scepter to end Beth's life, to provide his dragyra with mercy, the pagan king would still have to honor his promise to avenge Lord Dragos and free Gideon from eternal torment.

Without hesitation or further deliberation, Ghost instinctively leaped to his feet, raised the golden rod, and held it high in the air, even as the Great Hall narrowed, time stood still, and his eyes locked impossibly with his dragyra's.

I can learn to love you....

The words from her letter.

But no...

Ghost didn't love.

I will come to love you...

Too tragic, too late—Ghostaniaz Dragos *could not* love.

Yet, he had loved—once—perhaps in epochs past.

Ghost had dearly loved his brother, Gideon.

You are brave, strong, and incredibly faithful.

Absolutely not—Ghost wasn't any of that—never had been.

And more than that, you are worthy...

Ghost wasn't worthy; he had never been worthy.

But Beth...Gideon...*Beth...Gideon!*

I choose you, Ghost!

"I don't have a choice," he murmured beneath his breath.

I choose you!

Once again, Ghost whispered, "Forgive me." Then he tightened his fist around the base of the scepter and projected his voice like a volcanic eruption, channeling every ounce of rage, defiance, and reckless rebellion he had ever possessed into the desperate, inviolable command: "Fall prostrate on the floor and worship me without ceasing, until the sun that does not exist in this gods-forsaken hovel rises at *tierce* on the morrow." To the best of his knowledge, tierce was around 9 A.M., Ghost had no idea what would happen, since the command was not technically possible, and he still hadn't located Lord Drakkar, who was obviously immune to Ghost's audacious mutiny.

Yet to Ghost's surprise, both shades and demons fell to the floor before him. The hellhounds lay prostrate, the snakes stopped slithering, and even the fire in the great obsidian monstrosity quit flickering, crackling, and hissing.

Shiiit.

He didn't have a moment to spare.

He released his wings, shot forward like a rocket into the far northwest corner of the throne room, and bathed the sacrificial pit with ice-cold silver and blue fire, extinguishing the coals and instantly healing his writhing dragyra. He grasped the thick birchwood post with one hand, wrenched it out of the post hole, and dropped it like a heavy anchor to the throne room floor. And then he released his claws, lunged at the neck of a fallen prostrate demon, and beheaded the sin eater with one brutal swipe of his razor-sharp talons, snatching both chain and brass key from the blood-spurting stump.

Praying that somehow—someway—Gideon would accept his whispered apology, Ghost tore through Beth's bonds, wrapped both arms around her, and began to spin in violent circles, whirling faster and faster like a cyclone, until he had tunneled his way through stone, mortar, and crumbling granite, dropping ever downward into the castle's underbelly.

They landed just west of the castle's lower staircase and maybe three feet east of the high stone archway, the cordoned-off grotto that led to The Deep: the cistern...the well...the supernatural vortex that could provide them passage out of the underworld.

His heart beat a salvo in his chest as he set Beth down, focused like a laser, and shifted gears into supernatural overdrive: He shredded the stanchion rope with ease. He inserted the brass key into the ancient cryptic lock surrounded by the painting of a sword, a reversed numeric seven, and a witch's pentacle etched into the pommel; and then he twisted the key so hard, he almost broke it in half.

He reached for Beth's hand, kicked the door open, and flew into the forbidden chamber, dragging his dragyra behind him. And then his heart seized in his chest, and his mouth dropped open. Beth screamed a bloodcurdling cry before ducking behind him.

Lord Drakkar Hades hovered above the conical vortex—a swirling, undulating, kaleidoscope-colored vapor that demarcated the top of the well and shrouded the entrance to The Deep—like a fairy-tale dragon guarding an ancient treasure, only there was nothing reminiscent of a fairy tale about him.

The king's eyes were glowing like two coals of bewitched, molten lava.

His inky black wings were webbed, leathery, and flapping violently like agitated palms in a category-five hurricane, his wingspan stretching from one distant side of the musty cavern to the other. His talons were more like knives than spindly finger-nails, and his taut, reedy lips and his thin, narrow nose had trans-muted into an enormous, hard, scaly, smoldering snout.

Rage.

Wrath.

Savagery and retribution.

Obviously, in those last fateful moments in the throne room, the king had foreseen Ghost's decision and chosen to lie in wait rather than confront—and kill—the dragyri in front of his minions. What was it he had said the morning he had given Ghost the robe and the scepter? "No, Ghostaniaz, I want to catch my prey unaware. I want them to run and hide and, occasionally, provide a challenge. I want to outwit them, catch them, devour them with my claws, and tear their hearts out with my canines as sport, not as a matter of such inherent superiority."

Truer words had never been spoken.

Sulfur rose from the vortex like steam from a cauldron, static electricity prickled Ghost's skin, and an unholy calm—savage, wrathful, and singularly determined—settled over the king of the underworld as he fixed his powerful gaze on Ghost: "Alas, it has come to this," the king said, wearily. He lowered his heavy, scaly eyelids and shook his head in disappointment. "I offered you eternal exaltation, vengeance against your father, and clemency for your pathetic, suffering brother—the very keys to my kingdom, title to my dominion, and *my name!*—and you chose... what?" He sneered at Beth, and his snout curled upward. "This woman...this whore...this worthless, inferior creature." His serpentine tongue snaked out, and plumes of smoke swirled around it. "You have dishonored me before my entire court, and I shall defile you in equal measure. I will remove your spine from your body, just as I did the first night you were captured in my throne room, and use it as a fishing hook to extract your very soul. What your sire did to Gideon will look like child's play by comparison, as you shall live in this underworld, forever and ever, only not as a prince and not as my exalted blood lineage. Your soul will be traded and passed from one pagan vassal to another for all eternity, and then passed, violated, and defiled again, *eternities* upon eternities." He smiled softly, as if expressing some strange, incongruent pity. "And know, before I begin to...harm you...and your mind is no longer lucid, that your woman will suffer in kind. I shall bring her just to the edge of death, slowly, painfully...creatively...only to heal her, save her life, and begin again, so that her soul may never return to her own creator. She shall never be out of my reach. And every pagan in my kingdom will lie with her, use her, defile her in ways—and with implements—Wraith Sylvester never dreamed of. Ghostaniaz Dragos, you are a fool, and you are hereby sentenced to perpetual life, consisting of eternal death."

* * *

Ghost inhaled sharply as Lord Drakkar's words sank in, and his legs felt rubbery beneath him. He could never defeat the king of the underworld in combat, not even if he was willing to try.

He bit his bottom lip and cursed beneath his breath.

His whole life had been shit!

Since the day he had first emerged as a genesis hatchling, Ghost had been fated to suffer—and he had expected to suffer *and then some*—yet somehow, he had also believed the torment would one day end.

But this?

This was beyond anything he had ever imagined, and now, he had sentenced Beth to the same fate.

What the hell had he been thinking?

She could have been free. Gideon could have been free. Ghost could have used the scepter to give his dragyra a merciful death, allowing her soul to ascend to her heaven, avenged his brother with Lord Drakkar, and then later taken his own life. He had screwed this shit up, six ways to Sunday, and now, there was nothing he could do for anyone.

He had heard it said that a lifetime of memories, a millennium of regrets, and a treasure trove of awareness could come into focus, collectively suspended, in the blink of an eye—how deeply he felt the truth of this: Other than his early years with Gideon, Ghost had never bonded with anyone. Hatred had been his clan. Bitterness had been his family. Indifference, his best friend. And cold, hard emptiness the only arms he had ever clung to, the only soul he had ever embraced. On some level, it was fitting that his end would come in the bowels of the underworld, for he had never walked, lived, breathed...or emerged...into light. Yet there was a being of light cowering behind him, about to emerge into an unconscionable fate, and he didn't even know her

—he had never tried to care for her—and he was the cause of her eternal demise.

Regret.

Awareness.

Guilt and shame, like an avalanche of heavy boulders shot from an ancient catapult into an aged, crumbling fortress, demolished his defiance and pummeled his pride. "Beth." He turned his back on the murderous pagan king and searched his dragyra's terror-stricken eyes. Lord Drakkar would not get Ghost's last sentient moment; neither would Ghost die in silence, the same way he had lived.

I'm sorry could not be spoken.

It was far too inadequate.

But what he had, he would give, before it was too late.

Eternal Rest.

Eternal Peace.

An everlasting existence without torment or pain.

Lord Dragos had taught him well, and Ghost knew he could take Beth's life in a scintilla of a second—he could drain her heat, expunge her essence, and extinguish her anima faster than Lord Drakkar Hades could stop him. But there was something else, something she deserved...something, maybe, he deserved as well.

He cupped her face in his hands, as gently as he was able, and for the first time in his gods-forsaken existence, he let the walls of the fortress come down, and he completely bared his soul. A hot, angry tear, something both foreign and unbidden, streamed down his high, hard, angular cheek and he leaned forward. "For whatever it is worth, I want you to know that I chose you over the only thing that has ever mattered, the only soul I have ever loved." He pressed his forehead to hers and exhaled the words. "I chose you, Beth. *I chose you too.*" And then he released his fangs, bent to her neck, and sank them deep into her carotid artery.

CHAPTER THIRTY-EIGHT

Anne Liu's hands were sweating, and her heart was pounding.

Even as she sat in a field at the Arapahoe County Fairgrounds, surrounded by her dearest circle of friends—heads bowed, hands linked, praying silently in whatever way each knew how—she was drawn to another striking, impossible sight, something no one else could see.

Jax, Chance, and Roman Dragos were also standing in the wheat-colored field, maybe a hundred yards away, each dragyri male forming the point of a triangle, clasping their diamond amulets, and glowing like pillars of brilliant, supernatural light.

What the heck were they doing?

Why had they come to the fairgrounds, why were they clutching their amulets, and why couldn't Kari, Joy, or Nicole see them?

The ground beneath Anne's crisscrossed legs began to hum with vitality and pulse with energy, and the sky above thickened with clouds—no, not clouds, more like liquid vapor in a myriad of distinctive, celestial, jeweled configurations: Asscher, oval, baguette, and lozenge; round, radiant, pear, and marquis.

The heavens were dotted with stars and filled with...diamonds.

Anne turned her attention on Nicole Perez and the simple, unscented timberline candle set in the ground in front of her, and then she shivered: Nicole's eyes were closed—whatever she was praying was both heartfelt and earnest—and the flame in front of her was swaying back and forth, flickering in and out, glowing yellow, soft orange...then phantom blue.

Anne slowed her breaths, closed her eyes, and did the best she could at creative visualization until, within her mind's eye, the diamond clouds became individual plumes on the wings of angels, the phantom-blue flame became a shield of protection, and both imaginings were wrapped gently yet firmly around Beth's slender, elegant shoulders. She held the image and chanted in silence.

CHAPTER THIRTY-NINE

Everything happened at once.

Ghost held her face in his hands, a pure white light shone through his phantom-blue pupils, and his words emerged like a single diamond flame of glittering fire, igniting a spark of life in the grotto: "*For whatever it is worth, I want you to know that I chose you over the only thing that has ever mattered, the only soul I have ever loved.*" He pressed his forehead to hers, and a surge of energy filled the grotto. "*I chose you, Beth. I chose you too.*"

In a shocking flash, just a blink of an eye, Ghost released his fangs and sank them into Bethany's throat. Lord Drakkar Hades roared with fury, his inky black wings became two individual, dark, fallen angels, and each dark angel lunged forward at Bethany and Ghost.

The king's cruel mouth opened like a bottomless, hungry cavern, his tonsils glowed with pulsing, molten fire, and his snout discharged plume after plume of thick, swirling smoke. Then time stood still, oppression hovered over the mouth of The Deep, and King Drakkar Hades, a crazed primordial beast, unleashed the flames of hell.

Searing heat.

Red-hot agony.

Melting flesh and burning hair.

Ghost lost his purchase. Bethany cried out in anguish. And then a second pair of angel's wings—pure luminescent and ringed in gold, their aura reminiscent of Grandma Betsy's—enfolded the two burning bodies and swept them like a powerful gust of preternatural wind through the unrelenting flames, over the edge of the well, and into the swirling vapor of the vortex.

Falling.

Burning.

Screaming in agony.

Spiraling like two blazing comets through every shade of gray in the underworld, every shade of black, indigo, and cerulean in the infinite galaxy, then the deep, dark, midnight blue of the earth's unmistakable sky.

A sudden sphere of diamond-shaped clouds...

The Arapahoe County Fairgrounds!

And then finally, through the center of a glowing diamond triangle, a *portal* held open by three dazzling amulets, each talisman grasped in the fisted hand of a diamond-eyed mercenary with desperate, determined pupils and lines formed from concentration etched into their foreheads.

Bethany's screams scorched her throat, and her arms flailed wildly as she streamed through the second portal, still thrashing and burning. And then she felt the balls of her feet hit a hard, unyielding platform, a raised octagon dais, and her body stopped spinning, thrashing...falling.

She glimpsed a magnificent, high-coffered ceiling gilded in layers of sparkling jewels, and she somehow knew she was in a huge sanctuary, though the pain in her nerves along her skin...

within her marrow...was too great, too stark, too agonizing to think.

A hard-as-granite chest slammed against her back.

Two powerful, sweltering arms dragged her down to her knees.

Then a cloak, a shield of armor—*no, two strong, taut, leathery wings*—enfolded her like a fibrous vise inside a solid, immovable, yet blistering cocoon. Seven billowing streams of fire rushed over the dais like a converging onslaught of supernatural freight trains: Ghost tightened his grip, covered Bethany's head with his, then cried out in misery, again and again.

And then the room went black and still, and Bethany heard nothing—she felt nothing.

She knew...

Nothing.

The complete absence of being.

Pop!

A sharp, distant sound, followed by an ambient stream of light.

The light began to radiate all around her, first silver, then blue, then a resplendent combination of both luminescent colors, until her body felt like it was floating.

Floating...

Not burning!

In fact, nothing was hurting.

Her ears hummed with the vibration of distant music, her skin tingled with the joy of peaceful ecstasy—no fear, no worry, no pain, or anguish—her soul felt more alive than it had ever been, and her body felt invincible!

Ghost retracted his wings, which were no longer burning or smoldering, reached for her forearm, and hefted her onto her feet. As she glanced down at her body—her trunk, her legs, her arms, then her wrists—her eyes swept slightly forward, and she saw the most dazzling antique ring encircling the fourth finger of her left hand: The disk was shaped in the likeness of a dragon; the center diamond was surrounded by an emerald, an amethyst, an onyx, and a citrine...a magnificent sapphire and a brilliant topaz...all six gemstones like celestial planets orbiting around a diamond sun.

"Welcome to the Pantheon of Dragons." She heard Ghost's deep, gravelly brogue as he bent to her ear.

Bethany opened her mouth to speak, but her voice got caught in her throat. Along the western wall, maybe twenty feet in front of her, there were seven huge dragon lords seated on seven ornamental thrones, each immaculate cathedra constructed from one of the sacred gemstones, and all seven dragons were staring right at her.

Ghost cleared his throat and popped his neck. "Little late for the invocation, but considering the circumstances, it's the best I can do." He placed his left hand on the small of Bethany's back, then lowered his head and closed his eyes. "Great dragon lords, from the world beyond; fathers of mystery, keepers of time; I bring to you this mortal soul. Born of fire, bathed in light; to guard by day and watch by night; to live, and love, and breathe as one, the *fated* of a dragon's son—be gentle with her soul. Through sacred smoke and healing fire; a flesh-and-blood renewing pyre; I give my life with one desire—reanimate her soul." He stepped back and shrugged his shoulders. "Great dragon lords of the sacred stones; from the Temple of Seven, from your honored thrones; renew my dragyra, and bless"—his voice fell off with a snarl—"bless the *Diamond* Lair."

Bethany's spine stiffened.

If Ghost had spoken the word *Diamond* with any more contempt, venom would have spilled out on the dais.

A huge dragon god seated in the center of the row of thrones stood and gawked at Ghost, his diamond eyes and giant mortal appearance silhouetted by the image of a ferocious beast. He had to be Lord Dragos. "Son." He spoke the word with both anguish and reverence. "We accept your invocation."

Ghost chuckled, a low, caustic, abrasive sound. Then he shook his head and grinded his teeth. "Nah, not you. Wasn't asking you." He turned his head toward the far right throne and regarded the dragon deity on the topaz cathedra. "Lord Topenzi, can you speak for the Seven? Do you accept my...late...invocation?" He gestured with his chin toward Bethany. "And thank you for saving both me and my dragyra."

Lord Topenzi gasped, and the temple fell silent.

Then Lord Dragos' snarl shook the entire sanctuary, causing the high coffered ceiling to shudder. A blood-red, diamond-shaped tear fell from the dragon lord's eye, and then he nodded his head in somber anguish. "I have mourned you, son. I have sought you from the grave and back. I have searched the earth, the underworld, and the Oracle Pool to divine a way...any way... some way to save you, to return you home to my bosom. Did I not intervene on your behalf? Did I not show both you and your female mercy? Have I not brought you forth from the very fires of hell and saved you both in this temple?" His voice rose to a thunderous crescendo. "Yet you would mock your lord and defile this sanctuary with arrogant and brazen contempt. You would dare to defy and denigrate your own forbearing sire, even as you ask for his blessing? I will flay the skin from your bones, and your soul will be no more. You have broken my heart, Ghostaniaz."

Ghost laughed out loud.

He clapped both hands slowly, harshly, irreverently, at least five times, and then his upper lip turned up in a snarl. "Did you mourn my brother, Gideon? Did you search the earth, the underworld, and the Oracle Pool for a way to heal him or save him?"

"Profanity!" Lord Dragos shouted.

"Did you intervene on his behalf?"

"Lies! All lies."

"Where was your fucking mercy when you chained him up in a cave, left him to rot and starve? Where was your reverence for this sacred sanctuary or your deference to your fellow deities when you defiled the Laws of Harmony and hid Gideon's existence from your fellow lords? When you murdered your own Genesis Son and trapped his soul in this very temple, to suffer forever, his soul and his bones stacked like a human child's Legos inside a profane, twisted coffee table."

"Heresy, all of it! You will speak no further!"

Ghost turned to face Bethany, and his eyes were haunted. "I'm sorry, dragyra. I really did choose you, but now you know the truth of what's happened. You will live, Beth. The gods will see that your life goes on—live a good one for both of us, and please don't hold this against me. Earlier...at matins...that shit in the Sinners' Cave? It all came out on the screens. The fact that I once had a brother, a twin—I had forgotten all of it—the fact that my sire both tortured and killed him. But I could never forget again. And I cannot dishonor him." He turned to face Lord Dragos once more, and his features were as set, stern, and stoic as granite. "I loved my brother, Lord Dragos." His voice caught on a hitch. "Gideon was everything you weren't: stronger, wiser, worthy of respect, and on his behalf—with my very last breath—I curse you all the way down to my revolting DNA. You are neither a father nor a god, just a run-of-the-mill, everyday, narcissistic piece of shit."

Fire shot out of Lord Dragos' nostrils.

He launched so fast from his throne, his body shot forward like a cosmic blur, and then a loud crack of thunder, followed by six terrifying bolts of white-hot lightning, crossed in a blistering electric explosion, barring Lord Dragos from Ghost.

Bethany screamed, ducked, and hit the floor, cowering with her forearms crossed and covering her head.

Lord Dragos drew back in both rage and surprise and glared

over his shoulder at his brethren, before turning back to Ghost. "What is the meaning of this profane interference?" he bellowed, shaking the rafters with his rage.

The dragon lord with emerald eyes covered his face with his hands, shook his head slowly from side to side, then rose soberly from his throne and stepped forward. "The last time we were in this sanctuary together, I asked you, 'What have you done?' But I never imagined anything so...mendacious. I would have never counted treason among your various petty faults."

Lord Dragos spun around in a fury, balancing the bulk of his body on a large, wide, leathery tail. "Treason? *Treason?* Have you all gone mad? And who are *you* to speak of petty faults!?"

The remaining five dragon lords stood up, and Lord Topenzi strolled forward from his topaz throne before crossing the brilliant, light-refracting glass floor with a glide. "Brother of this sacred Temple of Seven." His voice sounded sad. "Ancient creator of the dragon sun, the dragon moon, and the Dragyr race; co-author and ruler of Dragons Domain; first of the Seven, Keeper of the Diamond, and Father of the Diamond Lair. What have you done, *indeed?*" He closed his topaz eyes, his features grew pensive, and when he reopened them, his pupils were icy and resigned. "You may have applied the First Law of Harmony, *Absolute Liberty*, when you hid your...disabled...son from the Pantheon, and you may have even had the right to *Sanctity in Privacy*, protection under the second law, when you concealed him in a cave, tortured both of your Genesis offspring, but surely, you had to know that you were violating the third law, *Preservation of the Species*, when you took the child's life without seeking counsel or permission from this body. You. Took. The. Life. Of. A. Genesis. Son. An original pure-blooded hatchling."

Lord Dragos rolled his large diamond eyes. "Oh, *whatever!* Are you simply going to take Ghost's word for all of this?"

The sapphire-eyed dragon clenched his fist. "Enough!" he

snarled, staring daggers through Lord Dragos. "Your Sanctity in Privacy, the fact that we would never profane to look inside your thoughts, your memories...your private chambers, has come and gone, Lord Dragos. You know damn well the moment Ghost spoke those words, the truth of them was known to all of us—we are, like you, divine, omniscient creatures, are we not? *Enough*." He turned to regard each of the remaining six dragons, one by one. "A thousand years. The law is law. We cannot let this stand."

"Blasphemy!" Lord Dragos roared, and the temple columns shook.

Ghost gasped, lunged toward Bethany, and yanked her off the floor by the arm. Then he backpedaled like an alligator was an inch away from his toes, and covered her body with his.

"What's happening?" she cried.

"Close your eyes! Don't look at Lord Dragos, or he could take you with him!"

"*Take me with him?* Where? What are they doing!"

"The Seven—no, the remaining six—are going to banish Lord Dragos," he panted in her ear, his voice thick with both terror and shock. "Back to the original swirling mass, the endless black hole of hot, burning gas, the place he first emerged from fourteen billion years ago!"

Before Bethany could respond or react, the sanctuary filled with heat. A blistering, multicolored vapor rose like neon methane gas from a violent volcano, snaked along the sanctuary floor, and coiled around Lord Dragos' thick hind-paw skeleton— his amalgamated mortal ankles and his bent dragon's heels.

Lord Dragos spun and thrashed and whipped his tail in savage fury, even as the remaining six dragon lords unleashed a terrible cone of sweltering fire, a wall of flames the size of a tsunami, which swept over—and consumed—the diamond deity in wrath, judgment, and damnation.

Hideous smoke, convulsing flames, and spiraling, exploding ash.

The overwhelming scent of acrid carnage and the earth-shattering roar of a dragon's feral lament...

Rage.

Rebellion.

Infinite...timeless...power, swirling like raw sewage down a putrid open drain.

Bethany's feet left the floor, and so did Ghost's. Then silence, the quaking temple settled, and "Holy shit, holy shit, holy shit!" Bethany burrowed her face in Ghost's rock-hard chest, wrapped her arms around his waist, and listened as his heart raced, shuddered, then finally returned to a steady, normal rhythm.

* * *

Banishment...

Are you fucking kidding me?

Ghost couldn't believe what had just taken place, but before his mind could process the breadth of it—the sheer unconscionable horror and truth of what the dragons had just done to his sire—the six remaining rulers of the Pantheon circled both Ghost and his dragyra.

"Ghostaniaz," Lord Topenzi said soberly, "the Temple of Seven cannot function without its full measure of power. An undivided quorum is needed to induct an eighteen-year-old dragyri into his permanent lair and to affix his eternal amulet. It is equally needed to usher a female dragyra into the sacred Pantheon, to perform the consecration...rebirth by fire...to say nothing of the demands on council..." His voice trailed off. "As your sire shall not return for a thousand years, there is only one way to remedy his absence."

"Sixty-six chromones," Lord Amarkyus added.

"Huh?" Ghost grunted, unable to follow. "What are you talking about?"

Lord Topenzi reverted into his full mortal persona and declined his head in deference. "The sons can never be greater than the father, but the power of sixty-six chromosomes, a complete set of divine genetic information, is not to be taken lightly either."

"Your spirit," Lord Saphyrius explained, "combined with that of Gideon's, even temporarily, would equal the sacred quantity of Father-Creator in both substance, form, and genetic material."

"With time...with teaching...with practice and magick," Lord Cytarius added, "should two original hatchlings of the same genome and principal genesis wield their alchemy correctly, then yes, the twins would possess power almost equal to a deity, certainly enough to complete the sacred ceremonies."

Lord Ethyron shook his head, and his dark emerald eyes grew cloudy with anger. "The stupid fuck just had to create one more extra hatchling, even if it meant inadvertently producing a dangerous metaphysical double." He waved an impatient hand through the air. "So be it. It is done. And we have no other option."

"I concur," said Lord Onyhanzian.

Ghost still couldn't track wherever this was going, but as far as he was concerned, he didn't have to: *The sons can never be greater than the father...your spirit combined with that of Gideon's...the twins would possess power almost equal to a deity... so be it.*

Sons.

Twins.

Gideon...

Ghost's breath hitched in his throat, his stomach twisted into a ball of knots, and his forehead began to bead with perspiration. Whatever the hell they were talking about, if it meant freeing

Gideon—if such a thing was even possible without the aid of Lord Drakkar's duplicitous promise, then Ghost would do anything.

Anything.

"I'll do it!" he exclaimed. "Whatever is asked of me. Whatever you need. Whatever you're implying, just please...*please*...if you are able, do not leave my twin's soul in that coffee table." He shivered innately, bent to one knee, and bowed his head with reverence, even as Beth stepped to his side and placed a gentle hand on his shoulder. "I'll do anything."

And then the glorious, coffered ceiling, bedazzled and plated with the seven jewels, began to shimmer like a liquid rainbow, the various gemstone panels taking on the consistency of liquid gold. The gold began to undulate, then float, and the apex of the cathedral started to part...and separate...exposing the upper residential floor.

Softly.

Gently.

Ever so reverently, the twisted, dreaded coffee table floated down in the air, came to rest on the center of the dais, and the ceiling closed above it.

Ghost stiffened and winced.

He closed his eyes and held his breath.

He would not look at the bones—he *could not* look at the bones. The very thought of what had happened to his brother still curdled his stomach and filled it with bile, threatening to come up...and out...all over the dais.

Then, in the blink of an eye—an eternity made manifest in a hallowed moment—the coffee table exploded into a thousand tiny particles, infinite specks of light and fairy-tale dust, and the specks of light became dancing sprinkles, the eddies fusing together into the outline of a small, translucent six-year-old boy.

Ghost gasped and unwittingly grabbed Beth's hand.

His mouth fell open, and his heart leaped in his chest.

And then the body of the boy filled in completely, though his mortal form remained ghostly luminescent, and his old crude metal braces remained intact: his muscles, yet frail, his frame, yet diminutive.

Eyes wide, mouth hanging open, Ghost licked his lips and tried to speak, but he couldn't.

The boy lumbered forward, his expression filled with both caution and wonder as he studied Ghost's features in earnest. He sucked in air. His eyes grew wide as saucers. He scrunched his nose, hunched his shoulders, and began to tremble with excitement. Finally, he stood as tall as he could, clapped his hands, and giggled with merriment, the whole of the temple lighting up from his countenance. "Ghost! You came to see me!"

Ghost sucked in air, and his shoulders began to tremble.

A serene, bright-eyed, six-year-old Gideon stepped forward on wobbly legs and held out his open arms. "Ghost, you came to *free* me."

Ghostaniaz Dragos sank to his knees, collapsed on the floor, and wept.

CHAPTER FORTY

The air was warm yet crisp, sweetened by a cool, gentle breeze. Bethany stood barefoot in the soft white granules of sand within the Cove of Dragon's fire. She pressed the side of her thumb and fingers against her forehead, shielding her eyes like a gentle salute, in order to gaze at the glorious pantheon sunset, and then she turned her attention to the distant waves in front of her. About a hundred yards away, rising, swelling, capping then receding, were at least a dozen surfs of aqua blue, the peaks dusted with luminescent white foam, and inside the deepest curves of each wave, subtle prisms appeared, refracting a brilliant underbody of diamond, emerald, sapphire, amethyst, onyx, citrine, and topaz light.

"Funny," Ghost said absently, tightening his strong arms around her, "as long as I've lived in the Diamond Lair, I never really noticed how...beautiful...that is."

Bethany leaned back against him and nodded her head, even as the colors in the waves grew more vivid, more intense, and the caps began to dance. She inhaled sharply. "They have rainbows above them! Like vapor...or gas...and it's rising upward."

"Keep watching," Ghost said.

Bethany watched in wonder as the gas expanded, drew upward into sharp, cresting arcs, sparked, then turned into fire, an ocean of dancing gemstone flames. "It's everywhere," she breathed in awe. "Above, below, and part of the water."

"Yep," Ghost said.

She shivered, ran her palms along his taut, sinewy forearms, then gestured with her chin toward the modern glass high-rise a couple of hundred yards away on the beach behind them. "This is your home." He didn't reply, yet she understood his silence. *Home*, for Ghost, had not been a place of peace and welcome, a refuge filled with countless good memories. It had been a prison... an ordeal...a house built on wicked, duplicitous, sadistic cards. No need to broach the subject. She laid her head against the crook in his shoulder and softly changed the subject: "So tell me again how all this works, for me and for you, with Gideon and your brothers."

"Lair mates," Ghost corrected.

Bethany smiled inwardly: It had been just over fifteen hours since she and Ghost had "arrived" in the Pantheon, Bethany had been changed...fully converted to dragyra...and Ghost had met the spirit of his long-lost little brother, Gideon. Bethany had had twelve hours at best, after catching a few hours of sleep, to talk to Ghost about the future, tour the Diamond Lair, and meet his awesome, powerful—*intimidating*—brothers of the lair. But it didn't require a wealth of time or an Oracle Pool to discern what she had seen in Chance's, Roman's, and Jax's diamond eyes: Ghost was dearly loved by his companions. In fact, Jax had jumped through hoops, tried to move heaven and earth, to get Ghost back from the underworld, to say nothing of the amazing, timely portal the males had held open at the fairgrounds. Ghost had a lot to take in, even more to process, and it might be a while before he saw some things clearly—specifically, the fact that he had always had a band of brothers, if not three more loving siblings. "Okay," she said, "your *lair mates*, but you are now the new leader of the Diamond Lair, its ruler so to speak. What does that mean?"

Ghost exhaled a whistle and rolled his shoulders. "Shit if I know," he said candidly.

Bethany squeezed his arm. "And you and Gideon are the seventh dragon deity. I mean, once you get that whole merging of your spirits and your energy perfected, right? That must feel crazy." Ghost shook his head, and she glanced over her shoulder to look at him. His eyes were glazed with...moisture...yet his jaw was set in a hard, firm line. He was trying to control his emotions —too much, too soon, too raw for this moment.

Again, Bethany understood.

Gideon would always remain as a six-year-old child, and unless and until he was merged with Ghost, he would maintain an ethereal, spiritual body. His body was still frail, his legs were still twisted, and his movements were still a bit...awkward, but there was no pain or illness, and as a living spirit, he could glide... transport...move objects with thought and telekinesis. In other words, he was more whole than he had ever been, yet Ghost still had to unpack the guilt of Gideon's millennia-long torture, the fact that he had forgotten his sibling—no, Lord Dragos had erased his memory—and make peace with a twin who would always be a child. To say nothing of learning to merge their power.

Yeah, it was a lot.

"So," she said, once again shifting the subject, "you, me, and Gideon; we'll all live in the Diamond Lair together, and with a little mental persuasion...*compulsion*...is that the right word?"

Ghost grunted.

"With a little compulsion to protect the secret, Jax no longer has to erase my best friends' memories, not even Anne's...correct? My girlfriends will all be able to keep their memories, and I—*we*

—will be able to travel back and forth. You will get to know my parents on Earth, and I can quit my job but still do something useful if I want to. Something meaningful. Something human. Maybe volunteering?"

At this, Ghost chuckled. "You're no longer human, dragyra; trust me on that one. But I told you back in the underworld—I have no desire to enslave you or restrict you. I'm not...entirely... my sire's son."

Bethany spun around and glared at him. "You are nothing like your sire, Ghostaniaz."

"*Ghostaniaz?*" He crooked both eyebrows.

"Nothing like him, *Ghost!*" she said sharply, and then she refused to let him look away. "You will get the hang of the whole sacred Seven thing, you will be a leader to your lair, and you and Gideon have forever and a day to make up for the time that was taken. And as for the two of us, we'll find our way. It may take time, but—"

"Love is a choice, not a feeling." His bluntness caught her off guard.

"Yes," she warbled, before nervously looking aside.

He reached out slowly, raised her chin with his hand, and once again merged their eyes, this time commanding her unbroken attention with a hypnotic, phantom-blue and diamond regard. "I see you, Beth." The words were a whisper. "Your mind, your heart, your character...your fidelity. The way you stand by my side. I see you."

She gulped and shivered inwardly, and then she forced a self-effacing smile. "I...well...you know, I'm learning too. I think—"

"Shh. Just let it happen, girl."

She pushed through her stubborn apprehension. "Let what happen?"

"This. You and me. The future."

She nodded slowly, finally understanding: He wanted to take

things slow, and she was probably talking too much, thinking too much, getting a little too personal, maybe a little too...intimate.

His top lip curved up in a semi-smile, and he brushed his thumb along her jaw. "Love is a choice, not a feeling, but one day soon, it's gonna be both. The gods knew that only an angel of light could get anywhere near my blackened soul." He leaned in closer. "They knew that only a virgin could capture my attention or hold my respect—fucked up, I realize, but it is what it is. I've seen too much bullshit in my lifetime, and I'm far too private... territorial...and reclusive to let anyone in who, well, ever let anyone else in." He ran his hand through a loose tousle of midnight-black hair before letting it fall through his fingers. "They knew she had to have dark brown eyes and hair I could wrap my hands around."

This time, Bethany shivered outwardly. She felt like a mouse in the hands of a lion, and wasn't sure how to respond. "I...you... I'm not sure—"

"Your innocence is beautiful." He brushed her lips with the pad of his thumb. "And your way with me...foreign, yeah, but... perfect." He bent to hover just above her mouth. "Bethany." He kissed her softly, just a brush of lips. "Kayla." He did it again. "Dragos." He grasped her by the small of her waist, tugged her hard against him, and kissed her with passion, parting her lips to taste her tongue, sucking her bottom lip into the cavern of his mouth, then nipping it gently with his elongated canines. "Fuu-uck," he groaned against her open mouth.

Then, "Ewww!" A child's bright, high-pitched voice. "If you're gonna do that, you have to warn me!" Bethany backed up, and Ghost spun around, just as Gideon Dragos approached them on the sand. "I came to see you, Ghost! But I didn't know you'd be kissing a girl."

Ghost's eyes lit up, and he laughed out loud. He dropped to one knee, held out an arm, and waited patiently as Gideon plodded to him. Then he sucked in air and drew back in surprise as the outstretched limb passed right through the child's midsection.

Gideon laughed uproariously, like he had just told the world's best joke. Then he reached out with a tentative hand, swiped the pads of his fingers over Ghost's, and drew a faint beam of crystal light from the male dragyri's fingers. "Lord Topenzi told me I could borrow your anima whenever I wanted to make a part of my body more solid." He held up two dense, nearly perfect corporeal arms, showing them off like newfound treasure, and then he dove at Ghost's chest like a swooping eagle coming in for a swift, sudden landing, and wrapped both solid limbs around Ghost's neck.

Ghost exhaled with relief and hugged him back.

"He also told me," Gideon said excitedly, taking a step back, "that one day soon, with lots of practice, the two of us can merge our essence and become a primordial dragon!" His eyes grew wide with wonder. "But in the meantime, he said I can step inside your body whenever I want, just like walking through an open door. And whenever I do, I will still have my own thoughts, but I'll be able to walk and run and feel whatever you feel. Like both of us are ghosts...but people...but really dragyri...all together."

Ghost stood up and smirked. "Yeah, well, that dragon thing... still to be determined. We'll have to take that shit slow."

"Language." Bethany slapped Ghost's forearm.

He rolled his eyes. "Beth, he's as old as I am!"

Gideon drew back his shoulders and raised his chin, and Bethany just shook her head.

"As for stepping in and out of my body like an open door," Ghost continued, "do me a solid, okay? Warn me before you try that shi—*stuff*—at least give me a little heads-up."

At this, Gideon giggled. Then he turned to look at Bethany.

"Yeah, but only if you do me a solid and tell me when you're going to kiss a girl."

Ghost chuckled. "We didn't even know you were here."

Gideon bobbed up and down, the equivalent of an excited spirit jumping for joy. "I know, right?! It's like I'm a ghost too. Mini me!"

Ghost stared at his brother. "*Mini* me..." His voice trailed off, and Bethany knew he was once again corralling his emotions. "*Better* me," he corrected, "but yeah, that's cool. And this girl has a name." He gestured toward Bethany.

"Princess!" Gideon blurted.

"No, her name—"

"*Dragyra!*"

"Well, yes, but—"

"Beth! Beth! *Beth!*" He bobbed up and down again, and then he grew suddenly, almost eerily still. "I saw her...in the Dream Weave...all those years, when I was trapped in the table, when the pain was too hard...or too much to handle...and my soul would drift just outside of the table. Every time a dragyri male would cross over on his way to the Garden of Grace, for an entire millennium, his soul would pass by and tell me, 'Hold on, be strong, someone is coming who has not yet been born.' And I knew they were talking about a girl! A pretty princess with long brown hair who was quiet enough, strong enough, and so filled with light and love that she would cover your soul in a place of only darkness. A girl whose grandma would love her so much, too, that she would cross worlds and dimensions—*even pantheons!*—to help her. To free her. And her freedom would mean our freedom too—Ghost and Gideon! And then, maybe, twenty-one years ago, another spirit passed by on her way to the most beautiful light-filled heaven, a smart, funny girl named Kimberly Johansson. She said that nothing was by accident, not even her own passing at seven years and seven months, that

Grandma Betsy would cross over soon, and everything would be set into motion: 'Gideon, you will temper Ghost's harshness, and my best friend, Beth, will teach him to love.' So, you see"—he shrugged his little shoulders and giggled again—"nothing was ever hopeless or random: I always knew Beth was coming."

Ghost opened his mouth to speak, then closed it.

He stared blankly at Bethany, then back at Gideon.

And even Bethany was at a loss for words: All this time, all these years, cherishing her dearest friendships yet remaining single, first losing Kimberly and then her grandparents, none of it had been random or without purpose. And that morning, in that narrow tin tub, when her heart had finally opened, and she had seen the statuesque soul of a timeless warrior, the male buried beneath all the splintered shards of glass, the night she had written that dangerous letter and left it on the chair for Ghostaniaz...

Fated.

Chosen.

Those weren't just words.

Born from the *soul* of the Pantheon...

And Lord Dragos, Ghost's sire, in all his wickedness and deceit, had still sped up the couple's mating without even knowing what he was doing or why he was *really* doing it.

"Love is not just a choice—or a feeling—it's a destiny," she whispered as she reached for Gideon's soft, small hand.

The child reached out, linked his fingers in hers, and brought both of their hands up to his strong beating heart.

Ghost closed his eyes and nodded.

EPILOGUE

The music was thumping, the barbeque grills were smoking, and heaven have mercy, the male dragyri of the Diamond Lair were moving in and out of Ghost's spacious private condo and the high, breathtaking balcony, talking with Bethany's *besties* and occasionally even dancing, moving their prime, perfect bodies in wondrous ways, certain to raise a female's blood pressure.

Now, as Bethany glanced outside at the private saltwater pool—every level of the sleek, sparkling Diamond Lair had one—and watched Ghost huddle up with Chance, Jax, and Roman, she knew he was telling them about the scrying screens in the Sinners' Cave, the information Lord Drakkar had gleaned from Ghost's memories, and the topographical map of the Pantheon that Killian Kross had drafted. Even though the night was supposed to be a celebration, a chance to unwind and bring two worlds together—Bethany's human friends with Ghost's dragyri brethren, something Lord Dragos would have never permitted—the powerful new leader of the Diamond Lair wanted his lair mates to be both aware of and alert to any potential danger.

"Guuurl..." Joy sidled up to Bethany with a tropical drink in her well-manicured right hand, her smoky brown eyes alight with mischief. "My mind is blown. *Blown!*" She gestured toward the balcony with the wrist that held the drink. "Ghost. You spent the last five days in another dimension with a beautiful, sexy, hot-as-hell...ghost."

Bethany chuckled softly. "He's not an actual ghost."

"Oh no!" Joy exclaimed. "That would be too...normal. A dragyri mercenary. A son of a dragon. A six-foot-five, black-haired Adonis with hard-cut muscle in places I didn't even know muscles existed. And those eyes—*those freakin' eyes!*—Beth, you're actually like his wife now, right?"

"Well, not exactly his—"

"What are we discussing?" Kari Baker sauntered up to the circle, put one arm around Bethany, the other around Joy, and leaned in with a bright, curious smile.

"Joy's talking about Ghost," Bethany said, playfully.

"Ohhh," Kari conjectured. "She's lusting after Ghost?"

"No, no," Joy swiftly corrected. "He's obviously taken. I'm *appreciating* Ghost, but I'm lusting after Roman, especially now that I have my memories back: you know, the day he saved me from that fake-ass Mitch Moretti." She shook her head from side to side, flipping a tuft of full bouncy curls behind her shoulders. "Have you ever...have any of you *ever*...seen anything like him?"

"Nope," Nicole said, joining the enclave. "That clean-shaven jaw, those saffron-diamond eyes, and that naughty...*wicked*...smile, all that honey-colored hair, and the way he pulls it back in that—what is that anyway—some sort of man sweep? A ponytail?"

"It's some sort of ancient Jupiter—you know, the Roman god —throwback," Joy answered. "But you can't have him."

Nicole laughed, just as Anne meandered toward them.

"How are you doing?" Bethany asked, turning her attention to the petite five-foot-four beauty.

"Jax is really sweet, isn't he?" Anne said.

Okaaay, well, that was random.

"Sweet?" Joy echoed.

"Mmm," Kari considered. "Yeah, really, *really* sweet, now that we've had a little more time to...behold him. Although, I don't think *sweet* is the first word that comes to mind."

Anne rolled her dark, inquisitive eyes. "Well, I meant, once you get to know him."

"Oh, shut up, chica!" Nicole said, teasing. "We can't all be deep philosophical Seers."

"With our own personal, supernatural bodyguards," Joy added.

"Checking in and out...meeting...texting...bringing us to an otherworldly temple, behind our best friends' backs," Joy chided.

"*Joy...*" Anne said, her voice thick with apology.

"I'm just kidding," Joy said. "If you had not been somewhat psychic or at least tuned in, you would've never woken up at 1:30 in the morning, told Jax about the ring of fire, or asked the three of us to go to the fairgrounds, to meet and pray for Beth."

"Yep," Nicole said, "your relationship with Jax ended up saving our Beth." She placed her hand in Bethany's full, wavy hair, tousled it, then laid her head on Bethany's shoulder. "But I still don't get how that happened—how Jax knew what to do next."

Bethany leaned into Nicole and smiled, feeling more love than she had ever felt from her besties. The girls had really gone to the mat for Bethany, meeting with Jax, exposing themselves to the Cult of Hades, even collecting an ancient tome, and the knowledge of all they had done still made her stomach feel queasy and her heart, well, unworthy. In a word, she felt humbled, even though she knew she would have done the same for any one of them. "Jax didn't actually put all the pieces together on his own," Bethany offered by way of an explanation. "After Anne called him, he alerted Lord Dragos, who alerted the Seven, but it was the Oracle Pool that interpreted Anne's dream, deciphered the omen, and put two and two together. Lord Dragos was the one who sent Ghost's lair mates to the Arapahoe County Fairgrounds with orders to wait and to be ready to open a portal."

"Maybe," Anne said, "but it was your sweet Grandma Betsy who told me to tell Jax about my dream in the first place: *Send a message to Jax, then awaken your girlfriends. Return as one in spiritual harmony to the Arapahoe County Fairgrounds and pray for Bethy.*"

A lump caught in Bethany's throat.

She still did not know what to make of all the supernatural sightings, divinely appointed interference...all the timely yet physically impossible occurrences orchestrated on her behalf by one beloved matriarch.

It would take a lifetime to unpack it.

Kari hummed the theme song to the *Twilight Zone.* "I still can't wrap my head around any of this."

"Don't try," Anne said softly. "Just let it settle. It's a lot to take in. I'm just glad Beth was loved so much by more than just the four of us. I'm just glad our bestie is back."

A reverent silence filled the circle as the weight of Anne's words settled in, and five high school, college, and twenty-something girlfriends embraced in what had to be their umpteenth group hug.

Finally, Kari broke the silence. "Can I at least have Chance?" she asked sheepishly.

All five women giggled.

"I don't think you can *have* any of them," Bethany said, still laughing. "I'm pretty sure it doesn't work that way."

"Well, just for tonight?" Kari persisted. "I mean, I don't care if he has to erase my memories. I just want to know what it's like to—"

"Shh," Joy cautioned as the circle of dragyri males broke up, and the gorgeous, sexy, predatory...*topics of conversation*...made their way back to the living room.

Ghost strode in first, like a sleek, stealthy, stunning jungle tiger, and padded straight to the circle of women. Then he slipped behind Bethany, hovered above her, and wrapped his heavily muscled arms around her shoulders.

Joy nearly swooned.

Nicole fanned her face.

While Kari just gawked, mouth hanging open, and Anne turned around to look for Jax.

"Didn't Beth tell you?" Ghost grunted, in that distinct, gruff, super-masculine way. "All sons of dragons have supernatural hearing. Unless you're miles away, or on the other end of the Pantheon, we can hear every word you say."

A collective gasp.

Bethany snorted her drink.

Joy covered her face in her hands.

And Kari turned a bright, almost luminescent shade of pink.

"But to answer your questions," Ghost continued, bluntly. "Nah. Nope. Already told the guys—not gonna happen. You all mean way too much to Beth, and I won't be responsible for any fallout...heartache...not in either direction. And as you all know by now, every dragyri has a chosen dragyra, just one chosen mate that he waits for." He absently tightened his grip around Bethany. "That said, brothers...sisters...friends...a little harmless flirting...as long as it's not anything that rises to the level of erasing memories, s'all good. Don't ask, don't tell." He actually winked.

Oh my gosh. Bethany cringed for her besties—she had completely forgotten about the supernatural hearing.

Luckily for all of them, Romani Dragos sauntered lazily over to the circle, locked eyes with Joy, and gestured with his chin toward the saltwater pool. "You swim?" he asked, flashing a devilish smile. Then he glared at Ghost, as if daring him to say something further.

Joy sucked in a harsh breath of air, closed her eyes to regain her composure, and smoothed the front of her blouse. "Um... yep...I do now."

Roman chuckled, and Joy followed him back to the patio, peeking behind her shoulder to flash an *oh-my-gosh, can-you-believe-this-shit!* expression.

Chance followed suit, a margarita in hand, holding it out to Kari. "Help me get the burgers off the grill?" Kari scrubbed her cheeks, feeling positively mortified, and for the first time, Bethany appreciated her own newfound, preternatural hearing as she heard Chance whisper, "Girl, don't I wish! But hey...please...we can still have fun anyway."

He was going out of his way to make Kari feel comfortable, to let her know the attraction was mutual, and to Kari's credit—she was embarrassed, not stupid—she accepted the drink and followed Chance to the barbeque.

Jax approached the circle next and regarded Nicole and Anne: "So, the guest bedroom at the end of the hall still needs to be made up for Gideon—last I checked, he was in the office, just discovered the Internet." He jacked up his eyebrows as if to imply that the child might be lost in cyberspace...forever. "Maybe the three of us can help him make a list of all the things he hasn't collected over the last, well, millennia; meet up next week, earthside; and make sure he gets everything he wants or needs."

"*Earthside,*" Nicole echoed absently, the disbelief still stark in her voice.

Ever the pragmatic one, Anne smiled, then thought it over.

"Well, I don't get off until late all next week—a lot of my massage clients come in the evenings—but sounds like a lot of fun."

At this, Jax chuckled. "Well, far be it from me to be the one who influences you to skip out on your therapeutic duties, play hooky from work, but if you want a day...a week...or a few months off, I think you can afford it now."

Nicole and Anne locked eyes and furrowed their brows.

"Ghost didn't tell you?" Jax asked.

"Tell us what?" Anne shrugged her shoulders.

"Money is not an object," Ghost cut in. "Not for any of you. Not anymore."

Jax smiled softly. "Purpose...self-fulfillment...pursuing your personal ambitions—that's all on you. But none of you will ever need money or want for anything again. Ghost and Beth have you covered, indefinitely."

Nicole's eyes grew wide, her mouth fell open, and she grabbed Anne's hand and squeezed it, even as Bethany's heart swelled with excitement and gratitude. She watched as two of her best friends in the world followed Jaxtapherion Dragos down the hall, and then she exhaled a breathless gasp as she witnessed a stark, yet tender, intimate exchange of prolonged eye contact pass between Jax and Anne.

That wasn't superficial at all.

She drew a long, deep breath, just trying to take it all in...

The Diamond Lair. Sweet little Gideon. Ghost being reunited with his long-lost brother.

The fact that Lord Dragos was gone, she and Ghost were finally free from the underworld, and now, her girlfriends would be taken care of forever. To say nothing of the electricity coursing between Jax and Anne—interesting, *very interesting*—or the stunning, powerful, possessive dragyri male, standing so close behind her, giving off heat like a furnace.

The moment the living room was empty, she turned around

and stared at Ghost. "This doesn't seem real. Any of it. I still can't believe all that's happened."

Ghost's mouth turned up in that almost-smile, and his witchy phantom-blue eyes nearly sparkled. "Five nights ago, I was standing in Lord Drakkar's throne room, when you were dragged in before him, and there was nothing I could do to stop it. An hour or two later, we were hovering under a ceiling, both outside our bodies, and my head was virtually spinning, trying to figure out how to protect you from Wraith, how to shield you from Lord Drakkar's vulgar...intentions. Even then, as time went by, and we settled on a plan, tried to figure a way out of there, I couldn't have imagined this moment. Me. You. Gideon, who I didn't even remember, just a couple dozen yards down the hall-way. My evil sire, gone. The rebirth by fire, behind us. You, standing here, looking like some kind of sublime, edible angel, and me, just trying to take it all in." He sucked in a harsh, ragged breath, held it, then released it slowly, a waft of smoke trailing the exhale. "In that letter you left, you said I was worthy, even if I didn't know it. I'm not, Beth. I never have been. Yet here we are, the two of us together, and for the first time in my entire gods-forsaken existence, I actually wanna be. Worthy, that is. Worthy of you. Worthy...for you. Someone you can look up to and, well, trust."

Bethany studied Ghost's eyes as if this was the first time she'd seen them, the arch of his brows, the cast of his forehead, and the striking ambient light behind those magnificent Siberian-husky-ish pupils, the way each phantom-blue sphere was orbited by pure celestial diamonds. And the soul that shined through their depths, reflecting so much timeless wisdom, purpose...*pain*... sacrifice, suffering, and overcoming. The brutality. The battles. Struggling and surviving. The brokenness, hatred, and the absence of...living. And finally, blessedly, the new rays of hope and even healing—loyalty, too long denied him, strength, always there within him—the promise of a better future that might just await them both.

All of it.

All of Ghost...

It was all right there in those spectacular, glorious eyes.

Bethany's heart skipped a beat, and her palms grew sweaty. "I can hardly breathe when I look at you, Ghost." Her words were few, but she hoped they at least conveyed the depth of her feelings. "I'm just...helpless...ruined, and I have no idea when it happened."

He cupped her face in his hands and stared right through her. "Ditto, dragyra. Ditto." Then he bent to her mouth and hovered above it, waiting for something Bethany couldn't quite articulate: perhaps her consent, perhaps her initiation, or maybe just a silent promise to always be with him.

"Just kiss him already," a sweet, elderly, feminine voice. "You don't have to wait. He is ready...he is willing...and his heart is open."

Grandma Betsy!

"I leave you in good hands," the matriarch continued. "Live well together. You are loved, sweet Bethy, both by me and by Ghostaniaz."

Bethany closed her eyes and shivered from the nape of her neck to the stern of her ankles. Then she rose to her toes, wrapped her arms around Ghost, and kissed him with a passion, fervor, and unrestrained longing she didn't know she had in her. He growled into her mouth, and she giggled. "Take me to our room, dragyri. I want to taste you...know you...love you, slowly. I want to feel your soul inside me."

His legs nearly buckled as he dipped down to scoop her up in his arms. "You sure, dragyra? You're ready for...all of this?"

"I'm more than ready," she whispered huskily. "Child of fire, daughter of flames." She traced his lips with the tip of her finger and giggled softly.

He sucked in air and raked his fingers along the front of her body, from the hollow of her throat, over her collarbone, between her breasts, and down to her stomach. "More than a woman; more than a name..."

She burrowed her head in his neck and sighed in utter contentment. "Born from the soul of the Pantheon."

JOIN THE MAILING LIST

A SNEAK PEEK FROM BLOOD DESTINY

(BOOK #1 – BLOOD CURSE SERIES)

Jocelyn was positively spellbound, unable to pull her eyes from the phenomenon appearing in the heavens above them. She had never seen anything so powerful or mysterious in all her life. How was it that they were viewing such an event without a telescope? How could any constellation appear so bright? And what in the world could cause the moon to turn the color of blood?

She slowly turned her head to look back at the creature standing beside her, and her heart began to pound in her chest.

The vampire stood motionless.

Transfixed by the magic before him.

He seemed to be lost in a daze; his eyes glazed over with wonder, and for the first time since she had met the self-assured male, he looked utterly...unsure of himself...completely caught off guard.

His eyes shot back and forth between the moon and her arm, until eventually, some primitive warning system began to go off inside her.

Something was wrong.

Really, really wrong.

Nathaniel was changing.

His eyes were narrowing, his posture stiffening, his counte-nance becoming all at once deathly serious. And then he caught at her wrist, flipping it over like a police officer about to slap on a pair of handcuffs, holding her captive in an iron grip.

Jocelyn cringed and tried to free her arm, but he only held on tighter.

Instinctively, she froze then, knowing he was no longer in full control of his actions. Curiously, her eyes followed his to the inside of her wrist, where the skin was beginning to burn and tingle. And then, like a microscope zooming in for a closer look, readjusting the lens to view something she couldn't have possibly seen correctly the first time, her gaze narrowed: The delicate skin on her inner arm was covered in cryptic markings. A strange series of discolorations taking the form of a brilliantly intricate tattoo.

This time, it was Jocelyn who looked back and forth between the sky and her arm as her mind began to connect the celestial dots. The exact position of the individual stars, the brilliant constellation in the sky, the very picture they were viewing in the heavens *was etched indelibly into her wrist*. And whatever the markings were—whatever they meant—Nathaniel was utterly captivated by them.

Jocelyn took a deep breath, trying to remain calm while she studied the obscure design. There was something important happening. Something magical that connected her and the man standing before her with that blood moon. It was both prophetic and foreboding. And although it felt odd—even frightening—it also felt strangely *familiar*.

She recognized a subtle stirring, almost like a faint awakening of...something...she couldn't name. And it was like being drawn into a dream, one she knew nothing about and wanted no part of.

She only knew that her once safe world had suddenly come

to an end. And that the vampire who had been so kind, almost human, just moments before was something altogether different now. Dangerous and predatory.

What in the world had happened?

Had the sky somehow triggered the monster? Was it the color of the moon? *The color of blood?* Had Nathaniel become like the creature she had seen in the dark chamber?

As the enchantment wore off, a perilous cry of terror rose in her throat. In one desperate moment of clarity, she yanked back her wrist and drew for her gun.

Nathaniel was far too fast for her.

Using only his mind to disarm the threat, the vampire jerked the gun from her hand and sent it flying hundreds of yards into the forest, smoldering like a glowing red coal as it left her fingers. A fierce growl of warning rumbled in his throat, and his eyes pierced hers with a harsh, reprimanding glare.

Jocelyn cried out as the tips of her fingers were burned by the blazing iron. "Nathaniel!" she shrieked, her terror no longer contained. "You promised!" It was a desperate plea for compassion. "You swore you weren't going to hurt me." It was a pitiful cry for mercy.

ALSO BY TESSA DAWN

Ghostaniaz ∼ Son of Dragons (Book 3)

(NIGHTWALKER SERIES)
Daywalker ∼ The Beginning
(A New Adult Short Story)

OTHER

Do You Have Any Advice for Aspiring Authors?
(A *free* booklet for my readers, who are also aspiring writers)

.

JOIN THE AUTHOR'S MAILING LIST

If you would like to receive a direct email notification each time Tessa releases a new book, please join the author's mailing list at...

www.tessadawn.com

ABOUT THE AUTHOR

Tessa Dawn grew up in Colorado, where she developed a deep affinity for the Rocky Mountains. After graduating with a degree in psychology, she worked for several years in criminal justice and mental health before returning to get her master's degree in nonprofit management.

Tessa began writing as a child and composed her first full-length novel at the age of eleven. By the time she graduated high school, she had a banker's box full of short stories and novels. Since then, she has published works as diverse as poetry, greeting cards, workbooks for kids with autism, and academic curricula. Her Dark Fantasy/Gothic Romance novels represent her long-desired return to her creative-writing roots and her passionate flair for storytelling.

Tessa currently splits her time between the Colorado suburbs and mountains with her husband, two children, and "one very crazy cat." She hopes to one day move to the country, where she can own horses and what she considers "the most beautiful creature ever created"—a German shepherd.

Writing is her bliss.